HUMAN FACE

a&b

HUMAN FACE

ALINE TEMPLETON

Allison & Busby Limited
12 Fitzroy Mews
London W1T 6DW
allisonandbusby.com

First published in Great Britain by Allison & Busby in 2018.
This paperback edition published by Allison & Busby in 2018.

A CIP catalogue record for this book is available from
the British Library.

10 9 8 7 6 5 4 3 2 1

ISBN 978-0-7490-2336-2

Typeset in 10.5/15.5 pt Sabon by
Allison & Busby Ltd

The paper used for this Allison & Busby publication
has been produced from trees that have been legally sourced
from well-managed and credibly certified forests.

Printed and bound by
CPI Group (UK) Ltd, Croydon, CR0 4YY

For Emma and Philip, with much love and joy

For Mercy has a human heart,
Pity a human face,
And Love, the human form divine,
And Peace, the human dress.

Songs of Innocence

And mutual fear brings peace;
Till the selfish loves increase,
Then Cruelty knits a snare
And spreads his baits with care.

Songs of Experience

William Blake

CHAPTER ONE

It was the moon that woke her, shining through the uncurtained casement window and flooding the attic bedroom with cold, pure light.

It summoned Beatrice like a call to worship. She came awake, muttering and groaning as she shifted her bulky body, propping herself up at last with a wheezing groan, then rolled out of bed to sit on the end of it for a moment with her eyes shut, moon bathing.

As the pale radiance washed over her she felt light, light and free, a gossamer thing, purged of the gross burdens of the flesh. But it was drawing her to the window and she stood up, flinching at the chill, then with infinite tenderness bent, crooning, to pick up the little shawled bundle that had lain beside her and padded across the bare boards, cradling it to her shoulder.

There was a film of condensation on the small square panes; she pulled down the sleeve of her thick flannelette nightgown and rubbed them clear.

Overhead, the moon was a bone-white disc in a black velvet sky that was thick with stars; there was not so much as a breath of wind. Below her, the bay was still and steely as a pool of mercury, and in late autumn some of the trees were black winter skeletons already. The garden was all shades of grey – dark grey, dove-grey, pearl-grey, dirty-white – and though it was almost as bright as day it looked sickly pale, eerie in the moonlight.

She loved the strangeness. It cloaked everything with magic, evoked a different reality, where she could imagine herself transformed – where she could be what she wished to be, not what she was.

'See, Rosamond, my precious. Wake up – see how beautiful! Come on, I'll hold you up,' she whispered, pulling back the cobweb-fine shawl.

The eyes opened obediently, blue and blank above the rounded cheeks that were delicately flushed with pink, staring sightlessly out at the dream-world where a doll could become a real live baby.

'You mustn't get cold, though,' she scolded lovingly. 'That would never do, my darling.' She swaddled it again, cradling it in her arms as the eyes shut with an audible click. 'There, that's better. I'll pop you back into bed.'

But she lingered a little longer, reluctant for the moment to pass, though she was beginning to shiver. She was just turning away when a movement caught her eye.

There was a boat pulling out from the pier across the bay, a small motorboat that was, however, being rowed as if to escape attention. The ripples from the oars spread out and out, breaking the mirror surface of the sea with concentric rings.

Her curiosity piqued, she turned to settle Rosamond gently back into bed then swathed herself in the duvet and returned to the window. The boat would arrive in a few minutes: it wasn't far across the bay.

There was movement below her too. Someone was coming from the house, running across the grass and down the steps to the jetty.

Even huddled in the warmth of the duvet, she felt a sudden chill run through her.

Adam wouldn't like this. He wouldn't like this at all.

Beatrice turned hastily away, climbed back into bed. She didn't want to know, didn't want anything to do with it. She wouldn't tell him, but he would find out. He always did.

As she turned away, a faint wisp of cloud drifted across the moon and a little breeze ruffled the surface of the sea.

Eva was shivering as she ran back across the lawn, leaving footprints in the deep dew that soaked her feet. Behind her she heard the cautious splash of the oars as Daniel rowed back towards the huddle of houses across the bay in the village, dark and silent in the eerie light.

To anyone watching it would have looked like a lover's tryst, and she gave a little, wry grimace. Of course he had talked of love, and the girl she once was might have believed him. Now, bruised and scarred by experience, she suspected that this was just the sort of thing men said when they were wanting something from you.

It had been a risk taking the key from Adam's drawer while he was away but she'd got it back safely, and now the copy Daniel had made was cold in her hand. As she went back into the silent house she found herself almost hoping it wouldn't work. But if it didn't . . .

The hall was bright with the moonlight pouring through the long stair window, and she glanced fearfully up the stairwell that rose above her as she scurried across. *I'm like a mouse*, she thought, *looking for the owl hovering overhead*. But there was no sound from the attic floor.

The back office, where even Beatrice did not go except in Adam's company, lay behind a door below the stairs and Eva winced as it squeaked on its hinges and she stepped into the windowless passage. No one would see her if she switched a light on here but somehow it felt safer to grope her way to the door in the faint light filtering through from the hall. Even though Adam was away for the night, dining and staying over, she felt a superstitious fear that he might suddenly appear as she fumbled for the lock and fitted the key into it, shouting 'Treachery!'

Click! It turned. Feeling sick with nerves, she let herself in, locking the door behind her before she switched on the light. It was barely bigger than a cupboard, Adam's office, created out of one of the old service rooms, probably, and just big enough for a desk with a computer on it, a couple of chairs and a large metal filing cabinet.

She went to the cabinet, ignoring the computer; Daniel had told her it would be protected so she wouldn't get in and that anyway the most important stuff wouldn't be where an enterprising hacker might find it – on disks if they were lucky, ordinary files if they weren't. The drawers, when she gave a tug, were locked and she fished in her pocket for the little bunch of metal keys he had given her.

This was treachery, of course – a dirty word. Add that to the list Eva would have to confess to the priest, if she hadn't stopped going to confession long ago.

Her dream of a better life hadn't seemed wicked at the time; it had seemed brave, the sort of feistiness Nënë had always encouraged. Her eyes prickled as she thought of her dead mother – what would she think of her daughter now, of what she had become?

Oh, she'd pretended to herself that the relationship with Adam was a genuine attraction. It wasn't hard, not at first; he was darkly good-looking, charming, and being the director of a charity for refugees surely vouched for his good intentions. But all along, at heart she had known it for what it was, and she had accepted 'housekeeper' status on his assurance that he would transform her into a Pole with a National Insurance number, entitled to her place in the West where the ordinary lifestyle represented barely imaginable luxury to someone who had lived in miserable poverty with a drunken father.

Now she was trapped in this weird situation, along with the poor, sad, obsessive woman who treated her with defensive hostility; apart from visits across to the pub, and sometimes to Portree for shopping, she had no life of her own.

She had nowhere else to go, though. She had been patient, waiting for Adam to give her the papers and leave with his blessing, but slowly the chilling realisation had dawned: that was only going to happen when he tired of her and he hadn't, so far. She'd made the big mistake of asking when she might be able to leave; she had seen the flicker of wounded pride on his face and the relationship had cooled rapidly after that. These days she was spending almost every night in her bare little bedsitter, not in Adam's luxurious flat.

Eva no longer trusted him to honour the unwritten agreement. He could just turn her out and then she would have no alternative but to become what at heart she knew she was already. A 'working girl', didn't they call it in Britain? There was a starker word for it back home.

And now she had sold herself, or at least her conscience, to another man. Daniel, too, was showing her a glimpse of the Promised Land; he could give her all that Adam had offered and more, but there needed to be what he liked to call the 'devil's bargain' – do evil that good may come. A Jesuit belief, he'd reassured her, playing on her Catholic education, but she was still uneasy.

Could she trust him, any more than she trusted Adam? And what if Adam found out? No – she daren't think of that, not even for a second. He wasn't going to find out, and then Daniel would spirit her away to her new life. For a moment she let herself dream, holding on to the vision like an amulet against fear.

She took a deep breath and began trying the keys. On the second try one of them worked, just as he had said it would, and she pulled open the top drawer, her hands shaking slightly. She couldn't see any disks – just files – but he'd given her a list of the sort of information he wanted and she began checking through. When she found one, she took it to the desk and sat down, copying the information into the notebook he'd given her as fast as she could.

It was boring work. There were two more drawers, and eventually the names and figures began to blur and in the unheated room her fingers were becoming stiff. There was one more file she should check, but it was very late; Daniel had waited until he saw Beatrice's light go off before he came across from the village, and after Eva had nodded off to sleep twice she decided to call it a day.

Beatrice never got up before half past seven if Adam was away, and when she did she would go straight to the main office and stay there, so if Eva set her alarm she'd have plenty of time to slip in unseen, finish off and slip out again long before Adam would be back from his leisurely country-house breakfast. With a yawn that almost dislocated her jaw, she put everything back and let herself out again.

The moon had gone down and the hall was in deep darkness. With her hand stretched out in front of her, Eva groped her way across, terrified of losing her bearings and knocking something over that would bring Beatrice out to see what was going on.

She wriggled down into her cold bed, desperate for sleep, but now the eyes that had kept shutting before stayed obstinately open. She was too frightened to sleep. How had her dream become the nightmare she was living now? There was a bird singing freedom somewhere, but listening to it felt like tempting fate and as she lay there the monsters of fear and guilt crept closer, closer in the darkness.

The whitewashed croft houses of the township at Balnasheil, scattered up the low hills rising to the Black Cuillin behind, and the cottages, huddled by the shoreline, had an embattled look; its tiny bay offered only slight protection against the Atlantic storms that came roaring in across the sea.

It was an ancient settlement, surrounded by the ghosts of its past: the Celtic standing stone; a hut circle from the Bronze Age; sad ruins that had once been houses, still bearing the marks of the fires of their destruction when the brutal Clearances drove their owners into exile.

A close-knit community with a dwindling population, it was set in its ways, polite and cool to strangers. Very cool, when it came to the present inhabitants of Balnasheil Lodge.

The penny-pinching Victorian magnate who had built it across the bay on the rough moorland for the shooting – 'with walls you could spit peas through', in scornful local opinion – had styled himself the laird. He had looked for forelock-tugging in vain from the Highlanders, who had only ever considered their own chiefs first among equals and had somehow missed out on the deference gene.

Over the years his successors had been viewed with a mixture of tolerant indifference and quiet amusement – and even sympathy in the case of the Danish businessman who had bought the Lodge, sight unseen, and been so dismayed that he visited once and never returned.

The Human Face charity had been welcomed at first, even admired for its canny approach in making its headquarters here instead of in fancy offices in one of the big cities, but gradually support drained away. They didn't make use of local businesses; the directors who dropped in occasionally for a drink or a meal in the little hotel were flash and toffee-nosed and the procession of 'housekeepers' who came across to the pub that provided Balnasheil's social scene didn't help either. The general verdict was that there was something 'not right' about it.

Vicky Macdonald had known she was taking a risk when she got a job at the Lodge doing the cleaning and cooking that the 'housekeepers' apparently couldn't manage. Coming from the Central Belt and not having the Gaelic, she'd been considered all but a Sassenach and was still working out her probation, despite having married one of the locals more than a year ago. She was left in no doubt that she was seen as tarnished by association, not least by her own husband.

This morning, when she said 'Murdo, it's time we were away. I'm running late as it is,' the response was unhelpful.

Murdo John Macdonald – so called to differentiate him from his father, John Murdo – was a big, quiet man, slow-spoken, dark-bearded and dark-eyed. He looked up from his mug of tea and grunted, 'Seen the weather?'

The view through the kitchen window was just a square of opaque white. Vicky ran her hand through her fair curly hair and sighed. 'You've been out when it's been worse than that. I can't afford to be unreliable – we need the money.'

She could have bitten her tongue off after she said it. She'd hurt him; under the heavy brows, his eyes were pained as he looked up at her, and she hurried on, 'I know you'd prefer I just did whatever the hotel could offer me but when the climbing season was over I was earning next to nothing for months. Anyway, I got really tired of Fiona Ross cheating me over the hours I'd worked and snaffling the tips and I hated having to waitress while Douglas's ministrations ruined good food. At least this is steady and I get to cook. I don't want to lose it.'

He didn't reply, but she saw his jaw set in a firmer line and sighed. Once Murdo John made up his mind, you'd be better working on a project to make water run uphill than trying to change it.

Vicky had been at a very low ebb after her mother died, feeling alone and vulnerable with the only family she had gone. She'd come to stay in the hotel for a holiday looking for comfort in the beauty and peace of the hills and then, reluctant to return to the stress of her pressured job in catering, she had taken a temporary job as a waitress. Her decision had a lot to do with Murdo John; he was very attractive, in that rugged Highland way, and he had pursued the relationship with a sort of devoted, unthreatening persistence that had soothed her aching sense of loss and won her heart. She'd have been happy just to move in with him, but it was marriage he wanted – marriage or nothing.

'I want to make sure you're mine,' he had said, and, happy and in love, she'd thought it very romantic at the time. And she would be part of a family again.

The problems only appeared when Murdo John lost his job in construction. With the downturn, work slowed to a trickle and then stopped; he'd been making good money for years and now he was dependent on bar work and a bit of fishing. It hurt his pride that he couldn't support her as, in his eyes, a husband should. He lost his self-respect; he felt humiliated, diminished and no amount of loving assurance could shift his view of himself as a failure.

As if in compensation he was becoming more controlling,

and now their relationship was showing signs of strain. He hated her associating with the dubious company on the other side of the bay, but she was digging in her toes. Even if he couldn't accept the concept of the New Man, she was a modern woman and no amount of passive coercion was going to make her give in. When the housekeeping job had come up, she'd jumped at the chance and she was keeping it even if Murdo John would all but spit on the ground when she so much as mentioned Adam Carnegie's name.

Vicky didn't like him either – creepy, even sinister, she thought – but she wasn't paid to socialise with him, or with the 'housekeepers' either, though Eva was all right – a sweet girl, a decent girl, even, unlike her predecessor, who'd been a cold, brassy-looking woman who obviously knew the score and who was using Adam just as much as he was using her.

'Maybe if it clears later,' Murdo John said grudgingly, his tone telling her this was his best offer.

She'd have to settle for that; if she tried driving round by the road, more like a track, that took you up into the foothills and across a narrow stone bridge before it dropped down to the other side of the bay, it would be nearly time to set off home again.

Perhaps the fog would lift as suddenly as it had settled. As they said around here, 'If you don't like the weather, wait a minute.'

'All right,' Vicky said, trying not to sound tight-lipped as she set about making her preparations for their own meal at night. If she had it ready, she could stay on a bit if the fog lifted and work her hours; Beatrice had pointed out to her that not to dock her for work she hadn't done was taking food out of the mouths of hungry children. Vicky could have suggested a few economies the directors could make towards the same noble end, but she didn't. She wasn't daft.

As she chopped onions, her mind was on the odd household across the bay. There had been a bad atmosphere of late and she was trying to figure it out. Last time she'd sensed that, it was because Adam was plainly getting bored with Eva's predecessor, who had left shortly afterwards, but this time wasn't like that. He'd seemed very taken with Eva until fairly recently, when there had been a sudden cooling – a sharpness in the way he spoke to her, no casual arm round the girl's shoulder, no laughter between them any more. And Eva was definitely on edge.

She'd noticed, too, that when Adam was on one of his frequent trips away Eva had been spending time in the pub with a man who'd been living in a rented cottage in the village for a month or two – a writer researching a book about hillwalking in the Inner Hebrides, apparently.

Eva claimed to be Polish – but then the last girl had, too. Vicky doubted it; when she'd tried to talk to Eva about Poland she'd shown the whites of her eyes and suffered a relapse in the standard of her English. She worried about Eva; she seemed so young and vulnerable and she was in a very unhealthy situation. Her strong protective instincts aroused, Vicky had tried to befriend her, but despite being happy enough to smile and chat, she shied away from anything approaching intimacy. When Vicky had asked how she had come into Adam's life she had clammed up immediately.

If her immigrant status was dodgy she'd be wise to keep Adam Carnegie sweet. And if he found out she was carrying on with someone behind his back, from what Vicky knew of the man, he wouldn't like it – wouldn't like it at all.

There wasn't a lot she could do about it, though. With another sigh, Vicky began peeling the carrots.

Beatrice Lacey looked out of her window with a sinking heart. The view had vanished this morning and she couldn't see anything – not the Black Cuillin across the bay, not the near hill, not even the lawns and shrubs in the garden, only a dense, vaporous blanket wrapping the house in a smothering silence.

On mornings like this she felt she could barely breathe, that she was in exile – a prisoner, even – stifled by the implacable strangeness of this place where she had found herself living, a fairly modest fishing lodge in a remote part of Skye. She hated it here, where the natives spoke another language, at least among themselves, and put up a wall of polite aloofness that barely concealed their dislike.

She'd been so happy when Human Face had been headquartered in Surrey, in what had been her own home until she had turned it over to Adam Carnegie's foundation. She'd had old friends there, a brother, even, and it had been quite a shock when, six years before, Adam had announced they were moving to Skye.

He'd been getting restless, she knew that. For some reason he didn't like her friends, and particularly not her brother. Well, she could understand that; Quentin, with his constant crises, was a problem and even she hadn't been pleased when he too moved to Skye, not long ago, and only a few miles away.

And there were the interruptions to their work, too, like the supporters who wanted to do charity events to raise funds – which, as Adam said, never raised more than a piffling amount that didn't pay for the time they had to spend helping with the arrangements – and the unheralded official visitations, making sure they weren't embezzling all the money. When world poverty was such a colossal challenge, the petty stuff was frustrating.

Certainly, they weren't plagued like that out here in the wilds and once Adam had explained, looking at her with those blue eyes, so dark that they were almost navy, that with property prices the way they were they really ought to liquidate their assets and cut their overheads at the same time, for the sake of the children. And she had agreed, of course: the photographs he had shown her of the refugee children with huge pleading eyes and malnourished infants with grotesquely swollen stomachs had haunted her ever since.

It had given her a pang to sell her house and move but it was a comfort to think that it would put food in a lot more hungry mouths, just as the monthly income from her trust fund did. And it had, most importantly, pleased Adam too.

Another benefit, he'd said, was that at Balnasheil Lodge he could offer fishing and a bit of rough shooting on the moor that went with it to promising sponsors, and from time to time a group of men would come to be wined and dined and flattered.

Not that she had much to do with them, though, apart

22

from making bookings for flights and transport from Glasgow. Adam had explained that he needed a housekeeper, someone to be a hostess when he entertained, who could charm the money out of their pockets. And it worked: she could see the evidence in the size of the donations they made afterwards.

The 'housekeepers' had all been immigrants, struggling to make their way in a hard world, and she'd have been pleased that this was giving them a chance to find their feet if she hadn't realised that they had – well – other duties. She managed to ignore it, though with pain, telling herself that one day he would tire of the shallow vapidity of these girls. None of them lasted long, and they were easily replaced: she would be here, at his side, long after the current one was gone.

Eva. She didn't want to think about Eva: Eva with her little pixie face and her bright smile. Though she'd tried to hate her she couldn't quite manage it. It was lucky Adam had been away last night, because—

She shied away from the thought and fixed her mind on the tasks of the day as she showered and dressed and chatted to the doll while she did her hair and put on make-up; it took her mind off the face she saw in the mirror. She'd got up a little earlier than usual today; several applications had come in late yesterday and she wanted to get on with them. Locking her door carefully behind her, she set off down the stairs from her attic flat to open up the charity office on the ground floor.

On a day like this, with little light coming through the staircase window, the hall looked even gloomier than usual, with its heavily varnished pitch pine and the brown and orange stained-glass window in the front door.

It was a dark and oppressive house, so unlike her bright and sunny Surrey villa. With its six bedrooms, plus servants' quarters, it was far too big, except when sponsors visited, and it wasn't as if the public rooms were handsome either. It had obviously been thrown up on the cheap by someone who only came in August for the shooting, and in bad weather the draughts whistled through the gaps round the windows. Today there was even a hint of the mist outside creeping into the hall.

Beatrice had reached the last few steps when the door to Adam's private flat on the left of the staircase opened and the man himself – stocky, with thick black hair and strongly marked brows – came out. He was frowning.

Her heavy face brightened. 'Adam! I thought you were staying over with the Lindsays last night. I didn't know you were back.' She couldn't disguise the yearning in her voice.

He stopped and the scowl vanished at once. 'Morning, sweetie! Yes, the company was deadly boring – dear God, once the colonel gets into his stride you lose the will to live. I couldn't face him again over breakfast so I drove back at some ungodly hour in the fog. I've quite a lot to see to anyway before I go off tomorrow.'

She was hurrying down when she saw the dog following him and stopped dead – not that the Dobermann took any notice of her. It never did, never showed any interest in anyone except its master.

It was, she had to admit, an elegant animal – sleek, muscular, its black and tan coat gleaming. She liked dogs well enough, in general – just not this particular dog. She waited, with an almost superstitious shudder, until it had passed.

Adam was going towards the private office, the one she only went into when they were working together. Her heart lifted. She'd put some papers for him in the box outside the door and they might need discussion.

Those were the happy times, when they talked about the next project. Once, gloriously and unforgettably, he had taken her with him to a refugee camp they were supporting in North Africa. It was the most – and, indeed, the only – romantic experience in her life and she lived on the dream that it would happen again – and perhaps this time she might be lucky with a real baby. It was a long time ago now, though, and she was losing heart.

'Adam,' she called as she went towards him. 'There's a couple of things—'

'Yes?' he said impatiently, over his shoulder.

He didn't sound enthusiastic and she hesitated. If he wasn't in the mood for a chat, there was no point.

'It doesn't matter,' she said hastily. 'I'll see you later.'

He nodded without turning round as he put a key into the lock, then wrestled with it, puzzled. He tried the handle and the door opened.

Adam stopped on the threshold. 'Have you been in here, Beatrice?'

His voice was icy and her hand went to her throat in dismay. 'No, Adam, no!' she cried. 'Of course I haven't! You know I never go to your office unless you're with me. And I keep the key in my bag so no one else could have used it. Perhaps you just forgot to lock it.'

He ignored that. He went into the room, the dog at his heels. It was empty but Beatrice, hovering uncertainly in the doorway, could see that the chair by the desk was pushed back and the edge of a piece of paper was sticking out of one of the drawers in the filing cabinet.

He didn't say anything. She was turning to leave when he said suddenly, 'Where did she go last night?'

'Go?' She was flustered. 'I – I don't know—'

Adam smiled. 'You do, don't you? You're a rotten liar, darling. I was out with Amber this morning and I saw the footsteps in the wet grass, going down to the jetty. It wasn't you, was it?'

Beatrice shook her head.

'No, I didn't think it would be. Who was she meeting?'

Her heart beating a little faster because he had called her 'darling', she told him what she had seen the night before.

'That's fine. You're my good girl.' He smiled at her and then went to open the top drawer of the filing cabinet as the dog, with a sigh, lay down in the corner of the room. He began piling files onto his desk, as if he was planning to move them somewhere else.

From what he said, from his smile, he should have sounded pleased. But he didn't, he sounded . . . grim.

Oh God, she mustn't think about it. With a hollow feeling in her stomach Beatrice went back to the main office on the right of the front door, a large draughty room with too many windows. She always dreaded the approach of winter.

She sat down at her desk in the bay window at the front, switched on the computer and checked her to-do list. Keep herself busy: that was the best thing. There was a flight to be confirmed; she could do that first. Her hands were trembling, though, and in the part of her mind she couldn't quite silence a voice was whispering, *Not again, not again.*

PC Livvy Murray sat up in bed and looked out of her window with no enthusiasm at all. She lay down again, pulled the duvet over her head and groaned. What was a nice Glasgow lassie like her doing in a place like this? And how long could she stand it before she cracked? After all, she could resign any day she wanted.

The trouble was, Livvy loved her job. At least, she'd loved the job she'd had in Glasgow, until it all went horribly wrong.

He'd said, 'Sorry, doll,' as they took him down, grinning at her stony face and giving her the cheeky-chappie wink that had been his stock-in-trade since they were at primary school together.

Bastard! But you had to give it to him, he wasn't one to bear grudges. She'd been the one who'd shafted him, after all, even if he'd shafted her first.

She hadn't known anything about his double life, though perhaps she should have: with the benefit of twenty-twenty hindsight she could see that there were questions she should have maybe asked, but she hadn't. She'd let herself be blinded by the looks and the gallus charm. It was amazing what you could choose not to see if you didn't want to.

When it all hit the fan, at Glasgow HQ they'd have been happy enough to sack chippy, sassy PC Murray, but once she found out what had been going on she'd grassed him up as best she could and was the star prosecution witness. She'd had no problem in court; she'd been totally honest about her own stupidity and she'd come out of it with this as the only stain on her character.

How humiliating was that, though? She'd never been as confident as she tried to sound, covering up the sense of inadequacy instilled by her endlessly critical mother – a mean drunk – with a bright, shiny armour of indifference. She'd had to stand there, in public view, exposed as such a rubbish police officer that she hadn't even spotted the crime syndicate operating right under her nose.

Her bosses couldn't pin anything on her, though they'd tried. Since they couldn't bust her for having rubbish taste in men they'd just moved her – no discussion, no appeal – to exile in the piddling wee police office in this place that would make Troon on a wet weekend in November seem buzzy by comparison, that didn't do any proper police work and that was going to be shut down any day now, along with a police house that was all but unheated and had so many leaks in the roof that you could barely see the tatty carpets for the basins put out to catch the drips.

Nothing happened here. Nothing. And now Police Scotland was scaling everything down so that in the unlikely event that something did happen, they'd have to call in someone qualified to deal with it and she wouldn't get a look-in even then. The highlight of her week was a Saturday night, when she might be called along to Portree to deal with a rammy in one of the pubs. There certainly wasn't much else to do if she was off on a Saturday around here.

But if the idea was that she'd just resign in disgust, they could get stuffed. Even if she was totally pissed off, she wasn't going to give them that satisfaction. She'd keep her head down for a bit, then she'd start very politely applying for a transfer to a place where the most interesting thing to do wasn't watching the grass growing down the middle of the road.

As Eva Havel slipped along the below-stairs passage, she was shaking so that her legs would hardly hold her up. He'd almost caught her red-handed.

All she'd had time to do was shove the files in the drawer, push it shut and flee when she heard Beatrice talking to Adam in the hall. There hadn't been time to lock either the drawer or the door and all she could hope for was that Adam, secure in his own house, was sometimes a bit casual about locking up himself.

She'd know about it soon enough if he wasn't. Like a frightened animal taking refuge in its den, she headed for her little bedsitter but before she reached it Marek Kaczka came out of the kitchen, eating a sandwich.

He too was an immigrant but he was much older and he'd been there for a couple of years, living in the gatehouse at the end of the drive and doing maintenance on the house and grounds. He never said much and he wasn't usually in the house unless he was sent for; he looked guilty and made a movement as if to hide his sandwich when he saw her. She just nodded to him as she passed and he went on towards the side door.

Reaching her room, she shut the door and leant against

it, her eyes shut. At least he hadn't come along in a towering rage; perhaps, after all, he hadn't noticed. She could get Daniel to fetch her tonight – but then she remembered that Adam was going away the next day, flying to Paris for a conference.

Once he'd gone, she could pack up everything, including the important notebook, and leave quietly so that he would just come back and find her gone. And until then, she would try to keep out of his way.

When she picked up her phone to text Daniel, she saw there were two anxious messages from him already. She hesitated, then tapped out a blandly reassuring reply; she had found the paper files, got the details he wanted. She didn't mention that Adam might have realised what she'd done – he might be annoyed. She could be out of here by tomorrow afternoon.

The fog was starting to clear now, but rain was taking its place, the relentless soft, wetting rain that could soak you to the skin in minutes. She couldn't wait to get away.

It was raining in Edinburgh too, though here the rain had come in on tearing winds, lashing the small windows of the fisherman's cottage at Newhaven where Kelso Strang lived. Even within the shelter of the stout stone walls of the harbour opposite, the little yachts were tugging at their moorings, rocking on the swell.

He was a tall man, dark-haired and hazel-eyed with a lean, intelligent face, currently disfigured by a neat scar running straight down the right-hand side. His expression was bleak as he stood in the silent house, staring out at the rain.

He'd wanted peace, had believed he was desperate for it, after the surreal, frantic activity of the past few days. He'd told his fussing, anxious family to leave him alone, unable to cope with their grief as well as his own, and at last he'd persuaded them to go.

Kelso had been thankful to see his father out before he said something that would wreck their already damaged relationship. Highly successful professional soldiers are not celebrated for their tact, and though Major General Sir Roderick Strang had made all the conventionally proper noises, he hadn't been able to resist saying, 'Things will be different now, of course. I'm sure I can still find a string or two to pull to get you back into the regiment.'

His tone suggested that there was a silver lining to every cloud. Kelso was digging his nails into the palms of his hands, struggling for control, when Mary Strang flew across the room like a small, heat-seeking missile. 'Leave the boy alone, Roddy. He's not wanting to think about anything more just now. I'm taking you home.'

Like any good soldier, he obeyed the command of his superior officer and left.

Kelso had often thought that if the army found itself suddenly short of a brigadier, his mother could have taken immediate command of a battalion with unruffled calm. She could cope with his father, after all, and sometimes in moments of extreme exasperation he had muttered the aphorism that any woman could manage a clever man but it took a very clever woman to manage a fool – even though he knew that was not entirely fair.

He'd never been forgiven for leaving the army after a

short-service commission, despite being offered another term and promotion, in favour of joining the police force. It had been bad enough that he'd volunteered as a sniper – pukka officers did not sully their hands with the dirty end of the business – but this was, to Roderick, social disgrace as well as being a calculated insult to him personally. And he had blamed Alexa, who should have been happy to abandon her medical career and follow the drum after a soldier husband.

Kelso had tried to explain: he'd enjoyed his time in the army but he'd never intended to make it his career. As an army brat himself, he had no wish to inflict that life on any children he might have – the changes of schools, the friends lost, the constant dislocation, the feeling of always being an outsider.

His father, sensitive to slights as many insensitive people are, took that as a direct criticism. Clearly this was That Woman's influence, corrupting his boy, the son he was so proud of, a graduate from Edinburgh University with a good degree then a top cadet in the Sovereign's Parade at Sandhurst, destined for glory. Their meetings became reduced to special family occasions, when he was, of course, icily polite to her.

Alexa, in her warm-hearted way, had been understanding. 'He didn't have your advantages, remember. He started out in the ranks and he worked his way up to where he finished entirely on his own merits. He feels he handed you success on a plate and you just threw it back in his face.'

Kelso had snorted. 'Rags to rags in three generations, you mean? You're far too generous – he's just a howling snob. And I paid my dues – surely a couple of tours in Afghanistan entitles me to tell him he can't dictate a life plan for me.'

But Roderick was still at it; he hadn't given up. Yes, it was certainly just as well his wife had strong-armed him out of the house.

Kelso was on his own at last but now he had peace, he didn't want it any more.

The ghosts were all about him, whispering at some times, wailing at others, and worst of all laughing, light-hearted and carefree. It could send him mad.

He fingered the scar running from cheekbone to jawline. It was still tender but healing well, the marks left by the stitches almost gone. A pity life couldn't knit itself together again in that easy way.

Tomorrow he'd go back to the job. The alternative was to look for oblivion at the bottom of a glass – or take a trip up Salisbury Crags and choose the quick way down.

CHAPTER TWO

It was a better morning in Skye today, with just a few wisps of morning mist draped flirtatiously round the shoulders of the Black Cuillin ridge. There had been a first fall of snow overnight and it lingered up there on the peaks, sparkling now as the sun started to peep through. In the icy pale aquamarine sky, an eagle was soaring, spiralling up and then away out of sight.

Sitting at her desk in the window of the main office, Beatrice didn't even notice. Though she could also see across the bay to Balnasheil village on her left, her gaze was directed the other way, to the view across the lawn to the rough ground and the moor on the hill that rose behind, where the heather bloom had long faded and the bracken was russet and limp after all the rain. The Black Cuillin ridge was a pale hazy blue today, its brutal lines softened by the hanging mist.

Adam was out with the dog, his habit at this time in the

morning, which explained why she was always at her desk so early when he was at home. Today the dog seemed excited, racing round and round in circles with its nose down, as if the damp morning scents were particularly strong. Then suddenly it was off, speeding in a straight line, and Beatrice saw with sick dismay a panic-stricken hare bounding out of cover, saw a moment later the chase abruptly stop. She couldn't see exactly what happened but she didn't need to. The dog's way with hares was always the same: a chop to the back of the head that broke its neck.

Adam would be pleased, anyway. He was calling the dog, petting it, stooping to take the limp carcass from its jaws then returning to the house, holding the hare by the ears, as the dog pranced at his side. The worst bit was that he would bring it in to show it off and Beatrice would have to look impressed.

He was beaming when he came in. 'Look at what this clever girl's done!' he crowed.

The dog, for once, was acting the way normal dogs did, bouncing around, wagging its docked tail in a frenzy of enthusiasm.

'Yes, Amber, you'll get your share, girl. Just be patient,' he scolded her jovially.

Trying not to look at the mutilated creature dripping blood on the carpet, Beatrice murmured something suitable. The dog's mouth was bloodied too, and she tried not to look at that either.

'I'll put it in the game pantry and Vicky can do us jugged hare once it's been hung. That'll be something to look forward to!'

Beatrice only just managed not to shudder – jugged hare, ugh, and he liked it high, too, so that the whole house stank. For once she wasn't sorry to see him leave. With the dog circling him, its eyes on its prey, he went to the door, then paused.

'You've made sure that the car will be at the pier when I go across later?'

'Yes, of course, Adam. Marek drove it round first thing this morning then got back in Murdo John's boat when he brought Vicky across.'

She didn't add that Marek had sworn at her because neither he nor anyone else liked having to make the long drive around the head of the bay, but it was only Adam and his guests who never had to.

She went on, 'Your flight's at seven tonight, so you really ought to leave before twelve o'clock to have plenty of time. You know what the traffic can be like around Glasgow.'

'Yes, yes,' he said testily. 'I do know how long it takes to get to the airport.'

Beatrice flinched. 'Sorry, sorry. Of course you do.'

'It's all right, sweetie.' His tone had changed and he was smiling. 'I know you only want to make absolutely sure I don't miss the conference. I'm just going to have a word with Harry before that – oh, did I tell you he'll be coming up the day after tomorrow? All right?'

'Of course,' Beatrice said dully. Harry Drummond, the other executive director, allegedly possessed of great charm which he never bothered to bestow on her, was always a demanding guest. 'Does Eva know?'

'You could tell her. But just check that she's done the

needful, would you? I know I can rely on you.' He gave her a smile and a wink.

'Of course, Adam,' she said, her heart in her voice. 'Always.'

She went off at once to check the drinks cabinet. Once, Eva had forgotten to order in Harry's particular Highland malt and he'd been furious. She'd better check his room too; Harry was fussy about everything and though Eva might be willing, she wasn't what you could call meticulous. She really wasn't needed – not for any domestic purpose, anyway. Beatrice would be happier – much happier – if she'd just go. She had a sort of fresh charm that had kept Adam amused for longer than usual, which made it worse if—

But she had work to do. She went back to the office and settled to checking through a pile of invoices. It would never do if the accounts weren't in perfect order when Harry arrived; she dreaded him finding some discrepancy, though he never had so far.

At ten o'clock she made herself a cup of coffee and had just got out a pack of Twixes when the door of her office opened. She hastily slipped it back in the drawer as Adam came in, looking bothered.

'We've got a problem in Oban, Beatrice. Harry's had an urgent request for supplies and he hasn't much confidence that the girl in the warehouse will get it turned round fast enough. Could you bear to get down there right away and sort it out? I know it's a bore, sweetie, but it really is vital that we get the stuff out without delay and if you're in charge I know it'll mean lives being saved.'

It was a bore; it was more than a bore, it was hours and hours of driving on difficult roads, and then the same back again. But he'd called her 'sweetie' and he needed her.

She smiled. 'Yes, of course, Adam. I'll just take ten minutes to finish up here and then I'll be on my way.'

'I really don't know what we'd do without you.' He smiled down at her, his hand on her shoulder. He was looking particularly attractive today, she thought, with a dark blue shirt that made his eyes look an even deeper blue.

'Oh – that's all right,' she said, blushing with gratification.

'But don't try to drive back tonight. Find yourself a hotel in Oban and treat yourself to a nice meal. Can't have you exhausted and falling asleep on the road, can we? Human Face would simply collapse.'

Treasuring another smile, Beatrice said goodbye to him, finished what she was doing then went through the door under the stairs, past the office – presumably securely locked now – to the big old-fashioned kitchen. They'd had to spend money on upgrading the bedrooms for visitors and this, like her own flat and the bedsitter by the kitchen, was somewhere they could economise to minimise expenses for the charity.

Vicky was sitting down at the table, having her break, but she got up when Beatrice came in.

'Kettle's just boiled,' she said, 'and there's shortbread there.'

Beatrice's eyes flickered to the open box Vicky indicated, but she shook her head. 'No thanks, Vicky. I just came to tell you I've got to go down to Oban and won't be back tonight. And Harry's coming the day after tomorrow, apparently, so we'll need you to stay on to prepare everything ready for supper that night anyway – don't know how long he'll be staying.'

Vicky pulled a face. 'That's a blow. I'd a few things planned for my afternoons. Still, the extra money's welcome, I suppose.'

'Well, you know how it is with these busy men – they don't always know what their plans are much in advance.' Beatrice spoke stiffly; she still had an upstairs-downstairs mentality and always quashed any discussion of the directors. 'Adam may even be back from Paris himself by then but I'm not sure – he hasn't said. And could you please check on Harry's room? You know how particular he is.'

Vicky laughed. 'Oh, you could say! The last time Eva forgot to put a bathrobe in his en suite you'd have thought it was the end of civilisation as we know it. Some folk just need to grow up.'

Beatrice smiled non-committally, though she certainly agreed. 'I'll just tell Eva that I'll be away. Is she in her room?'

'I haven't seen her around the house.'

Beatrice nodded and went out. As she reached Eva's door she could hear sounds of movement, but when she knocked there was a sudden silence, then a pause and a scuffle before her voice said, 'Come in!'

Eva was standing in front of her wardrobe – a sale-room purchase, like the rest of the furniture. The door was inclined to swing open if not properly shut and as Beatrice came towards her she could see that a lot of the hangers were empty.

Eva's face turned a dull red, but she said only, 'Hello, Beatrice. You want something?'

Beatrice explained and Eva nodded. 'Vicky and I take care of things, OK? Have a nice time.'

'It's not a jaunt, you know,' Beatrice said sharply. 'I'd much rather stay here and make sure the accounts are all in order for Harry to see when he comes. You know Adam will be away too? He's going to a conference in Paris.'

Eva said, 'Yes, I know,' and turned her back to fiddle with something on the dressing table.

'I'll see you tomorrow, then.' Beatrice went to the door. Then she noticed there was a suitcase standing just beside it and there was another smaller one, open and half filled, by the bed. She walked out, pretending she hadn't seen that.

If Eva was going to run out on them, it was the best thing she could possibly do. Her heart lifted a little. She'd have Adam to herself for a while and as always the hope that never quite died sprang up again.

It was getting harder to hope – much harder. Beatrice was getting on for forty now; she had started feeling panicky about the relentless ticking of the biological clock, and the agony of rejection when yet another 'housekeeper' appeared was getting harder to bear, too. Sometimes she even had to fight down her anger that Adam was so shallow as to think that a pretty face and a lithe body were worth more than the sort of soul-surrendered, for ever love that she was offering, a love that could transform both their lives – if he would only let it.

Just thinking about it was physically painful. But the pang of jealousy passed, and as she walked upstairs to her bedroom it occurred to her that if Eva went of her own accord, she wouldn't have to worry about – well, what she didn't want to have to worry about, and her spirits lifted.

'Wake up, Rosamond!' she said as she unlocked the door and went into her bedroom. 'We're going to go on a trip – isn't that nice? Now you can watch me while I pack.'

She picked up the doll from the little crib that stood in the corner of the room, draped in white layered tulle with a frilly canopy, and propped her in a chair. The blank blue eyes opened obligingly and under their sightless gaze Beatrice packed her own modest bag, then fetched a holdall from her wardrobe.

'I know you don't like going in the bag, darling, but it's just till we can get to the car. Then you can sit up and look at everything,' she said as she tucked the doll into the holdall. She zipped it shut; she might meet Vicky on the way downstairs – or worse, Adam . . .

And, indeed, he was in the hall as she came downstairs. She was touched that he was waiting to say goodbye to her.

'All ready?' he said jovially as she appeared. 'That's my girl.'

A frown crossed her face. 'Should I have booked a room for when you come back? If you come straight back from the conference it'll be quite a late flight.'

'No, no.' He sounded impatient, on edge. 'I'll probably go to Harry's flat – I'll see. Now off you go.'

Beatrice had opened the front door when he called to her, 'What time does Vicky leave?'

She turned, beaming. 'Oh, were you thinking you could take her across when Marek took you? It's so like you, to

41

think of that! But she won't be ready when you'll need to go. Don't worry – her husband always pops over to fetch her around half past twelve.'

'Right, right.' Adam turned to go back into his flat, then as an afterthought added, 'Safe journey, and thanks again, sweetie,' and Beatrice left, bathed in the sunshine of his approval.

DI Kelso Strang presented himself at DCS Jane Borthwick's office at nine-thirty. He hadn't wanted to go to see her, but DCI Chisholm had insisted.

'Didn't expect to see you back quite so soon, lad,' he'd said. 'Are you sure it's a good idea?' Then he'd added, 'Good to see you, of course.'

'Yes, I'm quite sure,' Strang said tautly. He was finding it hard to get used to the mixture of dismay, embarrassment and over-hearty goodwill he had encountered on every side that covered up an understandable wish that the difficult meeting hadn't happened. 'I've got a job to do.'

Of course, he had no reason to feel nervous going up to see Detective Chief Superintendent Borthwick. Her support and sympathy at the funeral had been perfectly judged, but even so . . . Alexa had once asked one of his colleagues what he thought of 'JB' and got the reply, 'Fair, firm and effing formidable.' It had made Alexa laugh, but it said it all, really. Strang took a deep breath before he knocked on the door.

Borthwick was sitting at her desk doing paperwork and glanced up when he came in. 'Kelso! Good to see you. Sit down – give me a moment just to finish this.'

After the funeral, Mary Strang had described her as a handsome woman, and her son had been surprised. He'd never really thought about JB's appearance at all, and looking at her now he suspected that wasn't an accident. She was always smartly dressed, mostly in well-cut trouser suits that looked as if she'd only swapped one uniform for another when she joined CID, and her appearance – neat dark hair, pale skin without noticeable make-up – was, he supposed, what you'd describe as professional.

You weren't meant to think about the woman behind the job. She was – he groped for the word – self-contained, that was it.

She scribbled a signature on a sheet of paper, then put it to one side with a muttered apology and looked directly at him. That was the one thing you did notice about her – her eyes. A clear, light grey, they had a very direct gaze.

She studied him for a moment then in her cool, brusque way, said, 'You felt like coming back – good. Coffee?'

It didn't matter that he was tongue-tied. She was talking on. 'I was going to speak to you anyway. The results have just come through to me – they've passed you for Senior Investigating Officer.'

It was lucky she had handed him the milk just at that moment and Strang was able to look down, swallowing the lump in his throat and blinking hard. It would have been a cause for serious celebration, before. His response was flat but she didn't react to that, just explained that though there wasn't a slot for him at the moment he would certainly be high on the waiting list.

'Of course, I ought to point out to you that there are other possibilities too. I suppose you might want to think about a promotion to another division, somewhere different—'

He felt something like panic. Leave Edinburgh, leave the familiar, leave the house, even the empty house— 'Not sure,' he mumbled.

Borthwick seemed pleased. 'No, no, of course you're not. You shouldn't make decisions of any kind at the moment.'

Then she paused, looking at him with those penetrating eyes. 'You think you're all right, but you're not. You're pretending to yourself that you are. I know, because I did exactly the same myself when my husband died suddenly. It's not the worst idea, actually, and I doubt if there's any method of getting through it that you could call good. You just need to be aware that this is what you're doing and not lie to yourself.

'The good thing is that being busy makes the days pass more quickly. If you're suddenly crippled, you get very proficient at using crutches over time. You've just joined the legion of the lame and, with the help of whatever crutches you find useful, you can live with the injury, even though it won't ever completely mend.'

He saw JB's eyes linger for a second on his scar, then swiftly pass on. He cleared his throat. 'Thanks – I'll remember that.'

'Right. More coffee? No? Are you sure you don't want to take a bit more time? I've signed you off on compassionate leave.'

Truth to tell, he was feeling shaky and even a bit light-headed; he recognised that he was still suffering from delayed shock, but being on his own with nothing to do except think would certainly be worse.

'No, I'm fine,' he said. 'I don't want that. Thanks for the coffee, ma'am.'

DCI Chisholm didn't look thrilled to see him when he reappeared but he made all the right noises. 'The team will be glad to see you back.'

Like hell they will, Kelso thought, but he played along. 'Great,' he said hollowly as they walked along to the CID room.

Beatrice Lacey was feeling very tired by the time she arrived at the warehouse in Oban. In her little Fiat, she had felt every bump and pothole in the roads, and there were plenty of those. Her back was aching and her arthritic knees had locked solid; it took her a few groaning minutes to prise herself out of the car and settle Rosamond.

'You've been such a good girl, sweetheart, on all that long journey. You go to sleep now. Mummy won't be long.' She put her into the holdall, zipped it up to conceal the doll from view, then locked the car and hobbled across to the entrance.

She liked going to the warehouse. It was always busy with workers filling packing cases with orders being sent off to refugees all over the world and she could take pride in seeing the shelves her money had helped to fill with mattresses, blankets, tents and boxes of basic foodstuffs. She didn't like the manager, though, who always seemed to resent Beatrice's supervisory visits – unless, of course, Adam was with her, in which case the woman was always as nice as pie.

Beatrice's arrival was obviously a surprise and not a

pleasant one. 'I didn't know you were coming,' she said with a sniff of annoyance. 'No one told me.'

'Oh sorry, Sandra. I don't mean to disturb you but Adam just asked me to pop down. There's an urgent order Harry was worried about and he wanted me to expedite it – you know what he's like.' She despised herself for sounding placatory; it never did any good.

Sandra bridled. 'And what order is this?'

Beatrice told her and the woman looked even more annoyed. 'No one told me that was urgent. Harry could just have picked up the phone and I'd have got it off at once. I don't know what the status is, just at the moment, whether it's ready to go or not.'

'Have you the note of exactly what's needed? Perhaps we could put some more workers directly onto it,' Beatrice suggested as delicately as she could. No wonder Adam wanted her to come down – Sandra was always so obstructive!

'Well, yes. Naturally. I had managed to work out that we'd need to do that,' Sandra snapped. 'I'll just check the details.'

She bustled off to the office at one side of the building, leaving Beatrice to follow more slowly, still stiff after the journey. Sandra was coming out again with a thick file of papers in her hand while Beatrice was still on her way across, and she saw the woman's contemptuous eyes flicker over her.

'Oh, there you are,' she said pointedly. 'I don't know what on earth this fuss is all about. That shipment went out last night, quite routinely. Looks as if you've had a wasted journey.' She gave a malicious smile.

'Oh – oh, that's excellent. It was just, well, you know, Harry was anxious,' Beatrice floundered.

'He should know by now he doesn't need to be. Anything else on your list for checking up on me?'

'No, no. That's fine. Thanks, Sandra – that was very efficient.'

The conciliatory attempt didn't succeed. 'No need to thank me – I don't do it for *you*.' She turned away, calling to one of the packers, 'There's a delivery arrived – can you sort it just now?'

Beatrice left, her face glowing with embarrassment. She was furious that Harry had put her in such an awkward position; what on earth had it all been about? She'd never liked Harry; she didn't trust him, and she didn't like the way Adam was when he was with him. He seemed to think he had to sound hard and cynical, not showing the wonderful, caring side that he showed to her. Harry had just wasted a whole lot of her valuable time, as well as the charity's money; now she'd have to look for somewhere to stay and somewhere to eat.

She loved her food. At the prospect of a nice meal her mouth always watered, but eating in a public restaurant . . . She felt all eyes were upon her, that the waiter would take her order with a curled lip if it was for the sort of thing she liked to eat and, with her courage failing, she would end up ordering cold, unappealing salad instead.

And even a B & B was expensive. Every penny spent on her was a penny less for the starving orphans who haunted her dreams. She looked at her watch.

It wasn't that late. She could find a KFC, buy what she

47

really wanted then park up somewhere to eat it and have a little rest before she drove home. It was a long way, but she'd be fine.

'Back in our own bed tonight, Rosamond,' she said cheerfully, and drove off.

She'd never known a day pass more slowly. Eva had busied herself checking the bedrooms and going through orders for supplies with Vicky, still a little on edge about the summons from Adam that so far hadn't come. She'd been terrified all of the previous day, but she was beginning to believe he hadn't noticed after all.

She'd heard him going away just before twelve, and then Vicky left a little later. With a sigh of relief, she finished her packing and was just about to phone Daniel when she heard a car engine and went through to the front of the house to see who it was. A delivery, perhaps . . .

But it wasn't. Adam's Mercedes was coming up the drive. She gave a gasp and fled back to her own room. He must have forgotten something – passport; ticket, perhaps. Poor Beatrice – he'd be sure to blame her for allowing that to happen.

Did that mean he'd missed his conference, that he wouldn't go? She would leave anyway; she'd only to contact Daniel and he'd come – but that would have to wait until dark. She couldn't risk going in broad daylight carrying luggage, and she hated the thought of leaving behind the few possessions that were all she had in the world.

It had worried her that Beatrice had seen the suitcases. Eva knew that she reported everything to Adam and it wouldn't be good if he knew she was planning to leave – he just wasn't the sort of man you walked out on.

But she hadn't commented on it at the time and apparently she hadn't said anything to Adam – probably glad to see the back of her. She felt sorry for Beatrice, who was obviously so desperately in love with him that she couldn't see what was right under her nose: that he was using her shamefully. She'd once let slip a remark that suggested she thought that one day Adam would settle down and marry her.

Well, he'd never actually discussed Beatrice with her but she'd once seen him look at her with a little shudder of revulsion. The happy ending wasn't going to come any time soon. Eva knew, none better, how many girls there were looking for an easy way into the country; Adam would replace her within a couple of weeks.

When the knock came on her bedroom door, she froze. She'd managed to avoid Adam pretty successfully yesterday; she'd hoped she'd never have to see him again. Perhaps he wanted her to arrange another flight for him or something, since Beatrice wasn't there to do it.

'Just – just a moment!' she called. As silently as she could, she shoved the smaller suitcase out of sight under the bed then picked up the bigger one and swung it into the wardrobe.

Taking a deep, calming breath, she went to open the door. Yes, there was Adam, but he was looking quite relaxed and smiling at her.

'Are you busy?' he said. 'There's something I want to show you.'

The wardrobe door, hastily shut, swung back a little but

mercifully not far enough to let him see the suitcase and the empty hangers. It was all right, he wasn't harking back to yesterday morning.

'Of course, if you want me, darling, I am not busy,' she said brightly.

'Good,' he said. 'I'll bring the jeep round.'

'I just get my coat.'

She did wonder, as she shut the wardrobe door more carefully and put on a jacket, what he could be taking her to see, but it was very reassuring that he was in such a good mood.

The dog was in the back of the jeep when it drew up outside the front door. She didn't like it; its total indifference to anything except its master was unnerving and when its amber eyes were looking straight at you without apparently seeing you, it was positively sinister.

'Where is it that we go, Adam?' she asked as he drove on a little further and then took the rough track that led up onto the moor. He didn't reply immediately and she went on, clearing her throat with a nervous cough, 'I thought you were going away to Paris today.'

'Oh yes, I am, but not just immediately. It was such a glorious afternoon, sweetie, I thought I really must take you up to see the best view in all of Skye. You've never been up there, have you?'

She shook her head. 'I – I don't think so.'

'It's pretty spectacular, I promise you, and I couldn't bear to waste the day. We won't have many more like this as the weather closes in and we have to take advantage of it, don't you think?'

There was no denying that it was a glorious day. As the jeep bumped up the track across the rising moorland, the scenery was a symphony of soft colour, the mountains off to her left shading through greens to greys to blue distance; above, the sky was clear azure, with just a few wispy clouds.

'Is very beautiful,' she murmured, but she was starting to feel uneasy, very uneasy. Why had he suddenly got this idea? She'd been living at Balnasheil Lodge since May and he hadn't demonstrated an interest in showing her any scenery at all apart from the ceiling in his bedroom. And for him to do this right now . . . The hairs on the back of her neck were starting to prickle and she could feel cold sweat beading her brow.

He turned off the track, the jeep lurching over the rough ground, with the summit of the hill just ahead of them.

'Here we are!' he said cheerfully. 'Out you get and take a look at this.' He went round to the back of the car to let the dog out and it raced off, relishing its freedom.

Eva got out, looking uncertainly about her, her hair blowing in the slight breeze. Adam was striding ahead and she followed him up to the ridge where there was a small level space.

'Amazing, isn't it?' he said as she joined him, and she gasped.

It was, indeed, amazing. The moor had petered out into rough, salt-stunted grass and low rocky outcrops; beyond, the land fell away with dramatic suddenness, down hundreds of feet of iron-grey cliffs to the sea below. It was calm today, a deep, deep blue, with a white froth of waves fringing a line of spiky rocks below in a curve at the foot of the cliff. The air was sharp with the sea-smell, and the gulls' cries, like shrieks of lost souls, came up from far below as they coasted on the air currents. The islands of the Outer Hebrides were dark smudges on the thin blue line of the horizon.

Eva's every nerve was shrieking *Danger!* She stopped a few feet from the edge, moved back, away from it. She gave a little nervous laugh and her voice was shaky as she said, 'Is wonderful, darling, but I'm not so good in high places. Dizzy, you know?'

Adam was looking at her, his eyes blank. 'You're such a fool,' he said, his tone almost conversational. 'Did you really think I wouldn't realise what was going on?'

CHAPTER THREE

Beatrice came out with her bucket of chicken and chips and found a lay-by on the way out of Oban where she could stop and tuck in. She needed her strength for the long journey ahead, she told herself.

She was still furious with Harry. He'd made her look a fool in front of Sandra and she'd have a few sharp words to say to him when she saw him the day after tomorrow. The way he treated her, he sometimes seemed to forget that she wasn't the hired help, she was Human Face's most committed patron.

The next few days were going to be interesting. It had been a huge relief when she saw that Eva was packing, and surely she'd take her chance to slip away quietly with the young man from Balnasheil when there was no one in the house. Adam might be angry that she'd walked out, but if he thought she was spying on him for some strange reason he'd be relieved he didn't have to deal with it – surely he would.

Then there would be one of the spells when she had Adam to herself. He was invited out a lot, of course, and even gave dinner parties sometimes for the county set, but every so often it meant a precious evening on their own.

One of these days he'd be ready, at last, to ask her to marry him. She'd explained that they could do so much more good if she had full control of her trust fund and she'd only get that once she was married; he'd given her that special smile and said, 'There's no rush. I'd hate you to think I'm going to marry you for money, sweetie.'

Whatever he might say, she knew it wouldn't be for any other reason, but she didn't care. Perhaps she had reason to thank her old-fashioned father for his demeaning provision.

It would actually have made a lot more sense if he'd tied up Quentin's trust fund as well. Then he might not have run through the money before he was thirty and had to live on dead-end jobs and handouts from his older sister ever since.

She'd kept trying to explain to him that the charity came first, but she couldn't let him starve in a gutter, whatever Adam might say. She knew perfectly well that he'd come to Skye because she found it harder to turn him down when they were face to face than if he was on the phone – but blood was thicker than water, after all.

Quentin had found a woman to move in with, someone from Cumbria who'd moved up here and bought a gift shop, and Beatrice hadn't seen so much of him lately – perhaps the handouts were coming from her. She could only hope that he'd stay away for the next bit before she had to compete for Adam's attention with another 'housekeeper'.

Beatrice nibbled daintily at the last chip, then cleaned her greasy fingers with the wipes she always carried in her bag. She turned to the doll, propped up in the passenger seat.

'It's time we got on our way again, my darling. I think you should have a little rest, don't you? I'll let you sit up again later on.'

She laid the doll down and then drove across to the litter bin so that she only had to open the window to drop in her rubbish, looking round disapprovingly at the mess of trays and bottles dumped by people too lazy to walk over and dispose of them properly, then pulled out into the traffic to begin the long drive back.

He was right; she had been a fool. How could she think he wouldn't have noticed that she'd been in the office? Eva could feel the blood drain from her face.

She gave a frightened little whinny of laughter. 'Adam, you are not nice! What do you mean?'

He fixed her with a cold, expressionless stare. 'Who is he? What does he want to know?'

Go on denying everything? Tell him? There was mortal danger now; her own safety hung on her reply and he seemed to know anyway. There really was no choice.

'I – I don't know. Daniel, he is called. He want me to look in the files.'

'Which?'

Her mind was numb with terror. There were only a couple she could remember; she told him those. 'I don't know all. Is written down—'

'Where?'

'Notebook. Is in my bag. I show you, Adam. Please, let's go back and I show you.'

'He hasn't seen it?'

She shook her head, biting her lip so hard that it began to bleed. 'We go back, I show you,' she said again, desperately.

He didn't reply. He gave her one last, contemptuous look and turned away. As she made to follow him he gave a short whistle and with mounting panic she saw the dog racing to his side.

'Adam!' she screamed. 'What are you doing?'

Again he ignored her. He gave an order to the dog and then stepped back.

The dog turned towards her and advanced, moving slowly and steadily towards her, not rushing, lifting first one black foot and setting it down slowly, deliberately, then another. Its eyes were locked on her and it was so close now that she could see saliva glistening on dark pink gums and bared white teeth and smell its gamey breath.

The dog in front, the void behind her. Eva's head was feeling light, as if it would float away. Was this real or was she dreaming, locked into some sort of hideous nightmare, unable to wake up?

She stepped back; the dog stepped forward. She stepped back again. And again. Soon there wouldn't be anything to step back onto except empty air.

Adam, with a thin smile on his face, was keeping his distance. Behind him there was nothing but moorland on every side, miles of it. No people, no friendly houses. No miraculous rescue. No one to hear her scream.

'Adam, please! Please, Adam!' She was crying

convulsively now, with high, frightened gasps like a child. There was no hope, nothing she could do. There was only a choice: the dog, or . . .

She'd seen what the dog did to the animals it caught. The other – it would be quick, at least.

There was a chirruping whistle from Adam and the dog gave several sharp, excited barks, snapping the pointed teeth, barely containing its excitement. Any second, it would be given the signal to attack.

Eva had long neglected her Catholic faith but now, lips stiff with terror, she gabbled, in her mother tongue, the old familiar words: '*Hail Mary, full of grace, the Lord is with thee. Blessed art thou among women and blessed is the fruit of thy womb, Jesus.*'

She took a step back. '*Holy Mary, Mother of God, pray for us sinners . . .*' Then another step. '*. . . now and at the hour of our death.*'

And one more step.

Gripping the steering wheel hard in concentration, Beatrice stared at the road unwinding ahead of her, screwing up her face against the lights of the oncoming cars. She yawned, feeling her eyes starting to itch, the lids beginning to droop. She stretched them wide open, and shook her head as if that might dislodge the treacherous longing for sleep.

It was half past seven. She hadn't taken a proper break in Oban and the long drive was taking its toll.

'Oh dear, Rosamond,' she said to the doll, now sitting propped in the passenger seat, 'Mummy's getting very, very tired. I think we're going to have to stop for a minute.'

She peered ahead into the darkness. She wasn't sure where she was, even, and all she could see was featureless rough ground on either side of the main road. There was only one petrol station with a shop and a little cafe attached around here, before the Skye Bridge, and she couldn't remember whether she'd passed it or not. Surely she'd have noticed it?

Beatrice drove on for a bit, uncertainly – and then there it was, the welcome lights an invitation. She turned into the forecourt, drove round to the cafe and got out, with a reassuring pat to Rosamond.

The cafe was more homely than the motorway chains and the thickly iced cakes were home-made; the sugar rush of a large slice of lemon sponge and a black coffee should keep her alert enough to get the two of them safely home. She carried her tray over to the window where she could keep an eye on Rosamond in the car.

With its position here in the wilds, the business did a good trade, with a lot of cars coming and going. Enjoying her cake, Beatrice didn't pay much attention to the big Mercedes by the petrol pumps – until Adam Carnegie came out of the shop and walked back towards it.

Beatrice gasped, and inhaled on a crumb. It was only after the paroxysm of coughing had subsided that she could mop her watering eyes and peer out. The car was just driving out, heading south.

Adam should have been on his way to Paris by now. What could have made him miss his flight? She rummaged in her bag for her mobile; her automatic reflex was to call him and find out what had gone wrong and ask whether there was something she could do.

Then she paused. Once or twice before she'd tried to be too helpful and had got a stinging rebuke. If Adam had wanted her help, he'd have asked for it – and anyway, what could she really do just at the moment? Perhaps he'd have left a message for her back at the Lodge. She'd be in a position to deal with it there.

And anyway, what if she'd been wrong? The lighting wasn't very good; what if it hadn't really been Adam at all, just someone who looked like him?

No, the best thing she could do was to get back as soon as possible. She finished the rest of her cake more carefully, drained the coffee and left. She had enough to think about now to make sure she wouldn't fall asleep at the wheel.

'Pick up, Eva, pick up!'

For the twentieth time, Daniel Tennant pressed redial. It rang briefly, then went to voicemail yet again. He ended the call, then slammed the phone down so hard on the table in front of him that he bruised his knuckles.

He had been texting, with increasing frustration at the lack of replies from her, off and on since the middle of the afternoon. There was a lot hanging on this. Eventually he had walked from his rented cottage to the pier and with a little frisson of disquiet saw that Carnegie's Mercedes, usually parked by the pier, had gone.

She'd said she would call him the minute the man left, but she hadn't. He went back to the cottage, just starting to worry.

Maybe she'd got cold feet. He phoned this time but she didn't pick up. He left a message, asking her what was happening – still no reply. When he phoned again, he left a more reassuring message; it didn't matter if she'd changed her mind, he just wanted to know that she was all right.

There was no response to any of the next calls, either. At last Daniel got up, unable to sit still, and paced over to the window that looked out across the bay. It was evening now and in the fast-fading light he could only just make out the bulk of Balnasheil Lodge against the hill on the other side. The windows were all in darkness.

He couldn't bear hanging around watching a phone that obstinately refused to ring. He had the use of a small boat; he pulled on his weatherproof jacket and then walked along to the wooden jetty where it was moored. He had no need for secrecy this time so he fired up the outboard and chugged across in less than ten minutes. He tied up at the wooden jetty and crossed the lawn; in the darkness he could see the paler colour of the drive going up to the front door, and went towards it.

There were no lights to be seen anywhere. When he rang the bell he thought fancifully that it sounded as if it was ringing in an empty house, and he didn't expect a response. He didn't get one. There were no cars parked outside either.

He walked round to the window Eva had told him was her bedsitter, but though he cupped his hands and peered through he couldn't make out anything in the darkness, except a white mass that was her bed. There was no one in it.

He hadn't really thought she would be. He could probably get in by the side door – no one locked doors around here – but he really couldn't afford to be caught inside the house. There wasn't much point anyway, when he could see her bed was empty.

He turned away, dismayed and helpless, then noticed a light in the little gatehouse at the foot of the drive. Marek might know something, though whether he'd tell Daniel was another matter.

He'd seen him drinking his beer in the pub from time to time but the man rebuffed all attempts to draw him into conversation. Perhaps it was a language problem, but on the other hand from the look of the man he wasn't likely to be chatty in any language.

The sudden, savage barking of a dog stopped him and he looked wildly round him. Surely the grounds weren't patrolled? But no, he was just walking past a cage in front of a huddle of outbuildings and he could make out a large dog there, even hear the snapping of its teeth as he passed. Lucky there was a stout padlock, he thought as he knocked on the gatehouse door.

Marek only opened it a few inches and he didn't look welcoming. In answer to Daniel's question, he shrugged.

'I don't see her,' he said flatly, then retreated, shutting the door again.

There was nothing more he could do. Amid another frenzy of barks, Daniel headed back to the boat. He was seriously, seriously worried now, almost sick with worry.

Where was she? Where could she be? And what could he do, if she wouldn't answer her phone – or chillingly, couldn't?

He knew the answer to that. Nothing. Except wait. And worry.

* * *

Beatrice drove faster than she usually liked to do over the narrowing roads. She was worried about what could have delayed Adam; he would be so upset if he missed his plane! It was only a one-day conference but it was a regular meeting that brought together agencies dealing with refugees in Europe as well as Africa and he always enjoyed those. What was haunting her was that maybe it was something she'd failed to do – that would be so awful, and she just wanted to check everything to make sure.

Muttering a checklist and pushing on, she lost concentration and rounding the corner before the old stone bridge she skidded on some loose gravel; she went on more cautiously after that with her heart in her mouth.

When she reached the drive, there was a light on in the gatehouse but Balnasheil Lodge itself was in total darkness. Eva was usually a night bird; perhaps she was in the kitchen, at the back.

Or perhaps she'd gone, really just gone. Beatrice's heart gave a little skip of pleasure at the thought.

But she had more important things to attend to. She climbed out, stiff after the journey, and limped to the front door. When she tried it, it opened – did that mean Eva was still in the house? If the house was actually to be empty they locked up, though they didn't bother otherwise.

She hurried into the office, dreading a reproachful note, but her desk was still in the pristine state she always left it in. There was no rebuke, but no instructions either; she was more puzzled than ever.

She switched on the computer to see if he had sent her an email but the only ones that had come in today were routine. She did an extra check of the arrangements in case she'd got it wrong about the time of the flight, but no; it was exactly as she had thought.

Adam would just have to get himself on to a later plane, if he'd missed that one for some reason. Or perhaps she really had been mistaken; perhaps it had been someone else at the service station who looked like him and she'd made an assumption because of the car. Plenty of people owned Mercs and surely if there had been a problem Adam would have let her know. Yes, that probably explained it.

Certainly there was nothing she needed to do tonight – except, of course, check to see if Eva really had gone. The dark house had been promising, and there was no light on in the back corridor. The kitchen door was standing open and she wasn't there.

Beatrice's heart was beating a little faster as she reached Eva's room. In case she was in after all and was just having an early night, Beatrice tapped on the door and opened it cautiously.

The room was empty and when she switched on the light she could see that there was none of Eva's usual clutter on the dressing table. She opened the wardrobe: empty. The drawers in the little chest: empty. Eva had gone, most likely run away with the young man she'd seen her with the other night. Beatrice made a little soft, triumphant sound.

Adam would be angry, humiliated, even, and she gave a shiver at the thought of how angry he would be. But she must work extra hard at making the Lodge a restful, pleasant place to be, an oasis in his busy life. Perhaps after this he'd see how deceitful these girls could be and he wouldn't see the need to find another 'housekeeper'.

And of course, poor Adam might have come looking for Eva and been worried that something had happened to her when she was nowhere to be found. That would explain why he was delayed. Beatrice's annoyance on his behalf mounted; it was so inconsiderate of Eva, and she'd probably made Adam miss the conference he'd been looking forward to.

Well, there was nothing she could do about it tonight. Perhaps he'd managed to get a standby ticket, or something. She gave a huge yawn and turned to go.

It was only then that she noticed the other smaller suitcase that had been pushed right under the bed. Why would Eva have gone and not taken that with her too?

Beatrice felt sick. The 'what ifs' were multiplying in her mind, forming more and more hideous pictures, like the flashbacks that had only recently stopped afflicting her.

Oh no, no, it couldn't be, she told herself. *Not again!* Suddenly the room seemed very, very cold.

Vicky was surprised when Daniel Tennant appeared on the doorstep first thing in the morning, asking if she would take him to Balnasheil Lodge when she went across. She didn't know him very well, had just chatted to him once or twice in the pub where Murdo John did shifts as a barman.

'Why?' she asked, puzzled.

'I've been trying to phone Eva since yesterday. She's not replying – it just goes to voicemail.' He seemed quite upset.

'Maybe it's just the signal's down. It's a bit iffy round here,' she said soothingly. She didn't like to say that maybe Adam Carnegie had found out about Eva's little flirtation and told her it had to stop.

'I'd still like to go across and see that she's all right.'

Vicky looked at him sharply. 'Is there some reason why she shouldn't be?'

'No, no, of course not. I just – just want to speak to her.' He didn't sound convincing.

He really was worried. Vicky felt a sudden qualm of nerves – she'd had that nasty feeling that things were going wrong at the Lodge between Adam and Eva. She said, 'Yes, I'm sure we can. You could wait and bring him back, couldn't you, Murdo?' She went to get her coat.

Murdo John, busy stacking the dishwasher, nodded, then gave Daniel a straight look. 'Do you think she'll be glad to see you?'

'I don't know,' Daniel said truthfully. 'But I know I'll be very glad to see *her*.'

From her bedroom window Beatrice saw Murdo John's boat coming across the bay to bring Vicky in to work. Then she stiffened; there was a man in the boat with them and she recognised him. What was that man doing coming here?

She'd passed a wretched night, with hideous dreams when she did get off to sleep and then wakefulness to a reality that didn't seem much better. She couldn't make up her mind what she should do; should she phone Adam to tell him Eva was gone? He might blame her if she didn't – but then again, he might blame her if she did.

If he was in Paris, if he'd caught his plane, perhaps she had just been mistaken about seeing him, and Eva herself had forgotten about the bag she'd put under the bed. Thinking of that explanation made her feel better, though she'd brought the bag up here anyway without letting herself consider why.

But this man, coming up to the house with Vicky, the man she'd seen with Eva that night – why wasn't he off somewhere with her? For a moment she felt so faint that she had to sit down.

Whatever it was, she'd have to deal with it – for Adam. Taking a deep breath, she got up and went downstairs.

As they had crossed the bay to Balnasheil Lodge the sun was still low in the sky, glinting on the sea and sending shafts of silver dancing on the waves. There was a touch of frost in the clear autumn air, making the colours particularly vivid and the outline of the surrounding hills as sharp as if it had been outlined with a fine-point pen.

Daniel Tennant was oblivious to the postcard-perfect scenery, sitting in the stern, drumming his fingers on the side of the boat. It seemed to be taking longer than usual to make the short crossing.

Vicky, feeling on edge, chattered on randomly. 'Beatrice is staying in Oban tonight, so Eva and I should have time to make sure we've got it right for Harry Drummond coming tomorrow before she gets back and starts fussing. She's always a bag of nerves in case he finds something to complain to Adam about – and believe me, he will unless everything's perfect.'

He barely heard her, and it had been difficult to make the right social responses. When they reached the jetty he had jumped out almost before Murdo John had tied up and waited with raging impatience for Vicky to follow.

Now as they walked up to the house, Vicky stopped

suddenly. There was a small Fiat parked round the front.

'Oh! Beatrice must have come back last night after all.' She didn't seem entirely delighted about that. 'Come in anyway.'

She opened a side door and ushered Daniel inside. 'This is her room here.' She gave a tap on the door but there was no answer. 'We can check in the kitchen – this way.'

Instead of following her, Daniel opened the door. 'I don't think so,' he said grimly. The room was empty of any sign of personal belongings.

Vicky turned. 'What! Has she – has she just *gone*? She didn't say anything to me about it yesterday. I thought I was her friend – why wouldn't she have said goodbye? I wonder if Beatrice knows?'

'If Beatrice knows what?'

Daniel turned. The woman coming along the corridor was hugely fat with a pale, flat face ringed with a layer of chins. She had muddy grey eyes and her hair hung in a thin, lank bob.

Before Vicky could answer, Beatrice went on, 'And who are you? What are you doing here? I saw you coming over to meet Eva the other night, didn't I?'

She was bristling with hostility. Daniel said, as pleasantly as he could, 'We were just wondering if you knew where Eva was?'

A sort of ripple passed over Beatrice's face but it was hard to tell what she was thinking. 'Gone,' she said harshly. 'Just taken off. Isn't she with you?'

'Did she tell you she was leaving?' he asked.

She gave a little snort. 'She didn't have to. I saw her suitcases, all packed. She was obviously just waiting till the coast was clear before she went. I'm just going to check around and see what else she may have taken with her.'

'I'm sure she wouldn't have taken anything that didn't belong to her!' Vicky cried, distressed. 'She was a nice girl, Beatrice.'

Daniel gritted his teeth. 'Did she say where she was going?'

'I didn't ask her. I'm sure she'll get in touch with you if she wants you to know. Perhaps she was *friendly* with someone else as well, someone that you didn't know about.'

She gave him a knowing little smirk that made him want to seize the old bat by the neck and squeeze hard. Right at this moment he'd be happy to think there might have been.

She was going on, 'Vicky, now that Eva's gone there will be quite a bit to get on with. So if there's nothing else . . . ?' She raised her eyebrows.

There wasn't, really. Feeling sicker than ever, he went back to the boat.

'Did you have a word with her?' Murdo John asked.

Daniel shook his head. 'The room was bare. She's gone.'

'Ah.' Murdo John pondered that for a moment. 'Not the first, you know. Not very – settled, these girls.'

'Perhaps not.'

They went back to the village in silence, but as Daniel got out he said, 'I'm not satisfied. I'm calling the police.'

When the phone rang, PC Livvy Murray scowled. She was on fire this morning; it looked as if she was going to get to the next level on Candy Crush and if this was Mrs Brodie again demanding to know why she hadn't found her cat, she'd tell her why instead of pretending that she was doing something about it.

Reluctantly she abandoned her game and took the call.

As she listened, her face brightened. 'I'm on it,' she said.

She pulled her hair back into a ponytail, jammed her hat down on her head, grabbed the keys and shut up shop.

Murray didn't exactly take to Daniel Tennant – that was the polite way of putting it. *Patronising git*, was what she'd thought as he explained to her how important it was to find his now presumably ex-girlfriend. He didn't seem much taken with her, either, when she said that women who packed their suitcases sometimes didn't choose to explain to absolutely everyone where they were going. She was proud of her restraint in not saying that this Eva probably just hadn't been that into him and if it'd been her, she too would have taken the first available opportunity to ditch him and disappear without a trace.

When she wouldn't promise an immediate investigation and he told her he had a problem with that, she probably shouldn't have said, 'Well, we all have our problems, sir.' But it slipped out, somehow.

Then she had to take the long and tedious road round the head of the bay to Balnasheil Lodge. She wouldn't fancy it in bad weather but fortunately today was clear and chilly and the views were certainly spectacular, if you went for that sort of thing. She preferred seeing them on one of those 'Great Scottish Views' calendars.

Her welcome at the Lodge was distinctly chilly. Murray was well used to getting a less than enthusiastic reception when she turned up on someone's doorstep, but there was no need for the woman who let her in to look at her as if she had a problem with personal hygiene.

She had the sort of posh voice you didn't usually hear from someone as fat as this – most of the toffs around here were skinny as rakes and wiry with it. It probably came from yomping around the hills in the rain, and maybe if Livvy did that herself a bit more often she wouldn't need to worry about the muffin top she was afraid would develop from sitting watching the rain with a packet of Tunnock's teacakes close at hand.

A case about a missing female had sounded promising to start with, but from what Daniel Tennant had told her it was pretty improbable that there would be anything for her to do. An adult woman who packed up then walked out without telling anyone where she was going – headline news, not.

Beatrice Lacey took her to Eva Havel's room, and all her effects had certainly gone.

'And you saw her packing – right? I'll just need a statement from you, if that's all right,' Murray said.

Beatrice, with a sigh of annoyance, led her to a sitting room on the first floor, a room with what might be called corporate furnishing – cream walls, oatmeal curtains and large leather chairs and sofas – but redeemed by its view up to the Black Cuillin, looking its majestic best on this sunny late autumn morning. Murray sat down and took out her notebook.

'I went to Eva's room yesterday to tell her I was going to Oban,' Beatrice said. 'She was obviously embarrassed to be caught packing and I didn't feel it was my business to interrogate her. To be honest with you, Constable, these girls that the charity tries to help with establishing themselves over here are often a bit unreliable. Adam Carnegie, who is our executive director, is too idealistic – I think they are sometimes less than truthful in the sob stories they tell him, to say the very least.

'Eva had a young man over in the village, and possibly more than one. I wouldn't put it past her – a flighty little thing. I think she'll be long gone by now – and of course she didn't have the courtesy to tell us where she was going. It would have saved all this nonsense.'

As she scribbled to keep up, Murray had to admit that it sounded plausible. Given the way Daniel Tennant was getting his knickers in a twist, she guessed that he wasn't just a 'concerned acquaintance' like he said – and if him, why not some other fella too?

'You don't know who else she might have been pals with?'

'No. I wasn't party to her – social life.' Beatrice's tone was scathing.

'So when did you leave yesterday?'

'Just before eleven, I think. I was to have been away overnight but I finished my business early and decided to drive back instead.'

'And she was gone by the time you got back?'

'There were no lights on so I imagine she was.'

'Right. Thanks for your time, madam.' Murray shut her notebook and tucked it away. 'There's a Mrs Macdonald who works here? That right?'

'Yes. I'll take you to find her, shall I?'

Beatrice Lacey rose with an alacrity surprising in one so bulky and led the way out, calling 'Vicky! Vicky!'

There was a reply from the kitchen and Beatrice pointed the way, then disappeared into a room on the farther side of the hall.

A cleaner who went across to do the rough work, Daniel Tennant had said, so Murray was surprised to find that Vicky Macdonald looked more the sort you'd find working in a hotel or an office: young and very pretty with her wavy fair hair and wide-set blue eyes, wearing smart-looking jeans and a neat checked shirt.

She had a worried crease between her brows, though, as she waved Murray to a seat at the kitchen table and made tea. The shortbread she offered melted in the mouth.

'That stuff's pure dead brilliant,' Murray said, and Vicky smiled.

'It's my job,' she said. 'Oh, I do the cleaning, and except when there's guests it's not very demanding. But I'm a trained cook and I do whatever catering needs doing here.'

'Not in the hotel?' Murray asked. The shortbread box was pushed towards her again and despite the muffin-top worry she couldn't resist.

'Not enough work there, except in high summer. The owner does most of it himself.'

'Right.' Murray got out her notebook. 'Eva say anything to you about leaving?'

Vicky shook her head. 'Nothing. I was surprised – not saying she was my BFF, or anything, but we always chatted and it wouldn't have been like her not to say goodbye.' Then she said with careful emphasis, 'I was worried about her, actually. She's the kind of gentle girl who could be very vulnerable and I don't think things have been going well between her and Adam lately.'

Murray looked enquiring but the only reply was a shrug and, 'Just a feeling, that's all.'

'So her position in the household – what was that?'

Vicky turned pink. 'Well – housekeeper, sort of.'

Murray raised an eyebrow. 'Bidie-in?'

She made an irritated noise. 'She was just a nice girl, all right?' she said. 'You don't know what her background was, to find herself in this position. You will be looking into it?'

'Mmm.' It was Murray's turn to be non-committal. This was sounding more and more like a girl who'd been a bit 'flighty' and had changed her mind about who was to be next. 'So – you last saw her when?'

'Yesterday. She was doing orders and checking stores through here in the back pantry and I didn't really see her after that. I don't know what she was doing.'

'Miss Lacey left at around eleven, she said.'

'That's right. Then Adam left just before twelve. Marek – Marek Kaczka, he's the handyman who lives in the gatehouse cottage – took him across by boat to Balnasheil. His car's always parked there because the road round the bay is so awful—'

'Tell me about it,' Murray said with feeling.

'I saw Marek come back, and then my husband came across to take me home at about one.'

'And Mr Carnegie's car had gone by that time? Right. So Eva was alone here?'

'Yes. The thing is, how did she get away? She'd told Daniel she was going to call him when she wanted to go.'

'Yes, he said. But there's nothing more you can add to that?'

'I wish there was. You are going to check it out?' She sounded almost as anxious as Daniel had.

Murray shut her notebook and sighed. 'When an adult disappears and there are no suspicious circumstances, I'm afraid we don't put an investigation in hand for several days anyway. And since we know Eva Havel was planning to leave I don't reckon there's much we would be able to do in this situation, to be honest.'

'You mean, because she was an immigrant and a bidie-in?'

Vicky, friendly before, was now glaring at her and Murray was taken aback by this sudden aggression. 'I didn't say that,' she said stiffly. 'I will certainly be making a report to my sergeant. And if there's any further information you think might be helpful, get in touch, OK?'

As she got back into her car and prepared for the long drive back, Murray felt her spirits sink. She'd been hopeful that here at last was a proper investigation, but she knew exactly what her sergeant would say when she made her report: that it wasn't Police Scotland's business to track down a girl who'd changed her mind about a fella.

CHAPTER FOUR

'Kelso Strang,' he said.

'Strang?' DCS Borthwick looked up at DCI Chisholm with a frown. 'Problems? Sit down, Brian.'

'I hate to say this, ma'am, but he's buggering up the team. Oh, he's not doing anything wrong. There's no problem with his operational performance, but he's going round like a zombie and it's draining the life out of everyone else. Don't think we don't sympathise. Everyone's sympathetic to the point of total paralysis. And it's only natural, for God's sake, but to be honest I don't think he should have come back so soon. No one can relax, there's no banter and it's starting to affect morale.'

'Hmm.' She was concerned. 'Have you talked to him?'

Chisholm grimaced. 'Talking's a two-way process. I ask him how he is and he says, "Fine." I suggested he should take more compassionate leave and he just says no. He was angry: I couldn't push it.'

'You can see why he might be. Life's a bitch. But we've all got a job to do – that has to be what comes first.'

Chisholm waited in respectful silence as she brooded for a moment. Then she said decisively, 'Right, I've taken that on board. Leave it with me.'

'Thanks, ma'am.' He left, she thought, reassured.

When the door shut behind DCI Chisholm, Borthwick sat back in her chair, still frowning. Yes, the job came first. As she'd said to Strang earlier, she'd used it to fill in the gaping hole in her life after John died and her career was now what defined her. Particularly now, with the upheaval of changing from multiple local constabularies to a single national force, there was serious pressure to deliver; one chief constable had already crashed and burnt and the leaders of the divisions were all nervous.

She had fellow feeling for Kelso Strang, of course she did. But sympathy was one thing, operational efficiency was another. If he was messing that up, she'd have to do something.

The trouble was, she didn't want to lose him. She believed in proactively spotting talent and she'd noticed him as a bright young constable in Armed Response who'd saved another officer's life and then handled the subsequent inquiry with aplomb. To the annoyance of his sergeant, she'd convinced Strang to transfer to CID and until now she'd congratulated herself on her own acumen: he'd made sergeant, then inspector and now SIO in record time – what age was he now? Thirty-one, thirty-two?

She'd been pleased when he'd said he wouldn't consider a transfer; he was by a distance the most able officer she had, the only one she reckoned was going places in the force. Too many officers, male and female, merely wanted a job; he saw it as a promising and satisfying career, just as she had – and probably even more so now.

Damage limitation. That was the priority. She'd have to see him. She leant forward and buzzed down. 'Make an appointment for DI Strang as soon as possible.'

Beatrice had tears in her eyes as she went along the corridor to the kitchen. It wasn't her place to serve up the meals Vicky had left ready; that had been Eva's job. She just couldn't get everything assembled and then carry a big heavy tray along to the dining room quickly, so it wasn't her fault if the food went cold.

Harry had been really rude about that and Adam, instead of standing up for her and pointing out that she was doing this as an obligement, had only said, 'It would be nice to get it before it congeals, Beatrice.'

She hadn't thought about this aspect of being without a housekeeper. It had never happened at a time when Harry was staying before and if Adam was on his own he usually ate in his own flat where there was a smart little kitchenette at one end of his sitting room. He mostly just microwaved a frozen meal but he rather prided himself on being a gourmet cook and on the rare, precious occasions when he'd invited Beatrice in, she would sit and watch admiringly while he chopped vegetables like a professional and then conjured up some delicious little something they'd share, sitting intimately at the breakfast bar. He'd hardly do that for Harry, though.

As she manoeuvred her way through the kitchen door, carrying the tray, she realised that the oven timer was bleeping. She didn't know how long it had been doing that, but she could smell that Vicky's self-saucing lemon sponge – 'Be sure not to let it overcook, Beatrice, or it'll be dry' – was not only going to be dry but a bit scorched as well.

Sniffing miserably, she retrieved it from the oven. It wasn't fair! Harry had been here for three days already, working on accounts or projections or something and he was in a filthy mood too – there had been raised voices when he and Adam were closeted away in the office. If he was going to stay much longer they'd have to make some other arrangement, that was all.

The only good thing was that nothing more had happened about Eva's disappearance. Adam had seemed to be annoyed but philosophical about it. 'Easy come, easy go, those girls,' he'd said, then added, with a glinting smile, 'Not like you, sweetie.'

And he'd said he'd got his plane to Paris all right, so obviously it had been a case of mistaken identity at the petrol station. And obviously Eva had been in a hurry to get away and had just forgotten the case under the bed, so there was nothing to worry about. Obviously.

The policewoman hadn't returned either, so that was all right, though she was getting a bit irritated with Vicky, who kept asking questions, clearly prompted by Eva's boyfriend. Had she noticed anything unusual when she came back that night? What about other girls – had any of them gone away suddenly like that?

'No,' she'd said firmly, but she had a feeling that the reply hadn't come out quite as slickly as she would have liked it to. Vicky had said sharply, 'Are you sure?' and she'd had to be quite abrupt with her.

They were waiting for their pudding. Burnt, and cold as well if she didn't hurry, wasn't going to be good, and then she'd have to clear everything up afterwards. Her eyes still blurred with tears, she was clumsy in picking up the hot dish to put on the tray; it tipped out of her hands and smashed on the stone floor. She stood staring at it, aghast.

Alerted by the crash, Adam appeared. 'Oh, for goodness' sake, Beatrice – what's happened now? And stop that damned thing bleeping, can you?'

She burst into sobs. He gave an exasperated sigh, then put his arm round her shoulders. 'Now, now. Cheer up – accidents happen. We can manage with cheese, if you just bring that through. But this won't do – we'll have get things sorted out.'

Beatrice sat down, fished out a handkerchief and blew her nose. Did that mean another housekeeper? She was more or less resigned to them by now, would almost welcome one this time, if it wasn't for—No, she was just being stupid again, obviously. She needed to put all that out of her mind.

She lumbered to her feet. They were waiting for their cheese. She'd better get on with it before Harry had another tantrum.

'I apologise, ma'am,' DI Strang said stiffly. 'I didn't mean to be a drag on the team.'

DCS Borthwick could see the rigidly suppressed anger

in the whiteness round his mouth. 'I'm not for a minute suggesting you are, Kelso. I'm just saying it's not only you that needs breathing space. Other people need to get over their shock about Alexa too – she was very popular with your mates, I know.'

'I – don't – want – leave.' Suddenly the anger erupted. 'Why would I get out of bed in the morning? What would I do when I got up – start drinking? No, hang on, perhaps I could just leave the bottle by the bed so I could poke my head out from under the duvet, have a swig and then pull it back over my head again? I need there to be something I have to do. For God's sake, it's all I have left!'

He was shaking. He bowed his head, struggling for control, then managed, 'Sorry, ma'am. I – I shouldn't have said that.'

'Better out than in,' she said calmly. 'No need to apologise. It's natural enough; in fact you're actually making progress – anger's the second stage in grief, after denial.

'I'm sorry, but I'm going to have to pull you from the team meantime. I'll expect you in tomorrow first thing, though; there's a lot of follow-up admin needing to be done on that rape in the Grassmarket for the report to the procurator fiscal. All right? I'll give some thought to another placement and I'll get back to you.'

'That policewoman's not doing anything, is she?' Daniel Tennant said. He was looking pale and strained as he sat at the kitchen table in the Macdonalds' cottage.

Vicky stopped rolling out pastry. 'It's outrageous. I don't think she's paid any attention to what we said. She hasn't even gone back to Balnasheil Lodge, as far as I know. They're just kicking the can down the road. How can we force them to take it seriously?'

Murdo John, who was sitting at a small desk in the window doing paperwork, looked up. 'Don't get involved,' he said.

'But I am involved, Murdo,' Vicky argued. 'I was very fond of Eva and if something's happened to her I'm not going to let them get away with pretending nothing's wrong.'

'If,' Murdo John said. 'The girl was packing to go away, wasn't she, and now she's gone away. That's all.'

'She was going to get me to collect her when she was ready,' Daniel repeated, for possibly the fortieth time. 'She didn't. She didn't answer her phone.'

'Yes, you said. It looks as if she changed her mind. What do you think happened – someone pushed her over a cliff or something?' He sounded irritable.

'Murdo, we're not saying that!' Vicky said. 'It's just—'

'Something happened,' Daniel insisted. 'And no one's doing anything about it. I spoke to one of the sergeants at Broadford and all he said was that he had it on file. What use is that?'

Vicky was distressed. 'Oh, I was hoping someone senior would come and investigate it! Is that all – they're just shrugging their shoulders? What can we do?'

'Try leaving it to the experts,' Murdo John said flatly. 'And if I did think harm had come to the girl, I'd forbid you to have anything more to do with them over there.'

The word 'forbid' fell into the conversation like a hand grenade going off.

'Forbid? Did you say *forbid*?' Vicky's voice rose.

Daniel got up hastily. 'I'll be off. I'm going to see what I can do.' He went out, shutting the door behind him with a silent whistle. That was going to be one hell of a marital spat.

The interview with Kelso Strang was a constant niggle at the back of DCS Borthwick's mind over the next couple of days, even as she dealt with the usual overload of papers on her desk and the fallout from an inquiry – or 'witch-hunt' as one of her more irascible inspectors had termed it – by the Police Investigation and Review Commissioner.

She could slot him into admin meantime but it wouldn't be the absorbing job he was needing right now and in his current volatile state he might just chuck it. That wouldn't be good for him, and losing talent wasn't good from her point of view either. She was still trying to think of a way round it when the phone call from the deputy chief constable came.

They'd been setting up a pilot scheme for a new initiative: the Serious Rural Crime Squad. With the pressure on budgets, financing CID expertise in low-crime rural areas was expensive so it would make sense to have officers from one of the larger units available to be seconded as necessary.

There was, he said, a case that the CC thought wanted looking into on Skye. When he described the circumstances Borthwick was surprised; a woman packing her bags and walking out without explanation wouldn't normally justify the expense of sending someone in, but if that was what the CC wanted . . .

And, she thought as she put down the phone, this just might be the answer for what to do with Kelso Strang. He'd be in an isolated position but she suspected that wouldn't bother him much. She'd always sensed a sort of independence in him, aloofness, even, as if what others thought or did mattered little to him. This would give him a brief breathing space – Skye, on his own, not much pressure. A bit of hillwalking in his spare time, even.

She was definitely warming to the idea. He was intelligent, too, so she could task him to produce a report on the viability of the new system before some major case came up.

As long as he was up to it. Was he? She wasn't a gambler by nature and if the case had been anything other than low-key she wouldn't have entertained the idea. But it wouldn't be for more than two or three days, surely, then he'd have a spell doing the feasibility study. It might be the chance he needed to let everything settle down – and let the team get back to normal too.

She buzzed her secretary. 'Get hold of DI Strang for me,' she said.

'They're going to parachute in a DI up from Edinburgh to check out that female who disappeared in Balnasheil,' Sergeant Buchanan said.

At the other end of the phone, PC Murray bristled. 'Edinburgh? What for? I've investigated. She just packed her bags and went and the guy who thought it was him she was going to go off with didn't like it, that's all. We're not needing some hotshot Edinbugger coming here and mucking us about.'

'Lassie, you're there to cooperate, right, not start some sort of civil war. Or uncivil war, since it's you. You'll get word when he's coming so you can be prepared. Have you got that?'

'Sir,' Murray said in as bolshie a tone as she dared, and banged the phone down. This was all she needed.

DI Strang went to the appointment with DCS Borthwick in no very receptive frame of mind. Doing nothing but office work, he could almost feel the moss growing as he sat there. This wasn't the job he'd loved; if what JB had in mind was putting him into admin, she could shove it, frankly. He went in to see her, determined to stand his ground whatever pressure she brought to bear.

So what she had to say took him aback. He hadn't even heard of the SRCS but it sounded like an interesting idea.

'You'd have to be prepared to be a bit of a maverick, operating on your own initiative,' she explained. 'Whatever help you got from the local force would be billed to the SRCS budget and the CC is very keen to keep costs down. Of course, if it was a major investigation we'd helicopter in whatever is necessary but to be honest this case looks like a cosmetic operation to placate someone who has pull – a soft start for what's still really a pilot project.'

She paused, looking at him a little uncertainly. 'Do you – do you feel you would be up to that at the moment, Kelso? It's a big responsibility.'

He almost bit her arm off. Solo operations held no fear for him and at least he'd get a break, however brief, from seeing the lads going home to spouses and partners every night, constantly reminding him that he had none. If he handled it well, it might lead to other opportunities. This job appealed to him. It appealed to him a lot.

For the sake of form, he hesitated as if he was giving it mature consideration, then he met her eyes squarely. 'I know you'd be taking a chance with me, ma'am, but I'd welcome the challenge.'

Borthwick held his glance for a moment, as if she were evaluating the chance she was taking. Then she said briskly, 'Good. Anyway, as I say, it looks like something you could wrap up in a couple of days. And you'll be reporting directly to me on your progress.' Then she added warningly, 'But you understand – this has to be your show and you'll be in charge.'

'Not a problem, ma'am. Thanks for giving me the chance.'

Kelso drove home, his mind already working on logistics. Liaise with the office about accommodation, check the route, pack ready to leave first thing tomorrow . . .

And phone his mother. He'd been bad about not returning her calls and there were dozens of other messages he hadn't even read. Sympathy only made him feel worse; even though Mary wouldn't be crass enough to offer it, he would sense her pity. If he told her he was being sent to Skye to do a job for a few days and would be out of touch, he wouldn't have to feel guilty about not responding.

He heard the relieved lift in Mary Strang's voice when he spoke but she was careful not to sound reproachful at his neglect, or to ask how he was.

'Getting away will be good, and Skye should be lovely

at this time of year – all that autumn colour,' she said cheerfully. 'Get some fresh air—'

'I know. It'll put some colour in my cheeks,' he finished for her, and heard her laugh. It had been her constant cry when her family showed couch-potato tendencies. 'I'll probably get that all right. Skye isn't famed for its balmy weather.'

'Don't be such a pessimist! I heard the forecast this morning and tomorrow's going to be nice. Lots of sunshine. And don't say they got it wrong today. Even if they did.'

'Shouldn't dream of contradicting my mother. But anyway, I'm not exactly going to be taking my bucket and spade – and talking about tools for the job, I'd better get on and sort some out.'

He was just about to ring off when she said, in a rush, 'Darling, try not to blame Dad too much. He's worried about you, you know—'

'Yes, Ma, I know.' He knew he sounded terse and he heard her give a tiny sigh, but he couldn't help that. At least he hadn't retorted that what his father was worried about was his masterplan for Kelso failing. 'Anyway, I've got a lot to do. If you need to get in touch, go through the office. The reception's probably not very good and I won't be checking calls.'

It was one of her virtues as a mother that she didn't believe in flogging dead horses, and Mary made no attempt to return to the subject of his father. 'Right. Let us know when you get back. Have a good drive up and – and take care.' The anxiety showed through when she said that.

Kelso swallowed hard. 'Yes. At least, I'll do my best.

Bye, Ma.' He didn't want to think about getting out onto the motorway again.

He busied himself with packing and checking through the reports that had been passed on to him. It sounded straightforward enough; he scribbled a few notes and sketched in a schedule. He was engaged, absorbed even, and when he looked at his watch he was surprised to see it was almost midnight.

He struggled with a foolish feeling of guilt that something of a healing process seemed to have begun.

CHAPTER FIVE

He hadn't realised how nervous he would be on the city bypass. It was the first time since the accident that Kelso Strang had driven outside the city streets and he found himself shaking, sweat forming on the back of his neck, eyeing every juggernaut that passed in the outer lane of the other carriageway, tensed up for a sudden swerve that would bring it smashing through the central barrier, imagining what he would do, what he would have done, if he had been driving instead of Alexa . . . He needed distraction.

The car was stocked with Alexa's CDs; he'd had no interest in classical music before he met her but she'd got him hooked. He couldn't listen to her music just now, though – not yet; he was too afraid of the emotion it would provoke. He switched on the radio, set to Radio Three, and hastily flipped to some sort of phone-in on Five Live instead, something about cuts to welfare benefits – that might do. He forced himself to listen until he felt his attention drifting and flipped again, finding a documentary on Afghanistan. There was a journo holding forth on how it was and he listened with a wry smile to the confident rubbish the man was spouting.

But as the long miles rolled on it became harder to concentrate on the voices coming from the little box in the dashboard, harder to suppress the memories that flooded in, taking him through it all over again.

'You're not killing her,' the doctor had said, reading his mind. She was very young and not far from tears. 'Alexa's dead already, Kelso.' Then she corrected herself. 'They're dead already. The baby too.'

At least she had acknowledged the baby. The consultant, professionally compassionate, seemed to have forgotten the other life – the child who would never exist but who had been so fondly imagined.

Alexa didn't look dead, though. The hand he was holding was warm and her chest rose and fell gently with each breath. Apart from the dressing on her head, where the corner of the roof had caved in on her after the crash and the bruising under her eyes, she looked as if at any moment she might sit up, look incredulously at the technology attached to her and shake it off, laughing.

'Can you leave us alone for a moment?' he said to the doctor.

'Of course. As long as you want.' She whisked out of the room and he knew she was going to cry when she got outside. Poor kid. She'd have to toughen up. He didn't feel like crying. He felt remote, detached, as if all this was happening to someone else.

He didn't feel like talking to Alexa either. They'd let him see the brain scans that showed no activity at all after the massive damage, and though he'd heard the theory that a familiar voice could get through even so, he didn't believe it. He didn't want to because if she could hear, it would mean she was in some sense still alive. He badly needed to believe what the doctor said – that she was dead already.

But she was warm and she was breathing, thanks to the tube in her throat, and once he gave the consent they were waiting for she wouldn't be breathing any more. She would go still and the ugly processes of death would start.

They would let him stay. He could wait until the breathing stopped, wait till the hand went cold in his.

Or he could go now to sign forms that would bring death to her and give life to someone else, then get out of this place that had started to smell of death to him so strongly that he gagged. He could get out before the rage, the agony and the despair – the total, blank, utter despair – kicked in.

He wasn't sure how long that would be. He could feel it building, like a sort of mental nausea, and he was afraid of what would happen when the numbness of shock that had carried him through this far began to wear off.

With a great, shuddering sigh he stood up. He kissed Alexa's hand and laid it down on the smooth white sheet. Her lips were cracked and dry; he kissed her forehead instead. The obstruction in his throat was almost choking him.

As he turned away, he said, 'Sleep well,' as he had said every night for all the years they had been together, though he knew he was saying it to empty air. Alexa had gone already.

Kelso Strang walked out without looking back, along to the nursing station where the doctor was waiting. She stood up with a brave smile but her eyes were red and puffy.

'Give me the forms,' he said harshly.

It hit home as he came out of the doors of the hospital into the watery sunshine, striking him with a force that doubled him over. A woman walking past eyed him nervously but he didn't even see her or hear her tentative, 'Are you all right?' Gasping, he managed to straighten up and staggered towards the car park.

He hadn't expected the physical pain that was crushing his lungs. He was sweating and breathless by the time he reached his car, finding it by instinct rather than conscious thought. Perhaps he was having a heart attack. He embraced the thought. The end. Nothing more to face, nothing more to feel.

But it hadn't been that easy. He had driven back blindly to the fisherman's cottage opposite the Newhaven harbour, the little house that still smelt of paint from the room they were painting yellow for the baby because Alexa couldn't bear to wait to see if it would be blue or pink.

He had crashed the front door closed and walked to the cupboard to fetch the Scotch and drunk himself into oblivion.

The memory of the hangover that followed, the worst he'd ever had in what had not exactly been an abstemious existence, jolted him out of the darker thoughts. He was setting off to start the next chapter of his life and that meant this sort of emotional overindulgence had to stop.

He'd learnt resilience in a hard school. To save his comrades in Afghanistan, it had been his job as a sniper to inflict death on an oblivious man miles away. Then, when he'd been in Armed Response, he'd dropped a Yardie who was high on smack as his finger was tightening on the trigger of the shotgun pointing at a policewoman. He'd learnt to live with that, learnt not to punish himself for what had been his duty to do.

He had to use that hard-won ability now to handle the soul-deep anguish of losing Alexa. He had to lock away the pain, the grief, the guilt that came from feeling as if he had killed his wife and child, no matter how authoritatively he was told that they had both been dead already. He had to lock all that out and get on with the job, just as he always had. As a soldier's son and a soldier himself, discipline was inbred; whether this was entirely healthy or not was a question he wasn't going to let himself debate.

Courtesy of JB's patronage, he had an absorbing new task. Here he was on the traditional Road to the Isles, even if only for a couple of days, and he owed it to her to get this absolutely right.

And what, he wondered, was the reaction at the other end going to be like? How happy would the local force be about someone being parachuted in over their heads? He grimaced. He had a nasty feeling that they wouldn't exactly be shaking out the bunting to string across the front of the station.

They were arguing. Beatrice Lacey could hear their raised voices in Adam's flat as she struggled in the kitchen trying to make sure she was perfectly organised for the evening meal. Vicky had just gone, leaving food that was as simple as possible – soup, a fish pie with a green salad and a cold pudding to follow – but she had to work out when to heat things up and how to stop them spoiling if the men wanted to linger over their drinks.

Rows between Adam and Harry were nothing new – they were both strong-willed men with their own very definite views – but this was going on longer and getting louder than anything she had heard before. She'd never known Harry stay so long, either, when there wasn't a house party, and he wasn't showing any sign of leaving. This wasn't normal; there was definitely something wrong.

Beatrice began to tremble and hastily set down the dish she was holding in case she dropped it. She was getting more and more scared, sleeping badly and waking shuddering at the dreams she'd had.

Harry was shouting now. 'I don't trust you!' she heard, then something about being compromised. Suddenly there was a series of sharp barks. Harry stopped mid word. There was a silence, then she heard Adam give a harsh laugh and what sounded like an instruction to the dog.

A few moments later a door slammed, then another one, and she heard footsteps going right across the hall, not climbing the staircase or heading towards the door underneath it.

Oh God, was Harry looking for her? Beatrice hurried out of the kitchen but before she was halfway across the hall Harry erupted from the main office, shouting, 'Beatrice! Where the hell is the woman?'

Harry Drummond was no taller than Adam but he was more powerfully built, wide-shouldered and deep-chested. He was, even Beatrice had to admit, quite a good-looking man, with thick dark hair and blue eyes, but he had what she described to herself as a cruel mouth, a straight line with corners that turned down in repose, and the jutting jaw of the bully.

She had tried to convince herself that she had no reason to be scared of him – what could he do, after all? He could hardly sack her, with the charity depending on her income. But it never worked.

She scuttled across to him. 'Here I am, Harry. What did you want?'

'There's a file I need. It's marked "Donors X-list". Find it for me, then bring it to the office.'

Colour flared in Beatrice's cheeks. 'I – I don't know where I'd find it, Harry. There isn't a file with that name on the computer.'

'Not on the *computer*.' He spoke as if she'd been a fool even to imagine it would be. 'A paper file. They've been moved out of the filing cabinet.'

Beatrice swallowed. 'I – I've never had anything to do with those files. I think Adam perhaps moved them.' She knew Adam had moved them, and she knew why. She was feeling sick.

Harry stared at her, the rather prominent blue eyes bulging. 'I see. Is there no limit to the damage that bloody idiot has done?' he said. 'Get it from him, then, and bring it to me.'

'I—'

He spun round. 'Yes? You *what*?'

She'd been going to go on, 'don't like to disturb him,' but she changed her mind. 'Nothing, Harry. I'll see what I can do.' Asking Adam, stirring up the memories of the morning when the files had been moved, worrying that he would see her fears in her face, was the lesser evil. She would just be very calm, very matter-of-fact.

She could sense the tension whenever she obeyed his call to come in. The dog was sensing it too; it was restless, its eyes always on its master who was standing by the window looking out.

'Yes, Beatrice,' he said without turning round. 'What is it?'

She was happy not to have to meet his eyes. 'Harry wants a paper file called "Donors X-list" and he wondered if you had it?'

'Oh – oh yes.' He went to a wall cupboard and when he opened it she could see that the shelves, set deep into the wall, were piled with untidy bundles. On the floor beside it was a stack of random books and papers that had clearly been dumped there to make space.

Adam looked helplessly at the confusion and with a reflex reaction she stepped forward. 'Would you like me to sort these out for you, Adam?'

'No!' It sounded like the crack of a whip and the dog gave a small whine.

She recoiled, but Adam went on hastily, 'Sorry, sorry, sweetie. I didn't mean it to sound like that. I've just had a difficult time with Harry – you and I both know how pig-headed he can be!'

He smiled at her, a conspiratorial smile, and suddenly she felt better. 'Of course. That's all right. But are you sure I can't . . . ?'

The 'no' this time was more polite but just as definite. 'Don't worry about it. I'll take it to Harry myself.'

Beatrice nodded. She was on her way out when she turned to say, 'What time are you going to want to have supper tonight, Adam? It's just—'

He was carrying a pile of files across to the coffee table in front of the fireplace. 'For God's sake, Beatrice, I don't know!' he snapped. 'Whenever.'

He didn't apologise this time. Biting her lip, she went out. It was all very well to say that but you couldn't produce a fish pie the way he liked it, with a nice crispy top, in five minutes, and if it wasn't ready when they wanted it, there would be another scene. Tears of self-pity gathered in her eyes as she went back to the kitchen.

But in a way, having something practical to worry about was a relief; it blotted out the terrible sense of foreboding that had possessed her, as if they were all just waiting for something to happen. She didn't know what it was, but she knew it was making her feel sick and sweaty.

For once she looked at Vicky's chocolate mousse with a shudder of revulsion as she put it into the fridge.

'He's driving up from Edinburgh today,' Sergeant Buchanan said. 'DI Kelso Strang.'

'What sort of a name is that – Kelso? Thought it was a town. Couldn't just be called something like Jimmie, could he?' PC Murray's hackles were up already.

'Perfectly good Border name,' Buchanan said. 'His mother's maiden name, maybe. Folk have all kinds of reasons for what they call their kids, *Olivia*.'

Murray could hear that he was grinning. She'd made the big mistake of telling him she'd been named after *Olivia Newton John*, for God's sake, and now she failed to think of a smart reply. What came to her instead was a sudden unwelcome thought. 'They're not expecting him to stay in the police house, are they? Because I don't take lodgers and that's flat.'

'We-ell, you know how tight the budget is . . .'

She was drawing in her breath to protest when he laughed. 'Winding you up's almost too easy to be fun. No, you're in luck – the locals around here are a bit straight-laced and the high heid yins have decided it wouldn't go down too well to have a man moving in with an innocent young girl. They obviously didn't know it was you.'

For what was very possibly the first time in her life, Murray found herself grateful to the top brass. She ignored the slur on her character, since there was a distinct lack of evidence to refute the allegation.

'So where's he staying, then?'

'The hotel. Just booked in for a couple of nights so I don't reckon he'll be bothering us long.'

'Can I just say, "Nothing to look at here, sir. Move along, please"?'

'You can. Not saying it would be a good idea though, Livvy.'

'Oh, I know.' She sighed. 'I'll get down there and say hello in the evening, maybe. OK, Sarge.'

Murray put the phone down and looked at her watch –

half past three. If he'd set off promptly in the morning, he could be arriving any time now. Maybe she should check that all her 'i's were dotted and all her 't's crossed; in her experience DIs tended to be picky types. She picked up the file from the basket on her desk and found Daniel Tennant's number.

He sounded eager when she identified herself. 'Any developments?'

'Sorry, no. Just checking – anything more you thought of that could be helpful?'

'Oh.' His voice went flat. 'Of course not. I'd have let you know immediately.'

'OK. There's a detective inspector arriving from Edinburgh later this afternoon and no doubt he'll want a word. Not going to disappear too, are you?'

'No, no. And thank God that there's someone competent coming to deal with it at last.' He rang off.

This was obviously her day for collecting slurs. She phoned Vicky Macdonald, who said much the same thing, if rather more politely.

That was her bases covered. She checked that the paperwork was in order, then decided she was entitled to a break; having a drink with an inspector this evening would count as work, in her book. What she liked to do in her spare time was to have a wee wander round the shops but since the only shop available was the local Spar, that wasn't on the cards. Still, it was a beautiful sunny day and she needed the exercise, so with a brief sigh for Sauchiehall Street she changed into a tracksuit and ran up the hill behind the police house. She'd award herself a teacake when she got back.

* * *

It was a relief for Beatrice to be back at her desk, doing the familiar routine things – vetting applications for funding to put in front of Adam, sending out grateful acknowledgements for donations, sorting through the household accounts which Eva, of course, had failed to write up before she left.

There was a list beside her now that she'd compiled giving details of different timings for the evening meal, depending on the time the men drifted towards the drawing room for drinks; lists always gave Beatrice a sense of security and she felt more confident about it now. She didn't know where Adam and Harry were – in the office, perhaps. She hadn't seen either of them all afternoon and the house had been quiet.

Absorbed in her work, she jumped when the doorbell rang, and then her heart jumped too. Unexpected visitors had been bad news lately. But it was her brother, Quentin, who stood on the doorstep, wearing a shabby Barbour jacket, red cords and an ingratiating smile.

'Hello there. How's Trix?' he said jovially.

Ignoring the tired joke, she said, 'What do you want?'

'Well, that's a nice welcome, after I've driven all that way round the bay to see my favourite sister.'

Beatrice didn't move. 'Your only sister.'

'Yes, well – look, can I come in? It's bloody freezing out here.'

There was a brisk breeze, whipping up whitecaps on the bay, and his brown floppy hair was blowing over his face; he shivered elaborately, huddling the jacket round himself.

'Oh, all right.' Beatrice stood aside with a bad grace and

led him back into the office, pulling forward a chair then going back to sit at her desk.

Quentin looked about him discontentedly. 'Why do I always have to see you in the office? You've got a flat, haven't you? Why don't we have a family chat up there?'

'Because I have work to do and I'm busy. What do you want?'

He sat down reluctantly. 'Where's Carnegie?'

'I don't know. He and Harry Drummond are around somewhere.'

'At home, then? Look, is he likely to come barging in? We need a proper talk.'

'If you're looking for a handout, I can't give you more than twenty pounds until the end of the month.'

'No, it's not that – though if you could manage that, wouldn't say no, I'm a bit short, actually. The thing is, Grayling's been in touch. He's not happy about what you're doing.'

Beatrice bristled. 'I fail to see what reason my trustee could have for being in touch with you. Or, indeed, what right he has to express an opinion about what I choose to do, provided it's within the provisions of the trust.'

'He wants to stop you being exploited, Trixie.' He caught her look of irritation and went on, 'Beatrice, then. Look, that's all it is. We both do – I'm your brother, after all! I don't like to see you being made a fool of.'

'What you mean is, you don't like to see my money going to people who really need it and will make good use of it, transforming lives, instead of handing it to you to squander. That's what it's about, Quentin.'

He flushed. He had a quick temper and she could see that she'd riled him. He persisted, though.

'He tells me you're not paid for the work you do here – in fact, that you're basically paying for the privilege. Carnegie conned you out of your house, now he's milking you for your income.'

She had a temper herself, when roused. 'It's not going to Adam, it's going to the charity, and it's my pleasure and privilege. You're a nasty, money-grubbing—'

'To the charity? Is it? What are they paid, him and his pal? And where did the money come from for the BMW at the front door, and the Mercedes that's sitting across in Balnasheil, waiting for him to come over in the natty little motorboat?'

She was pale with anger now. 'Snooping, were you? Charming!'

He held up his hands. 'Hey, hey! Let's not quarrel. There's just the two of us, we haven't anyone else, and if your own brother can't be trusted to look after you, along with the trustee Father appointed himself, who can? Why don't you let me take you down to London to see him? He wants to suggest you sort out the legal side of things—'

'You mean, make a will leaving everything to you?'

He didn't answer immediately.

'Aren't you going to say, "Blood's thicker than water"? You usually do when you talk about the charity. Anyway, Adam needs his comforts. There's a huge weight on his shoulders, running the whole global operation. I'm happy to do anything that makes it easier for him.'

'Haven't you noticed that he's keeping you a prisoner

here? Seeing to it that you're well away from your family and friends, from anyone who might give you sensible advice?'

It chimed with her own misgivings, that was the thing. Sometimes she'd felt that herself and she had a sudden vision now of the little bridge group she'd belonged to, of the chat and the laughter. When was the last time she'd actually laughed? But she suppressed the rebellious thought instantly. She had to, otherwise everything she'd built her life around was a con trick and she was a victim.

But Quentin spotted her hesitation and pounced. 'Wake up, Beatrice. He's not interested in you for your pretty face, is he?'

She caught the sneer that he wasn't smart enough to hide. She drew a deep breath and with a heady kind of bravado went on, 'Anyway, it will sort itself out. We're getting married.'

His jaw literally dropped. His eyes flickered across her and she knew he was seeing the rolls of flesh under her gathered skirt and long jersey top, the pudgy cheeks and the layers of chins.

'He's going to marry *you*?'

She used anger to keep the pain out of her voice. 'Oh, I know what you think, but looks aren't everything. We share the most important things, ideals and—'

'Money, your money.' Quentin had jumped to his feet in his agitation. 'As if he hadn't made enough of a fool of you already! If he's proposed, he's laughing at you. It's a joke. And a swindle – I take it he knows you get control of the lot once you marry?'

'No, he doesn't.' She lied bravely, but she could see he

wasn't convinced. She got up herself. 'Get out, Quentin. And don't come back. If there's anyone who's a swindler, it's you.' She picked up the bag that lay at her feet and found her purse.

'Oh, I seem to have a fifty. There you are – that's your pay-off. There's no more going to come your way.'

Beatrice was pleased that he took it. Confirmed in her moral superiority, she despised him. And saying those words – 'We're getting married' – had actually felt wonderful, wonderful. Spoken aloud to another person, they had made the dream more real, as if in some strange way that made it more likely to come true.

CHAPTER SIX

Tummel, Loch Rannoch, Lochaber – the familiar place names set 'The Road to the Isles' singing in Kelso Strang's head as he went on his way to Skye. It almost felt like setting off on one of the West Coast holidays his family had always taken when he was a kid and he smiled at the memories: fishing for mackerel off the end of a pier, damming a burn, skinning his knees on the scree scrambling up a hill . . .

It was an improbably glorious day. Loch Laggan was a mirror reflecting the snow-dusted peak above it and the dark pine forest on its shores; the great slabs of stone that were the surrounding hills had an ice-blue tinge where their tops pierced the skyline. The heather was past and the bracken no more than damp, dark orange swathes of rotting vegetation, but the miles and miles of bog and bleak moorland were still beautiful today, their greens and browns punctuated with the silver of burns and little lochans.

And then there, at last, was the scimitar curve of the

Skye Bridge, connecting the mainland to the famous island. There wasn't quite the same romance in crossing it as in taking a boat 'over the sea to Skye' like Bonnie Prince Charlie, but it was certainly quicker.

He'd naively expected the wildness to start as he came off the bridge, and as he drove through the little villages of Kyleakin and Broadford, that admittedly had pretty sea views and hills behind but were almost suburban in their ordinariness, he felt a sort of childish disappointment. It was too domestic, too tame . . .

Then round a corner, towering high above the lower mountains and making them look suddenly puny, was the Black Cuillin ridge shimmering in the strong sunlight, mottled with snow-filled corries. He actually gasped.

Nothing had prepared him for this – this stark, savage statement of power. It flung a challenge as crude and contemptuous as a street fighter's 'Come on, if you think you're hard enough.' The roll call of deaths on these mountains was eloquent testimony to the folly of accepting it.

As the foothills closed in around him he started to feel almost physically oppressed. It had been a long, tiring drive and he still wasn't as fit as he should be, even though he'd started running again; maybe he'd get in a bit of that before he left. He had reached a single track road now, with sheer slopes on either side, and he had to crane forward to see the sky above the tops.

He could tell the tourists on this road; they were the ones who hovered nervously beside passing places as he approached, like children playing musical chairs. Locals, on the other hand, hurtled towards him with a terrifying insouciance, and it needed good timing to adjust his speed so that whether the passing place was on his side or theirs, neither car had to stop. It was a definite skill and as a trained police driver he started to enjoy himself.

By the time Kelso saw the sign for Balnasheil he reckoned he had the technique cracked, and when he rounded a bend his spirits lifted at the sight of a glorious panorama opening up to more distant hills and sea, with the peaceful little township straggling below him that held the prospect of a bath, a meal and a good night's sleep before he started work in the morning.

Even having done all his homework he still wasn't sure why he'd been sent up to what looked like a straightforward case. The underlying story was probably illegal immigration; perhaps the missing woman who seemed to have been employed here had somehow got the offer of a better job and had taken some care that she couldn't be pursued, either by her former employer or the authorities.

He wasn't commissioned to investigate that side, only to check that there were no suspicious circumstances. He'd read through the report filed by the local PC, Olivia Murray, and it seemed competent enough. He could see a couple of areas that definitely needed more probing but on the evidence as presented he would probably have reached the same conclusion as she had.

The hotel was right on the shore, just along from the pier. It was an attractive building in the local style, white-harled with small square sash windows and tubs of flowers on either side of the door; there was a single-storey extension to one side with a pub sign, BLACK CUILLIN BAR. There had probably been an inn on this site for as long as there had been a township, serving the drove roads bringing sheep and cattle to market from the north-west of the island and now sympathetically extended to cater for the comparatively new-fangled passion for dicing with death on the mountains.

There were a couple of small fishing boats tied up to the pier and he parked his car near a pile of lobster creels, which boded well for the meal he was looking forward to already. An elderly man in navy overalls and sea boots who was coiling ropes looked up as Kelso got out.

'Grand day for you!' he said.

Kelso recognised the pure vowels and soft burr of a Gaelic speaker who'd had to go to school to learn to speak English, an accent which, he guessed, would be much rarer in the younger generations – sad, in its way.

'It's been a bonny drive up, with the views. I've been lucky.'

The man's rheumy blue eyes surveyed him narrowly. 'Up from the south, then?'

'That's right. Staying at the hotel.'

He nodded with satisfied certainty. 'Aye, right. You'll be from the polis, then.'

Kelso winced. What had they done – taken out an advert? He'd been prepared for word to get round quickly – but before he'd even arrived? He nodded with a fixed smile, took out his luggage and went into the hotel.

When he rang the bell at the little reception desk, a middle-aged woman with badly dyed dark hair and stark red lipstick appeared. She introduced herself as Fiona Ross –

no Highland accent here – and booked him in, greeting him effusively. Then she peered rudely into his face.

'Oh dear!' she said. 'Someone taken a knife to you, have they?'

'No,' he said coldly. 'Is that my key?'

'Oh, I'll take you up myself.' She led the way to the front of the first floor, keeping up a relentless flow of conversation about the weather and the drive from Edinburgh, but once she had pointed out that they'd given him the biggest room with a sofa and a table where he could work, she could contain herself no longer. 'You'll be here about the girl who disappeared, I suppose?'

Kelso pointedly didn't reply as he walked to the window with its view of the bay and across to the opposite shore, to what he guessed must be Balnasheil Lodge, where the missing woman had been working. When he turned he said dismissively, 'Thank you. That's fine.'

She didn't take the hint. 'Now, if there's anything at all you need, you just come straight to me. I'll be delighted to help you in any way I can.' There was no mistaking her eagerness; she actually licked her lips as she said that.

He should have been prepared for this, but the reality of working in a small place hit him forcibly. Coming from the big city he'd forgotten that his arrival would provoke huge curiosity in a place this size and that any scrap of inside information would be seized on quicker than a dog would snatch a dropped sausage. Fiona Ross was right there at his feet with her mouth wide open expectantly.

It was natural enough but there was something about

her – her avid eyes, her loose, gossip's mouth – that was particularly repellent.

'Now, dinner's from seven till nine,' she went on, 'but I could bring you up some tea and a scone now if you like. It's no trouble.'

'No, thank you. I'm all right.'

She nodded. 'The bar's open at six.' Then she said, with a little giggle, 'You're not really quite what I expected, you know. You don't sound like a policeman. I do like dealing with a gentleman.'

The snobbery set his teeth on edge. He didn't reply, only walked across to the open door, holding the edge and moving it slightly to suggest that he was ready to close it.

He wasn't escaping as lightly as that, though. Fiona did move towards it but stopped just beside him and leant forward to say confidentially, 'It's difficult when you come to a wee place like this. People tend to close up, when it's a stranger asking questions. So if there's anything you need to know about Balnasheil, you just come and ask me. We came up from Lanarkshire twenty years ago and I know where all the bodies are buried.'

He couldn't resist. 'Really?' he said with apparent shock. '*Bodies*?' and watched with reprehensible pleasure as her face turned an uncomfortable pink.

'Oh – oh no,' she stammered. 'I didn't mean real bodies. I just meant – well, there's things people maybe wouldn't want you to know.'

He'd had more than enough of her and her snide little remarks. 'Exaggeration really isn't helpful, Mrs Ross,' he said acidly and watched her shrink like a slug under a sprinkle of salt. 'Perhaps you could tell me, though, if you knew the woman who left Balnasheil Lodge unexpectedly?'

She wrestled for a moment with indignation but in the end couldn't resist the pleasure of retailing gossip. 'Oh yes! She was in the bar sometimes – though I never really had that much chance to talk to her.' That was a reluctant admission, but she went on, 'Probably who you want to speak to is Murdo John Macdonald. He often serves in the bar if we're busy because Douglas – that's my husband – does the cooking. And he'll have noticed her – Murdo John always had quite an eye for the ladies. The strong silent type, you know – sometimes women go for that.' She said it with a sidelong look.

'I'm not sure I understand,' he said, deliberately obtuse. 'Are you saying he had some sort of relationship with Ms Havel?'

Fiona backed off. 'No, no, I didn't mean that, exactly. Just, well – oh anyway, he's married now, to a girl who was waitressing here. But like I said, I saw Eva sometimes, having a drink up at the bar. Oh, very *friendly*, she always was, joining in the craic. We get a lot of climbers and hillwalkers around here, so there were plenty of young men around.' She rolled her eyes graphically. 'And, well, you know . . .'

Kelso's revulsion was like an itch he couldn't scratch. 'Are you saying she was promiscuous?'

She gave a silly little titter. 'Oh well, no, not exactly. But of course with her position over there—' She jerked her head at the window, indicating the Lodge across the bay.

'Which was?'

She smirked. 'Housekeeper. That's what they said. But we all know what *that* meant.'

He was getting very tired of playing games. 'And what did it mean?'

Fiona recoiled slightly, then gave him a hard stare. 'Oh, I think we both know the sort of thing I'm talking about. Anyway, like I said, dinner's from seven.' She walked out, shutting the door perhaps just a little more firmly than was strictly necessary.

He knew he had antagonised her and perhaps he should have controlled his disgust, but being forced to listen to her sly, slimy innuendos made him feel he was grubby too. Not waiting to unpack, he started to run a bath.

She had given him a couple of interesting pointers, though: that Murdo John Macdonald needed looking at and that there were other men in the frame as well as the writer who'd been stood up. If Murdo John had a boat it might well explain Eva's mysterious disappearance.

This was going to be a steep learning curve. He was used to city policing where it hardly mattered how hard you went in but he'd have to be a lot more diplomatic here.

Vicky Macdonald put her head round the door of their snug sitting room, where Murdo John was sitting reading the *Oban Times*. 'Are you working tonight? Do you need supper early?'

Murdo John nodded. 'Yes. I'm in six till nine. They've this policeman staying, and another couple of visitors, so Douglas will be in the kitchen till then.'

'Is it tonight he's coming?' Vicky's face brightened.

'Maybe we'll get some action at last. Daniel will be pleased – I'll just give him a ring.'

Murdo John said nothing, pointedly. As she went back to the kitchen, Vicky grimaced. The row they'd had over his stupid choice of words was the worst they'd ever had and though things had been patched up, theoretically at least, there was still an unhealed wound and anything to do with Eva Havel or Balnasheil Lodge was dangerous territory.

It was good news that at last something was being done about Eva. She had started to feel almost sick with worry about her and she'd had a terrible nightmare the previous night, where somehow she was Eva, or perhaps Eva was her, and Adam Carnegie had been trying to strangle her – or perhaps it was Murdo John. It had been one of those dreams that colours your mood long after you have woken up and she'd found herself looking at her husband askance this morning. Was the dream trying to tell her something about their relationship? Was his controlling tendency threatening to strangle her independence?

Or was she just possibly making far too much of it and should stop overreacting? She went to call Daniel.

To her surprise, he seemed a little guarded about her plan to meet in the bar at half past six, hoping to bump into the Edinburgh inspector.

'If we could just get in first and explain why we're worried before he gets the official version from that constable who couldn't have cared less, he might take it seriously,' she urged. 'Otherwise, you know, he'll probably just rubber-stamp her verdict and head back south tomorrow.'

Daniel did agree eventually but in view of his previous

eagerness for action it was puzzling, and she was frowning as she started breading the fish ready to fry for Murdo John's supper. That prompted her to wonder how poor Beatrice was coping with preparing for the supper that was to be served across the bay. She always left everything ready but she'd been complaining about the problem of getting it served up. The unacknowledged trouble was that with Beatrice's bulk she couldn't move swiftly, particularly if she was having to carry a loaded tray, and Adam, never noted for tolerating anything that impinged on his comfort, was getting seriously irritated.

He didn't, she'd noticed, take it out on Beatrice – from remarks that she had dropped occasionally Vicky had deduced that she was bankrolling much of the operation – but Harry seemed to have no such scruples. He didn't seem to realise that he wasn't going to make Beatrice less clumsy by making her nervous as well.

Beatrice was hard to like but she did feel very sorry for her. A lot of her social problems stemmed from awkwardness; she could never have been attractive and she had developed a sort of shell to protect herself that often made her seem snobby and stand-offish, but she cared about the children the charity worked to rescue with all her heart. Vicky had seen her in tears more than once over some particularly tragic story that had come in and she was utterly dedicated to her work – her passion for it had even persuaded Vicky herself to donate. It was just a pity that she was equally dedicated to Adam Carnegie, who was exploiting her ruthlessly, but there was nothing Vicky could do about that.

The big question was whether Harry was going to be making a long stay; if he was – well, she could see it coming. Adam would make her job conditional on her staying to serve up the evening meal as well. Her stomach churned at the thought of having to live in the atmosphere that seemed to get more toxic by the day but she wasn't going to give in. She was going to agree, whatever it might do to her marriage.

Livvy Murray stood peering into her wardrobe, then, not seeing what she was looking for, went across to rummage in the pile of clothes heaped on the chair in the corner of her bedroom.

She'd considered quite carefully what she was going to put on. She wanted to spell out that she didn't belong out here in the sticks but she'd left most of her smart-casual stuff at home in Glasgow – you didn't need smart up here. She might be irritated that the DI from Edinburgh had been sent at all but she wasn't going to be written off as one of the teuchters. So that merited her best jeans; she only hoped they weren't in the wash. No, there they were, and only a bit crumpled.

She'd a denim bomber jacket that was quite smart and then all she'd need was her Gap T-shirt, but that definitely wasn't around. She could only hope it was in the dry pile downstairs, waiting for a day when she felt like ironing. Days like that didn't come along often.

Luck was with her and she plugged in the iron, laid a couple of dish towels on the kitchen table and ironed the T-shirt – well, probably 'flattened' was a better word. No need to bother about the back when she'd be wearing a jacket.

If he'd come up as planned, he'd likely be in the pub for a drink after the journey, so if she wanted to catch him she ought to go now; it was six o'clock already. She changed quickly and put on a bit of slap. She was channelling professional, but on the other hand she didn't want to look as if she'd gone native and adopted weather-beaten as her style of choice.

When she was ready to go, she assessed herself in the badly lit mirror. Maybe she'd erred a wee bit on the tarty side but it was too late to remove it and start again.

She shrugged. He'd just have to take her as he found her. He'd be away again before long, once he realised what a waste of his time this was.

There was a cocktail bar just off the front hall and Kelso Strang looked in as he came downstairs before dinner. There were small dark wood tables with spindly legs on the patterned red carpet and there were framed etchings of what looked like Scottish castles on the walls; the style of the chairs upholstered in red nylon velvet owed something to Louis XIV – not in a good way – and an elderly couple were sitting at the table nearest the window. Fiona Ross was standing talking to them, a tray balanced on her hip.

He'd had enough of that lady and he made a neat swerve left instead into the extension with the pub sign outside that he'd noticed when he arrived.

The Black Cuillin was definitely catering for a very different clientele, with practical tile flooring and ropes, ice-axes and even climbing boots displayed by way of decoration. Here the framed pictures were enlarged Ordnance Survey maps and there was one impressive blown-up photo of the majestic ridge Kelso had seen on his way here. There were booths with benches round the walls and a couple of large round tables in the centre of the room.

There was a handful of people in already, one group obviously just back from a day on the hills, with heavy socks folded down over the sort of huge, clumpy boots you would only choose to wear for severely practical reasons. There was a cheer and some raucous laughter as one of their number made his way back to the booth with beer glasses and a jug.

Trained to observation, Kelso automatically flicked a glance round the room, registering that the man and woman sitting up at the bar had reacted as he came in. They had immediately looked away again and started talking animatedly, but his heart sank. Of course he'd been naive to think that the locals wouldn't have spotted a good chance to get ahead in the gossip stakes. He could hardly walk back out, though, so he took a seat at the farther end of the bar, giving them a cool nod. 'A pint of special,' he said.

The barman said, 'Sir,' and went to pull it. He was a big, dark-haired man with a beard and craggy features – Murdo John Macdonald, presumably, and he clearly wasn't in a chatty mood. In fact, he didn't seem the type to seek out the bright side of life, even at the best of times. Kelso was certainly planning to talk to him, but the public bar with the couple at the other end stealing sidelong glances at him wasn't the place. He'd drink his pint quickly and get out.

The woman was quite tall, young and attractive-looking with fair curly hair and clear blue eyes, set wide apart. She turned to smile at him. 'You're a visitor, are you?'

He gave a brief smile in return. 'Mmm,' he said, which could mean anything.

She persisted. 'Lovely weather today, anyway. I don't think the forecast's very good for tomorrow, though.'

'Mmm,' he said again, as discouragingly as he could. She paused, but he suspected she knew exactly who he was and now was figuring out her next move.

Just then the door opened and a young woman came in. She was quite small – not much more than five foot five – and small-boned. She was wearing jeans and a denim jacket and her curly hair was hennaed a deep shade of red that was almost pink. Her make-up suggested she was planning a night clubbing, which seemed unlikely in a place like this. In the present company, she looked like a parrot in a flock of sparrows.

She glanced round then to his dismay made straight for him. 'DI Strang? I'm PC Murray – Livvy. Welcome to Balnasheil.'

He didn't seem grateful that she'd come to see him settled in, Livvy thought resentfully as she took an inventory of Kelso Strang while he bought her a drink.

He wasn't classically good-looking – his face was a little too long and his eyes were slightly hooded, but they were an interesting colour, a sort of brownish-green. He was well over six foot, too, and broad-shouldered with it;

he looked as if he knew how to handle himself, the sort of guy you'd like to find yourself next to in the line if there was trouble brewing – even if it looked as if someone had glassed him. Maybe you needed to see what he'd done to the other fella.

Yes, she'd have to admit he was attractive. He had nice hands, too, she noticed as he set down her drink on the table – Livvy had a bit of a thing about hands – with long slim fingers. And a wedding ring. That figured. How come the buff guys were always married or gay – or both?

He'd look good if he was smiling but he seemed kind of stiff and buttoned-up. Probably this was what went for professional if you came from Edinburgh, but she felt as if she could have chipped ice cubes off him for her vodka and tonic to save Murdo John the trouble.

He'd made all the right noises when he thanked her for coming but it wasn't hard to work out that he'd have preferred that she hadn't and her back went up like a cat about to spit – *Oh yeah, typical Edinbugger*, she thought, *and so toffee-nosed that he feels drinking with a humble PC is beneath him*.

Actually, now she thought about it, she didn't really know why she had come except with a vague idea that she could explain to him that they'd done all that needed doing already, and maybe find out why he'd been sent all the way from Edinburgh to check up on them. But she could hardly do that with Vicky Macdonald and Daniel Tennant at the other end of the bar, earwigging so obviously you could almost see their wee feelers waving.

Asking him about his journey and whether his room

was comfortable kept them going for a few minutes, and answering his polite enquiries about her work here took up a bit more time. But the pauses grew longer and more uncomfortable and she started to feel anxious. Had there been some complaint about the way she'd dealt with the case, and was his reluctance to engage socially because tomorrow he was going to have to discipline her? She couldn't afford any more black marks on her record.

Nervousness prompted her to make more and more random contributions to the conversation to fill in the gaps, and it was a relief when he finished his beer and stood up.

'If you'll forgive me, I think I'd better go and find some supper. I've arranged to drive across to Broadford to talk to Sergeant Buchanan tomorrow morning – will I see you then?'

It was her day off but she'd insisted to Rab Buchanan that she'd come in anyway so she could emphasise how thorough she had been.

'Yes, sir. I'm going to be giving you my report.'

'Good. Thanks very much for taking the trouble to come in,' he said, and this time he smiled.

She was right – it was a nice smile.

As Kelso left the bar, Vicky Macdonald scrambled off her bar stool and hurried after him.

'Inspector!' she called.

He stopped, swore inwardly, and turned round. 'Yes?'

'Sorry, sorry,' she gabbled. 'It's just – you're here to investigate Eva Havel's disappearance, aren't you?'

'To review the investigation, yes.'

'I need to talk to you. I knew Eva, you see, and—'

'You are . . . ?'

'Vicky Macdonald. And Daniel Tennant is with me in the bar – he was to fetch her from Balnasheil Lodge the day she disappeared, so if you could bear to wait for your supper and come back to talk to us—'

'I will be very happy to hear what you both have to say once I have been briefed by my colleagues, madam. If you would like to phone the police station in Broadford and make an appointment—'

'Oh, I see.'

Her voice went flat. He saw her enthusiasm drain away, which was unfortunate, but a public bar was no place for interviews. He also had a strong suspicion that she wanted to complain about the local investigation and was trying to nobble him before he'd been briefed. He said a polite 'good evening' and walked on to the dining room.

She'd said her name was Macdonald, he thought suddenly. The barman's wife? They hadn't said a word to each other the whole time. Perhaps that was just coincidence: Skye was Macdonald country after all, but he made a mental note to check.

The elderly couple he'd seen earlier were in the dining room and there were two middle-aged men at another table. They didn't look like holidaymakers and Kelso glanced at them with mild interest as he waited to have his order taken.

It hadn't quite struck him that he'd be under the spotlight every moment he spent in a public place; thank God he'd thought of stashing a bottle of Scotch in his suitcase – he might be spending a fair amount of time in his bedroom. It could all get a bit suffocating, but it was quite likely that the case of Eva Havel's sudden departure would prove to be as straightforward as it looked on paper and he might be on his way by the day after tomorrow. He might even take time to fit in a bit of hillwalking before he left.

He hoped that Sergeant Buchanan, his liaison with the local force, would prove to be a more solid type than the flaky little PC who'd been trying to make an impression – which she had, of course, but perhaps not the one she'd been planning to make.

It had been a trying afternoon. When he'd removed the papers from the filing cabinet, Adam Carnegie had been possessed only by the need for damage limitation and he had made no effort to be systematic. The particular file that Harry needed to check had proved elusive and Harry, in any case, was running him ragged. He was blaming Adam for everything and Adam wasn't going to take it. They were in this together and Harry wasn't going to be allowed to forget it.

They were both on edge, of course. The police seemed to have lost interest in Eva, at least, but now they knew someone was sniffing around the charity, Harry was having to trawl through all the accounts to check that the barrier between official and unofficial – very unofficial – records was solidly in place and everything that should be destroyed had been destroyed. That would take a few days yet and Harry hadn't responded well to being cooped up here.

He liked city life and high living and the meals here had

proved a trigger point. Harry fancied himself as a gourmet and though Vicky Macdonald was a very good cook, the food after Beatrice's ministrations became all but inedible.

They'd pretty much smoothed over the blistering row they'd had this afternoon. At the time, he thought Harry would actually have decked him if it hadn't been for Amber, who wasn't about to let that happen. For the sake of peace he'd had to promise to keep her in the run when Harry was about.

If there wasn't to be another eruption, he'd better go and check on the situation in the kitchen. Beatrice was in a state about supper already, thanks to Harry. It simply couldn't go on like this; he'd have to tell Vicky she'd need to work evenings until he left.

That would please Beatrice and he was well aware of the need to keep her happy. There was more work to do on her; she hadn't yet made the will he wanted her to make and he knew why, too. She was using the marriage clause in her trust as a weapon to get him to marry her – as if! Sometimes he really loathed the fat cow.

And she was dangerous, too. She knew far too much and he had seen the constraint in her manner since he came back, and he knew what that was about. Sometimes he felt he was walking along the edge of a cliff himself. It didn't bear thinking about.

Harry would be looking for supper any time now. He went out of his flat and along to the kitchen where he could hear signs of activity, pinning a smile on his face.

The smell of burnt food hit him as he opened the door. Beatrice, her face streaked with tears, was scrubbing at the caked-on mess on top of the stove and a pot, burnt on the bottom, was sitting in the sink.

'It boiled over!' she wailed as she saw him. 'I thought I'd heat up the soup early so I could have it ready quickly when you wanted it, and then the phone rang with a query I had to check in the office and I just forgot about it and it was burnt and all over the stove when I came back.'

She burst into tears again. Adam gritted his teeth. 'You can't do everything, sweetie,' he said. 'I can't let this go on – it's upsetting you. We're going to have to get Vicky across instead.'

The sobs stopped and Beatrice's face brightened. 'Oh, Adam, that's so thoughtful of you! I just get so fussed, with Harry, you know—'

'Yes, I know. You won't have to do it any more. Never mind about the soup – we'll just have the rest and fill up on cheese. What's the timing?'

'Oh.' Beatrice gave a helpless look about her. 'Well, it'll be a good while. The oven needs to heat up before I put it in and with all this I forgot to do it—'

Adam's temper snapped. 'Oh, for goodness' sake, Beatrice! Just forget all about it. We'll go across to the hotel tonight.'

He had heard the tears start again as he left but he had been too annoyed to care. Harry wouldn't be pleased about that either – the food at the hotel was pretty dire.

Now, in the old-fashioned dining room at the back of the Balnasheil Hotel, Harry tasted the wine they had ordered and pulled a face. 'Which do you think will be worse tonight, the stew pretending to be boeuf bourguignon or the salmon in soggy croûte?' he said, rather too loudly.

Adam frowned him down. 'Shh! Here's Fiona coming.' He produced a charming smile as he looked up at her. 'So what specials has Douglas got in store for us tonight?'

She beamed. 'He's done his beef bourguignon, and he's been experimenting with a Thai green curry – unless you want the salmon *en croûte*, of course.'

'Difficult choice,' Adam said, trying not to catch Harry's eye.

'I'll be brave,' Harry said. 'Hit me with the curry.'

'I'll join him. Thanks, Fiona.'

She wrote it down but didn't move away, bending over to say confidentially, 'We've got the police in tonight, have you heard? That gentleman over there.' She contorted her neck in a gesture to indicate him without pointing or turning round. 'Come up from Edinburgh. Not very friendly.' She gave a little sniff of disapproval.

Adam saw Harry stiffen. 'From Edinburgh? What for?'

Fiona gave one of her little titters. 'Well – he didn't say, of course, but some folks have been wondering what happened to your housekeeper. Left very suddenly, didn't she?'

Adam felt cold sweat break out on the back of his neck. 'I was in Paris at the time,' he said stiffly. 'I don't really know anything about it.'

'Oh, of course.'

She still didn't move off, though; she just stood there, staring at him expectantly with those slightly protuberant eyes, her nose all but twitching. His right fist bunched in his lap and he could almost feel the delicious soft crunch it would make as it landed square in the middle of her face.

Harry said coldly, 'The curry, all right?'

As Fiona at last went off, he looked across the table at his companion. Adam found he couldn't look away, skewered by his unblinking stare.

'You got me into this,' Harry said. 'Now get me out. And eat up when it comes. We've a lot of work to do.'

CHAPTER SEVEN

Beatrice Lacey was feeling happier this morning. She'd been upset about the meal last night, but now Adam had promised that she'd never have to do it again she wouldn't have the worry hanging over her all day – and it showed he cared that she'd been unhappy, too. She enjoyed her toast, thickly spread with Nutella, then bathed Rosamond, dressed her in a pink frilly dress and settled her in her little crib and went down to the office.

Adam was about already. The door to his flat was standing open, as was the door to the cupboard where all those files had been yesterday, but it was empty now. She was glancing at it with mild curiosity when the front door opened and Adam himself appeared, looking preoccupied. It was raining gently outside and his hair was damp.

He jumped when he saw her. 'Oh – Beatrice. You're – you're down early today.'

Her happy mood started to evaporate. He was on edge, she could tell. She was surprised into saying, 'Is something wrong, Adam?' and saw his brow darken.

'No, certainly not,' he said sharply. 'Why should there be?'

Her glance went involuntarily to the open door and he followed her eyes. 'Oh – the cupboard. That was just some stuff that should have been cleared out long ago. All right?'

'Yes, of course.' Beatrice hoped her voice didn't reflect the hollow feeling inside. 'I'll – I'll just get on, then.'

As she went towards the office he called her back.

'Beatrice, those files in there – they were all from a business of Harry's, nothing to do with me. I know how discreet you are, sweetie, and of course I rely on that absolutely. I hope the day won't come when you would ever be anything else, but if you were to find yourself in a position when you had no alternative but to talk about it, remember they belonged to Harry.'

'Of course!' Beatrice cried. 'I would *never* say anything that would cause you trouble, Adam. You know that.'

She hadn't meant to put an extra emphasis on those last three words but somehow it had happened. She saw him register that, and stiffen.

'Yes,' he said, his voice flat. 'You've always been – very loyal.'

'Well, naturally.' She tried to lighten her tone and gave him a little, strained smile. When she reached the office and shut the door, she leant against it, her hand to her racing heart. Something was wrong, very badly wrong, and she could do nothing to help her idol. All she could do was wait, and fear.

* * *

Still feeling anxious, PC Murray presented herself at the Broadford police station before the night shift had gone off duty at eight and was left kicking her heels in the waiting room until Sergeant Buchanan arrived.

'Well, well, well, you're bright and early,' he said. 'Nervous?'

'Why should I be?' she snapped.

'You tell me. You're the one who met him last night, aren't you? What's he like?'

She thought for a minute. 'Cool – both kinds of cool, probably. Very polite, pure Edinburgh – you know, "east-windy-west-endy". Not just what you'd call a fun guy.'

'Right. So tell me – what's he going to say we've fallen down on?'

Murray bristled. 'By "we" you mean me, don't you? Nothing. Checked it all yesterday, couldn't see anything I missed. Eva left of her own accord and I couldn't see anything to suggest that she didn't. Daniel Tennant was just dumped and doesn't want to believe it. I don't have any need to defend my procedure.'

'Oh aye. Funny you gave up your day off to come in, then.'

'I came in,' she said bitterly, 'because there's nothing I want to do. I've got a brain and if I don't find something soon to occupy it in this dreary hole it'll start to rust and bits will fall off.'

He laughed. 'Fair enough. We'll be in his hands, though – I don't know how he'll want to play this. I'm still wondering why they sent someone up, and so quickly. There's something we're not getting, Livvy.'

She'd thought that herself and now she was feeling really uneasy – not that she was going to admit it. 'He's welcome to waste his time going over all the same ground I have,' she said defiantly. Then, pointing through the glass door to the car park, she said, 'That's him now,' and Buchanan went to let him in.

Sergeant Buchanan was, thankfully, as solid a citizen as DI Strang could have wished: middle-aged, big, burly, with close-cropped greyish hair and an outdoor complexion. He didn't look entirely comfortable in the new Lycra high-necked uniform shirt – they didn't flatter the older officers whose fitness standards possibly weren't quite what they might have been – but he was in the old-fashioned style of coppers whose very presence spelt reassurance. From his accent Strang guessed he was a local man and that like the old man at the pier he too would, as they said, 'have the Gaelic'.

There was coffee waiting for them in the sergeant's office though, having allowed himself to be seduced by the allure of a Scottish breakfast, Strang declined the biscuits that were also on offer. The effects of a fried potato scone might take some time to wear off.

PC Murray, though, attacked them with the enthusiasm of one whose own breakfast had been a cup of black coffee. She was looking more professional today with the dark pink hair scraped into a tight, scrubby ponytail under her hat; without her make-up she looked very young.

She showed signs of nervousness when he asked her to

make her report but she got more confident as she went on and it was quite intelligently presented. In the pause that followed, her eyes flicked first to her sergeant then back to Strang.

'Thank you, Constable,' he said. 'Good – very competent.' She gave a modest smirk and threw a triumphant glance at Buchanan as Strang looked at the papers he had taken out of his briefcase.

'The other contact you presume Eva Havel to have had – any evidence?'

'Er – no.'

'The barman at the Black Cuillin, Murdo John Macdonald – I don't see him mentioned in the report. Did you talk to him?'

'No, sir.' Murray's face was turning red.

'You didn't think he might have known if Eva Havel had been noticeably friendly with anyone else when she was in the bar?'

Murray went on the defensive. 'It wasn't necessarily someone she met here. I didn't think we were trying to trace her, just looking to see if there were any suspicious circumstances, and there weren't. It was clear she was intending to leave – she told Tennant she was, and Miss Lacey saw her packing. All her clothes had gone. Once Vicky Macdonald left she was alone in the house and she was a grown woman—'

'Yes, of course. I understand the reasoning and you may well be right. My concern is that the fact that she'd been packing and the absence of any indication of disturbance prompted a conclusion that ignores the breaking of the very specific arrangement Havel had made with Tennant – something that both he and Mrs Macdonald agreed was uncharacteristic. She didn't have a car or access to a boat herself so it would be reassuring to find some backup for the theory that she was fetched by someone else, wouldn't it?'

'Yes, sir,' Murray mumbled. She didn't look at him.

Buchanan gave her a sympathetic glance. 'I don't know how much background they've given you, sir, but the lassies that work over there at the charity never stay very long – here today, gone tomorrow, you know? *Foreign* lassies,' he added significantly.

Strang raised an eyebrow. 'Legal?'

'Never been asked to investigate, sir.'

'Right. I'll be doing an interview with Murdo John Macdonald first, if you can point me to his house, then I'll head over to Balnasheil Lodge.' He read from his list. 'Inhabitants: I understand that's Beatrice Lacey, Adam Carnegie, possibly Vicky Macdonald if she's at work today – that all?'

Buchanan glanced at Murray, whose head went down again. 'There's a handyman lives in the gate cottage in the grounds,' he said. 'Another foreigner. Don't know his name. Do you, Livvy?'

Murray shook her head.

'He wasn't interviewed?' Strang said sharply. 'So he may have helped her to get away, or at least seen her go?' He got up. 'Sooner we get on to that the better.'

The other officers stood up too. 'What help will you be needing, sir?' Buchanan asked. 'We've no CID at Broadford now, but there's a team in Portree.'

Strang smiled, shaking his head a little ruefully. 'I'm on my own. Budgets, you know? I'm hoping that it's just a question of ensuring all appropriate enquiries have been made. I'm not expecting to be here more than a couple of days.'

'It's all money these days, isn't it, sir,' Buchanan said. 'Anyway, you know where to find us.'

'I'll keep that in mind. Thanks.'

He had noticed, with mild irritation, that Murray had been looking mutinous – she should have done a more thorough job if she didn't want to be panned – so he was surprised when she said, 'It's my day off, sir. If you like I could come with you to take notes. I've nothing planned and it'll be good experience.'

Buchanan, too, looked taken aback. 'Not like you to give up time off, Livvy.'

She shot him a look. 'Some of us like learning stuff more than dossing about. Others of us don't,' she added pointedly.

Strang remembered a certain young DC who'd made a remark like that to his sarge and been given, as that redoubtable man had said, his head in his hands and his lugs to play with. He had to suppress a smile; she'd got spirit, certainly. She could be useful to guide him around and maybe he'd glean a bit of background info from her at the same time.

'Thanks, Murray. That could be very helpful,' he said and pretended not to notice the withering look she'd cast at her more tolerant sergeant.

* * *

When they parked at the Macdonalds' cottage the rain was falling steadily and even in the few steps to the front door Strang could feel it trickling down the back of his neck. When there was no immediate answer to Murray's knock he said impatiently, 'No one in, obviously. We'll try later,' and headed for the shelter of the car.

'Hang on,' Murray said, pointing to a boat crossing the bay. 'That'll maybe be him now, sir.'

They walked along to the pier and waited as the boat came in to tie up. Strang saw Macdonald look up and see them, then look down again to busy himself with the rope. His face was impassive and his movements unhurried. At last he came up the ladder and Strang moved forward.

'Could we have a word, sir?' They showed their warrant cards and Macdonald took them and studied them, which Strang found interesting. It wasn't something people often did; did he just have a slow, deliberate cast of mind or was it a delaying tactic? Or was it even, he wondered bitterly, prompted by a malicious pleasure in seeing him get soaked to the skin? This was a lesson about the unwisdom of leaving the car without his oilskin jacket.

Macdonald nodded at last, then led the way into the cottage. The front door opened into a pleasant sitting room but he didn't invite them to sit down; Strang sat down anyway and after a brief hesitation Murray did too. Macdonald stood like a rock, looming over them.

'Perhaps you could sit down as well,' Strang said. 'I'm not sure how long this will take.'

He wondered if the man would refuse, but after a moment he complied, giving Strang a hard look from under his heavy brows. He hadn't so far spoken a single word, which wasn't promising for the interview.

'You've been barman at the Black Cuillin for some time, haven't you?' As Macdonald only nodded, he added, 'How long?' and waited.

At last Macdonald said, 'I suppose about ten years, off and on. It's irregular work – I do it when I'm needed.'

'Do you have other work?'

'Sometimes. Used to work in construction.'

There was a touch of bitterness in his reply but that was an irrelevance Strang didn't pursue, only going on to establish that he knew Eva Havel, that she had come in quite frequently, if not regularly. And that recently she had spent quite a lot of her time with Daniel Tennant.

'Anyone else?' Strang asked, and saw Murray stop her note-taking and lean forward, as if she was willing the man to say yes. He said no, and she gave a small sigh as she wrote that down.

'The other women who have been housekeepers at Balnasheil Lodge recently – were they regular visitors to the bar?'

'Oh yes.' There was no mistaking his reserve.

Strang raised his eyebrows. 'Not welcome guests?'

'It's a public bar. Nothing to do with me,' Macdonald said stiffly.

'Did any of them leave without warning?'

He shrugged. 'I – I wouldn't know.' He shut his mouth as if he never intended to open it again.

He was uneasy and Strang was onto it immediately. 'There was something else?'

'No, nothing.'

'Oh, I think there was. I don't want this to take longer than it has to, Mr Macdonald. Am I to assume there was a question mark about another woman?' Macdonald was looking down, not meeting his eyes, and he went on, 'I've no doubt if there was talk someone else will know as well – Mrs Ross, perhaps?'

Macdonald shot Strang a look of dislike but after a moment's thought he spoke. 'There was one girl, Veruschka. Four years ago. There was a local woman did cleaning over there – she said she'd disappeared, but she was always one to exaggerate.'

'Her name?'

'Morag Soutar. Died last year.'

'And no one else knew anything about that?'

'Just gossip. Never believed it for a minute.'

'Right.' Strang thought for a moment. Relevant – not relevant? Something to follow up later, perhaps. Go for the important question now.

'How did you get on with Eva, Mr Macdonald?'

He shrugged. 'Barely spoke to her, except to ask what she wanted to drink.'

'Did you fetch her from Balnasheil Lodge the day she disappeared?'

'No.'

There was no obvious reaction. Naturally impassive, or expecting the question? 'There would be no crime in helping her,' Strang said. 'Still no?'

'No.'

Strang got up, taking Murray by surprise. As he said, 'Thank you for your time, sir. We may want to talk to you again later,' she scrambled up, dropping her notebook and going pink with embarrassment as she bent to pick it up.

When they were back in the car she said stiffly, 'All right, I screwed up. I should have interviewed him. Maybe something awful has happened to that girl and we could have done something if I'd picked up on it sooner.'

Strang cast her an impatient look. Self-flagellation was usually an oblique demand for reassurance that this was unnecessary and he wasn't going to be drawn into playing that game. 'Let's check the evidence before we start dramatising. All the indications still are that she'd decided to go and there's probably no more to it than that.'

But he was beginning to have a nasty feeling that actually, there very possibly was.

Daniel Tennant arrived at Broadford Police Station just after nine o'clock. He was looking tense and he drummed his fingers on the shelf by the hatch in the entrance hall as he waited for someone to answer the bell he had pressed.

He waited, fretting, then pressed it again. The woman who at last appeared was a civilian and she looked resentful at being summoned. When he said he wanted to speak to the officer who had come from Edinburgh she looked blank. 'What name?'

'I don't know,' he said impatiently. 'He came up yesterday and he's not at the hotel where he was staying so I thought he'd be here.'

'He didn't sign the book,' she said, pointing at the ledger on the shelf by the hatch with some triumph. 'You can't just walk in off the street, you know. There's security, so he'd need to press that bell and get OK'd by me or he wouldn't get in here. And he didn't, so he isn't.'

'And you don't know where he might be, I suppose?' She gave him a pitying look, and he went on, 'Perhaps there's someone here who would know. Could you ask, please?'

'What's his name?' she said again.

Tennant gritted his teeth. 'I – don't – know.'

'Then I can't really ask about him, can I? Sorry, sir.' She shut the hatch and disappeared.

Tennant shut his eyes and groaned. Vicky had told him he'd need to make an appointment but he'd ignored that. Now he'd just have to wait until Inspector Whoever-he-was decided to seek him out – in fact, he'd better return home in case he missed him.

'Shocking road,' DI Strang said as they went round the edge of the bay. Even by local single track standards it was bad, very narrow and seamed with potholes; it began to rise in a series of sharp corners and blind brows as they went further up into the lower slopes of the Black Cuillin. 'If someone's coming the other way we'll meet bumper to bumper.'

He kept his voice determinedly level but it was spooking him. The rain had eased off a little but the surface was greasy and he realised his knuckles were white. He had to force himself to loosen his grip on the steering wheel.

PC Murray hadn't noticed. 'Oh, there won't be anyone coming the other way,' she said with youthful overconfidence. 'It only leads to the Lodge and mostly if they're going out it's the motorboat across to the pier. Watch when you come to the bridge, though – it's on quite a sharp bend and it's pretty rickety.'

She had been subdued at first, dealing with her humiliation probably, but when he asked her about Balnasheil Lodge she was ready enough to talk. 'You know they have this charity – Human Face. Funny kind of name, that, isn't it?'

'Very suitable. "*Mercy has a human heart, / Pity a human face, / And Love, the human form divine, / And Peace, the human dress*,"' he quoted, then as she looked at him blankly added, 'Blake. William Blake.'

She pulled a face. 'Sorry. Doesn't mean anything to me.'

'Romantic poet. Never mind. It's just that I guess whoever gave the charity its name knew the poem.'

'Doesn't sound very romantic to me,' Murray said. 'You'd think romantic would be just about love and stuff.'

'Er – yes,' Strang said. 'You were telling me about the set-up?'

'It's run by this guy Adam Carnegie – I've never met him but he's not well-liked. Beatrice Lacey's the secretary or something – quite posh but she's really fat.' She paused. 'Are we allowed to say that now?'

'Probably not. But I get the picture.'

'She definitely had it in for Eva Havel. Sort of implied she was a wee hoor who'd go with anyone.'

'And was she?'

'Vicky Macdonald didn't think so – got quite huffy about

it. But there's stories about the girls who came from there – and they were mostly hard-faced bitches on the make and snooty with it, according to the locals. Well, they're a bit traditional here.'

Murray was clearly untroubled by considerations of political correctness. What she said might or might not be accurate but it would certainly be what she believed to be the truth. That could cut both ways.

'Watch out,' she said now, 'the bridge is just round the corner.'

He was grateful for the warning. They had climbed quite a bit and there was a deep fissure in the side of the mountain, cut over the centuries by a burn that sprang down over slabs of rock in a series of waterfalls and deep pools, the stone worn away and pitted. The lush ferns and the moss growing around it were a green that seemed shockingly violent in this grey, misty landscape.

It was magnificent, if you were in a position to admire it, but Strang was engaged in changing gear as he drove down onto a bridge with low stone walls that looked as if it was just clinging on to the sides of the gully, like one of the straggly silver birches that grew on the slopes above. Then there was the sharp corner on the other side to negotiate, with a sixty-foot drop to rocks on the seaward side.

Strang was breathing unevenly as he said, 'Thanks for the warning,' as lightly as he could. With the second bend safely negotiated, the road sloped down towards the shore and now he could see the Lodge and its outbuildings, together with a cottage beside the entrance to the short drive leading to the front door.

The grounds were wooded and lawns stretched on either side but it was less grand than it had seemed from the farther shore; indeed, looking from above he could see that some of the outbuilding roofs had collapsed and even on the cottage there were tiles missing, and it badly needed repainting.

He drew up just inside the gate. 'We'll try here first. Don't know his name, I suppose?'

Murray shook her head, colouring up again.

There was no answer when Strang knocked on the door but there was the sound of wood being chopped at the back and they followed it round to a yard with a shed stocked with wood and a peat stack.

The man who was wielding an axe on the huge logs was powerfully built with musculature that spoke to a lifetime of manual work. He had a shock of black hair and a black beard, shining with the moisture clinging to it; somewhere around fifty, Strang estimated. His eyes were dark, almost black, under heavy brows and he didn't look pleased to see them.

Strang took out his warrant card. 'DI Strang and PC Murray. Could we have a word?'

The man didn't respond. He drove the axe into a waiting log and stood up, his great rough hands on his hips.

'Your name is . . . ?'

'Marek Kaczka.' He had a heavy accent.

'Do you speak English?'

'Yes.'

'And your nationality?'

'Polish.'

Of course. You had the right to work in Britain if you were Polish. *If* you were Polish, which Strang doubted. But it wasn't his business, at the moment anyway.

'We wanted to ask some questions about the female who left here last week. Inside, perhaps?' The rain might be gentler now but it was unremitting.

He could see hostility in the dark eyes but the man, familiar perhaps with the wisdom of cooperating with the police, turned and led the way round to the front door.

It opened directly into a small, dark room that had an unmade bed with a sagging mattress, a small sofa with the stuffing hanging out and a hard chair, with a sink on the back wall and a small camping stove on a table beside it. There was a pile of dirty dishes in the sink and dirty ashes in the meagre fireplace; the mantelpiece was thick with dust and there were clothes piled up haphazardly in one corner. There was a smell of peat smoke and something more unpleasant – human sweat, unwashed clothing. As tied accommodation it was basic to an extreme degree.

'You knew Eva Havel?' Strang asked.

'Yes.'

'Was she Polish too?'

'I do not ask.'

Breakthrough! The man had actually said four words. 'Did you know that she was planning to leave?'

'No.'

'Do you know if she had friends in the area?'

'No.'

'Did you see her on the day she left?'

There was a pause. Then he said, 'What day?'

PC Murray, with a glance at Strang, told him.

'No.'

'You didn't see her leaving in a boat? Or driving past here in a car?'

For a moment Strang thought there was a flicker of something in his eyes, but he only said, 'No,' again.

Strang sighed. He had no idea whether or not the man knew anything but he was quite sure that if he did, he wouldn't tell them. That might be because of an inbuilt dislike and distrust of the police, or it might be that if he was in a vulnerable position with his employment, he wouldn't be saying anything that his employer might not want him to say. They were wasting their time.

They got back into the car to drive up to the Lodge, parking it up by the front door. As they were getting out, he heard sudden, savage barking and turned sharply.

There was a man walking down from the rough moorland beyond the house towards them, one of the men he had seen in the hotel the night before, with a shotgun broken over his arm. A Dobermann dog was racing ahead of him, snapping its pointed teeth. Murray, with a squeal of fright, jumped back into car and shut the door. Strang paused, holding his door open for a sudden retreat, but interested to know what the man would do.

After a moment, when the dog was less than a hundred yards away, the owner barked out a sharp command and the dog all but skidded to a stop, turned round and ran back.

It had been a long moment. Long, and quite deliberately

calculated. As the man, smiling and very apologetic, came up to them Strang studied him through narrowed eyes. If he was under the impression that playing little games like this with the police was clever, he was going to learn his mistake.

CHAPTER EIGHT

'Adam Carnegie,' he said, shaking DI Strang's hand and nodding to PC Murray. The dog stood by his side, looking up at its master, displaying no interest at all in the officers. 'Do forgive Amber – she's just a little overenthusiastic when it comes to strangers.'

'We noticed. Do you find you need a guard dog?' Strang's voice was cold.

The smile vanished. 'We do live very much out in the wilds here. We don't have the luxury of a squad car round the corner if there was a problem.'

Strang raised his eyebrows. 'You surprise me. I understood that around here people didn't even lock their doors at night. I didn't realise that the sort of violent crime that might call for an aggressive dog was a problem.' He enjoyed the flicker of annoyance that appeared on the man's face and went on smoothly, 'However, perhaps we could have a word about some concerns that have been raised about Eva Havel's departure.'

'Of course, though I doubt if I can be of much help. We'll go in this way.' He went round to the side of the house where a little patio led to open French doors. 'Come in and sit down. Coffee?'

He was quite a good-looking man, in his late forties, Strang guessed; not tall but strongly built and fit-looking, not carrying an ounce of excess weight. His mouth was ugly, though, when he wasn't actually smiling, thin-lipped and turned down at the corners, and there were strong frown marks between his dark brows. Though he was smiling now, his eyes were cold.

'No, thank you.' Strang nodded to Murray to take out her notebook. 'What was Ms Havel's position in the household?'

Carnegie had gone to pour himself out a mug of coffee from a very fancy machine on a unit that neatly divided what looked like a designer kitchen from the expensively furnished sitting room: sleek cream leather sofas on either side of the fireplace, a large oriental rug on top of the pale fitted carpet, a dark polished wood desk in the window, a huge TV and a couple of good modern prints on the walls.

'Position?' Carnegie said. 'She didn't exactly have a *position*, Inspector. She was my girlfriend.'

Murray looked up, opened her mouth to speak then thought the better of it. Strang said, 'Oh? She was described to me as the housekeeper.'

Carnegie brought over his coffee and sat on the sofa opposite and the dog lay down at his feet. 'Well, we tended to say that. The village is not, shall we say, terribly sophisticated when it comes to modern morals.' He sounded amused.

'So – no papers, no employment contract?'

Carnegie didn't like that. 'Do you give your girlfriends a contract, Inspector? Oh, sorry, I beg your pardon. I see you're a married man.'

God, that hurt. It took him all his strength not to gasp. There was a fraction of a beat too long before he managed to say, 'What nationality was Ms Havel?'

'Polish, I believe. Or so she said.'

'Like Mr Kaczka?'

That took him aback. 'Oh – oh yes, that's right. And before you ask, I do have employment papers for him.'

'They must have enjoyed having a fellow Pole to talk to.'

'Perhaps they might. I don't know. Their paths didn't cross very much.' Carnegie moved restlessly and the dog sat up. 'Look, I really can't help you about the day Eva left. I had no idea she was planning to go, but apparently there was a young man in the village that she'd been meeting behind my back. I'm away a lot on business, you know. And as it happened, I was away – flew to Paris that afternoon. When I came back she was gone. The person you want to talk to is Beatrice Lacey – she saw her packing.'

'We'll speak to her later. So – how did you feel about being dumped?'

Carnegie gave a short laugh. 'Indifferent, to be honest. She was obviously tired of me and I was tired of her too. It was never going to be a long-term relationship.'

'You seem to have had a number of "housekeepers", or girlfriends, if you prefer.'

'Yes,' he said flatly.

'All foreign?'

'I like foreign girls. You should try that sometime, Inspector – oh, sorry, but perhaps your wife is broad-minded?'

That was deliberate. He had spotted Strang's reaction to the mention of his wife and he was probing. It hurt again and Strang hesitated briefly.

Murray seized the opportunity to jump in. 'Where do you meet them all? Not a lot of them around here.'

Neither man seemed to welcome her interjection. Strang gave her a cool look and Carnegie scowled at her, as if she'd interrupted a private conversation or come between the foils in a fencing match. 'If it's any of your business, I am abroad at international conferences quite frequently.'

Strang returned to the fray. 'And have they all been "Polish"?' He made the inverted commas obvious.

Carnegie did not rise to the bait. 'No.'

Time to bring out the big guns. 'Did any of your other girlfriends just disappear?' He fixed his eyes intently on Carnegie's face and saw his sudden wariness.

Only for a second, though. The man bent over to stroke the dog at his feet then said smoothly, 'No, of course not.'

'Veruschka.'

The name dropped into the conversation like a stone. Carnegie seemed almost stunned. 'Veruschka?' he said slowly.

'You seem very uncomfortable about that. What happened to her?'

'Uncomfortable? No, just surprised. It was years ago – to be honest, I'd forgotten all about her.' He was definitely

147

rattled, fighting to regain his composure. 'We'd been together for a few months and one day she decided to move on. Fair enough – I had no problem with that.'

It was tempting to go down that track but so far Strang wasn't here to investigate Veruschka, whoever she might be, so he only said, 'You don't seem to be awfully lucky in love, Mr Carnegie. You must suffer a certain amount of wounded pride.'

That got to him, as he had guessed it would. His lips tightened, though he said lightly, 'Who's talking about love, Inspector?'

'Anyway, at the moment I'm interested in Eva Havel. Did she have any family connections, here or back in Poland?'

'I haven't the slightest idea. We didn't talk about that.' He gave a little, suggestive smirk. 'To be brutally honest, Inspector, we didn't talk much at all. I didn't bring her here for the charm of her conversation.'

It was a pity there was a prejudice in the police force against giving someone a punch in the face just because that was what they were asking for. Strang got up. 'That's all – at least for the moment. Thank you for your time. Perhaps we could speak to Miss Lacey since you seem to think she knows more about it than you do.'

'Of course.' He stood up, with a signal to the dog to stay, then led them out into the front hall. A man was coming through from a door under the stairs, a man who stopped dead when he saw them.

Carnegie greeted him, 'Looking for me, Harry? I'll be with you in just a moment.' Then he turned to Strang. 'This is my partner, Harry Drummond. I don't think he can help you over Eva's departure – he only arrived here after she'd gone. I doubt if you ever had a conversation with her alone, did you?'

Drummond was, like his partner, middle-aged and of middle height. His hair was dark and curly; he had very bright blue eyes and a small, mean mouth. 'Can hardly even picture her,' he said. 'Sorry.'

He went back the way he had come. Carnegie went across the hall and opened a door on the farther side. 'Some people to speak to you, sweetie. It's the fuzz – better be on your best behaviour.'

He waved them through the door and left them.

Beatrice Lacey felt as if the floor had opened beneath her. It seemed rude not to stand up and greet the policewoman and the man with her, who was presumably a detective, but she wasn't sure that if she did her legs would hold her up. Instead, she gestured towards the two seats that stood beside her desk as PC Murray reminded her that they'd met before and introduced Detective Inspector Strang.

'Would you like to sit down? Is this about Eva again? I told you everything I could already.' She managed to inject a note of irritation into her voice.

The detective had a penetrating gaze and he was looking at her now in a way that made her feel he could see right through her, through to all the sleep-troubling secrets. What did he know? Could she mount a defence against whatever he was going to ask her? She wasn't a good liar. She was beginning to hyperventilate, and he had noticed.

'Please don't worry, Miss Lacey,' he said. He had a very attractive voice, quite deep and rich, and he sounded sympathetic. 'I know that it's a bit intimidating when the police march in but all I want is to hear for myself what happened the day that Eva Havel left.'

Beatrice licked dry lips. 'I was actually away most of that day. I had to go down to Oban to check on an order and I only saw her very briefly. I went into her room to tell her I'd be away and I saw she was packing. That's all, really.'

'You didn't ask her why?'

'It wasn't my business.'

'And you didn't mention it to Mr Carnegie?'

'He's a busy man. He was just on his way to Paris for a conference and I didn't want to worry him.'

'Had there been any rows between them, to your knowledge?'

'None at all.' She was firm on that. 'I couldn't see any reason why she should want to leave, but—' She shrugged.

'Was he upset when he found she had left?'

'Of course not!' Beatrice said contemptuously. 'Their relationship – it didn't mean anything. She was just a – a temporary distraction for Adam. Nothing to do with his true feelings.'

'Which are?'

Oh dear God, he was looking at her and she knew she was blushing. 'You'd – you'd have to ask him,' she said feebly.

'You suggested to my colleague that Ms Havel might have been involved with other young men apart from Mr Tennant, who contacted us about her disappearance. Was there anyone you had in mind?'

'Well, no, not exactly. It was just – well, she had that sort of manner, I suppose. The sort who would encourage . . . well, you know.' She was getting flustered, and she wasn't even at the difficult bit yet.

'She never mentioned anyone to you?'

'No. We weren't really on terms like that.'

'I see.'

He had paused. She braced herself for questions about Adam's movements, but instead he asked her about her position here and she seized on that with relief.

'I'm the charity's patron, Inspector. I christened it – Blake, you know?' She saw him nod and went on, 'I do the administration that keeps it going so that Adam can get on with his vital work.'

Much happier now, she expounded on the aims and achievements of the charity, her eyes shining with fervour. 'And of course none of this could happen without Adam. He's a wonderful, wonderful man.'

She'd let herself get carried away – too much so. The inspector was looking at her very thoughtfully.

'Mr Carnegie was away in Paris the day Ms Havel left – is that right?'

'Yes.' She had managed to say it. If he left it at that, everything would be all right. And they were getting up, asking where to find Vicky Macdonald . . .

'By the way,' he said as he reached the door, 'do you remember someone called Veruschka?'

The cold horror of the question, she thought later, must have put her into shock. Beatrice heard her own voice saying quite calmly, 'Veruschka? Oh yes, she was here a

151

few years ago. Always very unsettled, I remember – I wasn't surprised when she went.'

It seemed to satisfy him. They left, and she was able to slump across her desk, feeling her heart beating so hard that it felt as if it might burst out of her chest. But she'd got through it. Perhaps she wasn't as bad a liar as she had thought.

The contrast between Adam Carnegie's designer kitchen and the dingy kitchen where Strang and Murray found Vicky Macdonald was stark. Here it looked as if nothing had been done in the past thirty years: a scrubbed wood table stood in the centre of the room, the walls were beige, the Formica units and surfaces were beige, the worn vinyl floor was beige and brown. The only touches of colour came from the bottle of lemon washing-up liquid and yellow rubber gloves by the stainless steel sink, a bright red tea towel and the vivid orange of the carrots she was chopping.

There was a similar contrast in the reactions they provoked. Adam Carnegie had been hostile, Beatrice Lacey terrified; Vicky Macdonald was effusive.

'Oh, Inspector, I'm so pleased to have a chance to talk to you! I'm sorry about last night—'

Strang cut her off. 'You clearly had something you were very keen to tell me. What was it?'

Vicky hesitated. 'It wasn't exactly something I had to tell you – I wish it had been. I just wanted to stress that I don't believe Eva would behave like this, telling Daniel to be ready waiting for her and then doing something else without explaining, without saying anything to me. She was a really nice person, honestly.'

A willing witness without anything to say – this was undoubtedly disappointing. He said, 'Do you actually know that there wasn't anyone else she might have been involved with? Did she confide in you?'

Vicky looked crestfallen. 'Not really, no. I felt she was isolated here, needed a friend, and I tried to be one but her English wasn't that good and I think she was a bit careful too about what she said – I guess she was probably here illegally.'

'Were she and Mr Carnegie on good terms? Any rows, arguments?'

She hesitated. 'Not rows, no. But there was – well, an atmosphere. The relationship had definitely cooled and you didn't see them together much any more and Eva seemed strained. But—' She glanced at the kitchen door to make sure it was shut, then said, 'I think there's something going on just now. Beatrice is behaving as if she's had advance notice that the sky's going to fall and Adam and Harry keep shouting at each other. I really think you should investigate—'

'At the moment I'm only concerned with Ms Havel's disappearance,' Strang said firmly. 'You saw Miss Lacey and Mr Carnegie leave before you did – is that right?'

She nodded.

'So she was alone in the house?'

She nodded again. Then she burst out, 'Oh, you're not going to take it seriously, are you? You're just going to repeat the line that she was a grown-up woman—'

'We're taking it seriously enough for me to have come up from Edinburgh to investigate and I am interviewing everyone who might have information. I am keeping an open mind, I assure you.'

'Talk to Daniel Tennant,' she urged.

'I had thought of that.' He tried not to sound sarcastic. 'I spoke to Murdo John Macdonald – your husband?'

'Yes. But he won't have told you anything useful. He thinks she just left.'

She sounded bitter. Domestic friction? Well, that wasn't any of his business. He went on, 'How long have you lived here, Mrs Macdonald?'

'I came here on holiday two, almost three years ago, then got a job waitressing. I married Murdo John about a year later.'

'So you wouldn't have known someone called Veruschka?'

She looked blank. 'No. Should I have?'

'Your husband mentioned her. She was a housekeeper here a few years back and there was some story about her having disappeared.'

'Disappeared?' A flush came to Vicky's face. 'And Murdo never told me about this?' She was wringing her hands. 'Inspector, I beg you – you've got to find out what happened to Eva! There's something wrong here, there really is. Adam Carnegie—' She stopped.

'Adam Carnegie?' he prompted her.

'Oh, I don't suppose there's anything you could really prove against him. I just have a feeling about him.' She gave a little shrug that somehow turned into a shudder.

She was a nice, concerned lady and he admired her crusading spirit, but she was absolutely useless. 'I'll remember everything you've said,' Strang assured her, getting up. 'But I'll get on my way now and hope to find Mr Tennant and see what he has to add.'

Vicky thanked him but her tone was flat. She was clearly as disappointed in him as he had been in her.

As they started out on the road back to Balnasheil, he turned to his silent shadow. 'You're very quiet. Any questions about the interviews?'

'Didn't think I was invited to ask – me being a humble plod.'

He was annoyed by the chippy tone. 'I don't see it like that, Murray.'

Her response was a slight shrug. 'I got the idea you didn't welcome my input – that I was just there to take notes.'

'Yes, you were. It's what a police constable does. I followed up the intervention you made in the Carnegie interview, but it wasn't a direction I had planned to take at that moment and it's my job to shape the line it takes. It didn't matter, as it happened, but it could be a distraction.

'But you said you wanted to learn, so I'm asking you now – were there things you wondered about, things you thought I'd missed?'

'No. No, there weren't.'

'So tell me – you'd interviewed Miss Lacey before. Did anything further emerge this time?'

'Yes, I suppose so,' she said grudgingly. 'She'd do anything for him. She's in love with him, isn't she?'

Strang thought of the woman's ungainly body, her flat face with its muddy complexion and double chins. 'Poor woman,' he said. 'Inevitable, of course. I'm sure he can be very charming.'

'Charming?' Murray looked at him in amazement. 'Sleaze bucket. I was thinking of asking if I could have a quick bath before the next interview.'

He smiled. 'I was thinking more in terms of physical violence myself. But it looks as if the man wasn't even there at the time when Eva left and it's easy enough to check. So how do you assess the situation now, Murray?'

For a moment she didn't answer. Then she said, 'To be honest, this stinks. But we've nothing to go on, so I still don't see what we can do.'

She might be irritating but she wasn't stupid. 'Yes,' he said heavily. 'I've got an unpleasant feeling that you're right.'

The door had barely shut behind him and Vicky was standing staring blankly at the carrots, thinking over what Strang had said, when it opened again and Adam Carnegie came in, smiling.

'Seen them off, have you?'

Vicky gave a feeble smile in return. 'They were perfectly pleasant but I don't think they're taking it seriously.'

'And you are?' The smile became a little more fixed. 'Oh, come on, Vicky! Eva was a very bright, vivacious girl – there might easily have been more than one young man hoping for her favours. She probably found it a bit dull over here when I'm away so much and I certainly don't hold it against her – though I wish she'd left a note or something and saved us all being interrogated about something we knew nothing about.

'Actually, I came in to ask you for a favour. Harry's going to be staying for a few more days – he's got problems with his own business so he's working on them up here where he can get some peace. He's not the easiest of guests and my poor Beatrice is falling apart with the stress of getting everything served up. Oh, I know you leave everything ready but she gets flustered and upset and we don't want that. Would you extend your duties to coming across and doing the evening meal, the way you do when there's a house party? Same rate, of course – and you could sleep in Eva's room if Murdo John drew the line at another trip to and fro.'

There was something in the way he looked at her, something in the way his eyes flicked from her face down to the V of her open-necked shirt that made her flesh crawl. She recoiled from the thought of sleeping under the same roof as this man, but Murdo John certainly wouldn't agree to ferrying her on an extra trip. He wouldn't want her to go at all. But she wasn't in a charitable mood at the moment where her husband was concerned.

'Yes, I can do that,' she said, as calmly as if there wasn't a voice inside her screaming, *No! Don't! Don't!* 'But there was something I wanted to ask you. The inspector was asking me about another girl who'd been housekeeper here – Veruschka, was it?'

'My dear girl, I can't imagine what all that was about.' There was a smile on Adam's face but it was more like a rictus. 'Veruschka was just a girl who worked here years ago then got tired of it, just the way Eva did. I can understand; it's very remote for a young person.'

'And did she just disappear too?'

The smile, such as it was, vanished. 'No,' he said curtly. 'She told me she was leaving – going to London, she said, if I remember rightly, and then she left. And before you ask me, no, after all that time I don't remember exactly what her travel arrangements were – Marek taking her across to catch the bus? Maybe, or perhaps she got a taxi. Oh, and I seem to remember we were having some building work done on one of the outbuildings around that time – she was always moaning about the dust, anyway. So maybe a workman gave her a lift – Murdo John was certainly one of them. Why don't you ask him? Anyway, I have other things to do. Are you prepared to do the suppers or not? Because—'

'Yes, of course, Adam,' she said, but she had gone back to chopping her carrots with particular venom before he left the room. She had been angry before but now she was burning with fury. Murdo John knew this had happened before with another girl but he hadn't told her, even though he knew how worried she was about Eva.

Things weren't right between them at the moment and this could just be the night when things went badly, badly wrong.

Daniel Tennant had the front door of his rented cottage open before Strang and Murray were halfway up the short path. He looked pale and tense and the two-day stubble on his cheeks looked like negligence rather than design.

'You've taken your time,' he said irritably. 'I tried to catch you at the police station in Broadford this morning but the woman on the desk wouldn't try to find you because I didn't know your name.'

It wasn't often you found a witness as keen as this. Strang raised his eyebrows as he took out his warrant card and introduced himself.

'Strang,' Tennant read. His eyes slid over the woman officer. 'Right. You'd better come in.'

The front door opened into a living room which ran right across the front of the house, with a kitchen area at one end and a fireplace at the other. The furnishings were functional rather than elegant – solid foam sofas and chairs upholstered in primary colours – and it was clear that this was a holiday let, but it was comfortable enough and there were papers piled up on a table in front of one of the small windows and books and personal clutter spread around on the coffee table by the fire. It wasn't lit, and with the dead ashes in the grate the place felt cheerless.

It was only when Strang and Murray were going to sit down that Tennant seemed to focus on Murray. He pointed. 'Not her,' he said.

Strang stared at him. 'PC Murray is here to take notes for me. There's no reason—'

'Yes, there is,' Tennant said. 'I need to speak to you alone.'

'Perhaps if you were to tell me what this is about—'

The man's face twitched as he sat down on the

incongruously cheerful bright red sofa and folded his arms. 'I'm not saying a word until she goes.'

Strang felt his hackles rise. 'I understood you wanted to talk to me urgently. It seems curious that now I'm here you're making conditions.'

Tennant didn't move, only closing his lips more tightly together.

Murray was standing her ground, looking ready for a fight, but Strang was always inclined to play the percentages and he could lose this one.

'If you don't mind, Murray,' he said, and though she pursed her lips and glared at Tennant she said, 'Sir,' and left. He heard her slam the car door unnecessarily hard. Strang took his seat on the bright blue sofa opposite. 'This had better be good. What was your problem with my constable?'

'For a start, she interviewed me before and she didn't take me seriously.'

'I have reviewed her report and she proceeded perfectly properly, sir. PC Murray found no sign that there had been anything untoward about Ms Havel leaving, apart from the fact that you had expected her to call on you to bring her across from Balnasheil Lodge, but she was alone there after everyone else had left and had every opportunity to do so if she had wanted to. I have found nothing to suggest that this is wrong, though we are pursuing our investigation to try to establish who might have helped her to leave, since you didn't.'

'You won't find anyone,' he said wildly. 'She didn't leave. He's killed her – don't you understand?'

He could play dumb but there wasn't much point. 'If you mean Mr Carnegie, he was in Paris at the time.'

'Was he? Can he prove it?'

'I expect he can. We will be checking up. But why would he want to kill her? They were apparently on perfectly good terms—'

Tennant groaned, leaning forward and putting his head in his hands. 'I'm guilty, you see. I should never have done it.'

This was getting more and more confusing. Was the man unbalanced, accusing Carnegie of murder one minute and then confessing to it the next?

'Mr Tennant,' he said gently, 'you seem upset. Did you do something to Eva?'

'Oh yes. Oh yes, I did something, something that's led her to a shallow grave somewhere on the moors over there.'

Strang felt a chill go down his spine. 'What do you mean?'

Tennant flung himself back in his chair. 'Did you not pause to wonder why you've been sent up here to investigate a woman who had packed her own bags and gone without there being – what did you call it, "anything untoward" about it?'

'Yes,' Strang said slowly. 'Yes, I did.'

'She was a spy,' he said harshly. 'I persuaded her to do it. She didn't want to, but I promised her the sort of life she'd always wanted, wherever she wanted to be, if she got details of what Carnegie and Drummond are up to – money laundering on a grand scale, we think. I'm with a fraud department in the Met, and I've managed

161

to get her killed. She was a lovely, gentle, decent kid and she trusted me.'

He put his hands over his face and gave a groan that was almost a sob.

CHAPTER NINE

It was a long time before DI Strang reappeared. PC Murray longed to say, 'Well?' when he got back into the car, but taking a glance at the grim line of his mouth she thought better of it.

She was expecting him to drive back through the village to the hotel but he said, 'Where is the local station? Want a lift back?'

'Thanks, sir. It's not very far, but since it's raining . . .' she said and directed him up the hill. Maybe he might tell her something on the way.

When he pulled up, still silent, she decided to take a chance. If you don't ask, you don't get. 'What was Mr Tennant after, wanting me not there when he spoke to you, sir? Has he a problem with me?'

He glanced at her almost as if he was surprised to find her sitting there. 'Oh, sorry, Murray. I was just thinking. No, it's nothing personal. But I have to say there are certainly grounds for concern now. Write up the report from the interviews this morning and file it for me, would you, please? Thanks for your help.'

And that was it, was it? As she let herself back into the police station, its damp, stuffy atmosphere felt like a physical manifestation of the gloom that was sweeping over her. She'd never considered CID when she was in Glasgow and with the blot on her record it wouldn't have been a realistic proposition anyway, but now she was hooked. There was something, well, almost romantic about it – a challenge, a battle of wits against the forces of darkness.

Livvy was suffering from a severe case of wounded pride. When she'd known the DI was coming, she'd worked over her report on her original investigation to make sure there was nothing he could find fault with and he'd poked so many holes in it today that it looked like a lace curtain.

She'd let herself down and she'd let that girl down too. Something had happened to her, she was sure of it, and she'd put money on Strang being sure of it too. Adam Carnegie gave her the grue; she'd been on court duty once when a serial killer was in the dock and he'd eyes just like that. But she was out of it now and she wouldn't even know what Strang was planning. It was like being allowed to watch the first half-hour of *Psycho* and then being taken out of the cinema because it was past her bedtime.

Strang was good, though she hated to admit it. It had been an education, watching him persuade the Lacey woman to open up – she'd been closed as a clam when Livvy had been the one asking her questions. In fact, when she looked back at them now, they seemed perfunctory, almost offhand.

She knew why too, now. Her big sin had been making up her mind about what had happened with Eva, because that was the normal thing – the woman would turn up a couple of weeks later, furious about the fuss – and hadn't even tried to look for confirmatory evidence. She wouldn't do that again.

But of course, she wouldn't have the chance to put what she'd learnt into practice. She'd been dismissed, while her brain was still fizzing with ideas. Now here she was, back to the boring little office where the highlights of her day were queries about household security and lost cats.

The rain had stopped and little patches of tender blue sky were appearing as the clouds parted and the scenery, so grey before, suddenly burst into colour: all hazy blues and greens and the occasional little patch of flaring orange and red from such leaves as still clung on in a brave show of autumn colour before the next gale stripped the trees completely bare. Above, the looming bulk of the Black Cuillin was visible only as a shadow in the hanging cloud.

Vicky Macdonald glanced up at The Presence, as she sometimes thought of it. Today it seemed a manifestation of the cloud hanging over them as Murdo John brought her back across the bay after she'd finished her work. She didn't speak; that was unlike her, and she saw him look at her uneasily once or twice – as well he might. She didn't want to have the tearing row she was planning until they were within the privacy of their own home, but she went on the attack the moment they were in the cottage with the door shut. Murdo John was just hanging up his oilskin jacket when she said, knowing what his reaction would be, 'I'll have to go across again in the late afternoon. Adam needs me to do suppers while Harry's there.'

Murdo John swung round, his face dark with anger. 'That finishes it. You can just give in your notice. You're not his slave.'

'No, Murdo. But I'm not yours, either. I'm an independent woman and I decide what I'm going to do. He's my employer and it's a good job.'

'We don't need the money that much. I don't want you having anything to do with them. I didn't want you to take the job in the first place.'

'And why is that?' Vicky asked silkily. 'Is it because things have happened there, things you haven't told me about before?'

Murdo John went very still. Then he said, 'Like . . . ?'

'Like Veruschka.'

She saw the tension in his shoulders. 'What about her?'

'She disappeared, didn't she?' As he opened his mouth to speak she spoke across him. 'And don't try to deny it. The police told me. Daniel doesn't know; Adam wasn't going to volunteer that and neither was Beatrice. So where did they get it from, I wonder? Did they have a chat with you this morning before they came across to the Lodge?'

'I told them there was gossip, that's all.' There was a line of white round his lips; he was furiously angry. 'And I told them that the woman who started it was an attention-seeker who made a drama out of everything. She was just another of Adam's girls who left, that's all.'

'To go where?'

'How do I know? Look—'

'What was she like, this Veruschka who didn't disappear?'

'I don't remember.'

'Tall, short, dark, fair?'

'Oh – dark, I think. Brown eyes. I told you I don't really remember. It was years ago.'

'Do you remember Eva? She only disappeared a few days ago but I expect very shortly you'll have forgotten her as well.' Vicky paused and then said, less aggressively, 'Look, Murdo, I'm really worried about Eva and if there's another of Adam's housekeepers who has a question mark about her leaving, it makes me more worried still. Please, why didn't you want to tell me about this?'

Her softened voice had no effect. 'Because I didn't sodding well think the last girl "disappeared" and I don't think Eva did either. I think you and Tennant have created a storm in a teacup and there's going to be trouble. I don't want you mixed up in it and you can just give up that job right now.'

Vicky put her hands up to her hot cheeks. 'Is that an order?'

'If I take you across, you can stay there.' He folded his arms, standing with his legs apart. With his size and bulk, in that small room, it was an intimidating posture.

Something in her died at that moment. She stared at him, then said quietly, 'Fine. I'll go and pack.'

When she had reached the bedroom she flung herself onto the bed and sobbed, pulling a pillow over her head so he wouldn't hear the sound.

Strang drove back to the hotel, his mind in a ferment. It was coming home to him, with some force, how different this job was going to be. In Edinburgh he had been a member of a team and to get any idea actioned, he had to argue his case. It was a luxury to have full control; he had only to decide and he could put it into practice. And what Tennant had said made it easy; he would be pulling all the stops out.

Tennant had seemed almost distraught. Strang had tried to establish if he'd been sleeping with the missing girl and he'd denied it, but then he would, wouldn't he? There had been a case recently when an undercover officer had developed a relationship with one of the group he had infiltrated and it hadn't gone well. Strang had let that go, only asking if he was in love with her anyway, but Tennant had denied that too.

'This isn't some romantic agony because she ditched me,' he'd said angrily. 'This is guilt, man! She'd still be alive if I hadn't made use of her.'

Strang wasn't at all sure that he believed him – his reaction suggested there was both, perhaps – but he didn't doubt that if the Met was involved they would have good grounds for investigating Carnegie. And if Eva Havel had indeed been caught spying on her boss, it gave him a very solid reason for getting rid of her.

It was easy enough to check the man's claim that he'd been in Paris – a phone call to HQ would set that in motion.

But what if he hadn't needed to be there in person? What if the only person left at Balnasheil Lodge with Eva Havel that day, Marek Kaczka in the cottage by the gate, had been deputed to carry out an instruction from his boss?

He parked the car and, still deep in thought, went into the hotel. Fiona Ross, as ill luck would have it, was busy at the reception desk and her face brightened when she saw him.

'Hello, Inspector. Have you had a successful morning?'

He nodded an acknowledgement and walked on but she came round from behind the reception desk and followed him.

'You're a bit late for lunch, I'm afraid, but I can bring you up some sandwiches, if you like. I expect you're quite hungry, after doing all those interviews.'

How the hell did she know? Did the woman have spies everywhere? Yes, was probably the answer, because everyone in the place was watching what he was doing and talking about it. The Black Cuillin bar had probably done good business this morning. He realised that he'd better eat something, and with her intelligence network she might even be useful.

'Thank you, Mrs Ross. Ham, if you have it? One round.'

'Of course. Won't be long.' She bustled off and Strang climbed the stairs, his mind still buzzing.

He would reinterview Kaczka, of course, but he had little hope that he would get any more out of him next time. He could check his immigration status in the hope that there might be some sort of lever there but all the case was adding up to so far was unsubstantiated allegations, and he wouldn't be popular with JB if he mounted an expensive operation – and attracted press attention too – only to fall flat on his face.

He mustn't allow himself to fall into the trap of prejudging the situation. It was still logically possible that Eva had left of her own accord. Perhaps she'd decided it wasn't smart to spy on Carnegie and wanted to escape the pressure that Tennant was probably putting on her. He'd need checks done on the local taxis, buses, boats, even; he could see if anyone had a photo of the girl so they could flash it around. He was jotting that down when a knock on the door heralded Fiona and the sandwiches. She beamed at him.

'Here you are. Glad to see you survived the drive round that awful road. The potholes are dreadful – I think there's some dispute between the council and the charity about who's responsible. What you really need is a boat. If you're going to be to and fro to Balnasheil Lodge, Douglas could certainly arrange one for you.'

She was quite right, but it was a leading question and he said only, 'There was something I did want to ask you, Mrs Ross. Someone mentioned a young woman called Veruschka who was a housekeeper at the Lodge a few years ago and said there had been some talk about her when she left. Do you remember anything about that?'

Fiona's eyes lit up. 'Yes, indeed I do! When was it, now – three years ago, maybe, or four. Time just seems to go by quicker and quicker, doesn't it? She was very striking, I seem to remember, tall, dark, with those very long legs that these Middle European girls seem to have.

She was around the bar quite a lot and I think there were one or two young men who were very smitten—'

'Do you remember their names?'

She looked crestfallen and shook her head. 'They weren't local, I don't think. Murdo John had rather a soft spot for her too, if I remember rightly. But then, he did have an eye for the ladies – you wouldn't think it, him being so quiet, but he fairly snapped up Vicky after she joined us.'

Strang filed away the information. 'And after this Veruschka left . . . ?'

He watched with misgiving as Fiona sat down on a nearby chair, clearly settling in to enjoy her story.

'Well, it was the cleaner who was there at that time. She started the rumour that there was something funny about her going but – well, not wanting to speak ill of the dead, Inspector, but Morag Soutar would make a sensation out of the post van being five minutes late on its rounds.

'She said she'd seen clothes that belonged to Veruschka still hanging in her wardrobe when she was cleaning the room after she'd gone, but she had to admit afterwards that the girl had asked Miss Lacey to post them on to her later because she didn't want to have to carry them with her. That was it, and it didn't seem much to make a fuss about. I don't think any of us believed her.'

Was that a note of regret in her voice? 'I see,' he said. 'But you haven't heard any more about Eva Havel leaving, apart from the complaint to the police?'

Fiona shook her head. 'No, not really.' That was definite regret this time. 'Just, Daniel Tennant was awfully sure that she wouldn't have stood him up and he's got Vicky

Macdonald worked up about it too. But a girl like that – oh, you know—' She gave him a significant look.

Strang picked up a sandwich and bit into it. 'Well, thank you very much for your time, Mrs Ross. I think that's all.'

Fiona rose with a certain reluctance. 'Any time – it's no trouble. And if I hear anything, I'll report to you, shall I?'

His mouth being full saved him from having to respond and she left. Dreadful woman, but useful.

He added another note to his jottings then set about making his calls and checks. He'd better give JB an update once he'd done that to keep her on side; she would certainly be interested and even, he suspected, a bit nervous. He just hoped she wouldn't decide to interfere. He was relishing this maverick business – though he'd better get it right.

Beatrice Lacey was feeling terrible. Ever since the visit from the police in the morning she had been suffering from a splitting headache that even Paracetamol Plus couldn't shift. She'd tried to immerse herself in her work but the memories kept intruding and then she'd be seized with a shivering fit.

Eventually, at two o'clock, she gave in. At least she hadn't the horror of getting the evening meal to the table; Vicky had confirmed that she'd be coming over to do it. With her office work up to date there was no reason why she shouldn't just go and have a lie-down – and indeed, she needn't even appear at supper if she didn't want to.

She climbed the stairs wearily to her flat, then picked up Rosamond from her crib and cuddled her.

'We're just going back to bed to have a nice rest,' she told her. 'Mummy's very, very tired and she's had a horrid day.'

Tears welled up in her eyes as she said that but she brushed them away determinedly. She needed to cheer herself up or the rest wouldn't do her any good at all. She opened the little cupboard where she kept her stash of sweets and took out a bag of Minstrels – chocolate was always good for lifting the spirits – and chose her favourite from the shelf of Mills and Boon novels, then went through to her little bedroom.

It was a spartan room, with a cheap single divan and a second-hand wardrobe with matching chest of drawers that was only slightly better quality than the one in what had been Eva's room downstairs, but the deep burgundy coverlet on the bed was incongruously expensive-looking silk and there were little silver boxes and a silver toilet set on the chest of drawers. Beatrice sank onto her bed, tucked Rosamond in beside her then pulled over the cover with a sigh of relief and switched on her electric blanket.

Her headache receded a little and she could feel the soothing chocolate and the comforting, familiar story settling her nerves; she was just drifting off to sleep when there was a knock on the door of her flat. She sat bolt upright, tense again.

It couldn't be Vicky. She'd gone across with Murdo John at the usual time and she wouldn't be back until late afternoon. It could only be Adam or Harry and she didn't really want to see either of them just now.

But 'Just coming,' she shouted, and heaved herself out of bed with a groan – the cheap mattress did nothing for her back – and grabbed a hairbrush as she passed to smooth down the bit she could feel sticking up at the back. No time to put on a bit of lipstick, though. She patted her cheeks and bit her lips as she went to open the door.

Adam stood there, smiling at her. 'Oh, I'm so sorry – did I disturb you? Poor sweetie. I just thought you might be upset after having the plods trample all over you with their flat feet and I wanted to check that you were all right. May I come in?'

He'd never come to her room before; no one had come into her room before. She gave a nervous glance at Rosamond's crib there in the corner, but she really had no alternative but to let him come in. And he'd come because he was worried about her; Beatrice's heart melted.

'Oh, Adam, that's so like you!' she cried. 'Come in, come in – can I make you tea or something?'

'No, no, darling, no tea. You just sit down.' He sat down himself on a Victorian button-back chair she had brought with her from Surrey that mercifully meant he had his back to the crib; his frame was too large to look comfortable in it but he insisted she take her usual cushioned armchair. 'How are you feeling?'

'A little bit shaken, to be honest.' For a moment she contemplated shedding a tear or two in the hope that he would comfort her but, remembering how much he hated any show of emotion, she only gave a little, brave smile.

'Oh, I can understand it. I felt quite taken aback myself. There seems to be someone with an interest in stirring up trouble. But there's no need to worry about it, sweetie. If they come back, you know what to say – just what I'm sure

174

you've said already so they don't get the wrong idea and make a nuisance of themselves.'

Adam was eyeing her narrowly. She swallowed hard, but her voice trembled a little as she said, 'Do you think they will come back?'

'Oh, probably. They always like to confirm everything, even if it means that they end up crossing all the 'i's and dotting all the 't's. So don't tell them anything that might muddle their little brains, will you? I was quite surprised when they started talking about Veruschka this morning, weren't you?'

'Yes!' That came out a bit too loudly, and she blushed. 'I mean, well, I just said she'd been here, and then she'd gone.'

'Absolutely right, sweetie.' He leant forward to pat her hand. 'And if they ask again, you remember how when Morag asked about her clothes, we told her you had posted them on to the address she'd left?'

'In London. Yes.' Beatrice couldn't look at him.

'That's right. Do you remember what it was?'

'No.' She could say that with perfect truth.

'That's fine. How would you remember, after all this time? So there you are – that's all you need to say if they ask you about it. No need to worry any more, eh? That's my good girl.'

He stood up, bent forward and kissed her on the cheek. 'I'm so sorry you've had all this, darling – and all the fuss with Harry being here too, just because he's made a mess of some of his business affairs and wanted somewhere peaceful to get them all sorted out.'

He sighed and shook his head. 'To be honest, Beatrice, I've been wondering whether we were wise to have Harry involved in Human Face after all. I'm not convinced that he has quite the ideals that we both share. Maybe if it was just us two, working together towards our future—'

Adam looked at her, his head on one side enquiringly, then smiled. 'Not the time to think about it just now. Later, though, we'll have a good talk. Now, I don't want you going back to the office today. Have a nice rest and I'll see you at supper.'

Beatrice didn't move after he'd gone. She sat staring straight ahead of her, her mind spinning with conflicting thoughts. She should have been happy; he'd actually kissed her, mentioned long talks together about their future, suggested the hated Harry might go . . .

But she wasn't happy. She knew what she knew and it was getting harder to pretend that she didn't. She felt sick and even a little bit frightened. No, more than a little bit. She felt very frightened, and she didn't know what was going to happen next.

DCS Jane Borthwick was pleased when DI Strang's call came through. It had been on her mind: she'd been worrying that plunging a man in a vulnerable emotional state into such an exposed position had been an uncharacteristically risky thing to do.

But it did look as if a fairly straightforward situation had been bigged up, probably in response to a complaint from some pompous local councillor who was feeling put out at the CID reforms; it should just be a matter of showing the flag and checking there really was nothing untoward about the woman's disappearance – a way to ease Strang back into work again without too much stress on all sides. At least, she hoped it was.

His report was a shock. She offered a mental apology to the pompous councillor; if the Met was involved, that explained the order for further investigation and from what Strang was saying now, there was a definite question mark over the disappearance of not one but two women.

'The thing is,' Strang was saying, 'there's no proof of any of this at all. The rumour about the first female – Veruschka, no surname – disappearing isn't only unsubstantiated, it isn't believed by the locals. Eva Havel didn't keep to her spying arrangement with Tennant but she could just have decided to duck out of a situation she wasn't happy with. I've run some checks but there's no immediate record of her. She could be an illegal immigrant . . .'

With a hollow feeling in her stomach, Borthwick said, 'Or a perfectly legal visitor who isn't registered because she wasn't actually working.' Please God let that be all it was, a visitor who'd left of her own accord.

'Of course, ma'am,' he said politely, but she could tell he didn't believe that. 'I was hoping we might have got an in through the fraud inquiry, but they're not ready yet, apparently. It's a major investigation, links all over the country, and if we screw it up for them we'll really be in the doghouse.'

'I see. It would have been helpful, though, if we'd known about this before, instead of going in blind.' Making a mental note to have a terse word with the assistant chief constable, Borthwick went on, 'So where does this leave us, then?'

She was expecting a request for direction, but his reply was immediate, and confident.

'Reinterview. The woman who seems to run the charity admin, Beatrice Lacey, is the most promising – very nervy, but has stars in her eyes when it comes to her boss. We might get something out of her if we lean a bit. There's an allegedly Polish handyman who's been monosyllabic so far but I'll lean on him a bit more next time too – check immigrant status and so on, see if we can get a bit more out of him. Adam Carnegie, the boss, and his sidekick Harry Drummond, both of them under surveillance – I can rattle the cage but they'll be clued in so I can't imagine that will get us anywhere. The barman, Murdo John Macdonald—'

'That's really his name?'

'Lives up to it – big, black-bearded, strong silent type. Knows more than he's prepared to admit about the previous woman but I can have another go. And I'm going to want authorisation to task a local PC with dredging for gossip and checking out possible sightings of Eva after she is supposed to have left – buses, taxis, boats, lifts from the locals, all that sort of thing.'

'Certainly, in the circumstances. PCs come cheap, anyway. Have you one in mind?'

'Yes, I suppose so.' She could hear reluctance in Strang's voice. 'PC Livvy Murray – she gave up her day off to take notes for me. She's from Glasgow – the Scots Thistle type.'

Borthwick smiled. 'You mean "Wha daur meddle wi' me?"'

'Printed right through her, like a stick of Rothesay rock. She was smarting because I was critical of her initial investigation of Havel's disappearance but she's not stupid and she wants to learn. I don't think she likes me very much – you know what they say about Edinburgh and Glasgow not speaking?'

'Indeed, I do. Can you call a truce?'

'Easier just to run up the white flag, in my experience. Anyway, there's Tennant too. He's offered to be co-opted and of course his experience can be useful to me at the Met's expense. He doesn't seem to be worried about breaking his cover.'

'He's presumably competent. That should give you a bit more scope.'

'Yes. But if none of this yields anything . . .'

Borthwick could almost hear the shrug at the other end. 'Then what?'

'I don't see what else we can do.' His voice was flat.

She wouldn't lose sleep if this just petered out but in case it didn't, she wanted to be sure he could cope. 'How are you finding it, working without a team?' she asked.

He gave a short laugh. 'Interesting,' he said. 'It's high-wire stuff, isn't it? I'm relying on my own judgement and if it's wrong it's a long way down.'

He didn't sound, though, as if that was getting to him; it sounded as if he was enjoying it. Intrigued, she said, 'So, have you a gut feeling about this?'

His reply came back like a bullet. 'It's bad. The set-up stinks – there's something sick and evil going on there. And from my brief acquaintance with Carnegie I'd be more surprised if you told me he wasn't a psychopath than that he was, but I can't see yet how I could nail him.'

She was taken aback. 'I see. You certainly know your own mind. Fair enough. But I want to be kept in the picture.'

Borthwick sat thinking for some time after she put the phone down. With all her years of service she knew all too well how often you knew what had happened but couldn't prove it, and this sounded like one of those situations.

Strang seemed to have been landed with a lot more than she had envisaged but he was sounding good, exhilarated, almost. He certainly hadn't looked to her for guidance – indeed, she'd had the distinct impression that he wouldn't have welcomed it. Was that good or bad? The trouble was she wouldn't know which it was going to turn out to be until it was too late to do anything about it.

Murdo John Macdonald got out of the boat to carry Vicky's suitcase up to the house in silence. She stalked ahead of him; he followed her through the little lobby behind the kitchen where the pantry and the game larder were and set it down on the kitchen floor, then walked off without a farewell or a backward glance.

Her skin still felt sore and stiff after the tears; there was a huge, painful lump in her throat and she was feeling sick with nerves as she went to shut the back door behind him.

She could smell the distinctive whiff of corruption beginning in the hare that was hanging there and its rank, sweetish smell made her feel sicker still. She'd have to hang it for days more before it was rotten enough for Adam's taste.

When she walked through the kitchen to the room that had been Eva's, down the corridor beside the side door, she almost thought the smell from the hare still lingered, though that was nonsense, of course. It was just that in her own mind the house itself was tainted by something evil right at its heart.

CHAPTER TEN

Quentin Lacey hadn't had a good night. He was grumpy at breakfast and his partner, Karen Prescott, gave him an acid look. They'd got on fine when he'd first moved in with her – he could be quite a good laugh when he'd had a few – but he seemed gloomier and gloomier as he'd got more and more obsessive about his sister and this charity lately.

'I'd a nightmare last night,' he said morosely, cradling his coffee mug. 'Dreamt I was at their wedding. Horrible!' He gave a shudder.

'Whose wedding?' she said, just to be irritating.

'Beatrice's, of course. To that – that creature—'

'Oh, that wedding. Well, if she's made her mind up there's not a lot that you can do about it, is there? She's old enough to know what she wants and she's got a right to do whatever she likes with her own money, doesn't she?'

'This isn't about the money,' he said unconvincingly. 'It's about her. He's preying on her with this charity of his and if he's marrying her it's only so the trust can be broken and he can get his hands on it. You don't think it's a love match, do you?'

Karen had met Beatrice once; she was quite like her brother, in fact, and though you wouldn't call Quentin good-looking, features like theirs definitely looked better on a man – and she could give him a stone or two as well. 'No,' she admitted. 'And Adam Thing is quite buff, you said?'

'Slimy charm personified. She's mesmerised by him, lost all powers of reason. She's handing over every penny she can to a charity that's just the Bank of Carnegie. Like to have a look at its books, I tell you.'

'You're not likely to get that anyway. Oh, give it a rest!' She stood up. 'Time I went to open up the shop. Come in at ten to take over, will you? I've got a hair appointment.'

'I suppose so,' he said gloomily.

'Right. You could do some hoovering, if you like – take your mind off your sister.'

He flared up. 'It's all very well for you to say that. But what happens if he marries her? How long do you think it would be before she had a nasty accident, or a sudden heart attack, or something? I wouldn't put anything past him.'

Karen stopped at that. 'Are you serious?'

'Yes, I'm serious. I don't suppose I can actually forbid the banns but I'm not going to let him just get away with it.'

'Doesn't sound as if she's going to listen to reason, and you haven't enough money to buy him off so I don't see that you can do anything. Anyway, I've got to go. See you at ten.'

She left Quentin to stare at his empty coffee mug, as if the answer to his problems lay there in the dregs.

PC Murray went to her desk in no very positive frame of mind and booted up her computer. To her surprise, there was a message from DI Strang asking her to be available this morning.

Result! She'd been sure she'd blown it with him, but maybe she'd done enough to let him see what an asset she could be. She pinged back her assurance that she was ready when he was and prepared to be patient.

In fact, it was only a quarter of an hour later that she saw his car pulling up in the car park outside, and she prepared a bright, cooperative smile to greet him. Then Daniel Tennant got out behind him and her smile faded a little. It disappeared entirely when she discovered that he was a DC with the Met. They didn't explain why a DC from London should have been up here writing a book.

So he'd presumably only been 'writing a book', and if he was undercover it wasn't hard to work out who he had in his sights – and if he was this agitated about Eva having stood him up, she'd likely been involved in that too. If something had happened to her as a result of that . . .

Tennant's manner was frosty and she could guess why: he was blaming her because she hadn't taken his word for it at the time that there was a reason to worry about Eva. But he hadn't been exactly straight with her either, and even supposing she'd pulled out all the stops they wouldn't be any further on than they were now. She gave him a narrow-eyed look as payback.

She was royally pissed off when she realised that he'd be the one going poncing off on interviews with Strang while she shovelled coal back here at the pit, but she was wise enough not to show it. At least she was in on the discussion meantime.

Strang had managed to establish that Carnegie had indeed been in Paris as he had claimed but there was no further information about Eva Havel, and the likelihood was that it wasn't even her real name.

He was wanting now to find out more about the exotic-sounding Veruschka, whoever she might be.

'I thought perhaps you could spend some time in the pub this evening,' Strang said to her. 'Just chatting to people, you know . . .'

'Oh, I'm sure she'll be up for that,' Tennant said nastily.

Murray was opening her mouth, ready to give as good as she got, but then catching the look of distaste that Strang shot at Tennant, shut it again hastily. If it would pay her to be dignified, she could be dignified.

'No problem, sir,' she said and made notes as he detailed the enquiries he wanted made to establish whether there had been any sightings of Eva after the time Vicky Macdonald had left the Lodge.

It was frustrating to be left here while they went off to do the interesting stuff, but she'd plenty to keep her busy. She'd do the most meticulous search that had ever been done in the history of Scottish policing; if she could find just one person who could say they'd seen Eva leaving, it would prove she'd been right about this just being a case of a woman who'd changed her mind.

The thing was, though, she didn't now believe that she would.

* * *

Beatrice was still feeling groggy this morning. She hadn't gone down to supper, just gone to bed and taken a sleeping pill, but even though she'd made herself a hearty breakfast and drunk three cups of black coffee, her head seemed to be stuffed with cotton wool.

It was a sunny morning but very cold, with the icy wind whipping in from the sea finding the gaps in the window frames with a low, whistling sound. Adam was walking on the moor with Amber, and Beatrice watched them nervously. She really thought that if he came in this morning to show off another bleeding hare the beastly animal had caught, she wouldn't be able to stop herself screaming.

Mercifully, he walked back empty-handed. He did come in, but only to tell her that he had business in Glasgow and would be away all day.

'Yes, Adam,' she said obediently. 'When do you want to go? Do you need me to tell Marek to drive the car round to the other side and bring the boat back for you?'

'No, it's all right, I saw him and he did that earlier. I'll leave once I've grabbed a cup of coffee and a piece of toast. Have a good day, sweetie!'

A good day! Had he forgotten that the police were going to come and interrogate them again? Or had he remembered all too well, and that was why he'd suddenly had business in Glasgow?

He was leaving her to hold the fort. It was because he relied on her, she told herself fiercely. She had to be his rock, totally loyal when people like Harry and the wretched Eva had caused trouble for him. He'd told her what she needed to do when they asked their prying questions and she had to do it, for his sake. Then all this would be over and the future he had talked of, with just the two of them together, would be her dream come true.

She had to believe that, had to believe in him. If she didn't, all the sacrifices she'd made – not least the sacrifice of a quiet conscience – had been for nothing and hers would be a worthless life.

Marek Kaczka quite clearly distrusted the police. Perhaps he'd had reason to in some previous existence but it didn't make him any easier to deal with now.

When DC Tennant showed his warrant card, surprise showed on the man's face and then it darkened, but he said nothing.

'We've met before, of course,' Tennant said. 'I've seen you in the bar sometimes and I came to your door as well to ask if you knew anything about Eva Havel leaving that day, you remember.'

Kaczka only stared.

'Do you?' DI Strang said.

'No.'

'You didn't speak to her, didn't see her?'

'No.'

'Didn't do something to her, that Adam Carnegie told you to do?' Tennant said brutally. 'Because you see, we think you did. Knock her on the head and drop her over the side of the boat, maybe?'

'No! No! I do nothing!'

At last a response. The man's head was lowered and he

was swinging it from side to side, looking from one to the other like a baited bull.

'I think we'd better go in and talk about this,' Strang said, and they trooped in behind Kaczka to the squalid little room. The air smelt frowsty and there was something on the worn carpet that stuck to his feet as he walked.

Tennant leapt in. 'Let's see your papers. Come on.'

He'd made it sound uncomfortably like the sort of thing the Gestapo said in a bad Second World War film. Strang gave Tennant a sharp, warning glance and added, 'It's nothing to worry about, sir – just your National Insurance, passport, anything like that.'

'No paper. Mr Carnegie – he have papers.'

'You claim you're Polish.' Tennant was unabashed. 'Are you?'

'Yes.'

Tennant said, 'Maybe we'll get a Polish interpreter. Would you like that?'

'No! No! I speak English.' The man looked alarmed, frightened, even.

'Oh, really?' Tennant said with heavy emphasis. 'Maybe you'd prefer Ukrainian or Albanian, say?'

Getting no reply, he went on, 'Still not know anything about Eva?'

Kaczka stared back woodenly. 'No.'

Strang had had enough. He didn't like crude bullying and it wasn't working either. As Tennant opened his mouth to speak he cut in, 'Look, if you did nothing you're not in any trouble. We won't tell your boss what you tell us, and it could be very important.' Again he saw the flicker in the man's eyes that he had noticed before and he said encouragingly, 'I'm going to ask you again if you saw Eva, and think carefully about your answer.'

'Oh, very carefully.' Tennant's voice was heavy with threat. 'Very carefully indeed.'

Kaczka's face went blank and he shrugged. 'No.'

Seething that the moment had been spoilt, Strang said, 'Thank you for your time, sir,' and nodded curtly to Tennant. 'That's all, Constable.'

He walked out ahead, trying to contain his anger. Tennant caught up with him, looking quizzical.

'Something on your mind, Strang?'

Strang stopped. 'That was bullying. It was unpleasant and counterproductive, and it concerns me that you paid no attention when I indicated that you should stop.'

Tennant smiled. 'Well – I'd started so I thought I'd finish. Something fishy about his status, obviously, and if you press that button it's surprising what you get.'

'Nothing, as it happened,' Strang pointed out, tight-lipped. 'And you undermined any chance I might have had of persuading him to talk. Look, Tennant, I have no brief to investigate the man's immigration status at the moment and I'm conducting this operation my way. Is that clear?'

'For God's sake!' Tennant cried. 'Have you any idea what this case is about? You're talking about tiptoeing round in dancing pumps while they're laundering millions—'

'No,' Strang said. 'That's not what this case is about. This is about a young woman called Eva Havel. Anything else is subordinate to that.'

Tennant glared at him. 'You don't have to tell me that. I got you called in, remember? I'm gutted about Eva. But my bosses expect you to fall in line with the operation I've established here—'

'Sorry – hold it right there. Your bosses' wishes are irrelevant until they have agreed them with my boss and she has issued her orders to me. Until then, your operation and mine are entirely separate. So, no bullying and no threats when we do the interviews up at the house. I warn you, if you start I shall pull you up publicly. Is that clear, Tennant?'

Tennant's face was dark. 'Sir,' he muttered sullenly.

Strang walked on without waiting for him. He didn't enjoy pulling rank but he wasn't about to compromise his own standards of policing. If Tennant wasn't prepared to do things his way, he'd take Murray with him next time. He preferred stroppy to nasty.

When the phone rang, Beatrice was reading through an application for funds and she was sufficiently absorbed to have forgotten her own anxieties. It was something she always enjoyed doing, assessing whether there was genuine need or whether this was one of the many chancers who besiege any charity. With her experience she was good at weeding them out, but this one seemed genuine enough: a bush hospital, servicing a ridiculously large area of Ethiopia with very few resources.

There were pictures of mothers and babies whose lives had been saved and she smiled as she lingered over those, cheered that here was somewhere they could make a difference to the dreadful childbirth mortality statistics they quoted. She was scribbling a recommendation for Adam to consider when the phone rang.

'Beatrice?'

The sound of Quentin's voice wiped the smile off her face. 'What do you want?'

'I don't want to talk to you,' he said. 'Is Adam in?'

'Why do you want to speak to him?'

'None of your business. Just put me through, will you?'

'No, I won't. Anyway, he's in Glasgow for the day.'

'OK, I'll come out to see him later. You can't stop me.'

She felt positively ill at the thought of Quentin coming to see Adam, telling him she'd said they were getting married, demanding to know his intentions. What would Adam think? It might ruin all her dreams, just when he'd been talking as if the day might be getting closer.

'Look, Quentin,' she said awkwardly, 'I don't really want to fall out with you. I'm not going to get married the day after tomorrow. There's no need to drag Adam into it at this stage.'

'Trixie, I'm your brother. I'd be failing in my duty if I didn't have a proper talk with him to make sure he's not only interested in your money—'

'If you do that,' she cried wildly, 'I'll write a will this minute, leaving everything to him whether we're married or not.'

There was silence at the other end of the phone. Then he said, 'All right, calm down. I'll leave it for the moment. But we need to have a really proper discussion, without you flying off the handle and throwing me out after five minutes.'

'Yes, yes of course,' she said.

When she put down the phone her hands were shaking and slimy with sweat. Just one more thing to stress her out. And then she heard the doorbell. That must be the police.

It was understandable that a foreigner who might well be in the country illegally should be wary of the police, but Strang found it surprising that a respectable lady of mature years should also greet their arrival with a coldly forbidding look and a greeting that was positively hostile, particularly when he introduced Tennant as his colleague.

'I don't know what you think you're doing, harassing us like this. We've told you everything we can twice over.'

Beatrice Lacey's tone certainly was angry but her hands, clasped tightly in front of her, were shaking and she was blinking nervously. As she stood aside to let them in, Tennant nudged Strang, glancing pointedly at the telltale hands.

Did he think he was likely to miss something as obvious as that? Answer: probably, yes. Perhaps it was meant to be helpful, but the man had really begun to annoy him. If you worked for the Met perhaps a sense of superiority came with the badge.

'We just wanted to run over one or two points with you, Miss Lacey, and with Mr Carnegie too. Would you like us to speak to him first?'

'You can't, I'm afraid. He's in Glasgow all day, on business.'

'Oh. That's unfortunate.' Strang hadn't expected that, but he couldn't complain; he hadn't actually told Carnegie to stick around. Damn! He'd slipped up there.

'Never mind, perhaps we can clear things up with you first so we won't have to trouble you next time. It's this way, isn't it?'

He went purposefully towards the office where they had been before, followed by Tennant, though Beatrice hung back as if she still hoped to keep them standing in the hall. They were waiting beside the chairs by her desk before she lumbered in; she seemed breathless, but Strang wasn't sure whether this was nerves or the usual result of mild exertion.

Beatrice sat down in her cushioned chair with a little groan. 'Well? What do you want to ask me?' She was trying to sound aggressive but her voice shook a little and her muddy-grey eyes were round and frightened.

Again, Strang got a significant, go-for-the-jugular look from Tennant which he pretended not to see. 'Miss Lacey,' he said gently, 'you're obviously very nervous, which puzzles me. What is it that you're worried about?'

She looked more frightened than ever. 'Nothing! I don't know what you mean! I just don't like being harassed, that's all.'

Tennant didn't wait for Strang to ask the next question. 'This isn't harassment. Are you making a formal complaint?' He was leaning across the desk so that she shrank back.

'No, no, of course not,' Beatrice bleated. 'I just meant—'

'Miss Lacey, is Mrs Macdonald in the house just now? Yes? Then, Constable, please could you go and check up with her that she hasn't thought of anything else to add to what she told us yesterday? That will save us a bit of time.'

Tennant gave him an incredulous look. 'But—'

Strang stared him out. 'Thanks, Tennant.'

He waited until the man, his face set, left the room then said, 'We need to talk about this, don't we? Shall I tell you what I think? I know from what you told me last time that you have a great respect and affection for Adam Carnegie. I think that perhaps there are things that are worrying you, that you think he might not want you to talk about.'

Her eyes were filling and she was struggling to hold on to her composure. 'No, no.' Then there was a pause before she said, so quietly that she could barely hear him. 'Not really.'

He sank back in his chair, as if he were relaxing, making his body language as unthreatening as possible. 'You know, "Not really" sounds as if it's not anything very important and you're probably worrying needlessly – or putting two and two together and making five. It's easily done, when you're a very scrupulous person.'

The tears were spilling over, but she seized on that. 'Oh yes, that's what I keep telling myself!' She grabbed a tissue from a box on her desk, dabbed at her eyes and blew her nose. 'It was probably just a case of mistaken identity. I thought that at the time – that I'd jumped to conclusions because of the car.'

'Hold on!' Strang gave an easy laugh. 'You've lost me – mistaken identity?'

'It was just that I'd been to Oban – to check an order

at the warehouse. I don't know why there was a problem – failure in communication, probably – but anyway, I decided to drive back instead of staying the night. It's expensive, accommodation, you know, and the work the charity does needs every spare penny.' Beatrice was in full flow now, like a pent-up stream bursting the dam. 'But it was a long drive and I began to worry that I was going to fall asleep – you know how it is. So I decided to take a break.'

Strang nodded. 'Very wise.'

'Yes. There's this service station not far from the bridge with a cafe at the back – very nice, not the usual stuff at all, really proper home-baking. So we stopped—'

'We?' he said sharply. 'You weren't alone?'

She flushed scarlet. 'Oh – sorry, yes, of course I was alone. Why did I say that?'

Why indeed, he wondered, but he didn't want to distract her now.

'I was sitting by the window and I noticed a man coming out of the shop and going towards his car – a blue Mercedes, just like the one Adam has. And – and I thought it was Adam.' She stopped.

He was almost frightened to say anything, but he had to ask. 'This was the day Eva left, was it?'

She nodded. 'Yes. But Adam was in Paris at the time – I booked his ticket myself and he told me he caught the plane all right, so it couldn't have been him, could it? That's how I know it was just a silly mistake – easy to make a mistake like that, isn't it? It was quite dark, and with the car I just jumped to the wrong conclusion – two and two making five, like you said. I should just put it out of my mind, shouldn't I?' She gave him a watery smile.

He hated to do this to her. 'Absolutely. But I think you'd have put it out of your mind, if that was all. Was there something else to worry you, some signs of a disturbance back here, say?'

'Oh no, if there had been anything like that I'd have told the police at once!' She sounded horrified. 'I wouldn't—' Then she stopped.

He let the pause develop, without saying anything.

With an obvious effort she went on, 'It was just another silly little thing. Eva had forgotten one of her suitcases when she went, that was all. It was under the bed – just a few clothes in it; she could easily have forgotten it. Nothing much.'

'And why was that so worrying?'

It was one question too far. Suddenly there was alarm in those round eyes. 'Oh, just because I'm silly,' she said. 'I worry about everything, and with everyone asking me all these questions I've got things out of proportion, just like you said. But if that's all—' She heaved herself up out of the chair.

Strang didn't move. 'Just one more thing. There was another girl who left suddenly – you remember we mentioned her before – Veruschka?'

She went very still. Then her hands went across in front of her chest, clutching her sides as if she was trying physically to hold herself together.

'She left. That's all. I told you.' Her voice was harder now.

'She left her clothes too, didn't she?'

Beatrice went so white that he thought for a moment she was going to faint. She even swayed a little and sat back down on the chair.

'Did – did she? I – I don't remember.'

'So I believe. You had to post them on.'

'Oh – oh yes, I remember now. That's right. She didn't want to take them with her and I was to send them on to somewhere – a London address, I think, though I can't remember what it was.'

He recognised a practised response. 'Is that what Adam told you to say?'

At the mention of his name, her face changed. 'No, that's what happened. That's all I can tell you.'

He had one more try. 'Odd that they should both leave clothes behind,' he said, though not very hopefully.

'If you're going on public transport clothes are very heavy to carry.'

She'd retreated now to where he couldn't reach her, behind the shield that was her devotion to Adam. The answers to his next questions were monosyllabic; he decided to cut his losses.

'Thank you for your help,' he said. 'And – do you have a mobile phone?'

Beatrice, looking a little puzzled, produced it.

'Let me just enter my number. Then, if you think of anything else, you can reach me direct. All right?' He smiled, keyed it in and left her.

Tennant was waiting for him in the hall. He looked at him sullenly. 'Got her to confess she'd bumped them both off out of jealousy, did you?'

'Not exactly. Back to Balnasheil?'

'Fine,' Tennant said, but as they walked back to the jetty where he had moored his boat he said, 'OK. You tell me what she said and I'll tell you about Harry Drummond. I think things are coming to the boil.'

CHAPTER ELEVEN

It had been the smell that had led Tennant to Vicky Macdonald. She wasn't in the kitchen but there was an open door at the farther side of the room. When he went through into a small lobby by the back door, he was assailed by a rank, sickening smell like suppurating flesh.

Alarmed and all but gagging, he found Vicky Macdonald standing in a walk-in larder checking supplies with a pen and notebook in her hand, apparently oblivious.

'Dear God, what is that stink?' he choked.

She turned, surprised to see him, then laughed. 'Just a hare. The dog caught it. You think that's high? Adam will want it hung for at least another couple of days. You should smell what it's like once it hits the heat of the oven.'

Tennant opened the door she indicated into what must have been the game larder for the hunting lodge in its heyday. It had bare stone walls and a whistling draught came through the slatted windows; lines of pegs and hooks where rows of pheasants and grouse would once have hung lined the walls above zinc-topped shelves. Now there was only the carcass of a hare that had dripped blood into a bowl below, and he shut the door hastily.

'What are you doing here anyway?' Vicky asked.

'Well,' he began, then said, 'Look, do you mind if we carry on our conversation in the kitchen? If I stay here any longer I'll throw up. How do you stand it?'

'Oh, you get used to it. Adam loves his jugged hare and the dog's a very effective killing machine.'

It was all right once the heavy kitchen door was shut but the smell lingered in his nostrils with its sickly-sweet note of corruption. There was a certain fitness to that, Tennant thought grimly.

'So – why are you here?' Vicky said.

'Er – I'd better show you this.' He produced his warrant card.

She stared at it incredulously. 'What – you're a *policeman*?'

'Well, sort of, at the moment. I took unpaid leave from the Met because I've always wanted to write this book—'

She didn't believe him. 'Really? And all those times we talked about Eva's disappearance you didn't think to mention it?'

She wasn't taking it well. The temperature in the room seemed to have dropped about ten degrees. 'I know, I know. Sorry. The problem was, it's under Police Scotland's jurisdiction. You'd have expected me to get involved and I couldn't, but I did pull strings to get some more action.'

'Oh, well done.' Her tone was sweetly poisonous. 'And are they getting anywhere, now they've turned up after any sort of possible trail was cold? Or aren't you allowed to tell me now you've gone all official?'

'Look, we're still on the same side,' he said irritably. OK, she felt betrayed, but he had apologised. What did she want – blood? 'We're working on it but we still don't know what happened. Is there anything at all that you've remembered that might help?'

'No, there bloody isn't.' She was irritated too. 'I just wish there was something – I've racked my brains, but there simply isn't. I'd have told them immediately if there was. And what about this Veruschka who disappeared mysteriously as well – what are you doing about her?'

'Not a lot, at the moment, until we get this sorted out—'

'That's not good enough.' She thumped her fist on the kitchen table for emphasis. 'She's just been wiped out, as if she didn't exist! You knew Eva so you want to know what happened to her, but don't you think this girl has the same rights? You're just not going to bother, are you? Even if she was an immigrant it doesn't mean you can treat her as if she was a – a nothing—'

He reacted to her belligerence with aggression of his own. 'For God's sake, Vicky, no one's treating her like a nothing. Of course we're asking questions. You could try asking Miss Lacey about her – she might tell you what she wouldn't tell us.'

'I did. She said she couldn't remember. But you could put on pressure—'

Tennant snorted. 'Not the way the DI wants to work. Just ask nicely and they'll tell you everything you want to know.'

'Fat lot of use that is.' Vicky was scornful.

'I'm not going to argue with you on that but there's not a lot I can do about it. Anyway, if there's nothing more—?'

For a moment she glared at him and then her shoulders sagged. 'No. No, there isn't.' She was looking deflated when Tennant left.

He had hesitated as he reached the hall, hearing the voices from Beatrice Lacey's study. He'd like to be in on the interview but Strang had a sort of authority that wasn't only derived from his superior rank; the man wouldn't hesitate to cut him out altogether if he pushed his luck. Perhaps, if he went in quietly and kept his mouth shut . . .

He took a step towards the study door but at that moment a door at the other side of the hall below the staircase opened and Harry Drummond appeared, frowning. Tennant recognised him – the dark hair, the vivid blue eyes, the thin-lipped mouth; there was a photo of the man stapled to a file lying on his desk at the cottage.

Drummond stopped, looking startled, but only for a minute. Then he came over, smiling, his hand outstretched and introduced himself. 'You must be from the police. I heard you were expected. Getting any further with your investigations? I do trust nothing has happened to that poor girl.'

Knowing what he did of Drummond's associates, Tennant was tempted to count his fingers when he got his hand back. 'DC Tennant. What do you think might have happened to her, sir?'

'Oh – well, I don't know. These days, the things you hear . . . And these foreign girls are very unsettled. Never last here long – not that I blame them. Back of beyond, no shops, no cinemas – says a lot for Adam's charms that he gets these babes to come here at all!' He laughed heartily. 'Well, good hunting.'

He was turning to go when Tennant, seizing the moment, said, 'I wonder if I could just ask you a little about the background here, sir? Might be helpful.'

Drummond's smile faded and the bright blue eyes went very cold. 'I'm hardly ever here, Constable. I can't think what I could say that might be useful.'

Tennant was ready for a refusal when Drummond's tone suddenly changed. 'On the other hand, I'm keen to cooperate, naturally, if you think I can be helpful in any way. Look, why don't we go through to Adam's flat? He's away today and I know he won't mind.'

So what was it that Drummond wanted to put on record? And was this, he thought with a sudden chill, confirmation that they had indeed realised what was going on, knew about the part Eva had been playing?

'You know, Human Face is very much Adam's baby,' Drummond said confidentially as they both sat down in the sitting room. 'Adam's, and Beatrice's too, I suppose. As I said, I'm not here very often – I'm just the charity's accountant and I mastermind a lot of the distribution for them as well. Go abroad occasionally to monitor the sites we – they' – he stumbled revealingly – 'support, to make sure the money's being used the best way. That sort of thing.'

Yes, he did go abroad quite a lot and made quite a lot of interesting contacts too when he did. His digital trail and Carnegie's criss-crossed constantly, which was one of the things that had made them so difficult for investigators to pin down. He'd come back from the conference in Paris with Carnegie but Tennant couldn't ask him about his movements directly without explaining how he knew and he wasn't ready to do that yet. Maybe a little surprise for later.

Drummond's intentions were blatant so the answer he got to his question, 'You must rely on a considerable inflow of donations, presumably?' wasn't unexpected.

'Oh yes, but all that is Adam's territory, going through Adam's office here. I don't take anything to do with the money or the sponsors. Beatrice processes them and then I audit the books afterwards. All open and above board, as far as I can see, if that's what you're asking. Though of course—' He stopped.

'Of course . . . ?' Tennant prompted.

'Sorry? Oh, nothing, nothing. Human Face does a great deal of good, I promise you that. And if you're still concerned about this girl – well, she obviously decided that Adam's bonny blue eyes weren't enough compensation for the lack of nightclubs.'

Mindful of Vicky's prodding, he said, 'Did you know one called Veruschka, sir?'

'Good grief, I can only just remember the name of the last one, let alone any before that. Sorry, not much use, I'm afraid.' Drummond got up.

He'd said his say. Tennant hadn't tried to prolong the interview and was waiting in the hall when Strang came out of the study a few minutes later.

Conversation in the boat on the way back was impossible with the noise of the boat's engine and the muttering of a rising sea that was flecked with white caps under a leaden sky. Strang cast an uneasy look around; it almost felt as if there was a sort of pent-up rage that might erupt into a tempest of destruction. He didn't like those brooding, cloud-veiled mountains all around; it was making him fanciful, and he was glad to reach the Balnasheil shore. He waited as Tennant tied up at a small wooden pier, then went back with him to the cottage.

'It was pretty repellent, to be honest,' Tennant said when he had reported the conversation with Drummond. 'He was clearing his lines – nothing to do with me, all Adam's fault whatever it is, that sort of thing. They know we're onto them – and what does that say about my poor, poor Eva?' He bit his lip.

'I have to say I was surprised when you said you wanted to break cover today,' Strang said. 'It's going to generate a lot of talk in the village.'

'Not to mention hostility,' Tennant said. 'Vicky Macdonald's madder than a wet hen and she didn't buy the story about me happening to be here on leave. But my bosses reckon that in the circumstances it's time to pressure them. Drummond's started ratting already so it looks as if that just may give us leverage. Now – your turn. Did you get anything out of Lacey?'

Strang repeated what Beatrice had said but when Tennant seemed ready to seize on it as an excuse for a search warrant he shook his head. 'Forget it. She says she *thought* she saw Carnegie long after he was supposed to have gone but she couldn't have – we checked it out and he flew to Paris on the flight as scheduled. She was a little vague anyway – talked about "we" but then said she was alone. There's an odd question mark about clothes left behind by both those girls but nothing like the sort of evidence we'd need to persuade a sheriff to grant a warrant to search the premises of an established charity – unless you have something that could swing it?'

'You think we'd still be hanging about if we did? Not a chance. All circumstantial and nothing that you could actually describe as criminal,' Tennant said gloomily. 'You can't arrest someone for keeping bad company, unfortunately – our job would be a walk in the park if you could. But anyway, what now?'

'I'm going to call my boss in Edinburgh. See what she says.'

But he knew already what she would say. They were trying to make bricks without straw and unless there was a major breakthrough somewhere in the next twenty-four hours or so he'd be heading back south with nothing to show for his investigations.

There was still an interview to be done with Adam Carnegie once he got back from Glasgow, and he was going to take him head on. Maybe he'd let Tennant off the leash this time.

When the policeman had gone, Beatrice Lacey collapsed forward onto her desk. Her head felt as if it might float away off her shoulders, she was hot and cold all over and her heart was beating so frantically that she thought it might stop at any moment. She lay there, spread-eagled, until the blood started coming back to her brain and her heart rate slowed down a little. Then she sat up gingerly.

What had she said? She couldn't remember clearly, could only remember the kindly voice of the policeman and the relief she'd felt at telling him what had been bothering her. She hadn't betrayed Adam, had she? Even saying the words made her gulp nervously, but the inspector had agreed with her that she'd just got things out of proportion – exactly what she'd kept telling herself. She was sure of that.

And when it came to Veruschka, she was on firmer ground. She hadn't said more than she should, hadn't been drawn into saying anything that Adam wouldn't like; she'd kept to what he'd told her. She could comfort herself with that.

But – could she? She was still feeling strange and her mind, so obligingly ready to erect barriers in the past, was entertaining ideas that were as novel as they were unwelcome.

'The police are our friends,' her mother had told the little Beatrice, all these years ago. The police were men like the nice inspector, who'd been so understanding. She wanted to cooperate, to be on the side of the law as all decent folk should be – yet she'd lied to him.

She tried to argue with herself. It wasn't her lie – it was Adam's lie that she'd just repeated, and Adam came first, Adam was her life and anyway, if she'd been going to betray him (that word again) she should have done it long ago. If they found out now – she caught her breath – it wasn't only Adam they'd be after.

No, she needed to pull herself together, stick to what they had agreed. No one could prove anything – and perhaps she'd jumped to the wrong conclusions last time too. She was feeling a little better and once she'd dug out a Twix she managed to go back to the report she'd been working on.

She was still worried about Quentin, though. Somehow she'd have to see to it that he didn't get his talk with Adam. After all she'd been through for his sake, she couldn't bear it if Adam got angry and told her bluntly that all her dreams were at an end.

Vicky's second visitor that day was Marek. When he came into the kitchen he left the doors open behind him so she could see that the dog was with him, sitting obediently on the doorstep, though sniffing the rich aroma wafting from the game larder. When Adam was away it was Marek who walked it; it did as it was told but showed not the slightest interest in him. Amber was a one-man dog.

She had worked out at least some of her anger on her cleaning duties and finished them in record time; now she was sitting with a mug of tea. She offered him one but he shook his head.

'I am with the dog,' he said.

He was just standing there. 'Did you come over to do something?' Vicky said at last.

'No, I—you know policeman?'

'Not know, really. If you mean Daniel Tennant, I was friendly with him before – at least, I naively thought I was. I didn't know at the time he was a policeman. He didn't tell me.'

Marek scowled. 'He is bad man. Make trouble for me. You tell him – I like Eva, I not hurt her.'

Vicky's eyebrows shot up. 'Did he say you did?'

'Mr Carnegie, maybe make me do something, he says.'

She struggled to take that in. 'Are they actually saying she's been murdered?'

The man shrugged his shoulders.

'Daniel didn't say anything like that to me. Maybe he was just trying to catch you out. If there was any proof they'd be searching the house – not that it would do any good,' she added, more or less to herself. She'd tried that; with her housekeeper duties she'd been all over the house apart from Adam's flat, which she only cleaned in his presence, and Beatrice's, which she'd never even been inside.

The man shrugged again. 'You tell him,' he repeated. 'I do nothing. But Carnegie—' He stopped.

Vicky prompted, 'Carnegie?'

'Just – bad man.' Marek walked to the door then turned. 'You be careful.'

She found herself staring at the closing door. Just voicing the word 'murdered' had shocked her. She had, she realised, been shielding herself from the thought and everyone until now had colluded: they had all been saying 'something might have happened' to Eva.

That left open the possibility that the something that had happened might turn out to be a misunderstanding or even a deliberate deception; 'murdered' finished that hope. Eva dead, Veruschka dead too?

She felt deathly sick suddenly. Her heart was hammering in her chest and she was panting so hard that she couldn't force breath back into her lungs.

Panic attack – she'd had one before. She cupped her hands and breathed into them, telling herself *slow down, slow down*. At last her racing pulse slowed and she was able to sit back, trying to think.

She had seized an opportunity to try to find out for herself what had happened to those girls – the disappeared ones, and who knew if there had been others before? But had she just run herself into the same sort of danger? She could still feel the way her skin had crawled as Carnegie's lascivious look slid over her. Could he be lining her up as another victim? There were serial killers for whom it became an addiction.

She could go right now to Marek, get him to take her back meekly to Murdo John and try to mend their marriage, but something in her rebelled. She had proclaimed herself an independent woman who could look after herself and she still believed that as long as she was here she could hope to discover something more.

Vicky picked up the mug of tea in front of her and walked, on shaky legs, to the cupboard where she kept the cooking brandy and poured in a hefty slug. It was what was called Dutch courage, she thought as the rough mixture burnt warmth down her throat, but if she was to stay true to herself she needed any sort of courage she could get.

It hadn't been a rewarding day for PC Murray, at least not so far. CID work wasn't as interesting as she had thought it would be. Calling round taxi firms and checking bus timetables with a dodgy connection that kept cutting out was mind-numbing and she'd spent much of the afternoon kicking the desk and swearing.

She'd hung around the harbour in the morning, checking

up with boat owners – and, to be truthful, hoping she might bump into Strang and get an update – but all she'd got from them was blank stares, and she hadn't seen Strang or Tennant either. There were still a couple of day boats out at the lobster pots; she'd have to get the fishermen later but she wasn't hopeful.

None of the taxi drivers had seen Eva and now she was going to have to persuade the bus company, who seemed to have an obsession about data protection, to give her a contact number for the drivers on the service buses that called up at the top of the road twice a day. When she eventually extracted the information she needed, it was as she had thought. They hadn't seen her.

They wouldn't have. Because she hadn't left.

Yes, she'd been wrong at the beginning, but she was convinced of it now and she was pretty sure that Strang believed the same – and Daniel Tennant probably even knew why Adam Carnegie might have seen to it that Eva couldn't leave. But even if they spoke to every living soul on the whole of the Isle of Skye and none of them had seen Eva, it wouldn't prove anything. You can't prove a negative and that was what she'd spent the whole pointless day trying to do.

Her instructions were to spend time in the pub, in the hope of finding someone who remembered Eva having some sort of friendship with someone else, to give them a new lead – which, in her opinion, was only going to take them further down a dead-end road.

But she'd sat in on the interview with Murdo John and she'd seen his edgy reaction when Strang had asked him about this Veruschka girl. It had been a distraction from the question of Eva at the time and he hadn't followed it up; if she went in before the bar actually opened, while Murdo John was setting up, she could tackle him directly about her.

She'd seen how Strang worked and she'd picked up some ideas from that; this would be her chance to put them into practice. It wasn't exactly what he'd told her to do but if you waited for top brass to OK everything you did, all you'd be was a little pawn being pushed round the board and Livvy Murray wanted more than that.

Maybe he'd be impressed if she showed her initiative and maybe he wouldn't; she didn't much care. It was what she wanted to do and she was going to do it. She'd have plenty of time to chat up the punters like he'd wanted her to after that.

No matter how bad you were feeling, there was still an evening meal to be made. Vicky Macdonald paused as she looked at the vegetable rack, wondering how many potatoes she would need for the gratin dauphinoise. She'd had food left over last night because Beatrice hadn't appeared for supper and Vicky wasn't even sure if Adam, who was away today, would be back in time.

She decided to go through to check. It would give her an excuse to ask what the police had said to her and their relationship wasn't the sort where she could just wander in and ask anyway.

Beatrice was on the phone when she went in, talking to a donor, obviously; she was explaining how important their work was and how little money was wasted on admin.

'I'm a donor myself,' she was saying, 'and I work here for love. That's how much I value what we do and I make absolutely every penny work for us.'

She was good, Vicky thought; her sincerity shone through and if she'd been the person on the other end she'd have signed the cheque there and then.

As, indeed, the caller seemed about to do too. Beatrice was warmly expressing thanks and she was smiling as she finished the call and turned to speak to Vicky.

'That's good! Adam will be pleased. We've been trying to get him signed up for some time.'

'Well done,' Vicky said. 'You're very persuasive. Beatrice, are you planning to come for supper tonight? And what about Adam?'

'Oh – he didn't say. If it's just Harry, I'll take a tray upstairs. He's so rude it makes conversation very trying. But of course Adam might be back, so—' She broke off as the phone rang. 'I'd better take this.

'Human Face?' she said, then, 'Sorry. Who did you say?'

Vicky, standing back in the awkward way people do when trying not to seem to be listening when there is no alternative to hearing, saw Beatrice's face go blank.

'I'm sorry,' she said, 'could you repeat that?'

Vicky could hear that it was a woman's voice and it sounded a little querulous, she thought, though she couldn't make out what it was being said. Whatever it was, it was having an extraordinary effect on Beatrice. She was starting to shake and when she spoke again her voice was high and strange.

'Right. No, I didn't realise. I'm sorry. Goodbye.' The receiver rattled on the base as she tried to set it down.

'Good gracious,' Vicky said. 'Whatever was that, Beatrice? Are you all right?'

Beatrice slumped back in her chair. 'I – I don't know. I can't believe it—' She burst into tears, loud, uninhibited sobs.

Vicky looked at her helplessly. 'Tell me what's wrong,' she urged. There was a box of tissues lying on the desk; she thrust a handful at Beatrice, tentatively putting an arm round her heaving shoulders.

The other woman took it and started mopping at her face, fighting down the sobs. 'Sorry, sorry,' she muttered. 'It's the shock! I just can't believe it, I can't!'

'Is something wrong? Has something happened to Adam – your brother—?'

'No, no,' she wailed. 'It was this – this woman. She said she wanted to speak to Adam. And when I asked her who she was, she said she was—' The sobs began again. 'She had to repeat it because I didn't take it in the first time. She said she was Mrs Carnegie. And she wanted to speak to her husband.'

CHAPTER TWELVE

Beatrice seemed almost to be on the verge of collapse. She was half-falling out of her chair, moaning, and her face had gone a worrying greyish-purple colour.

Was she having a heart attack? At a loss to know what to do, Vicky looked round about her frantically. There was a bottle of water standing on a table beside a small kettle and a cup and saucer; she splashed some into the cup and held it to Beatrice's lips.

'Try and take this,' she urged her. 'I think what you really need is brandy – you're in shock. I've got some in the kitchen—'

Beatrice grabbed on to her hand. 'Don't leave me!' she begged. 'I can't bear to be left alone!' She sat up enough to take a sip or two of water though her teeth chattered against the cup.

'You need to lie down,' Vicky said. 'Do you think you can stand? I could take you to my room—'

'No, no – my own bed, I want my own bed. If you would help me upstairs . . .'

Vicky looked doubtfully at the woman's bulk as she staggered to her feet, swaying, but moved to her side so that Beatrice could put her arm across her supporter's shoulder. It meant stooping so that she herself was bent almost double – not the ideal position for taking a considerable strain. But somehow they made it across the hall and once Beatrice could grasp the banister on her other side it helped. Even so, it was slow progress.

Halfway up she remembered that her key was in her handbag. Vicky ran down and fetched it, but when she got back Beatrice had subsided onto the floor and was in tears again; it took three attempts to get her back onto her feet. Vicky would have gone to enlist Harry's help if she hadn't thought he was more likely to make things worse than better.

At last, with Beatrice gasping as if she might breathe her last and Vicky out of breath herself, they reached the flat and on instruction Vicky rooted in her bag for the key and opened the door. Even in the present situation, she had some curiosity to see what it was like, expecting it to be a slightly more modest version of Adam's. To her surprise, the sitting room was as shabby as the little bedsitter she was sleeping in herself, with an uncurtained window and a cheap nylon carpet on the floor. There were a few good pieces she recognised as antiques – a nice Victorian chair, a piecrust table, some porcelain on display, but that was in a tatty glass cabinet with a chipped leg, and the big armchair Beatrice had collapsed into had sagging cushions and a worn chintz loose cover.

And then there was the crib. As Beatrice leant back with her eyes closed, Vicky glanced at it curiously. It was the sort of toy a yummy mummy would buy for her little princess, canopied and frilled with layers of immaculate white lace, the pink lining beneath showing through. The doll lying there was large, almost the size of a real baby, and clearly expensive with its rosebud mouth and sweeping eyelashes closed on pale cheeks delicately flushed with pink.

Beatrice's colour was a little better but now she was moaning again. In some desperation Vicky said, 'Do you keep brandy or anything up here? I think it would help.'

'Sherry.' Beatrice managed to indicate a cupboard in the corner.

It seemed mainly to hold the contents of a small sweet shop but on a lower shelf there was a litre bottle of Croft Original, half empty. She found a glass – a little tumbler really – and poured in a hearty measure.

Beatrice stretched out a trembling hand to take it from her. 'Have some yourself,' she said shakily. 'This must have been quite a shock for you too.'

More of a *fino* woman herself, Vicky looked at the bottle doubtfully, but sharing a drink might loosen Beatrice's tongue and give her a chance to get answers to the questions she had been desperate to ask for so long. She poured a token amount into another glass and sat down.

Beatrice took a gulp from hers and choked a little, then sat staring silently ahead before taking another swig, as if it was medicine. Trying to keep communication going, Vicky said brightly, 'What a lovely doll! Is she an old friend from childhood?'

217

Beatrice's reaction astonished her. Her face, which had been pale, went bright red. Then she started to cry again, but silently this time, the tears streaming down her cheeks. 'Rosamond,' she wailed. 'Give her to me.'

Obediently, Vicky fetched the doll. Its eyelids flipped open with a click, revealing sky-blue eyes; it was wearing a beautifully smocked Liberty print dress with a hand-embroidered white cardigan that by the feel of it was cashmere. She brought it across to Beatrice, who grabbed it, cradling it in her arms and making a crooning noise as if soothing a real baby. There was something very disturbing about it.

'You're – you're obviously very fond of it – her,' Vicky said uneasily.

'Oh yes, oh yes!' Beatrice was rocking to and fro. 'It should have been my real baby, you see. I hoped and hoped, after that time in Africa – the most wonderful time of my life.' She looked up, her eyes dreamy. 'And if it happened once, it could happen again, couldn't it?'

Vicky didn't know what to say. 'Well—' she temporised.

'But now,' Beatrice said, reminded of her affliction, 'it seems he's *married*!'

'Were you – were you hoping he'd marry you?'

'Yes.' It was a bald statement, delivered with a defiant look. 'Oh, I'm not stupid. I don't think he's in love with me, but then I'm not sure he's capable of that – certainly not with any of the parade of whores who've gone through here.' She spat the words. 'But my money's tied up. The only way we can get control of it for the charity is if he marries me. And I could make him happy – I know I could.'

She was drinking the sherry now and she had stopped shaking. As Vicky topped up the glass, Beatrice said with sudden ferocity, 'How could he? How could he deceive me like that? After all I've done for him, all we've been to each other—'

'What exactly did the woman say on the phone?'

'She just said she wanted to speak to Adam, that it was Mrs Carnegie. I queried it and she said it was – was it Sheila, Shona? I was so shocked I didn't take it in properly. Anyway, she said she was Adam's wife, hadn't I heard of her? And when I said no, she sounded a bit huffy, just said she'd speak to him later and put the phone down.'

'Perhaps he's divorced,' Vicky suggested a little feebly. 'Perhaps she meant *ex*-wife.' She wasn't surprised, really; a man like Adam was unlikely to have reached his age without baggage of some kind. 'Why don't you ask him about it?'

'Oh, I couldn't!' Beatrice cried. She bent her head over the doll, clutching it to her face, and when she looked up, her eyes were fierce. 'It's – it's probably true and do you know this? I'm not sure I care any more. There's too much – he's asked too much of me. I've been so worried – and I'm beginning to see things in a different light now.'

She should be making the supper now, but Vicky didn't move. She'd find something later to put on the table and if they didn't like it they could sack her. She was angry for poor, vulnerable Beatrice; it was wicked the way she'd been preyed on by Adam Carnegie. He was – yes, evil, and as she listened she could almost see the shadows of that evil gathering about them.

It was good that Beatrice was starting to see what he really was, but what would he do if he came to believe she was of no further use to him?

'It's becoming clearer and clearer, ma'am. In my opinion Carnegie's killed two women,' DI Kelso Strang said to DCS Jane Borthwick.

'That's a bold statement,' she said, sounding taken aback. 'Are you sure?'

'Yes. I can't prove it and I don't know how he did it – perhaps using the man Kaczka, who works as a sort of odd-job man on the estate. Certainly we know he was still on the premises with Eva Havel after the others seem to have left. I suppose Kaczka could have done it on his own account but there's no way Beatrice Lacey would be covering up for him and that she certainly is doing.'

'So, you're positing that if Kaczka killed her he was carrying out an order, that Carnegie perhaps has paid him to do it?'

'Or has a hold over him. Illegal immigrant being exploited, I suspect. He's living in a hovel. I think the Border Authority might need to know.'

'Leave that with me. You have enough on your plate. So – next step?'

'Carnegie was away today. I'm going to pull him in for questioning tomorrow though frankly it's just a gesture – can't see a chance of breaking him with what we have. But I'm going to see Kaczka without Tennant – he scared him into total silence last time and I want to see if I can draw a bit more out of him. So we need to hold off the BA heavies until after that.'

'Noted,' she dryly, and he realised he'd just given an order to a DCS. Not the smartest idea, but there was nothing he could do about it now. After all, she'd told him he was in charge so she couldn't complain if he behaved as if he was.

Anyway, she didn't seem to be about to call him on it. She was going on, 'Are you suggesting the Al Capone strategy – get Carnegie on illegal immigration and see what crawls out of the woodwork? The Met would be pleased. But you need to think beyond that, Kelso—'

He jumped in before she could tell him what he was meant to think. 'Oh yes, I certainly have, ma'am. My problem is that I can't see what more I can do here unless something dramatic emerges from the interviews tomorrow, and I'm not betting the farm on that. I can try chatting up Beatrice again but I think she's told me all she's prepared to. So I suppose . . .'

'Yes. Sometimes you just hit the buffers and there's nothing more you can do.'

Did he imagine it, or did she sound just faintly relieved at that thought? If this did blow up into a double murder investigation, her decision to appoint someone with his lack of experience and personal baggage would be a gift to the police-bashing media.

But she left it at that, only adding, 'If you do have to wind it up tomorrow, it would do you good to take a break before you come back. Go and yomp up a hill, or something.'

He looked out of the window. That inexorable Highland rain had been falling almost all day and now it was dark it seemed to be gathering itself into a more solid form; the street lamps each had their nimbus of cloud and the other side of the bay had disappeared.

'Not really the weather for it,' he said. 'Thanks, ma'am. I'll give you an update tomorrow.'

And shortly, in all probability, he'd be back in his own house – the shell of the place it had once been, the rooms that were furnished but empty even so, lacking what had made it a home.

Kelso's throat constricted and the black despair that he had ruthlessly banished threatened to return. But giving way to it would be a form of self-indulgence that he had to force himself to resist; going back would be hard enough without letting himself go through agony in anticipation.

Get on with his work, that was the answer. He took out the notes he had made after today's interviews. It was proving his salvation and he'd plenty to do now.

He found himself going over his conversation with JB. Had he sounded cocksure, overconfident in his assertion about Adam Carnegie? He would hate to think he'd based it simply on 'gut feeling' – what would be mockingly called 'feminine intuition' in a woman. It could be useful, admittedly, but only when it had a sound rational base.

Strang leafed through his papers until he found the notes about the interview with Carnegie. Had he demonstrated behaviours that according to the classic Hare's test were the marks of the psychopath?

He could recall quite a few of them from his psychology lectures: glibness and superficial charm was one, shallowness and lack of empathy another. Carnegie certainly had those. And yes, he had a grandiose sense of self-worth as evidenced by his attitude to the string of girlfriends, only there to serve his sexual appetite and to Marek Kaczka, who seemed to be treated like a slave.

He wasn't wrong. Carnegie was a casebook study. There was a sort of hideous fascination about this man: there was simply no limit to what he might do, unchecked.

Strang shifted uncomfortably in his seat. It was his job to stop him and right at the moment he couldn't see how that could be achieved.

'Not up to her usual standard,' Harry Drummond said discontentedly, pushing his food around the plate. 'She's just made a white sauce and chopped up that slimy packet ham in it. And the so-called pâté was a tin of tuna mushed up. What happened to the jugged hare?'

'Could do with another day.' Adam's tone was curt.

'This won't do, Adam. You'll need to have a word with her.'

'For God's sake, Harry, have another glass of wine and shut up,' he snapped. He was clearly in a bad mood, for some reason; he'd been cheerful enough when he got back.

'What were you doing in Glasgow today, anyway?' Harry asked.

Adam shrugged. 'Couple of things to do.'

'What kind of things? Did you see MacNab?'

When he mentioned their lawyer, Harry caught a fleeting look on Adam's face that told him he was lying when he said, 'No. I was just dodging the police until I knew what they wanted. I was planning to pump Beatrice but she's in her flat and when I knocked she didn't answer. Of course, she wasn't well yesterday – she's probably sleeping.'

He sounded as if he was trying to reassure himself – that probably explained his bad mood. Harry didn't comment, though, only saying blandly, 'Actually, I'd a word with one of them myself.'

Adam stiffened. 'Oh? What about?'

'Just routine stuff. Nothing much I could tell them, really, was there?'

'I suppose not. We just need to hold our nerve. How much longer before you're confident about the books? You're taking a long time.'

'Shouldn't have dumped them in a mess, then, should you? You're not talking charity commission audits – these guys smell your sweat and won't leave till they've found out why you're sweating. So we have to be rock solid – give me another twenty-four hours and I'll be sure. Have you destroyed everything that needs destroying?'

'You think I'm stupid? Of course I have.' Adam's tone was glacial.

'Good. Oh, by the way, who was Veruschka?'

'Veruschka?'

'Yeah, the other girl they're asking about. What did you do to her, Adam?' Harry's blue eyes were hard and cold.

'Nothing!' Adam protested. 'Absolutely nothing! She was just a girl who went off without telling anyone she was leaving and someone's dredged up some local gossip, that's all.'

'Just like Eva did?' Harry's voice was mocking.

Adam was on a short fuse anyway. He jumped to his feet. 'That does it! I've had as much as I'm prepared to take from you. You were in on this too, Harry, and if I go down don't think I won't take you with me. Indeed, if you're thinking of shoving me into the pit with the lions I'll do just that.'

'Oh, don't tempt me,' Harry muttered as Adam slammed the door behind him. One of the lions in question seemed to have swallowed the little titbit he'd offered it this morning already; perhaps it was time to work out what else could be offered without implicating himself.

He pushed aside his plate and topped up his glass. He was confident that he was almost there with filtering the accounts but the problem was Adam and his women. He'd never heard anything about this Veruschka until this morning; to lose one mistress might be considered a misfortune, but . . .

Beatrice would know about her. Beatrice knew about far too much – a lot more than Harry did, certainly. It was Adam's job to keep her sweet and if they'd fallen out she could be dangerous – very dangerous, indeed. He didn't want to have to neutralise that particular threat too; they were in enough trouble already.

Harry brooded for a moment. He needed to find out what was going on. Maybe the cook – what was her name again? Vicky, that was it. She might know.

He got up and walked through to the kitchen. Vicky seemed startled when he came in; she was holding a tub of ice cream and a scoop and there were two pudding plates laid out on the table.

She flushed. 'Sorry, were you waiting for this? I'll bring it through in a moment.' She didn't sound apologetic, though;

pissed off, more like, and glacial enough to keep the ice cream she was holding rock solid.

'Don't bother,' he said. 'We've both had enough.'

'Right. I'll put this back in the freezer, then.' She opened the door to the back premises and as the rotting smell wafted through Harry pulled a face.

'Is that Adam's hare? I like it gamey but I think that's going a bit far.'

She came back in and shut the door. 'I'll cook it tomorrow. Was there something you wanted?'

'No, no, not really. I was just wondering if Beatrice was all right. Adam said she was in her flat.'

'How kind of you to ask!' She didn't try to hide the sarcasm. 'She's a bit upset. Very upset, indeed.'

'So what's her problem?'

Vicky gave him another icy look. 'She's just discovered that Adam's married. He never told her.'

'*Married*?' Harry stared at her. 'First I've heard of it.'

'His wife phoned this afternoon wanting to speak to him. If there isn't anything else, I'll just go and clear next door—'

He interrupted her. 'What do you know about someone called Veruschka?'

She stopped. 'What do you know about her?'

'Absolutely nothing. Heard her name for the first time this morning.'

'Oh. Well, I don't know anything either. Sorry.'

She picked up a tray and walked out, leaving Harry standing there, his eyes narrowed in thought. Married? Adam? What else was there that Adam hadn't told him?

He was going to phone MacNab tonight, find out what Adam had been doing there that he hadn't wanted Harry to know about.

Adam was a clever man, dangerously clever and totally amoral; was he playing some double game, setting up Harry to take the fall? If that was what he was up to, he wouldn't succeed. Harry had never been overburdened with scruples himself and if ruthlessness was required he would do whatever needed to be done.

CHAPTER THIRTEEN

Livvy Murray huddled inside her oilskin jacket as she hurried down the hill to the pub. It was raining in earnest now; sheets of rain were sweeping in across the sea, the hills were blotted out and the blurred pinpoints of street lamps spaced along the Balnasheil main street were the only light in the deepening murk.

She put on her flashlight. When it was as dark as this it was easy to find yourself walking off the road into the ditch that bordered it, now streaming with water. As she reached the shore she could hear the muttering and grumbling of the incoming tide and dodged as a bolder wave broke right across the side of the road.

Even so it splashed her and she swore. Oh, she should be used to it by now; this was nothing out of the ordinary. There wasn't much wind so they wouldn't be putting the sandbags out across the thresholds of the houses yet.

The door to the Black Cuillin wasn't open but the lights

were on and she could see Murdo John was behind the counter polishing glasses. She went in through the hotel entrance; the door to the bar on that side wasn't locked and she walked in.

He looked up and scowled. 'We're closed. The bar doesn't open till six.'

Ignoring his hostility, Murray said, 'That's just fine. Gives me – what – quarter of an hour for a wee chat before we're interrupted? Brilliant.'

She took up her position on a bar stool. Murdo John turned his back on her and went on polishing glasses.

'If you're trying to do an impression of a man who isn't there, I have to tell you it's not working,' she said. 'I'm needing answers to a few questions.'

'Do I have to give you them?' he said over his shoulder.

'You will if you're smart.'

'Maybe I'm not wanting to be smart. I've said all I'm going to say.' He took down an almost-empty bottle of whisky from the optic and picked up a replacement.

'You didn't say much about Veruschka.'

There was a momentary pause, then he very deliberately went on fitting the replacement into the stand. 'Nothing more to say.'

'Even if she was murdered, like Eva's been?'

The bottle slipped out of his hand. Only his lightning reaction stopped it falling on the stone floor and shattering. Whisky slopped over his hand and, swearing, he set it down and bent over the sink to wash it. The drying towel still in his hand, he turned to face her.

'Is that the truth?'

'Oh yes.' Murray crossed her fingers below the counter, though it didn't really count as a lie if you believed it was true.

'That's what the inspector's saying?'

'Yes.' Well, what she was sure he was thinking, anyway, which was much the same.

He was looking totally gobsmacked. 'Morag said that something had happened, but I didn't believe her,' he said as if he was talking to himself. 'We none of us believed her. We thought she'd just – gone. Found something, someone, that was a better bet.'

Murray picked up instantly on the note of bitterness. 'Your girlfriend?'

He reddened. 'She was living with Carnegie.'

'That's not an answer, but I've got the message. So – she was pretty hot, then? That's the way he likes them, isn't it? Was she on the make?'

He gave her a look of loathing. 'She wasn't like that. She wasn't mercenary, just someone who was escaping from a life where there was no future for her in the only way she could.'

She was tempted to say, 'Illegally?' but said instead, 'So what was she like, then?'

'She was straight – bright, honest, direct. Bonny, yes, right enough, but she'd a sort of warmth, a sort of innocence that none of the others ever had. And she was so – so *alive*. I'd never met anyone who just flared with so much energy, it lit up the room. Veruschka—'

He stopped and she thought he was going to clam up. Then he suddenly began talking again as if compelled, as if talking about her was a temptation he couldn't resist.

230

Startled, Murray realised he was a man still in love who just wanted to speak the name of the beloved, a name he probably hadn't spoken for years.

'Veruschka was desperate to get away from Carnegie. I don't know, perhaps she'd been in love with him at one time but she wasn't by then – hated him, really. She wouldn't tell me the things he did but I think he was abusive. And then, we fell in love – at least I believed we had. But she was so lovely – and why would someone like her want someone like me?'

Because you have a British passport, Murray thought cynically, but she knew better than to say it.

'I didn't deserve her. How could I expect her to settle for what little I could give her?' The bitterness was back in Murdo John's voice. 'It was only natural she'd just decided there was a world out there with a lot more to offer. A London address, Morag said they'd sent her luggage to. It hurt – God, how it hurt, her just vanishing without a word to me. But I never thought – even when Eva—' It was as if he'd only now realised what Murray had said. 'Do you mean that he – that Carnegie actually *killed* them?'

Murray couldn't risk that. 'What do you think?' she said instead.

He didn't answer. He took refuge in remoteness once more, turning away to wipe the whisky bottle, and set it in place. 'That's all I know. I don't have anything more I could tell you. I've said too much already.' He looked at the clock above the bar then went to unlock the door.

'Great. If it's opening time, I'll have a pint,' she said. But as he went back behind the bar she couldn't resist saying, 'So where does all that leave your wife?'

'My wife makes her own decisions. I hope she doesn't live to regret them,' was all he said, then, 'Evening, Donald. The usual?' as one of the regulars walked in.

Daniel Tennant was sitting by the window staring blankly out, his hands wrapped around a glass of whisky, his mood as black as the fog-thickened darkness outside.

He had only been doing his job, but that was a lame excuse. He'd known the sort of man Carnegie was, yet he had put Eva, so vulnerable, so naive, in harm's way – had lured her into it, indeed, playing on her particular insecurities to persuade her. He'd cut a few corners in his time, without compunction and without remorse, but – how could he have done that to her, to his Eva, with her shining, hopeful face? There was a special circle of hell reserved for those who betrayed the innocent.

He couldn't get her out of his head. Feeling guilt was a new and very unpleasant experience.

He owed it to her to make Carnegie pay, but the man seemed impregnable. His alibi was rock solid; he'd even checked for himself that Carnegie was on that flight in case Strang had managed to miss something. He had no faith at all in his superior officer's ability to get the evidence they would need: when he'd tried to go in hard on Kaczka, he'd been called off as if he was an overenthusiastic and ill-trained dog.

And Kaczka was the key to it, he was certain: he'd been alone with Eva at the Lodge when the others had left and even Strang had agreed that he could have been paid or coerced into doing Carnegie's dirty work for him.

They ought to be giving the man a going-over, breaking him down. His hands clenched involuntarily around the glass, as if it was Kaczka's throat. Strang was feeble, that was his problem, and because they were outside English jurisdiction his own hands were tied, at least officially. Strang had 'principles'. His lip curled in a sneer. There were no rules in a knife fight and if you were a crime-fighting officer, 'principles' were an indulgence you couldn't afford.

There was a lot at stake here, too, for him personally. He'd been kicking his heels for weeks now and he'd be expected to have something to show for it at the end – something apart from getting a nice kid rubbed out. God, this guilt shtick was painful.

His mobile rang. He glanced at the ID, then answered it with little enthusiasm. If Vicky was just going to give him another earful he didn't want to hear it.

But his mood lifted as he heard what she had to say. Yes! At last! They'd got him.

'She'll testify to this?' he said eagerly.

But Vicky's voice was flat. 'That's the problem. She won't. Maybe the sherry I gave her combined with shock loosened her tongue, but she was pouring it all out when she just suddenly stopped and started back-tracking – she didn't know what had made her say such a stupid thing, it wasn't really like that, she'd put two and two together and made five. She got angry, actually. If you question her about it, she's going to say she doesn't know what you're talking about, that I made it up. To be honest, I think she just suddenly realised she would be implicated and she was scared.'

'Oh,' Tennant said heavily. 'No use, then.'

'But I can testify to what she told me—'

'You can testify that you heard her say she saw him do something that she now denies she saw, or even said. We can hardly charge Carnegie on that basis – it's not proof. We can't do anything without proof.'

Vicky was incredulous. 'You mean you're just going to let him get away with it?'

'No, of course I don't,' he said irritably. 'We'll question her again, naturally, but from what you said it won't do any good. We can challenge him with it, try to break him and work for a confession. But I can tell you now we won't get it. He's not the breaking type.'

'And what happens to Beatrice afterwards?' Vicky demanded. 'A tragic accident when she falls downstairs and breaks her neck? Her brakes fail and the car goes off the road into the sea?'

God, the woman was impossible. 'We will of course warn her and tell her to clear out.'

'Terrific! And when you fail to pin it on him, you give her a permanent bodyguard, do you?'

'Not exactly,' he said through tightened lips. 'This doesn't help, Vicky.'

'Oh, sorry I bothered you with it. I was naive enough to think this was useful information.'

'Of course it is, Vicky. But—'

He was talking to empty air. He sat back with a groan, drained his glass then in a fit of temper threw it at the wall. The splintering crash was in its small way satisfying.

His hopes having been raised at first made the subsequent

disappointment worse. Yes, what Vicky said had confirmed what they believed already but unless Beatrice could either be coaxed or coerced into testifying – and from the sound of it he didn't believe she could – they were stuffed. He could still hope that the Fraud Squad would come up with what was needed to put Carnegie away but he couldn't see his Eva, and the other girl too, getting the justice they deserved that way.

The grey afternoon had given way to the encroaching gloom early tonight, but Beatrice didn't get up to switch on the light, just sat rocking her doll and mourning for her dreams in the darkness of her room, hearing the evening sounds as night came on: voices from downstairs and doors closing, a drift of raucous music wafting from somewhere across the bay, a motorboat's engine, the low keening of the wind.

At last, Beatrice got up, staggering a little, stiff with sitting for so long; perhaps it had something to do with finishing the sherry as well. She was dry-eyed now but pale and shivery.

She picked up the doll. 'Nearly time for bed, Rosamond,' she said. 'Your mummy's been very, very silly. We just need to think what we're going to do now.'

Silly she might be, but she wasn't stupid. She knew the trouble she was in, the dangers surrounding her on every side – and she knew she needed to think about things in a very different way now.

She'd made a fool of herself tonight and she didn't for a moment trust Vicky not to run to the police and tell them what had been said. She couldn't think why she'd said all that, except that she was in shock; now they'd come and question her again. She shrank from the thought, but as long as she just denied it, said that Vicky was making all this up and held firm to that, there would be nothing they could do. They couldn't actually force her to say anything she didn't want to, and if she stuck to it, didn't let herself be drawn into discussion, she would be safe enough.

The thought of facing Adam was worse. Could she really tell him it was all over, that she was walking out and would ruin the charity they had worked so hard to build together, while he looked at her with his navy-blue eyes and told her that it was all somehow a mistake, that even if he was married she still meant more to him than any wife ever could? Could she?

Just then she heard a door open below and, alert as always to Adam's movements, she recognised it as the one that led from his flat to the patio. Beatrice laid down the doll, levered herself out of the chair and went to the window to look down.

She couldn't see Adam, just the dog, streaking out into the misty darkness. A few minutes later she heard his voice calling, 'Amber!'

Usually the dog obeyed any command instantly but tonight it seemed reluctant and there was a sharp whistle, then Adam called, 'Amber! Amber!' with his voice rising in annoyance.

A moment later the dog appeared, licking its lips and casting a glance backwards before it trotted in. She heard Adam saying, 'What did you find out there, eh? Inside!' then the door shut again.

She was really very tired now. 'Come on, Rosamond,' she said. 'Time we were both asleep. We'll see how things are in the morning.'

The wind dropped later that night, making way for the slithering fog, rolling down from the mountains in drifting waves of vapour. In the stifling stillness, any sound of movement was muffled, even the perpetual muttering of the waves by the shore. A little later, there came what might have been the startled cry of a seagull, but even that was muted and then the silence returned.

CHAPTER FOURTEEN

After a wakeful night, Vicky fell into a troubled sleep in the early hours of the morning, a sleep punctuated by horrifying dreams, so that at first the sound of screams and a barking dog seemed only part of them. When it broke into her consciousness it brought her out of bed with her feet on the floor before she was fully awake.

As she shoved her feet in slippers and ran along the back corridor, a door slammed and the furious barking became more muted but the screams continued unabated. She heard Harry Drummond's voice shouting, 'Beatrice, for God's sake! What's happened?' just as she reached the hall.

Beatrice was hysterical, giving scream after piercing scream. She was cradling her arm and there was blood all over it and her hand and her clothes. Inside Adam's flat the dog was barking in a sort of frenzy, hurling itself against the door so that it bent under each impact.

Harry was on the way downstairs in his pyjamas, his

hair ruffled from sleep. He reached Beatrice before Vicky did and without hesitation slapped her across the face. 'You're in hysterics! Stop this!'

It worked. The screaming stopped, but she began a sort of high-pitched keening. Her arm, Vicky saw, was lacerated from wrist to elbow and with a cry of dismay she grabbed a hall chair; between them they got Beatrice onto it.

Her face was ashen and she was swaying, as if she might pass out at any moment. With ruthless efficiency, Harry grabbed the back of her neck and pushed her head forward onto her knees. She struggled, but he held her firm. 'Stay there for a moment. You'll feel better.'

'The pain!' Beatrice moaned. 'The pain!'

Harry turned to Vicky. 'Is there something you can do – first-aid kit, painkillers? Get them.'

Vicky sped away, her own heart racing. The dog had stopped barking but it was whining now, with the occasional spine-chilling howl. She heard Harry say, 'Can you sit up now? That's better. Now tell me what the hell is going on.'

It took Vicky a couple of minutes to grab a clean towel along with the paracetamol and a glass of water but Beatrice was still struggling to frame the words.

'I – I don't know. I went in, no, I listened first. But, oh God! Adam—' She choked. 'It – it just sprang at me—'

Vicky handed her the water as Harry said sharply, 'Has something happened to Adam? Beatrice, what have you done?'

She looked at him as if she didn't understand what he had said. 'The blood – everywhere! And it just attacked—'

Harry looked at Vicky. 'I can't open the door with that

brute in there. I'm going to go out and look in the window. Let's just hope the patio door isn't open.' He went out through the front door.

Vicky put an arm round Beatrice's shoulders, offering her the painkillers and helping her to drink. 'You're safe now. We'll get that washed and bandaged properly once you're fit to walk,' she said, gently wrapping the towel around the arm.

It was only a moment later that Harry came back, his face grim. 'Adam's sitting there at his desk in a pool of blood – and I mean a pool. There's blood everywhere. The dog's guarding him. I'll phone the police – they'll need to shoot it to get in.'

'What about—?' Vicky gestured to Beatrice, who still seemed to be unaware of what was going on.

'We should get her to a doctor. Dirty things, dog bites – infect the bloodstream just like that. Defending its master, I suppose. Given what you told me last night we have to assume she just lost it. Balance of her mind disturbed, all that.'

That seemed to penetrate. Suddenly Beatrice sat up. '*I* didn't do it! I wouldn't—!'

'Of course not,' Harry said soothingly. 'We'll get everything sorted out. Now let's get you more comfortable – there's a sofa in the office, isn't there? And meanwhile Vicky's going to make you some hot sweet tea, for the shock. OK, Vicky?'

Vicky nodded and turned to go. Harry had got Beatrice to her feet and was taking her across to the office. As she crossed the hall and went down the passage she heard him say, 'Don't worry. The police will be here soon and you can just tell them what happened. They'll be very understanding – if they don't realise what a bastard he was to you, I'll tell them myself.'

She heard Beatrice give a frightened little bleat. 'I know, he was, he was. But I didn't do it, Harry, I didn't!' and Harry's voice saying, 'It'll be all right. You'll be fine.'

The phone rang while Kelso Strang was sitting at breakfast. It was quite hard to stay impassive at the startling news but Fiona Ross's head had swivelled when she heard it ring and she was even now making her way over, with a pot of coffee ready in her hand by way of excuse.

'Thank you, Sergeant. Yes, go ahead. That's fine,' he said and forced himself to stay at the table long enough to refuse a refill of his cup and finish his toast before standing up. The news would break soon enough, but he hoped not to be there when it happened.

He took the staircase up to his room two steps at a time. So Adam Carnegie, the man he believed to be a double murderer, was dead – brutally slaughtered, by the sound of it.

His first case as Senior Investigating Officer, the lynchpin of the operation. It was a challenge, yes, but he wasn't nervous – except, perhaps, in the way an actor feels before they go onstage.

He'd always had a fastidious distaste for detectives who positively licked their lips at the thought of a murder investigation. Murder was an ugly business and in your task of finding the killer you had to trawl through the sordid depths of human experience in a way that often left

241

you feeling dirty yourself, but that was the job. The victim deserved the justice of a successful prosecution.

But this one . . . He was struggling not to feel that justice, in its most primitive form, had been done already.

Sergeant Buchanan had given him the bare facts over the phone. The emergency call had come to him and now, with Strang's authorisation, he would get across to Balnasheil Lodge with a couple of officers as backup, but it would take some time for them to arrive. There was a problem with Carnegie's dog, apparently, and there was a vet being summoned as well – that would cause delay too. But he was right here on the spot and in Tennant's boat the crossing would only take ten minutes – on a clear day.

It wasn't a clear day, though. It was anything but. Looking out of his window he could barely see the pier immediately below, let alone see across the bay. Set off in that and you could find yourself out in the Minch or driving on to the rocks.

And anyway, did he want to involve Tennant in this? Buchanan had said that Adam Carnegie was dead and according to Harry Drummond, Beatrice Lacey had killed him so it might be as straightforward as that. On the other hand, it might not be and he wasn't sure he wanted Tennant, with a different agenda and a different police status, complicating matters. Backup from Broadford would arrive soon enough.

No, he'd have to take the car. It would be a long, slow drive in weather like this on a difficult and dangerous road; he quailed just a little at the thought, but there wasn't any alternative. He paused long enough to tell Sergeant

Buchanan his decision and to leave a message for DCS Borthwick, who wasn't yet at her desk in Edinburgh, then walked out into the mist.

It almost seemed to put up resistance to his passage, clinging to exposed skin as if slimy hands were pulling him back. He was shivering by the time he reached his car and climbed in thankfully, turning the heater up to full as he drove off.

The news reached Balnasheil before Kelso Strang had left his bedroom. The wife of one of the constables at Broadford worked in the local shop and she was eager to tell Daniel Tennant when he came in for his newspaper and half a pint of milk.

Without completing his purchases, he hurried along to the hotel, looking for Strang, reaching it just in time to see him driving away. He stopped dead, staring helplessly as the rear lights of the car disappeared into the fog. Then he swore.

Was he being cut out of the investigation, then? Was it personal dislike – or had Strang already labelled him a suspect? Despite the cold damp air, Tennant's face flared with anger. He had a right to consultation, surely, and he'd get his bosses to insist that Strang had no authority to keep another officer out of the loop. He needed to know what was happening.

His boat was moored not a hundred yards from where he was standing – at least he assumed it was, not that he could see it yet. To go out in it on a day like this was the purest folly but it wasn't far across the bay and the sea was flat; steer a straight enough course and he'd be first on the scene, without a doubt.

Pausing only to fetch his oilskins from the cottage, he unhitched the boat and fired the outboard motor. The sound was almost shocking in the breathless stillness of the morning.

Beatrice Lacey lay on the couch in the office, nursing her arm. She couldn't bring herself to look at her wounds but Vicky had brought a bowl of water with disinfectant to clean them up and then bandaged her arm, but she'd said they'd certainly need to get her to the doctor for a tetanus shot.

Certainly it was hot and throbbing now and even the painkillers that Vicky had given her earlier had done little to blunt the pain. She'd made an attempt at the tea she'd been brought but once Vicky went to get dressed, leaving her to rest, she abandoned it and it sat cooling now on the table beside her, with a thin skin of milk congealing on the top. But every time she lay back and shut her eyes, she started going through it all over again.

Beatrice had dragged herself out of bed at the usual time. She was feeling wretched but if she decided this really was the day to walk out, there were requisitions to be signed off and every day's delay in a shipment meant another day's hunger for a starving child. She was crossing the hall to her office when she heard the dog whining, a strange, groaning whine that went on and on.

She paused, waiting to hear Adam speak to it, tell it to stop, but he didn't. Perhaps the dog was in there on its own, complaining about being shut in, but that was strange – usually at this time Adam would be taking it for its morning walk.

It was definitely odd. She walked over to the door of the flat and listened. It sounded as if the dog was running to and fro. She hesitated, then knocked at the door and called, 'Adam!' Then again, louder, 'Adam!'

There was no answer. Had something happened to him? Had he fallen, say, and banged his head on the fender, and the dog was calling for help? She tapped on the door again as she opened it.

The attack was instantaneous. She barely had time to take in what was in front of her – Adam, sprawled across his desk, blood everywhere, splashed on the walls, on the carpet – before the dog was on her, barking furiously, slashing at the arm she had thrown up to protect herself, then closing its teeth and shaking it like a hare to be killed.

Even now as she thought about it she could hear herself screaming, feel the tearing agony and blind panic. She had tried to shake it off, beating it frantically over the head with the bag she was carrying in her other hand as she retreated backwards.

It seemed to be knocked off balance. Staggering a little as if its legs were uncertain, it had let go and somehow she managed to put the door between them before it returned to the attack. Even once the door was safely shut, the screaming had possessed her like some external force until Harry slapped her, and still she could feel it bubbling under the surface, waiting to burst out again.

She mustn't let that happen. She needed to rest, to stay calm, to get her strength back. The police would be here soon—

The police. Harry had summoned them – Harry, who had said something about her . . . In her distress it had hardly registered at the time, but now she remembered – he'd been talking as if she'd done it, as if she'd somehow killed Adam and the dog had attacked her to protect him.

And Vicky had seen her too, coming out with blood all over her. How could Beatrice prove to anyone that it was her own blood, not his? She'd talked to Vicky last night too when she was so upset, told her far too much. She was in trouble, terrible trouble.

Her heart was starting to flutter, like a trapped sparrow beating its wings against a windowpane. She felt hot and sweaty and burning pain knifed through her every time she moved her arm. What was she to do?

Run. The thought came to her as clearly as if someone had spoken it into her ear. *Go. Harry's going to tell the police you did it because he killed Adam himself, and if you try to convince them you didn't, he'll have to kill you too.*

Even getting to her feet was a struggle but she had to go up to the flat. She couldn't go without Rosamond and she would need one or two things – nightie, toothbrush. She picked up the bloodstained handbag that held her credit cards and walked unsteadily to the door, opening it cautiously.

Apart from the dog's mourning whimpering, the hall was quiet and there was no sign of Harry or Vicky. With the cloud down at sea level today it could take quite some time for the police to arrive, though she couldn't count on it. She needed to move fast – not easy for her at the best of times and much, much harder for her now.

She hauled herself up the stairs to the flat, dizzy and breathless. Bending over to pick up Rosamond from her crib, she felt so faint she had to sit on the bed but she allowed herself only a moment before she forced herself to her feet. She fetched the holdall and piled in a few things along with the doll, then very quietly she opened her door again and stepped out onto the landing.

The doorbell rang. She shrank back, ready to retreat as she heard Harry's brisk steps going across the hall below. He'd got dressed and she could see his hair was still wet from the shower. She heard him say, 'That's impressively quick! Come in, come in. We've got a right mess here.'

Beatrice risked another couple of steps forward until she could peer down between the banisters. If it was the nice inspector, perhaps after all she could talk to him, explain, and he would understand. It wasn't, though. It was the rude, unpleasant one who'd been carrying on with Eva, making trouble.

No, she would have to go, especially since Harry was saying now, 'Come up to the sitting room and I'll explain. Beatrice just flipped, I think, then the dog went for her, defending its master, I suppose. You'd better come up to the sitting room—' His voice sounded high and nervous.

Beatrice shrank back out of sight as they climbed the stairs to the first floor.

'You'll want to interview her, of course,' Harry said. 'She's resting in the office there but I'd better put you in the picture first. I could hardly blame her, you know – he treated her like dirt then laughed about it afterwards.' The sitting-room door shut and she couldn't hear any more.

She didn't need to. She felt awful, hot and cold at the same time, but there was one thing clear in her fuddled head. She had to go. She didn't know where she would go – not time to think about that now. Just – away.

Halfway down the stairs she stopped. Her car – it was parked round that side, right below the sitting-room window. They'd hear her go and come after her.

Adam's car, his treasured Merc, was always parked near the top of the drive – and he wouldn't be needing it any more, would he? she thought, surprising herself with her cold cynicism. Once, what Harry had just said about Adam laughing at her would have cut Beatrice to the heart but she seemed numb, somehow, as if she was floating above it all, detached. She had seen the man she had loved for so long lying dead in a pool of blood and she felt absolutely nothing.

The key was kept on a panel at the back of the hall so that Marek could drive it round to the other side for Adam if he was going away. Feeling very shaky, she had to cling to the banisters as she crept down the final flight of stairs, took it off its hook and let herself out, wincing as the lock clicked when she shut the front door behind her and stepped out into the embrace of the mist.

It bathed her face like a cold wet flannel and she felt herself revive a little; she walked a bit more briskly to the car. It had seemed so hot inside, she'd felt as if she was burning up.

The driver's door shut with a quiet, well-bred click. She looked at the controls, a little daunted; her head felt so muzzy inside and it was hard to remember what she'd done on the couple of occasions when she'd driven it.

There was a special way of starting it – yes, that was right.

The engine purred into action and she propped Rosamond up on the seat beside her then drove off down the drive. As she reached the road, she stopped and lowered the window to listen for the sounds of pursuit but there was only suffocating silence, as if the thickened air was a layer of cotton wool. She had escaped.

'I'd better explain the situation before I take you round to see for yourself,' Drummond said.

'He's definitely dead?' Tennant asked.

Drummond was looking grim but at that he gave a short laugh. 'You could say. It's pretty gory – place is like an abattoir. Couldn't see exactly what had happened from the window but piecing it together I reckon that Beatrice killed him, then the dog went for her. Adam had it trained like a hand-gun dog, you know – dangerous brute. It didn't like me – wouldn't have let me get within ten feet, but I guess it probably knew her better and it was only when she actually attacked Adam that it reacted.'

'Was she carrying a weapon?'

Drummond shook his head. 'Dropped it, I suppose. From the mess, I'd guess a knife. She was standing there, blood all over her, her arm savaged – completely hysterical. She's resting now, but she's probably still in shock. If you're hoping to get some sense out of her you might be as well to wait for a bit.'

'I'd want to wait till DI Strang arrives in any case. I think he's on his way. But did Miss Lacey have some problem with Carnegie?'

'Not until yesterday. Far from it, but – well, Vicky Macdonald will tell you about it, but it seems she discovered last night that Adam was married and she was distraught, absolutely beside herself, I imagine.'

Tennant raised his eyebrows.

'Oh yes, I know, I know. But basically he'd strung her along, keeping her sweet by hinting at marriage sometime, believe it or not. And this certainly took me by surprise too – never heard him mention a wife. Anyway, I'd better take you down and show you.'

Tennant followed him downstairs and out through a side door towards a small patio with French doors opening onto it, fortunately closed, but as they reached it the dog appeared on the other side, barking and snapping white, pointed teeth. As they stood their ground, it hurled itself against the panes.

They both retreated. 'I'm not sure how sturdy those doors are,' Drummond said nervously. 'Better not provoke it. There's a higher window I looked through before – it'd be safer.'

Cupping his hands against the glass, Tennant peered into the room. The desk where the body of Adam Carnegie was slumped lay below him and there was, indeed, blood everywhere. He couldn't see a wound but craning his neck he could see that there was a knife lying on the desk beside him. It looked like the ordinary kitchen variety.

He stepped back. 'The knife – do you recognise it?'

'Is there a knife?' Drummond said. 'I didn't notice – a bit shocked, I suppose.'

He was shorter than Tennant and he had to stand on

250

tiptoe. 'Oh yes, I see it now. Could have been his own –
fancied himself as a bit of a chef, did Adam. There was
one of those wooden block things in his kitchen. And that
would fit, if you think about it,' he said as he stepped back.
'Beatrice comes in first thing, spoiling for a fight, loses her
temper, grabs the knife—'

'It's one theory,' Tennant said coolly. 'We'd better let
the dog calm down before it barks itself into a fit. It's
sounding hoarse already. Perhaps I could speak to Vicky
Macdonald now?'

They found her in the kitchen, sitting at the table with a
mug of coffee in front of her, though she looked as if she'd
been staring at it rather than drinking it. She was very pale
and tired-looking and the look she gave Tennant wasn't
particularly friendly.

'Oh, it's you,' she said. 'Have you seen – him? What are
you going to do about it?'

'Not a lot, at the moment, until the vet arrives to deal
with the dog.' Tennant sat down at the table, nodding to
Drummond, who was holding up the coffee pot enquiringly.

'Oh.' She gave a little shudder. 'It's just I don't like to
think of the dog, you know, in there with him, the blood . . .'

Both had a struggle to put the image she had conjured
up out of their minds. Tennant spoke first, questioning
her about the morning's events. Her account squared with
Drummond's but she wasn't prepared to go along with his
accusation.

'You can't say Beatrice did it,' she argued. 'She had
blood on her, yes, but her own arm was bleeding. And I
can't see Beatrice as the sort to go berserk like that.'

'Tell me about her reaction to the news that Carnegie was married,' Tennant said.

Vicky looked accusingly at Drummond. 'Oh, you told him that, did you? She wasn't angry, Daniel, she was just very sad and upset – broken, more. You can't just assume that would make her a murderer.'

'Tell me about it,' Tennant said, and rather stiffly she described the phone call from Carnegie's wife. She seemed reluctant to go into detail; even when he probed, she said no more than that it was natural for Beatrice to feel hurt.

'And you could just as well say that his wife came and killed him because she discovered he had kept the marriage secret.' Vicky's voice was rising. 'You don't know, that's the point. You don't even know when it happened, really.'

'True enough,' Tennant said soothingly. 'Did you hear anything last night, then, either of you?'

Drummond, setting the coffee mug down in front of him, shook his head. Vicky said, 'No,' then hesitated.

Tennant's ears pricked up. 'Yes?'

'I did hear a car coming up the drive in the evening – nine, half past, probably. I wasn't paying much attention – I was watching a film on my iPad – and I think I just assumed you or Adam had been out somewhere, Harry. I didn't hear it going away again but then I wasn't listening. Marek at the gate cottage should be able to tell you.'

'I'll want to speak to him, certainly. And the last time you both saw him alive?'

They both spoke at once; Drummond waved Vicky on.

'I served supper to Adam and Harry, then came back to the kitchen. I didn't see him after that.'

'Much the same for me,' Drummond said. 'We finished eating and neither of us wanted a sweet so I came in and spoke to Vicky and I didn't see him again. After that I was working in the office – I'd been hoping to finish up in time to get back to Glasgow today.' He looked at his watch. 'When do you think your inspector friend will arrive? I'd like to get on with it.'

'Shouldn't be long now,' Tennant said. 'Indeed, I'd have thought he'd be here by now.'

She had set off without a thought in her head, except that she had to get away. But now as she drove into the grey murk, Beatrice could feel panic mounting. She'd never driven before when she couldn't see the verge more than a few feet ahead, with the headlamps reflecting back and making the mist look like a solid yellow wall in front of her.

Mercifully the car was an automatic – how could Beatrice have changed gear, when even turning the steering wheel inflicted acute agony? – but despite being power-assisted it seemed heavy and clumsy compared to the little Fiat she was used to, and that didn't help either.

She was feeling light-headed and strange as she inched forward along the narrow road. She should be thinking out what she was going to do but somehow her head felt funny and she couldn't seem to keep track of her thoughts; they twisted and wriggled away and disappeared before she could pursue them to any sort of conclusion. And the bends were so abrupt; she oversteered on one and the car swung across the road, mercifully right towards the hill, not towards the drop on her left that she knew was getting steeper – twenty, thirty, forty, fifty feet – though she couldn't see it today, Probably just as well.

The right-angle bend before the old bridge couldn't be far away. Yes, that looked like it now. She sounded her horn as a warning to oncoming traffic.

The roe deer, browsing on the hill above, took a sudden fright and jumped down onto the road, skittering away with a clatter of pebbles as the car rounded the corner. Beatrice screamed, jerked and the big car skidded on the wet road, slewing across it till it hit the stonework of the bridge, long in need of repair. With a rumble of masonry, one side collapsed.

CHAPTER FIFTEEN

Livvy Murray sat moodily staring at the opaque square in her kitchen wall that purported to be a window, trying to plot her day over a cup of black coffee. She hated it black but somehow the milk was sour again which meant she couldn't have cereal either and she'd forgotten to get bread so she couldn't have toast.

She had the report to file for Strang about Murdo John Macdonald and she was proud of it, but she wasn't getting her hopes up. Tennant had got in there like a rat up a drainpipe and Strang wasn't going to ditch someone from the oh-so-wonderful Met in favour of a wee Glasgow PC who couldn't even keep her job in Glasgow.

The old feeling of inadequacy overwhelmed her. Sometimes it seemed that no matter what she did, she'd never be anything more than that, just the way her mother had always said. She could just give up—

No, she couldn't! She was worth more than that; she

was tough, she'd done a good job so far, and if the snooty sod didn't recognise it, too bad.

The thing was, if she could just work with him she knew she could learn, and more than anything she wanted that – wanted to know the right way to do stuff and get results. She'd plenty to offer, she told herself; all she needed was training.

But she was stuck here, trapped. Her mouth drooped.

Then the phone rang, and that changed everything. She listened with astonishment to Sergeant Buchanan, who was sounding harassed and was tetchy when she demanded more details.

'Never mind that. Just be down the pier in twenty minutes, right?' he said, ringing off before she could give him her enthusiastic assent.

As she scrambled into full uniform and looked out her wet weather gear, her mind was racing. If ever a man had it coming to him, it was Adam Carnegie, but life was unfair and usually people who had it coming to them somehow didn't get it. He, it seemed, had, and she couldn't help herself giving a mental high five to whoever'd had the guts to do it. They weren't getting anywhere with nailing him for murdering those two poor girls – and who was to say he wouldn't go on to bump off one or two more if he wasn't stopped?

But if you were in the polis you weren't meant to think like that and she'd have to give the hunt for his killer her best shot – it could even be her big chance, and moral issues weren't part of her job description. Whatever – it would certainly beat manning an office in what was basically a service point for trivial enquiries and feeling the cobwebs starting to form all over her.

Anyway, she just wanted to know who'd done it. She was inquisitive by nature; not knowing a secret was like having an itch she couldn't scratch. Right off the cuff, she could think of several people who might have hated Carnegie enough to kill him.

And, she suddenly realised with unholy joy, DC bloody Smarty-Pants Tennant was one of them.

After the scream of brakes, the small explosion of the airbag inflating and the bang of the impact, the silence that followed was almost shocking. Half-stunned, Beatrice stayed pinned back in her seat as the bag slowly deflated. She moved, cautiously; she didn't think she'd been injured because everything seemed to work all right but Rosamond had pitched forward onto the floor and with a cry of dismay she strained forward awkwardly to pick her up, yelping at the pain in her arm as she did so.

'There, there, my darling! That was a nasty fright, wasn't it, but you're all right. Come to Mummy.' She put the doll on her lap, patting its back soothingly as she looked helplessly about her.

The car had ended up completely blocking the road, its bonnet crumpled into the bridge wall on the inner side of the road, but the rear end had completely demolished the left-hand side of the bridge and part of one tyre was actually on the edge. Still, it was a heavy car; it seemed stable enough and the driver's door was unaffected.

Another foot and it would have gone over the drop, down

and down into the sea below. Beatrice grasped dimly that she had been lucky but all she could think was how dreadful she was feeling, sweaty and clammy at the same time, and tears of pain, weakness and self-pity came to her eyes.

'What are we to do, Rosamond? It's not fair, is it?'

Then she smelt oil. There was something about oil, she remembered. Oil and fire, yes, that was it: the car could go on fire and they'd be burnt up. They had to get out of here.

She tucked Rosamond under her arm and reached to open the door with a trembling hand. It was always a bit of a struggle getting out of a car and not being able to use her injured arm to lever herself up made it worse. But somehow fear gave her strength and she managed to extricate herself, feeble, whimpering with the pain from her throbbing, swollen arm and pouring sweat.

But what was she to do now? She was finding it harder and harder to think clearly. The car was blocking the bridge so that she couldn't get past but there was some reason why she couldn't go back the other way, towards the Lodge. She couldn't think exactly what it was just at the moment but she knew she had to go on. To escape, that was it.

If she couldn't get past the car, she'd have to go round it. Beatrice could hear the rushing of the burn, see it springing down the stones in little waterfalls when she looked over the inside edge of the damaged bridge.

'We can't cross here, sweetie. It's too wide and steep – we'll have to go a bit higher up to where it's narrower, won't we?' she murmured to the doll. She'd have to take it slowly but the exercise would warm her up. She was starting to shiver convulsively now in the cold, damp air.

She slipped on the wet grass as she set off up the hill, giving a yell of pain as it jarred her arm, but she recovered her balance and with dogged, insane persistence struggled on.

It was infuriatingly slow driving. Kelso Strang was used to the haars that came in to the East Coast off the grey North Sea, but he'd never seen anything approaching this. It was like being in an aeroplane passing through a cloud layer – which, he supposed, was exactly what it was.

Even with the fog lamp on he couldn't see more than fifteen feet and on a road like this where anticipation was essential if you weren't to be caught out by a sudden bend, it became an endurance test. It seemed claustrophobic, too, with the shroud of mist blotting out the surroundings; even though he knew that he could stop and get out any time he liked, he still felt half smothered.

When his mobile rang he pulled in to a passing place to answer it, guessing correctly that it might be JB returning his call.

He thought he could hear tension in her voice. She listened in silence while he told her as much as he knew himself about what had happened at Balnasheil Lodge, then said, 'Not quite what I expected you to have to deal with. Still, they think it's straightforward enough? Have they arrested the woman?'

He found himself bridling at the implied lack of confidence. 'I don't think anyone will have got there yet. I'm on my way there now and there's fog like you wouldn't believe so unless there's a local prepared to risk life and limb to take them across by boat I'll be the first to arrive.'

'Hmm. Your ETA?'

'Hard to say, ma'am. Twenty minutes, maybe? There may be a delay anyway while they find a vet to deal with the dog – as I understand it, it's standing guard.'

'You'll take over as SIO, of course. Your big break.' There was a touch of mockery in her voice. 'I'll put in a priority request for a chopper to bring in your SOCO team, but from what you say they won't be able to get to you.'

'Not right now, certainly, but it can change quickly around here and it's probably very local, around the Cuillins. They may be able to put down somewhere else on Skye and take it from there.'

'Right. I'll work with that. Report back when you can.'

It was reasonable enough for her to be edgy, Strang told himself as he drove on. All the bad press Police Scotland had been getting had left the top brass reeling, and leaving a totally inexperienced SIO to deal with this new-style murder investigation was definitely high risk. But she'd been quite clear at the start that he was to be in charge – in naval parlance, she had said, 'You have the ship' – and he wasn't going to allow himself just to be elbowed aside the moment it got tricky.

Was it his imagination, or was the mist starting to lift just a tiny bit? It would be good if it was; he must be near that awkward bridge with the nasty right-angle bend and the drop below, and he realised he was gripping the wheel a little tighter at the thought of it.

He slowed down and saw that ahead of him the mist was discoloured in a muddy yellowish patch to one side of the road. It took him a couple of seconds to work out what he was seeing and then he braked abruptly. The yellow glow was the headlights of a car, being reflected back against the mist, and judging by the angle of the road, it was a car in a very odd position.

Strang got out of the car, feeling sick and starting to shake, his hand going unconsciously to the scar on his face. Blood, smashed bodies – Alexa, crumpled sideways against him—

But he forced himself towards it, his heart racing. It came into clearer view: a big blue car, a Mercedes, straddling the road with its nose embedded in the hill and its tail right on the brink of the crumbling edge. He couldn't tell how close the whole bridge might be to collapse and he stopped just short to assess the situation.

There seemed to be no damage except to the bodywork and the car was empty; the airbag had deployed so with luck no one had been hurt. The lights had been left on and the driver's door was standing open as if someone had got out in a hurry – as you would, if you thought you might find the road beneath you suddenly subsiding into the gulf below.

There was no indication how long it had been standing there. Strang edged his way forward cautiously, keeping close to the inside of the road, and felt the bonnet. It wasn't quite cold; perhaps ten, fifteen minutes since the engine was switched off? He hoped it was off; there was an oily smell in the air and he couldn't get past to check without climbing over the car – and who knew what effect that might have?

It was very, very quiet. Even the sound of the burn

splashing down the side of the mountain was muffled and there was no sign of anyone – presumably they had walked back towards Balnasheil Lodge. He called, 'Hello? Is anyone there?' but he didn't really expect an answer.

It was only then, with the assurance that there were no casualties and with his heartbeat steady again, that he took in the implications. The road was firmly blocked. They would need a recovery truck at the very least; even once they got it moved, the bridge wouldn't be safe without repairs – and Fiona Ross had said there was some sort of dispute about who was responsible anyway. It could be weeks – months, even, and as he stood there he could hear a rattle of small stones slipping off the gaping hole at the side of the road, making the damage worse.

What was certain was that he wasn't going to get to Balnasheil Lodge this way today. He'd have to back up round all those bends, with a limited view of the road behind him, until he got to one of the passing places that would grudgingly offer a barely adequate space for turning round. He groaned, and went back to the car. He took his mobile out of his pocket; he'd have to let Buchanan know what had happened.

Just as he reached the car again, he felt a faint breath of wind, sensed a movement of the air, and a gap opened in the cloud with dramatic suddenness to show him the ground dropping away just by his feet to the sea, a dizzying sixty feet below. It was only a moment before it was blotted out again but it did look as if the mist might be thinning out down below. Perhaps they'd get across in the boat shortly.

They already had, he discovered when Buchanan answered. The cloud was clearing at sea level and Murdo John Macdonald had agreed to take them over.

'In fact,' Buchanan said in what Strang recognised as carefully neutral tones, 'DC Tennant was here already when we arrived.'

'I . . . see.' Strang's response was equally careful. 'I'll get back to Balnasheil as quickly as I can and once I get there I'll phone for Macdonald to come across and fetch me.'

He rang off. He was just about to get back into the car when he heard a little scream from somewhere high above his head. His first startled thought was, *A seagull, surely?* but then he heard what was unmistakably a woman sobbing.

With the distorting effect of the mist it was hard to work out where it came from. He swivelled round, trying to pinpoint the sound, but the heavy air made it difficult. 'Hello!' he called. 'Who is that? Where are you?'

The sobbing stopped instantly and there was silence, as if she was holding her breath. Then he heard, 'No! No! Go away! Leave me alone!'

Strang had seen the hill on that side – a gradual ascent between scrubby trees from the road at first, but then steeper, rockier and more unforgiving as it rose into the mountain itself. It was crazy to be out there in weather like this and whoever this was had plainly got herself into trouble already.

'Stay where you are,' he called. 'You'll be all right. I'm coming to help you down.'

He pulled on his heavy jacket, then with considerable

misgiving clambered over the damaged wall beside the nose of the car and began the climb up the side of the burn.

'What do you know about what's happened at the Lodge?' DC Tennant said.

Marek Kaczka looked at him impassively, then shrugged. He had allowed the detective into his house reluctantly and was standing only a few feet inside the door, his arms folded and his legs apart, so that to get in further Tennant would have to push him aside.

He didn't; he merely stepped up close and the man took an involuntary step backwards, as he had calculated that he would. Then another step, and another, until Tennant had established who was in charge of the choreography. Then he smiled.

'Not good enough. What do you know?'

Kaczka was showing definite signs of unease. 'Nothing. I know nothing.'

'Why are you looking shifty, then? After what's happened, you're acting evasive – what are we going to think?'

'No! No! I don't know!'

He'd got him going now. He changed tack. 'You're not Polish, are you. What are you? Serbian? Albanian?'

The man had started sweating, Tennant noted with satisfaction. He wasn't saying anything, though, just shaking his head.

'Oh, we'll find out soon enough. And you don't like policemen, do you? Criminal record back home, maybe?'

The man's dark eyes spat hate. 'Mr Carnegie – he tell you. He has my papers.'

'But he's dead, isn't he? Dead in a pool of blood. Can't tell us anything now, can he?'

Kaczka's face was impassive. He said nothing.

'Don't want to talk about it, eh?' Tennant jeered. 'We'll get you in the end – you might as well make it better for yourself and confess now. Only way to get a lighter sentence.'

He realised suddenly there was someone standing behind him, someone who had come in the open door without him noticing.

'Sorry – could I have a word?' PC Murray said.

Furious, he turned on her. 'Not right now, for God's sake, Constable! I'm busy here.'

Murray stood her ground. 'I'm to take you back to the house, *Constable*.'

'I don't take orders from plods,' he snarled.

Even under this provocation, she didn't lose her temper. 'You've no authority here,' she said sweetly. 'This is a Police Scotland investigation and in any case, I don't know what you do down at the Met but here being CID doesn't give you a right to pull rank. Anyway, I just pointed out to my sarge that you have to be a suspect in this case and he wants a wee chat, right now.'

Tennant stared at her, then swore at her violently.

'The C-word? Nice,' Murray said. 'But abuse won't help. You'll find Sergeant Buchanan up at the Lodge.'

He had no alternative. Boiling with frustration and rage, he left and stormed off up the drive. Behind him he heard Murray saying, 'Good morning, Mr Kaczka. We're trying to find out if you noticed anything last night – any cars coming up the drive, say, anyone moving about, that sort of thing?' and him replying, 'Just car – it come, then go back after.'

The mist had lifted now. Ahead of him he could see a knot of people standing on the patio outside Carnegie's flat and he could hear a dog's frenzied barking.

Then there was the sound of a shot, and the barking stopped.

Beatrice wanted to wake up now. It was a horrible, horrible dream: she was outside, somewhere wild and scary, and she couldn't see where she was going, as if she was walking through sheets of gauze. It was steep and slippery under her feet and she was first hot then terribly, terribly cold and her arm was on fire. She'd fallen more than once and now it was getting rocky and her leg was grazed and bleeding. She'd even dropped Rosamond, twice, wailing in dismay as she grabbed her up. She had to go somewhere, do something, though she didn't know what it was, and there were people chasing her. And a dog – there had been a dog somewhere too. A terrible dog.

Beatrice tried hard to jolt herself out of it, shaking her head, shutting her eyes, opening them again, but it still went on. She could hear running water somewhere, and she remembered something about that. A burn – that was why she was here. She had to go up, that was right, and cross it, but she couldn't work out if it should be on her right or her left. Had she crossed it already? She didn't know. And now she couldn't even tell if she was going up or down. The ground under her feet was bumpy; sometimes it went down and sometimes it went up so with all this gauzy stuff everywhere she couldn't tell.

There was something you did to wake up – oh yes, pinch yourself. She reached down to pinch herself hard on the leg, then cried out at the pain – but the nightmare still went on.

Was she awake, then? So why would she be here? Disconnected images started tumbling through her mind. There was something about Adam, something awful – blood. Blood everywhere. And the dog – the sharp white teeth, the bared pink gums, the pain—

Her legs were wobbling with tiredness, the muscles twitching. Beatrice sat down heavily and toppled sideways, finding herself lying with her head and shoulders over some sort of drop – a foot or twenty feet, she didn't know. She gave a scream of fright and began to cry.

Then she heard the voice, someone calling. 'Where are you?' it said.

They were right there, chasing her. Somehow she muffled her sobs. There was a spindly alder tree growing almost out of the rock just beside her and panic gave her the strength to grab it and pull herself to her feet. She had to get away, hide from Them or—

She didn't know 'or what'; she only knew she had to go. Stumbling and tripping, she forced herself on into the damp greyness. But now there were voices talking to her: Adam, saying, 'What *are* you doing, sweetie?'; her mother scolding her for playing outside and getting dirty.

She argued with them, but very, very softly, so that They wouldn't hear, and talked, too, to the doll still cradled in her arm, though it was very muddy now. 'Shush, Rosamond. You must be mousy quiet for Mummy, like a good girl.'

She was so tired, though, so exhausted and she felt so

ill and shaky. She would have to sit down soon; just a few more steps up. Or down, maybe. She still didn't know.

Listening for any betraying sound, Kelso Strang began climbing up the side of the burn. There was mossy grass at this level as well as the stunted silver birches, and though it was steep and greasy underfoot it wasn't challenging for a fit young man.

His mind was busy. It was a reasonable supposition that the woman who had cried out had come from the wrecked car, reasonable too to guess that this might be the Mercedes he had noticed outside the Lodge when he was last there and had assumed to be Adam Carnegie's. So who was the woman who had crashed it?

Buchanan had said that Beatrice Lacey had been accused of the murder. Could she have been overcome with panic at what she'd done and decided to make a run for it?

Not a clever idea, whichever way you looked at it. Having met the lady, he could be sure she wasn't at all the sort to feel at home on a mountain in the best of weathers, let alone in conditions like this. If she had been trying to get away, the crashed car would have prevented her from continuing along the road but she must have been desperate indeed if she was thinking about crossing the burn higher up. And now Strang thought about it, Buchanan had said she was injured as well, after an attack by the dog.

He paused, still listening, but beyond the sound of the burn and the whisper of a breeze getting up, there was an eerie silence. He took a deep breath, then shouted as loudly as he could, 'Beatrice? Are you there? Call back and I'll come and help you.'

He waited, but there was no response. He tried again. 'Beatrice, it's dangerous. Don't move, just call to me and I'll fetch you down.' Still no response.

She could be anywhere – this side of the burn, the other side. And there were no paths on the higher slopes, just ledges and ravines and cliffs and steep scree, slithering away down to the sea below. An injured, frightened, clumsy woman would be lucky to get out of this alive. Even if she just stayed hidden somewhere without moving, she'd get hypothermia unless she was wearing proper weather gear, which seemed unlikely.

What they needed was a tracker dog. Surely they must have one round about here? People were always getting themselves lost in the mountains. Until they had one there was little point in pursuing her.

He called Buchanan when he got back to the car and it seemed his guess had been right. Beatrice Lacey was indeed missing, but there was good news too: there was a mountain rescue team based nearby, with an experienced dog, and they could be scrambled immediately. The helicopter with a scene-of-crime team from Edinburgh was on its way already and should be able to land right on the lawn by Balnasheil Lodge.

He could see that the mist was definitely less dense even where he was and the sun, which had been a ball of silver in the mist, was showing a gleam of stronger gold. That was something, at least.

* * *

She couldn't go on any longer, she just couldn't. But what if They were right behind her, creeping up on her already? Steadying herself against a rocky face, she turned fearfully to look.

She wanted to scream but the sound died in her throat. Looming behind her in the mist was a terrible shadowy figure, hugely tall, a glow of light round about its head. She shrank away backwards, and it moved after her. Forgetting her injury, she flailed about frantically then howled in pain.

Jerked out of her arms, the doll flew up, describing an arc in the air as it fell down, down, and disappeared. With a wail of anguish, Beatrice stumbled after it.

CHAPTER SIXTEEN

DCS Jane Borthwick looked out of the window as the helicopter banked and came in across the bay between the little township of scattered houses and what must be, from the group of ant-sized people clustered outside it, Balnasheil Lodge on the other side. It was clear enough here and the sun was even shining, but for all she could see of the Black Cuillin there might have been nothing there at all, beyond cloud and more cloud – the Misty Isle, indeed. They'd been worried they wouldn't be able to put down within miles of the crime scene.

She was very much on edge. This was going to be something of a test case for the Serious Rural Crime Squad – the first murder to have to be dealt with from such a distance. Certainly, the team she was bringing up with her was better equipped and much more experienced than any local constabulary could have hoped to be, and they would be in direct computer contact with forensic expertise. High priority too – the chief constable was very keen that his cost-cutting brainchild should work; the media would certainly be onto this in a flash. So – no pressure, then.

Borthwick was feeling uncomfortably exposed. She'd read the situation here wrongly to begin with and to leave Kelso Strang, a newly qualified SIO who was still in a vulnerable emotional state, in charge of what would inevitably be a high-profile investigation could be a costly mistake. She'd cleared her desk at record speed and been first to board the chopper.

It landed neatly on the upper lawn in front of the house and as she climbed down a uniformed sergeant came towards her, a big, burly man.

'Sergeant Buchanan, ma'am.' Then he gestured towards the group she had seen from the air standing on the patio beside the house, which included three or four uniforms and a woman holding a gun. 'The vet's taken care of the dog that wouldn't let us in, but everyone's been kept out since, as instructed.'

'Thanks, Sergeant. That's excellent.' She pointed to the group of three men and a woman that had emerged from the helicopter. 'I've brought the SOCOs with me. I imagine DI Strang will be keen to deploy them as soon as possible.'

Borthwick made to go towards the house but Buchanan said uneasily, 'I'm afraid there's a complication, ma'am. Miss Lacey – that's the lady who's been accused of killing Mr Carnegie. She's gone.'

'Gone?' Her eyebrows shot up. 'Gone where?'

'Well, we think – Mr Carnegie's Mercedes has gone, you

see, and DI Strang has called in to say that it's crashed on a bridge and it's blocking the road round from Balnasheil.'

'Is she injured?'

'He doesn't think so. But she seems to have gone up the mountain—'

'Up the *mountain*?' Borthwick gave an incredulous look in that direction. The sun was shining brightly now, and the outline of the ridge was showing as an ominous shape in the mist. 'Whatever for?'

The sergeant gave a sort of helpless shrug. 'Anyway, mountain rescue is on its way with a trained dog so we're hoping they can find her before she harms herself. It's no place to be on a day like this.'

'I can well imagine,' she said. This was certainly an unwelcome complication. 'So where is DI Strang now?'

'He's going to show them where she's gone. He'll maybe be a wee while, if they've a problem finding her and bringing her down. She's not just a very' – he hesitated, choosing his words – 'athletic kind of lady.'

'I see. Well, we'd better get on with things at this end as best we can.'

The SOCOs, together with a pathologist and a photographer, were unloading equipment as she walked over to the patio. It wasn't Strang's fault, of course it wasn't. He could hardly wander off and leave a murder suspect stranded halfway up a mountain, but her own anxieties made her feel a certain unreasonable irritation that Strang had allowed himself to get embroiled in this. It was lucky she'd decided to come herself immediately and that the investigation wouldn't have to be held up right at the start. Delays cost money.

The smell assaulted her as she approached, that unmistakable sickly waft on the air that you didn't forget no matter how many years you'd spent behind a desk. One window in the French doors had been knocked out and she could see the body of the dog lying across the threshold, a Dobermann Pinscher. It had been a handsome animal, lean and well-muscled, its black and chestnut coat smooth and glossy.

Poor creature! It wasn't to know that it was doing the wrong thing by guarding its fallen master. At least it had been killed with a clean shot to the head.

The vet was hovering, waiting to speak to her. She was a fresh-faced woman, not much more than thirty, and she was looking distressed. 'Do you want me to stay or can I go now? I've got patients waiting for me.'

'Yes, by all means. We know where to find you, presumably.' As the woman turned to go, Borthwick said sympathetically, 'Sorry you've had to do that – a nasty thing to ask of a vet.'

She grimaced. 'You could say. If I had my way I'd shoot the people who train them like that, not the poor dogs.'

It wouldn't really do to give wholehearted agreement to this when you were a chief superintendent, so Borthwick only made a sympathetic noise as she peered through the glass. The desk where the man's body lay was to the left but, craning her neck, she could see that it was a gruesome spectacle – a severed artery, judging by the amount of blood.

One of the SOCOs came over to her. 'We've got everything out of the chopper now and the pilot needs to get back, ma'am. He's asking if you'll be wanting him to pick you up later.'

Borthwick hesitated. 'Hard to say, at the moment, until you can tell me what the situation is. I'll call in later.'

There was nothing she could do here now except get in the way. In a house this size there must be somewhere they could set up; perhaps Buchanan had seen to that already. As she turned round to ask him she realised that there was a man waiting to speak to her and she looked at him enquiringly.

'Can I introduce myself, ma'am? I'm DC Daniel Tennant, from the Met. I think my bosses may have spoken to you.'

'Oh yes,' Borthwick said coolly. Police Scotland hadn't taken kindly to finding that London had installed an undercover officer to spy on Adam Carnegie without having the courtesy to mention it.

'I'm happy to be of any assistance that I can,' he said. 'I've had a fair bit of useful CID experience and I'm sure they would agree if you wanted to co-opt me to this investigation.'

Borthwick suddenly became aware that there was a young uniformed constable who seemed to be jiggling about behind Tennant's back, trying to catch her eye. She was quite short, pale-skinned and brown-eyed, with hennaed hair that was almost pink scraped back in a scrubby ponytail under her cap, and now Borthwick had noticed her she mouthed something urgently.

Tennant, unaware, was looking at her expectantly, but she said only, 'I appreciate the offer, but we have a team in place now. I can understand that there are investigations the Met may want to undertake but I'm afraid that will have to take second place.'

Over his shoulder she saw the antsy PC relax, then edge away. Tennant said petulantly, 'I think that's a pity, ma'am, because—'

She cut him short. 'Sorry – excuse me. Sergeant Buchanan! Is there a room we can use?'

As she walked into the house with him she said, 'Tell me, who was the young policewoman who seemed to be trying to warn me about Tennant?'

Buchanan smiled. 'That's Livvy Murray, ma'am. With the local force, but doesn't much like it. She's from Glasgow and she's got a mouth on her but she's not daft. She's sort of taken a scunner to Tennant – he's that wee bit superior, maybe, and she's prickly. She's insisting he has to be a suspect because he'd some sort of relationship with this female that disappeared, Eva Havel.'

'Yes, I know all about her. And could PC Murray have a point?'

Buchanan looked doubtful. 'In theory, maybe. But the eyewitnesses saw Lacey coming out covered with blood, having been attacked by the dog, and taking off like that does look like an admission of guilt.'

'I suppose so. We'll just have to hope we get her back in a condition to be questioned. Now, find us coffee and then you can talk me through it.'

The dog was a neat black-and-white Border collie with sharp bright eyes that darted about, assessing its surroundings, while constantly checking its master's face for instructions.

'Looks an intelligent animal,' DI Strang said to the owner,

a middle-aged man with a weather-beaten complexion, who smiled proudly.

'Oh aye, he's clever lad, Moss,' he said. 'Loves a callout. Not exactly a tracker, mebbe, but he'll ken fine if someone's been past and it's hardly going to be busy up there the day, is it?'

There were three in the team, all men in heavy anoraks wearing serious climbing boots and carrying emergency gear.

'No,' Strang agreed. 'To be honest, I don't think Beatrice – that's her name – can be far away. She's a lady of – how can I put this? – a certain girth, but she thinks she's in trouble and may well be hiding. If she's just cowering somewhere we should get her quite quickly but I can't see her coping with this terrain. She's carrying an injury and I'm afraid she may be a bit confused so I'm worried about what might happen to her if she's moving about. I think she was probably trying to cross the burn higher up, so we could follow that line to start with.'

'You're coming up, sir?' The team leader gave a doubtful look at Strang's footwear.

'You lead on and I'll follow. Don't worry – I won't do something stupid and lumber you with someone else to bring down.'

'Och, not a bit – we'll just leave you lying there,' the man said jovially. 'Anyway, the wind's picking up. We'll have better visibility any time now. Right, lads, off we go. Moss!'

At the first sign of movement the collie had started racing round them, tail wagging so hard it was almost moving in a circle, giving joyous barks. As the men climbed over the low wall on the inside of the bridge it streaked up the side of the burn, low to the ground.

Strang followed. There was indeed a swirling wind, capriciously clearing the mist in patches, then letting it surge back, but it was definitely thinning now and the sun was tinting the grey with a sullen ochre.

The men ahead were moving with that steady, swinging mountaineer's gait and though he'd done a bit of hillwalking himself he was left behind, following the sound of their steps and voices, and the occasional excited whining of the dog.

She must have been asleep, or something, because Beatrice couldn't think how she'd got here. She was slumped against a rock, as if she'd fallen, and she felt hot and very, very cold at the same time. It hurt to breathe, as well. She crossed her arms to try to hold herself together and a terrible spasm of pain shot through her. Her right arm seemed clumsy, huge; she looked at it, bewildered.

Rosamond. She suddenly remembered Rosamond. Something terrible had happened to her; she'd gone to get her but the ground just dropped away. She'd almost fallen herself – that was right. She could see the edge from here; the mist wasn't nearly so thick now. She must have crawled back, sat down and fallen asleep.

But she remembered something else too, the great menacing thing that was coming after her and the terror that possessed her before convulsed her again. She daren't look round, she daren't—

And there was something else, too, something that had wakened her – and now she heard it again. A dog, barking. She knew what was going to happen next.

Somehow she got herself up, though every single bit of her hurt and her head was swimming so that she felt sick. What was she to do? If she hid, maybe the monster and the dog would pass without seeing her. It was her only hope. She shrank into a cleft in the rock.

But They weren't passing. They were coming closer and closer; she could hear Them talking, hear the terrible, eager whining of the dog and she backed away, back and back, the way she had come, towards the place where Rosamond had fallen.

Strang had somehow missed the line the others were taking. He could hear them above him now and he stopped to try to get his bearings.

He was only about twenty feet above the road and the mist was lifting every minute. He was standing at the foot of a small rock face, perhaps fifteen feet high, and it sounded as if the mountain rescue team was above it. He was turning to retrace his steps when he saw a flash of white at the bottom and went across to investigate.

There was a doll lying there, a doll whose lacy clothes were stiff with mud and whose delicate face had been smashed in on one side. It lay against the rock that had done the damage, one eye missing and the other eye open, its blank blue gaze directed up to the clearing sky.

He paused, frowning. What would a doll be doing in a place like this? It was muddy, certainly, but it didn't show any sign of having been exposed to the elements for any length of time. Could it have anything to do with Beatrice?

The mist had swirled back again round here and he couldn't see all the way along below the bluff; could she have fallen with the doll and be lying somewhere further along?

He heard the dog giving a couple of excited barks, suggesting that it thought they were closing in. With a hollow feeling in his stomach, he walked on.

'Do you think I could have a word with her, Sarge?'

PC Livvy Murray had been hanging around outside the upstairs sitting room where DCS Borthwick was establishing an incident room, waiting for Sergeant Buchanan to come out.

He looked down at her, amused. 'You can always try. She hasn't bitten anyone yet.'

'Maybe you could just introduce me. Just, you know, say I don't want to interrupt her or anything—?'

'It's not like you to be backward in coming forward. What's happened to the gallus Glasgow spirit?'

She pulled a face at him. 'I know, but I'm needing to get to her before Strang tells her I'm rubbish. I'm not wanting just to be shoved aside but I'm not wanting her to think I'm just being pushy or anything.'

'How on earth could anyone imagine that?' he said with heavy sarcasm, but he was grinning as he opened the door again. 'Would it be convenient for you to have a word with PC Murray, ma'am?'

Borthwick looked up from the laptop she was working on at the dining table brought up from downstairs to act as a desk. 'Yes, fine,' she said, and turned to wave Murray to one of the upright chairs placed in front of it.

It had been plain that Murray had been trying to tell her something while she'd been talking to Tennant, and then had slipped away; it had been quite a bold action for a humble PC and she was curious.

'What was it all about, Constable?' she said with her usual directness.

Murray coloured. 'I just wanted you to know DC Tennant shouldn't be involved in this, that was all. But you told him he couldn't, so that was all right.'

'You see him as a possible suspect?'

'It's logical, ma'am. We don't have a time of death yet and Miss Lacey could just have gone in and found him.'

She could even be right, at that. 'So – you're accusing DC Tennant?'

'I'm not accusing anybody. It's just he went radge about us not pulling out all the stops when Eva Havel disappeared and I think she was his girlfriend. That's a motive.'

This wasn't the time to play guessing games. Borthwick said repressively, 'I think we'll just follow the normal investigative procedure of establishing the facts before we indulge in theories. Thank you, Constable—'

'There's something else,' Murray said hastily. 'Marek Kaczka – he's the sort of handyman, and he heard a car coming up the drive last night, and then leaving again not long after.'

Borthwick pricked up her ears. 'Oh? Have you reported that?'

'I haven't seen DI Strang. I'm not sure who else is working on it so I thought I should report directly to you. There's another thing too. I did an interview with Murdo

281

John Macdonald – he's the barman at the hotel. He's married to Vicky, who's the housekeeper here, but I got him to admit to me that he'd been in love with another girl who disappeared. Still is, if you ask me, so if he thinks Adam Carnegie killed her too—'

Borthwick cut her short. The girl was obviously trying to get her piece said before she was dismissed; it sounded as if she had in fact come up with useful information but she hadn't time at the moment to indulge a PC whose experience of investigations had obviously been derived from too many crime series on TV. Still, she was always on the lookout for talent and there was no need to discourage her.

'All right, Constable. Speculating is pointless at the moment. Record whatever information you have and see that DI Strang gets it in an easily digestible form and then we can take it from there.'

She could see Murray trying not to look too gauchely pleased. 'Thank you, ma'am. Does – does that mean I'm to be working on the case?'

'In a very junior capacity,' she said dryly. 'Just do what you're told. You're not Sarah Lund.'

Murray said demurely, 'No, ma'am. Haven't the sweater for it. Thank you, ma'am.'

When she had gone, Borthwick smiled to herself and when Buchanan came back in she said, 'PC Murray – bit of a live wire?'

Buchanan groaned. 'Goes off like a firecracker. Needs to be sat on sometimes.'

'She seems to have come up with some useful stuff,

though. Find her a slot where she doesn't get too discouraged but she can't do too much harm.'

'Yes, ma'am,' Buchanan was saying when the door opened and one of the SOCOs in his white suit came in.

'Thought I'd give you a snapshot of the preliminary stuff, ma'am. Carnegie's throat was cut – severed carotid artery on the right-hand side. The doc won't be specific but time of death is certainly a lot earlier than first thing this morning.'

PC Murray had been right about that, anyway. 'Surely he can do better than that?' Borthwick pressed.

'Could be yesterday evening. He did say it wasn't likely to be after 2 a.m. but he's still doing tests. The other thing is that the weapon is a kitchen knife that's lying on the desk just beside him. We've printed him and we've just dusted the knife for prints. As far as we can tell, they're all his.'

Borthwick's first thought was how disappointed PC Murray was going to be.

DC Tennant had gone back across the bay, furiously angry. He'd had to phone his guv'nor and tell him what had happened, and he hadn't been best pleased.

Admittedly, it would surely mean they could get in on a search warrant – if the old bag who'd taken control didn't freeze them out. But what the Met might want clearly cut no ice up here – bloody Scots – and he wasn't going to have a chance to shape the way the investigation developed. There wouldn't be any urgency about seizing the records and Harry Drummond, who was as smart as he was slippery, was probably even now making sure that no one could lay a glove on him.

Tennant sat at the window, looking balefully across to Balnasheil Lodge. Somehow he had to play himself back in or he would be dangerously ignorant about their thinking.

He opened his laptop, more or less idly, and clicked on the extensive file labelled 'Adam Carnegie'. And then it struck him: if they offered Police Scotland access to this it would save hours of police time replicating the research, which would provide a powerful incentive to cooperate, in these cost-conscious times. He scrolled through it, checking the details, then stopped, frowning.

The man's life history was there, in some detail. There seemed to have been little problem about establishing the basic facts; it was only his patterns of travelling and his business transactions that had been obfuscated by the criss-crossing of his and Drummond's electronic footprints and proved impossibly difficult to unscramble.

What wasn't there was any mention of the wife who had sent Beatrice Lacey into meltdown. She could be a recent acquisition, and he put in a request to have that checked, but this was certainly something else he could raise with Borthwick.

No point in waiting. He grabbed his jacket and went back down to the boat.

As PC Livvy Murray went away, glowing with satisfaction after her meeting with DCS Borthwick, her stomach gave a hungry growl and she realised she was starving. Models might get through the day on black coffee for breakfast but she was more the full-Scottish-with-double-black-pudding type.

With fond memories of Vicky Macdonald's shortbread,

she headed for the kitchen, hoping that if Vicky was there she could persuade her to break out the box – if the other greedy beggars who were buzzing around hadn't got there before her.

She certainly wasn't the first. When she came in, Vicky, looking very weary, was filling an insulated Thermos flask and pointed out another with a tray of mugs on the table.

'I'm keeping these topped up. They're going through drinks like there's no tomorrow,' she said. 'If you want something to eat, they've brought in a couple of boxes of sandwiches – over on the floor there.'

It wasn't shortbread but it was better than starving. Murray grabbed a sandwich and a bag of crisps, then said sympathetically, 'Are you having to cater for this lot?'

'No. They make all the arrangements. It's just the coffee.' She screwed the top on the second flask and set it down, then went through to the larder and came back with another tin and measured some into the filter machine. 'Have you heard anything about poor Beatrice yet?'

'Beatrice? What's she done?'

'You haven't heard? Oh, Harry Drummond accused her of having killed Adam and she got scared and disappeared. I don't believe she did, not for a moment.'

'Who do you think did, then?' Murray asked hopefully.

She gave a short laugh. 'Harry himself, probably. They were having a tearing row yesterday and it wasn't the first time either—' Then she broke off. 'Oh, I don't mean that, really.'

Murray stopped mid mouthful. 'What was the row about?' she asked indistinctly.

'Couldn't hear. Probably something about the business

side of the charity. Daniel definitely thought there was something going on there.'

This was proving to be quite a useful chat. 'He was very upset about Eva, wasn't he?' she prompted, but just at that moment one of the detectives from Portree came in.

'Any chance of a coffee, miss?' he said, and the moment passed.

She simply couldn't take any more. Beatrice could hear Them coming nearer and nearer, hear the dog whining. They had brought it to attack her again, and now They were calling her name, 'Beatrice! Beatrice!' and the dog was barking.

They might not see her round the rock but the dog would smell her. She knew what would happen; there was a picture playing in her head, an echo of something she had seen: blood on the dog's mouth and chest . . . It would go for her throat this time and anything would be better than that.

She had retreated as far as she could and now she was right at the edge of the rock face, where Rosamond had fallen. They were almost on her now; she could hear the dog, panting as it came closer and closer. She stepped off.

CHAPTER SEVENTEEN

It was the tree that had saved her: a mountain ash, its gnarled, wizened branches spread wide, clinging to a cranny in the rock face, and it did enough to break Beatrice Lacey's fall so that Kelso Strang was able to move below and cushion her landing with his own body. He lay for a moment, winded, half stunned and pinned down by her weight, then he called for help, afraid to move in case she was badly injured.

It took the rescuers, and Moss, only minutes to reach them and at the sound of barking, Beatrice, who had been moaning feebly, started struggling to get up.

'It's going to kill me!' she screamed. 'Keep it away! Keep it away!'

At a gesture from its master the dog lay down, silent, and he moved forward.

'It's all right, Beatrice, you're safe now. Gently, gently.' He directed an anxious look at Strang, still trapped below her. 'You OK?'

'Fine,' he said, a bit breathlessly. 'Is she all right?'

The leader bent over Beatrice. 'There's blood on her clothes but it's not fresh. What hurts, love?'

She looked up at him in bewilderment, then groaned, 'Arm, my arm.'

'Nowhere else? Back? Legs?'

'Don't know. Everything. My head,' she said, but she was sitting up now and with infinite gentleness they managed to slide her off Strang.

'Phew! Thanks,' he said, taking a deep, shaky breath, and stood up, rubbing his head.

'Must have been quite an impact,' the leader said dryly.

'Tree broke her fall,' Strang said, pointing. The little ash lay, broken, at the foot of the bluff.

'Lucky for you,' he said, and one of the other men said, 'I don't think she's been much hurt in the fall, just scratches and bruising, but she's very hot and from the look of the arm it's infected and we don't want septicaemia. Better call out the ambulance and we'll start getting her down to the level.'

He turned to Strang. 'Want me to take a wee look at you? You've a nasty bump there.'

'Nah. Like they say, it's only my head. If you don't mind, I'll leave you lot in charge. I've this and that to do at the other end.'

Limping, Strang hurried back down to the car. His head was painful and he could feel the bruises developing down his back and legs; he'd pay for this tomorrow but he'd had worse dealing with a stramash in the Grassmarket on a Saturday night. He was desperate to get to Balnasheil Lodge: his first murder investigation as SIO and he hadn't even got to the scene yet – and it didn't help to know that Tennant was there screwing everything up with his aggression.

He'd better let JB know he was on his way now, though. When he called the Edinburgh number he was dismayed to learn that she was at the Lodge herself ahead of him.

That was bad news. She'd obviously come up the minute she heard about it, which didn't suggest total confidence in his ability to cope, and if she was concerned it didn't look good that he wasn't there, on the spot, however good his reason for that might be.

Was she going to take control, usurp him? He would, he realised, mind that very much indeed, would feel it was a betrayal. And he wasn't going to accept it meekly – not without putting up a fight.

Sitting on the jetty beside his boat, Murdo John Macdonald caught Sergeant Rab Buchanan's eye. He must have been there for at least two hours and he didn't look as if he'd changed his position, huddled in his oilskins and just sitting staring out to sea as if he was lost in his own thoughts.

He went over to him. 'Come on, Murdo John! No need to sit out here. I don't know when we'll be needing you again and you must be perished. Away in and get a cup of coffee from your wife. She's doing a rare job there in the kitchen and there's sandwiches too.'

The man looked up at him blankly, almost as if he hadn't understood what had been said, and Buchanan went on, 'On you go, man!'

Murdo John only shrugged, but he did get up and walked off towards the kitchen. Buchanan looked after him, shaking his head. He'd heard the rumours that Vicky was away from her husband, and under his stolid exterior beat a profoundly romantic heart; he might be an unlikely Cupid but you never knew what could happen if you got folk talking again.

It was lucky he didn't follow him into the kitchen. The elevenses rush had died down and Vicky was alone there when Murdo John came in.

She greeted him coolly. 'Coffee's there. And a sandwich, if you want it.'

He nodded and went over to take one. With his back turned to her, he said, 'I hear your friend Adam's got what he deserved.'

'He's not my friend!' she cried angrily. 'He was my boss and he was a profoundly unpleasant man – I think we can agree about that, at least.'

'Are you wanting to come back?' he said, still without looking at her.

'Crawl back, do you mean? Despite the gracious invitation, no thank you. I'll stay here meantime.'

He poured milk into his coffee, added two sugars with meticulous care. After a moment he said, 'Why did you marry me, Vicky?'

It took her aback. 'What do you mean? The usual reasons, I suppose. Why did you marry me, come to that?'

Murdo John's eyes went to her face for the first time. 'I don't know,' he said slowly. He stared at her for a long moment. 'Perhaps . . .' Then he stopped.

Vicky frowned. 'Perhaps what?'

'Perhaps it was a mistake, on both our parts.' It

290

didn't sound as if that was what he meant to say.

She glanced at him sideways as she collected coffee mugs for washing. 'There isn't much point in prolonging this discussion now, is there?'

'No. I'll take this outside – they'll maybe be wanting me at the boat.' He went to the door with the mug in his hand.

'Bring it back when you've finished with it, then. We're desperately short with all these folk wanting coffees.'

As the door shut behind him Vicky gave a great, shaky sob. It was really getting to her, and there was no sign that things would improve any time soon.

It was around midday that the news reached Broadford. The elderly woman who came into Karen Prescott's gift shop barely paused to pick up the birthday card that would provide her with an excuse for coming in before she burst out, 'Terrible thing at that charity in Balnasheil – what's it called? Human something – funny-like name for a charity. Did you hear about it?'

'Human Face? No – what's happened?' She was only mildly interested. A terrible thing could be someone having broken their leg – or, given the woman who was speaking, their fingernail.

'Well!' The woman propped her hip against the counter, licked her lips and prepared to enjoy herself. 'See that man – him that owns it – can't mind the name—'

'Adam Carnegie?' She had Karen's full attention now.

'That's right. Found murdered – blood everywhere, they're saying. And there's this woman that works there – Miss someone – she's done it!'

'Lacey?' Karen said faintly. 'How do they know?'

'Scarpered, hasn't she? Took off before the police could get to her. They're chasing her now.'

'Where are you getting all this stuff from?' Karen spoke sharply but her legs were shaking. 'It's probably wildly exaggerated. A cold in Portree's pneumonia by the time it reaches Broadford.'

The woman bridled. 'Oh, it's right enough. One of the polis told his girlfriend, her that works in the Co-op, and I've just come from there.'

'Oh.' Karen didn't know what else she could say; she just knew she had to get the woman out of here, shut up shop and get back home to Quentin. At least the Broadford gossip machine seemed to have slipped up on that connection so far, but it wouldn't take long. She reached for the card the woman was holding.

'Were you wanting this?'

'Oh – oh aye, I suppose so.' She produced the money, clearly disappointed by the muted reaction to what she had felt was a morsel of gossip of the choicest sort. 'I'd better get on. I've a lot of messages to do.'

I'll bet you have, Karen thought grimly as she put up the 'Closed' sign and locked the door and drove back to the house.

Quentin jumped guiltily to his feet when she came in. 'I didn't think you'd be back so early,' he said. There was a bottle of beer on the table in front of him.

'Evidently. I wasn't actually planning to.'

When she told him, he went white and sat down again as if his legs had given way. 'What – what on earth would make her do a thing like that?'

292

'Oh, I think we both know, Quentin, don't we? And I want to know what we're going to do about it.'

He sank his head in his hands. 'Oh my God! Bloody woman—'

'Not the best word to use, in the circumstances,' she said coldly. 'I just want you to know that I'm going to make it plain I was only doing that because you made me.'

'I didn't!' he protested. 'I'd like to see who could make you do anything you didn't want to. Anyway, it was only a joke.'

'Tell that to the police. And come to that, I've only your word for it about what happened last night.'

He went whiter than ever. 'But I told you,' he cried. 'I wanted to see how Beatrice had reacted—'

'I don't want to know more about this than I have to. You're sure he was still alive then? You and Beatrice didn't get together—'

'No!' he howled. 'Of course not! That makes no sense at all!'

'So what are you going to tell the police? I want this sorted out.'

He glared at her. 'I may not have to tell them anything. This may never come out. Who's going to tell them?'

'If you don't, I will.'

'But that's just plain stupid. No one knows I went out there and the phone call could have come from anyone.'

Karen looked at him pityingly. 'Did you never watch CSI? They'll be checking through the phone records as we speak. That phone could ring any moment now—'

He eyed it as if it were a poisonous snake. 'I – I could

just have been phoning her for a friendly chat.'

'And you think she won't tell them? When they catch up with her – and don't kid yourself, they will – and ask her why she suddenly decided to murder the man she loved, she'll say it was just a sudden impulse? That she just got up this morning at a bit of a loose end and thought, "Oh, I know what I'll do, I'll murder him"?'

'That's not funny.' Quentin was angry now.

'This whole thing isn't funny. Go to them before they come to get you. And find yourself somewhere else to stay – I don't want to be involved in this any more than I am already. I'll have your things packed up and waiting for you when you get back.'

DCS Borthwick glanced up as DI Strang came into the room. 'Oh, there you are! That's good. There's a lot you need to catch up on.' Then, taking a closer look at him, she raised her brows. 'Been in the wars?'

Strang pulled a rueful face. 'I'd have to say that as a method of apprehending a suspect it was – unusual. But we both lived to tell the tale.'

She listened as he told her what had happened, then briefed him on what had led to Beatrice being accused. 'But at least the poor woman will be getting proper medical attention now. The thing is, it's looking as if the man actually killed himself.'

'What? Slit his own throat?' Strang was incredulous. 'When he had a shotgun available?'

'They'll do lab tests on the knife, of course. But the team leader is pretty definite – the knife was lying beside the body and apart from a few slight smudges the fingerprints were all his and the grip pattern was right, apparently.'

Strang digested that. 'Did he know they were after him for fraud? Seems drastic, even so.'

'We've spoken to his partner, who did a lot of tooth-sucking then said he'd had dark suspicions about Carnegie – the sort, apparently, that you wouldn't think of sharing with the Charity Commission. The sound of hands being washed was almost deafening.'

'So I suppose we have to bring Tennant in on this?' he said reluctantly.

'It won't please your little PC,' she said, smiling. 'They don't seem to have hit it off.'

'Murray, do you mean? She's nothing to do with me. It's just she's been desperate to get in on the case – bored here, I suppose.'

'Quite a bright spark, I thought. Keen to point out that Tennant was a suspect, when we still thought it was murder.'

'I hadn't thought of that, I admit, though I suppose she'd have been right. But he could be useful now, even if I don't like his methods.'

'He's been useful already. He's been able to tell us that there's no record of Carnegie being married, despite the phone call from his alleged wife, which was what set off the whole thing about Beatrice. I've agreed to let him loose on whatever paperwork we find as a sort of quid pro quo.'

It really was Sod's Law that so much should have happened in the time he was away. He could feel his chance to take back control slipping away. 'So what's the current situation?' he asked, sounding as positive as he could.

'I authorised the SOCOs to get started and they've got all they need from the body so I've agreed to release it to be taken back for tests. The current estimate for time of death is late evening, early morning, and the pathologist and the photographer have both finished now. The chopper's on its way and I've recommended they send off anything they can – I've arranged for top priority, so it shouldn't take too long to get some results.'

It was hard not to let her see how irritated he felt. It was his job as SIO to give all the permissions and he would have preferred to see the body in situ for himself, but you didn't argue with a DCS. Particularly not this one.

'No problem,' he said.

Borthwick wasn't fooled. She looked at him with a faint, ironic smile. 'It's all right, I'm going back with them. You're still in charge.'

'Oh – er—' he stammered.

She laughed, giving him one of her direct looks. 'Oh, you're not wrong – taking over, parachuting in someone with more experience, was a temptation. But the whole point of the pilot scheme is that it should be possible to operate within the structure that's been set up. So over to you.'

Would she, he wondered cynically, have taken the same decision if it hadn't been suicide? He doubted it, which made him feel defensive, but he said gracefully, 'I appreciate your confidence in me, ma'am.'

'Mmm,' she said. There was still a hint of a smile lurking round her mouth. 'So, Inspector, what happens now?'

He didn't hesitate. 'This may have been suicide, but there are still two girls who went missing, presumed dead. I just want to see if anyone has changed their story now the threat of Adam Carnegie's displeasure isn't hanging over them.'

Not having been SIO before, Strang had never visited a crime scene in the immediate aftermath. His detective work had been done from photographs and computer film, and graphic though these were it wasn't anything like this. He put on a white suit and overshoes from the pile by the door then paused on the threshold for a moment, fighting down his visceral reaction.

There was the smell of blood, for a start, sweet and cloying. And here was blood, indeed; it looked like a scene from the Grand Guignol.

The body had gone already but its position was sketched in chalk on the desk, where Carnegie had fallen forward, arms outstretched. The wall above had been sprayed with blood and the saturated carpet below looked as if it was rust-red, not pale gold.

In the rest of the room there was a pattern of red paw prints where the frantic dog had raced round and round, spreading the blood even onto the woodwork and the French doors.

It was gruesome, horrifying. But then the shocking secondary impact hit him: how normal everything else was. The ambience was calm, attractive; a gleaming kitchen at one end, expensive sofas and table lamps, still burning, good prints on the walls – Rothko's *Rust and Blue* above the desk, spattered with the rust-red of blood now.

A laptop lay on one of the sofas, as if Carnegie had just set it down to fetch the knife that had killed him – Strang could see the expensive hardwood block, with one slot empty, standing on the work surface. The knife itself was lying bagged on the desk and covered with fingerprint powder beside the chalk outline of where it had been found.

The SOCOs seemed to be starting to pack up. He turned to the team leader, a dour-looking man with a sour expression.

'That's definitely what was used?' Strang said, pointing to it. He was still sceptical.

The man looked at him askance. 'The prints match perfectly and they're in a grip pattern as well. It's certainly big enough and sharp enough – it was quite a neat little slit in exactly the right place, just severing the carotid artery. Not a bad way to go – he'd be dead in minutes, seconds, even, and lose consciousness before that. And there's no sign at all of any disturbance.'

Strang nodded, then indicated the laptop. 'Anything on that? Note, email, anything?'

'No. Watching hard porn. Must've just closed it down and gone to the desk,' he said firmly as he picked up the bagged knife. 'The chopper's due shortly. We've got what we need so we're close to finished here now.'

'Really?' Strang swivelled again to survey the room. He just wasn't buying this. Here was this man, sitting in his comfortable room, indulging in his sleazy little pleasure, who then gets up and sits down at his desk to slit his throat? Hard to bring yourself to slice your own skin; much easier to pull a trigger, and he'd had a gun readily available. No, whatever the immediate evidence might say, he reckoned this was a crime scene.

'Other prints around the room?' he asked.

'Any number. We'd need to get prints from everyone with legitimate access if we were planning to take it further.' He sounded discouraging.

Strang wasn't discouraged. 'What about the handle of the patio door?'

The man pulled a face. 'Smudges. You couldn't take anything from that.'

'But not a clear print from Carnegie?'

'Not clear, no. Plenty round about on the woodwork.'

He looked round about him again. Certainly, there hadn't been any sort of altercation; if Carnegie had been killed, he'd been taken by surprise. Even so . . .

'But wouldn't you have expected to find that, if he'd shut it himself?'

'Not necessarily. Could just have been the way he did it. You can't go reading anything into it.'

His tone was dismissive and the message was clear: the expert has spoken.

Strang wasn't about to accept that. 'I don't want anything scamped. Treat this as a crime scene.'

The man glared at him. 'It'll cost, you know. Take us into the second day.'

'I've noted your objection. Carry on.'

This whole thing could blow up in his face. Strang knew all about the budget constraints, but JB had told him he'd have to be a maverick; it was his job to cause trouble.

He spent a little more time there, wondering if he was right: would the dog have permitted the attack on its master, for instance? But he'd made his decision and, satisfied that his orders were being, however reluctantly, carried out, he left and headed down the drive towards Kaczka's gatehouse.

At the interview Tennant had sabotaged with his aggression, Strang had been convinced that the man knew something useful that he had been frightened to say, and his position might be quite different now.

PC Murray had been lying in wait for DI Strang and when he emerged from Carnegie's flat she called after him. 'DI Strang!'

He turned. 'Yes, Murray?'

He didn't exactly look overjoyed to see her, but she fell into step beside him. 'DCS Borthwick told me to report to you, sir. I've found out there was a car that came here last night. Are you going to see Kaczka?'

'Yes, I had planned to.'

She shot him a sideways look. OK, he'd a lot on his mind and he was trying to get rid of her but if there was one thing her earlier police experience had taught her, it was that you stuck your foot in the door when someone tried to shut it in your face.

'This morning Sergeant Buchanan detailed me to ask him if he'd noticed anything last night and he said he'd heard a car come up the drive and then it went away a bit later. So maybe we should be considering that as the time of death, not first thing in the morning. That would mean—'

He cut her short. 'Forensics will be able to establish an

approximate time of death very shortly so there's not much point in playing guessing games, is there? In any case, at the moment the evidence suggests he took his own life.'

'You mean – it isn't a murder investigation after all?' She couldn't disguise her disappointment.

With some acerbity, he said, 'Murder isn't an entertainment, Constable. Anyway, we're still trying to establish what happened to those two girls, so—'

He broke off. A car came up the drive and stopped, about fifty yards from the house. A man was getting out, an overweight man, who was staring at the activity going on outside Carnegie's flat. Even at this distance, Murray could see that he had a strong resemblance to Beatrice Lacey and the expression on his face was anguished.

Strang walked over to him. 'Looking for someone?'

'Yes. I need to speak to the person in charge – there's something I need to tell them.'

'You're speaking to him. DI Strang. And you are?'

'My name's Quentin Lacey. My sister—'

'Right. Look, I think you'd better come inside so we can talk, sir,' Strang said, and with Murray, unbidden, following them, he took Lacey into the house and, looking round, saw the door to Beatrice's office was open.

'This will do,' he said. 'Do you know what's happened to her?'

Quentin sank onto a chair beside the desk, taking out a handkerchief to mop his forehead. 'I know she's murdered Adam and done a runner,' he said.

'She ran away, yes, but the evidence at present doesn't suggest she did anything else.'

Lacey's jaw dropped. 'You mean – she didn't do it?'

'I can't comment. The investigation is still at a very early stage, but we have no reason to believe that she did.'

'Oh.' He assimilated that. 'So where is she now?'

'In hospital.' Strang explained what had happened and to his surprise and disgust the man burst out laughing. 'Something funny?'

'Oh God, it's just that it's so like Trixie, to do something bloody stupid like that! Her up a mountain—'

'She was in a fevered state with what looks like blood poisoning from dog bites,' he said coldly. 'I'll be getting a report on her progress later from Broadford Hospital. I expect you'll want to go and see her.'

'Of course, of course,' Lacey said hastily. 'Thank you for letting me know.' He got up with some alacrity.

'Just a moment,' Strang said. 'You said you had something to tell us. What was it?'

He licked his lips nervously. 'Oh – nothing, really. Just – I wanted to say I was her brother, you know, and if I could be of any help—'

'I don't think that's true,' Strang said flatly. 'Could you tell me your movements last night?'

'Last night?' The handkerchief came out again and Lacey wiped his brow. 'I – I was at home, with my partner.'

'All evening?'

'Er – yes.' He didn't meet Strang's eyes.

'And she will confirm that?'

He gulped, then said shakily, 'Yes, of course.' He couldn't have made it clearer that she wouldn't if he'd said, 'No, she won't.'

Murray chipped in. 'It was you who came up to the house last night, wasn't it?'

Lacey, whose head had been bowed, looked up with a certain defiance. 'Oh, all right then, yes, it was. But what was wrong with that? I came out to see my sister; Adam Carnegie came out with his dog and warned me off the premises, so I left. That was all.'

'I think we had better get a formal statement from you. You may have been the last person to see Mr Carnegie alive.' Strang glanced at his watch and then stood up. 'PC Murray, perhaps you could do that and report back to me later.'

'Yes, sir,' she said, and drew a deep breath. This was her chance to make him realise that she was every bit as good as Tennant could be at squeezing the truth out of a witness.

'Maybe you should sit down again, sir. This may take a wee while.' Murray took the chair opposite him and took out her notebook.

Lacey cast her a look of dislike, but obeyed. 'I hope it won't take too long. I've a lot to do today.'

'I'll need to take the full background. Did you know your sister was hoping to marry Mr Carnegie?'

He looked as if she had struck him in the face. 'What – what do you mean? Of – of course not.' Realising the denial was unconvincing, he blundered on, 'She's – well – she's not exactly—the idea would be preposterous.'

'Preposterous? That's not a very nice thing to say about your own sister.'

'Well, she – he wouldn't—' He was floundering. 'Look, can we get back to the business in hand?'

303

'Did you know he was married?'

'No – how would I know? He might have been – nothing to do with me, anyway.'

She noticed, with sharpened interest, that he was literally twitching. 'Why are you twitching? Is that a difficult question?'

'No, no, of course it's not.'

He'd started sweating again too. 'It is, though,' she insisted. 'You're sweating now.'

Lacey opened his mouth but no sound came out. He just looked at her helplessly.

For the first time in her police career, she scented blood. She could *make* him tell her. This was heady stuff.

'You're a rubbish liar,' she said scornfully. 'We didn't believe you when you said you'd just come to offer to help. What did you come for?'

He was staring at her now like a rabbit transfixed by a stoat. Then he groaned. 'Look, there was something I was going to tell you but when you said Beatrice hadn't done it, there was no need. It's just a personal, private thing, that's all—'

'He didn't say she hadn't done it, just that it was unlikely.' She ignored a warning twinge of conscience and went on brazenly, 'No such thing as private, in a murder investigation.'

'Oh, all right then. Beatrice told me she was going to marry Adam and I didn't trust him – didn't think he would make her happy, you know?'

The concerned brother bit wasn't very convincing in the light of what he'd said already but since he was going on she let that pass.

'So I asked my partner if she would phone up, just as a sort of joke, really, and say she was Adam's wife. I'm convinced the man's a crook and I thought that would make Beatrice realise how little she knew about him. He'd probably deny it if she challenged him but I was going to point out that he would, wouldn't he. And that was all it was. Nothing for you there, is there?'

Oh, he was a right little sweetheart. Murray didn't even try to hide her distaste when she said, 'Nice brother, you are. You didn't think she might be a wee bit upset about that?'

He seized on it. 'Yes, of course I did. That was why I was coming out to see her, to comfort her.'

'Having got her all wrochit up in the first place? That's nice.'

Lacey glared at her. 'It's not your place to lecture me. I thought you were just meant to be taking a statement? This seems a very unprofessional way to be going on.'

She paused; perhaps he was right. The sense of power had gone to her head a bit, maybe. 'Anyway,' she said, 'what happened when you got here last night? What time was it?'

'I'm not sure – sometime after nine, I think. I had just parked the car when Adam appeared and I said I wanted to speak to Beatrice. He said she wasn't feeling well and I said I wanted to see her anyway. And I – well, I may have said something about him trying to cut Beatrice off from her friends and family and then he got very aggressive, accused me of only being interested in – oh well, that doesn't matter.'

Murray had quite a good idea of what the accusation might have been, but mindful of the 'unprofessional' remark didn't push it.

'He told me to get off his land. He'd that brute of a dog with him and he just made a gesture and it snarled at me – said he'd "explain to the dog" he didn't want to see me again. So I didn't stay to argue. All right?'

'You were probably the last person to see him alive.'

'Apart from the murderer,' Lacey pointed out.

She made a non-committal noise. Evidence about Carnegie's state of mind before he decided to kill himself was important, but she'd painted herself into a corner; the question was difficult to frame, after what she'd said about murder.

She tried, 'What sort of mood was he in?' and got an incredulous stare in return.

'Aggressive. I told you.'

She tried again. 'Yes, I got that. But did he seem upset, agitated, anything like that when he came to the door?'

'Why would he be? He didn't know someone was going to pop in and kill him, did he?'

Defeated, Murray said, 'Well, I think that's all my questions. Now if I can take you through a formal statement—'

She had to listen to Lacey's grumbles on the way through it, but she hardly heard them. She'd tidied up one small mystery and if it did turn out not to be suicide after all, she'd scored off one suspect from the list. Having thought he'd put paid to Beatrice's marriage plans, he wouldn't need to kill Carnegie.

She was well pleased with her success. *Eat your heart out, Tennant!*

* * *

Marek Kaczka wasn't at the gatehouse. That was annoying; he could be anywhere around the estate. DI Strang shielded his eyes against the watery sunshine to look around.

In a characteristic change of mood, it was a pleasant day now. The air was clear and the sky benign; there were sun sparks glinting on the sea and a soft breeze was blowing. He looked across the bay to the Black Cuillin ridge, almost clear of mist now though with a few patches still lingering in the corries. The rain the previous night had fallen as snow up on the tops and the slopes were white, mottled with black rocks still showing through. It was a magnificent and oppressive presence; he would hate to live in its shadow, himself.

He heard the sound of an engine, somewhere down by the shore. The tide was out, exposing the green-yellow tangle of seaweed by the rocks and the mudflats beyond, and a mini-tractor with a trailer full of bladderwrack was driving up towards the outbuildings with Kaczka at the wheel. As Strang went back up the drive the sharp, fishy smell drifted towards him, the nostalgic tang of a hundred childhood visits to the beach.

Kaczka switched off the engine as he approached but didn't get down, only giving him a guarded look from under heavy brows.

Strang smiled at him, gesturing to the cargo. 'Fertiliser?'

The man nodded. He didn't smile back.

'Could I have a word, sir?'

To his surprise, Kaczka said, 'Yes. Good,' as he climbed down to stand beside him.

'There's something you want to tell me?'

'You ask before. I not can say.'

'What was it about?'

'Girl. Eva.'

'Yes?' Strang found he was holding his breath.

'That day – he take her. In jeep. He come back – no girl.'

'Where did he take her?'

Kaczka pointed down the drive, then sketched a curve up onto the hill that rose behind the house.

'What's up there?' Strang asked sharply.

The man dropped his head. 'Cliff,' he said.

He commandeered the jeep. Had Eva known what was coming, as it lurched over the rising moorland, just as it was doing now? Had she tried to get out, had he restrained her or even knocked her out beforehand – or had she thought no more than that her lover was taking her out for a drive?

Strang had thought all along that she was dead, and dead at Adam Carnegie's hands, but thinking and knowing were two different things. This was the perfect disposal method for a body – tipped into the sea where the currents could take it and even if it came ashore there would be nothing to connect it to this place. There were hundreds of unidentified bodies washed up all over the world – no, thousands, probably.

The moor was thinning out now, its vegetation burnt off by the salt spray, with clumps of short rough grass taking its place around the outcrops of grey rock. It was springy under his feet as he left the car and climbed the last few yards to the top.

The cliff edge was abrupt, a shocking sheer drop of a

couple of hundred feet, and to the left it ran for about two hundred yards to where a tail of rocks formed one side of a shallow bay. To the right, it rose steadily and it looked as if the cliff might continue round the corner, out of sight. It was, he supposed, possible that Carnegie might have driven on over there, but the logical assumption would be that nearer was more likely.

Strang walked along, a discreet ten yards from the edge, scanning the ground for any signs. The jeep's wheels had bitten in today after all the rain, though perhaps if it had been dry and hard when Carnegie came up on his murderous errand there would be nothing to mark the place. But you had to think that at this time of year on Skye conditions like that would be rare.

And there it was: a set of wheel tracks coming up from the moor not far from where he'd parked himself, with a turning circle where the jeep must have headed back down. He went along to where they stopped and, taking that as his mark, walked in a straight line up to the edge. The land on either side rose but here there was a small, flatter dip almost like a platform. He stood there, looking down.

Here the sea was deeper, grey-green, with waves that were just tipped with white. The wind was stronger in this exposed position too, though it was still little more than a light breeze. There were a few herring gulls drifting by below, the young birds still in their mottled plumage, but the colonies on the cliffs were empty and silent now.

She must have been so terrified. Had she stood here, knowing what was coming, or had she been taken unawares – or even been mercifully unconscious when Carnegie threw her over? Strang could only hope so, though mercy was probably a concept foreign to the man's nature.

Then with a creeping horror he remembered the dog that was always at the man's heels, the dog trained to be slave to its master's ugly will. Had he given her a choice of deaths? And if so, which had she chosen? It made him sick to think of it. Was it possible it had sickened even Carnegie at the last, sickened him to the point where he could no longer live with the monster he had become?

So was this where it would all end – in an assumption? No body, no grave?

There was something mesmeric about looking down over a naked drop like this. There seemed to be a sort of magnetic pull, drawing you down, down into the abyss and onto the savage teeth of a protruding ridge of jagged rocks below. With a little shudder, he took a step back.

Just then something caught his eye, something right down there at the foot, between the cliff and that curving line of rocks, something caught there – clothes, fabric of some kind.

Strang stared at it for a moment, then broke into a run back to the jeep.

CHAPTER EIGHTEEN

Harry Drummond had proved elusive. With permission now to examine the files that had probably cost Eva her life, DC Tennant had gone in search of him. The communal sitting room was now DCS Borthwick's incident room and when he found out which was Harry's bedroom, he wasn't there either.

He was standing in the hall, wondering where to look next when a door at the back of the hall opened and Drummond came out. He was scowling but when he saw Tennant the frown vanished immediately. He even managed a small social smile as he reached him.

'Well, how are things going? Any sign of Beatrice yet?'

'Yes, I understand she's been found. But we're being told that the likelihood is that Mr Carnegie took his own life. Can you think of any reason why he might have done that?'

Harry seemed appropriately shocked. 'Adam – killed himself? Poor fellow!' He shook his head, then said, 'But—' and stopped.

'Yes?' Tennant prompted him.

'I hesitate to say this, but you may remember that yesterday when we spoke I mentioned that there were one or two aspects to his running of the charity that made me a little uneasy. It was nothing I could quite put my finger on, of course – if there had been, naturally I wouldn't have let it go on—'

'Naturally,' Tennant said with heavy sarcasm.

Drummond ignored that. 'I wonder if it's possible he was mixed up in something, got himself in too deep, perhaps. If, say, he felt that the authorities were onto him—'

'Oh, we were. Are, in fact.'

He didn't blink. 'Really? You must be very much on the ball, considering that he managed to cover it up from me. What are the charges?'

'We prefer to review the evidence before we charge anyone. So – access?'

'Certainly. Let me take you through to the little office. There's a filing cabinet there with paperwork – I'll give you the key. And then of course Beatrice will have the passwords for the charity admin files, through on the main office computer.' He seemed entirely unmoved by the request.

He'd had plenty of notice and presumably the files were squeaky clean now, Tennant reflected with some chagrin as he followed him across the hall.

'Did you see Mr Carnegie last night?' he asked.

'Oh yes, we had supper together.'

'And what sort of mood was he in?'

Drummond stopped, considering. 'Now I think of it, he was a bit on edge. Yes, very definitely on edge, in fact. He had gone to Glasgow for some reason, so perhaps something had happened there that upset him. I remember the meal wasn't up to the cook's usual standards and he was complaining about that – certainly out of temper. And yes, I suppose he could have been worried. If he'd just confided in me, perhaps this wouldn't have happened.' He shook his head again, giving a small, sad smile.

Tennant had a strong stomach but this was testing it. The man had been doing his best to smear his associate and the hypocrisy was nauseating. With malice aforethought, he said, 'We'll be checking on your documents too – bank statements, credit card accounts, tax returns, travel records and so on.'

The smile vanished. 'Accounts? Travel records? What do you mean? I can understand that you need to look into Adam's affairs to see if there could be some motive for his suicide but I fail to see what mine could have to do with it!'

'Ah, that inquiry is only tangential to my own inquiry. I'm cooperating with Police Scotland, but I'm from the Met, investigating fraud. We've been trailing you both for months.'

He took enormous pleasure from seeing Drummond's jaw drop and his face turn a sickly shade of grey.

As a police motorboat took him back across the bay, DI Strang was mentally ticking off his next steps. He'd alerted the coastguard immediately; they'd need to get a boat round there before the next storm blew in and dislodged whatever it was that he had seen at the foot of the cliff. And they would need a command centre on the mainland; they'd got a couple of police boats on site at the moment and it only took ten minutes to cross, but they'd be taking a lot of equipment now.

He wasn't sure if JB would be back in her office yet, but as he got out of the boat he was dialling the number. She wasn't, but he left a message to ask her to call him back.

The police office was the obvious place to establish an incident room. It had been downgraded to little more than an information centre and soon even that would be closed down, but whatever they needed could be brought there. He set off along the shore road towards it, and when he saw PC Murray ahead of him climbing the hill he called to her.

She stopped obediently. 'Sir?'

'Is the police office open just now? I want to have a look at it. We need a base on this side.'

Murray looked appalled. 'But it's minging, sir! There's rooms no one's been in for months and there's buckets everywhere if it rains. They won't spend any money on it because it's being closed soon.'

'But you're living there, aren't you?'

'I'm used to it. If it's tipping it down I can sleep on the sofa downstairs – and at least I get a bathroom to myself. In fact, if the leaks are bad enough I can shower without leaving my bed.'

He smiled. 'It'll only be short term. We'll manage.'

'I'll let you in.' She fell into step beside him. 'I've a report to make on Quentin Lacey anyway.'

'His statement? Oh yes, write it up, file it and I'll see it later.'

She wasn't going to be brushed aside. 'There's some points you might like to hear about,' she persisted.

He glanced at her. She had a cat-that-got-the-cream expression on her face; he'd enough on his mind without pursuing the irrelevance that was Quentin Lacey, but it was probably easier just to listen than to try to stop her.

'All right. Give me the broad outline.'

'He's a real creep, that man. I asked him if he knew his sister had been planning to marry Carnegie, and he just laughed at her. "Nice sort of brother, you are," I said to him.'

He winced at the lack of professionalism. She noticed, and said defensively. 'Oh, I know it was just a statement about his movements you wanted but I decided to use my initiative and push him a bit.'

'Did you?' he said, without enthusiasm.

'Well, I could see he was getting sweaty and twitchy so I asked him why he should be so nervous. He said it was just a private matter so I said nothing was private in a murder inquiry—'

Strang stopped. 'You said *what*?'

She coloured a little, but went on defiantly, 'Well, I knew it wasn't really, but I got him to tell me what it was all about, didn't I? He'd got his partner to phone and tell Beatrice that she was Adam's wife. Nice, like I said, eh?' She looked at him in triumph.

He said coldly, 'I had told you that present evidence suggests suicide. You deliberately lied to a witness. We don't do that.'

She didn't back down. 'It got him to tell me what I wanted to know.'

'I authorised you to take a statement, not conduct an interview. There is a difference.' Strang started walking on up the hill, with Murray trailing behind. 'And shall I explain to you why we don't use lies to pressure witnesses? Some police officers do it but personally I don't like feeling grubby and I don't think it's necessary. Apart from anything else, let's say this turned out to be murder after all. We charge him and he tells his brief that he was tricked into a damaging admission by an officer who told him a lie – we're in trouble. The case could even fall. In any case, I expect decent standards from anyone under my command – no lying, no bullying. Is that clear?'

She didn't respond. When they reached the police office she unlocked the door in silence, her face still set in mutinous lines.

Strang looked around him. Her ethics might be seriously flawed but her judgement about the police office was spot on. The front desk where Murray worked was in good repair with a waiting area and a computer, but the rooms behind in what had been the small police station were thick with dust. The wastepaper baskets hadn't been emptied and the floor around was littered with old forms and files that no one had bothered to remove.

There were two decent-sized offices that he could press into service, but cleaners would have to be drafted in before anyone could use them. Apart from that there were what could only be called cubbyholes, mainly in use for storage, as well as the traditional lock-up where a drunk could sleep it off if necessary. Poorly ventilated, it still seemed to have retained a sort of foetid smell. It might serve its turn as a temporary morgue, if that was needed.

As they stood together in the larger of the offices he

said, 'You were right about the state of the place anyway. Minging it is. Can I put you in charge tomorrow to see the cleaners get started? We'll be bringing in what we need for a major incident.'

Murray looked up sharply. 'You mean it is murder? Because—'

He shook his head. 'Nothing's changed there. But Kaczka gave me information about seeing Carnegie take Eva Havel up towards a cliff in his jeep and he didn't bring her back. There's some debris that we will have to investigate in the sea below the cliff. The coastguard are dealing with it now.'

'*He pushed her off*?' She was aghast.

'I guess. Pushed her, threw her – who knows? She may even have been dead or unconscious at the time – let's hope she was. Anyway, I've a lot to do. I'll leave it to you to arrange the cleaners.'

As Strang walked back down the hill, he scanned the sky anxiously. It was still looking calm enough – fairly settled, he would have said, if by now he hadn't realised that you never said that around here. But the coastguards would only have – what? A couple of hours, maybe, before it got dark.

Would they even be able to reach the spot today, let alone get a diver down? A sudden storm could sweep every scrap of evidence away.

When the door shut behind him, Livvy erupted. She kicked the wastepaper baskets across the room and when even that didn't satisfy her she began kicking at the wainscot. She was furious with herself, even more furious than with

317

him. She'd left herself open to his lecture on police ethics, demonstrating what a pathetic lowlife he thought she was.

Ethics were all very well but the villains weren't bound by ethics, were they, and if you let them put one over on you without doing whatever you could to stop them, you were a mug. She'd got from Lacey what she'd set out to get, so Strang could get stuffed.

Oh, she took his point about not falling foul of the laws of evidence – which were all rigged to favour the criminal anyway – and that was just a matter of training, if she could get it. This whole thing was a manufactured fuss, frankly. So why was she feeling uncomfortable?

She remembered the delicious feeling of having power over that sad old bastard. She'd enjoyed seeing that he was afraid of her, enjoyed seeing him squirm. And what did that say about her as a person?

There had been a sergeant at the station in Glasgow who'd got off on scaring kids. She'd loathed him, and cheered when he got in trouble for it. Grubby, Strang had said, and he was right.

Oh, sod it! She looked round the room; all that her explosion had achieved was to create more mess and now she'd stopped kicking the furniture she'd just have to pick it up.

She did that, then went through to the main desk to arrange for the cleaners and to write up a suitably careful report on Lacey, leaving out any mention of the way the information had been obtained.

But her thoughts kept returning to the poor girl who'd ended her days at the bottom of the cliff. She'd believed Eva was dead, sure, but that wasn't the same as knowing how it had happened.

And she didn't for a moment believe that remorse had driven Carnegie to kill himself. More likely he'd done some dirty deal and reckoned the guys who were coming after him had even less appealing ways of getting their revenge. Good riddance!

The ward round started at six o'clock in the morning. Beatrice Lacey, waking out of a drug-induced sleep, was completely disorientated at first. She was in an unfamiliar room, there was a nurse taking her temperature and when she looked around there was a splint immobilising one arm where a needle was feeding in something from a drip bag on a stand beside the bed she was lying in. Her other arm was bandaged and a bit sore.

The nurse was smiling as she filled in the chart at the foot of the bed. 'That's good!' she said cheerfully. 'The doctor will be pleased with you. Feeling better this morning?'

She ached all over but she definitely was feeling better. She'd been so confused, so frightened the night before but this morning her head was clear.

'Yes, I think so,' she said cautiously. 'My mouth's very dry.'

'That'll be the painkillers. They'll be round with the tea trolley in a minute. Want me to help you sit up?'

With movement, the aches became sharply painful, but propped against the pillows and sipping a cup of tea, Beatrice began the struggle to separate reality from nightmare.

Adam was dead. That was reality. Her throat constricted but the tears didn't come. He'd betrayed her; she knew that too. He had led her on to think of marriage when he had a wife already. And the dog – that was real too. The horror of the blood, the attack, her own screaming, her savaged arm – all too real. She still didn't know how she had escaped, except that the dog had seemed shaky on its feet.

She remembered Harry slapping her and then accusing her of killing Adam – as if she would, whatever he had done – and she remembered her escape, even her own reasoning for taking the bigger, more comfortable car.

It was after that everything got confused. There was thick mist, and a mountain – surely she wouldn't have been climbing a mountain? Then Rosamond, something had happened to Rosamond – and now the tears did come to her eyes. She couldn't remember properly what had happened to her baby.

Then there was the other memory – a terrible, shadowy figure that had pursued her. That must be nightmare, surely? But then she'd fallen – that was why she was so sore.

Now she was in hospital, so the police must have found her. She must have been mad to try to run away; perhaps she'd been in shock after what happened. She needed to talk to the police, explain . . .

And then Beatrice remembered the other reason she had fled. Her hand began to shake so that she had to set down her cup.

She should have gone to them long ago with what she knew. That she hadn't, made her – what was the phrase? An accessory after the fact, that was it. But it wasn't like that, really. It was just that she hadn't permitted herself to think what the implications were of what she had seen; it would destroy everything she had lived for if she was forced to believe Adam was so entirely wicked.

But he was, wasn't he? And because Beatrice had so determinedly shut her eyes, another innocent girl had died. Worse than that, while she was upset, she'd told Vicky things she shouldn't have and even though she'd taken it all back when she realised the implications for herself, she didn't trust Vicky not to tell the police.

Even before all this she'd half thought she might confide in the nice inspector. She'd be wise to take her chance to explain everything, before they came to accuse her.

And she could ask for protection from Harry. He'd always scared her; he was so aggressive, such a bully. She wasn't going to tell the police what she suspected – indeed, knew in a sort of way, if she'd allowed herself to admit it – because that would involve her, but Harry wasn't to know that. And she didn't have the slightest doubt that if he thought she was a danger to him, something would happen to her. Just as it had to Adam.

The next time the nurse looked in, she said, 'Please can you get a message to the police that I want to talk to Inspector Strang urgently? It's very important.'

Strang opened the curtains the next morning with some anxiety. Everything hinged on the weather; nothing could happen if the storm they'd been talking about had come in more quickly than expected. At least he hadn't heard the wind blowing.

There was condensation on the pane and as he rubbed it away he realised it had got very much colder overnight.

The sun was barely up, the dawn sky showing fiery streaks of red and purple and the still sea a muddy blue-grey. Each blade of grass along the verge on the road below was distinct, defined by hoar frost, and the outline of the hill above the Lodge on the farther side was crisp as an etching.

He gave a sigh of relief. They had got a boat to assess the site late yesterday and there should be nothing to stop them getting a diver down today; with the price of hand-dived scallops there was no shortage of experts around.

Fiona Ross was lying in wait for him as he came into the dining room. 'What a tragic, tragic thing,' she said, eyes gleaming with prurience. 'That poor, poor girl! Who could have believed a thing like that about Adam? He was here quite often, you know, and always the gentleman. And of course, he must have been remorseful, or he wouldn't have killed himself, would he?'

It had been, Strang thought, naive to imagine that it wouldn't be common knowledge by now. 'Mmm,' he said, his voice discouraging.

Impervious, Fiona went on. 'Will they manage to raise the body today? We had a couple of the coastguard lads in last night and they were saying they were hoping there'd be' – she hesitated delicately – 'well, *enough* to bring in. Where would you be taking it? I wish I could say we'd make a room available but you know – the guests might not like it.'

'There won't be any need for that,' Strang said curtly. 'I wonder if you could bring me toast and coffee quickly, please? As you can imagine, I have a lot to do today.'

She said, 'Of course,' but the look she gave him

suggested that in the gentlemanly stakes he came well below Adam Carnegie.

It was quarter to eight when he finished and stepped outside to see if the police boats had arrived from Broadford. He shivered as the biting air hit him but it was invigorating too, with a sparkling clarity that piqued his throat like the bubbles in champagne. Looking out to sea, he spotted a promising-looking large motorboat rounding the headland at the side of the bay and went back inside to fetch his jacket.

Sergeant Rab Buchanan was waiting for him on the pier when he came out again. He greeted him briefly and gestured him back on board.

'DCS Borthwick will be arriving later on but I want to take the jeep up to the cliff first to see if they've started the operation yet,' he said as they set off across the bay.

'I think they will have, sir,' Buchanan said. 'The officer in charge came in last night and said they were hoping to be on station at first light.'

'Good, good. Sooner the better, before the weather changes.'

'There's a bit of a blow forecast, unless the wind veers. They'll get as much done as they can today.'

'Hard to say how much that will be. Anyway, I've got a meeting scheduled with the super when she arrives.'

As they drew in to the jetty below the Lodge, the constable who had been on the night shift was waiting for them, poised for departure at the earliest possible moment.

'Morning, sir, Sarge,' he said.

'All quiet last night?' Buchanan asked. 'Good lad. OK, you can be away to your breakfast. I'll take over.'

Beaming, he was into the boat almost before his superior officers had left it.

Strang walked over to the jeep, parked in front of the house. 'Keys still in it? Good,' he said.

Buchanan climbed in, then said, 'You'll want these, sir,' taking a pair of binoculars out of his jacket.

It wasn't much more than ten minutes across the moorland and this time Strang knew where to park, carefully avoiding the old tracks. They'd be bringing up the materials to make casts later on.

There was quite a brisk breeze blowing off the sea and as they came near the edge, Buchanan hung back. 'I'm just not that taken with heights, if you see what I mean.'

'Oh, I do – don't blame you. I'm not sure how good I am with them myself,' Strang said, but when he looked over the cliff the sight of the coastguard rescue boat below took his mind off the sickening drop at his feet.

They seemed to have got a line round a rocky pinnacle, mooring on the inside of the ridge of rocks. That was good; it would mean that even if a swell developed they could stay in place, and as he watched he saw a diver, sleek as a seal in his wetsuit, slip over the side. He took out Buchanan's binoculars and focused in.

The man was under for no more than three minutes when he surfaced again at the side of the boat. He was holding up something that looked like a jacket; he was having a conversation with one of the men in the boat, who nodded, and at a gesture from him another man in a wetsuit came forward and sat on the edge of the boat, putting on goggles and flippers and an oxygen cylinder.

So what Strang had seen yesterday was more than a random piece of fabric. With a hollow feeling in his stomach, he watched both men submerge again. He lowered the binoculars. He wasn't sure how much he wanted to see what poor Eva might have become.

It took longer than he had thought it would. Perhaps the body had caught on something – indeed, it must have, otherwise it would have been swept away.

Buchanan came to stand beside him, looking down apprehensively. 'Have they got anything yet?'

'A jacket, I think.' As he spoke, there was a disturbance in the water and one of the divers appeared, and then the other. They were raising something between them – something pale and grossly bloated with a little floating fringe of hair, sea-bleached to almost white.

With a queasy feeling, Strang lifted the binoculars to his eyes again. 'They've got her,' he said thickly and turned back towards the car.

Human Face, they had called the charity. It was a sick sort of irony that the human face had been only a mask that concealed the monster beneath. It was as well that Adam Carnegie was dead. If he hadn't been, Strang would almost be prepared to take care of that himself.

CHAPTER NINETEEN

He hadn't expected to be able to speak to Beatrice Lacey so soon. Her message that she wanted to speak to him 'urgently' reached DI Strang just after he came down from the clifftop and he set off immediately for the Broadford hospital.

According to the nurse who had shown him to the side ward she was in, her blood poisoning had responded well to intravenous antibiotics and as there were no other major problems it seemed likely she would be discharged later. She did have a fair few bruises to show for her adventures; one side of her face was scratched and she had only just escaped a black eye, but Beatrice was certainly looking better than he had expected after the state she'd been in yesterday.

When he appeared, she looked flustered and reluctant to meet his eye and for a moment he was afraid that someone had told her about his role in her rescue, but mercifully not. Her embarrassment, it seemed, was linked to a bad conscience.

And well it might be. She was so keen to purge it that he

barely had time to sit down before she began. He listened with a sort of astonished horror to her account of the weak and foolish self-deception that had cost Eva Havel her life.

'It was the time Veruschka went missing,' she said. 'I knew they'd quarrelled – I couldn't help it! They were screaming at each other. She'd found someone else – Murdo John, she said. And naturally Adam was angry – he felt totally betrayed. She was a flibbertigibbet, that girl, very demanding, very headstrong. I never liked her.'

There was contempt in her voice, a hint of sympathy, even, for Carnegie, but she noticed Strang shifting uncomfortably in his seat and changed her tone. 'Of course, she'd every right to leave if she wanted. As a matter of fact, I thought she'd be gone when I came back – I'd been in Portree doing an errand for Adam. He'd told me to take an afternoon off, go to the cinema or something, but I'd so much work piling up I didn't want to, so I came back early. And then—' She stopped, biting her lip.

'I went to Adam's flat to tell him I was back – just went round to the French doors when I'd parked my car. He was outside on the patio with the dog – there was a pail of water – he was – he was' – her voice was so low now that he had to strain forward to hear her – 'it was covered in blood and he was on his knees, washing it off.'

An inarticulate sound escaped Strang and she looked up, on the defensive now. 'Well, *I* didn't know! He said there had been a deer, that the dog had chased it and the blood was the deer's. That's what he told me. It was only when I realised Veruschka had gone that – well, I wondered. But he said he'd taken her across in the boat and she'd asked to have her cases sent on. And he was the man I loved, the man I had given up everything for—'

Strang had reproved Livvy Murray for being judgemental, but the words slipped out before he could stop them. 'So you were determined to believe him.'

Tears came to her eyes. 'Yes, I suppose I was. If he was lying about this, then I was – I was nothing. Worse than nothing. It worried me, of course it did, but then time passed and nothing happened and I was able to tell myself I was being silly. Why shouldn't what he said be true? Then – then when it happened again . . . You see, I knew Eva had a young man too. I saw him, he was rowing across to her one night, that Daniel Tennant, and they were very lovey-dovey. And she'd been doing some spying as well, going through Adam's filing cabinet. I don't know what she thought she was looking for. *I* wouldn't let anything wrong go through *my* books.'

She paused for a second, then said with a sidelong look at him, 'Of course, I couldn't vouch for anything *Harry* might have been responsible for.'

Strang could tell she thought she was being very subtle but at the moment he wasn't going to be diverted. 'Eva Havel,' he said. 'Tell me about her.'

'It was – it was like history repeating itself. I told you what happened when I was coming back.'

He nodded. 'You thought you saw Adam when he should have been on his way to Paris.'

She seized on that. 'Yes, but then he said he'd caught the plane. So I – I thought I must have been wrong. And the case that was left behind – well, she could just have forgotten it, couldn't she? That was the thing, you see, Inspector – there was always a sort of reason.'

'So you just fought down your anxieties?'

'Yes.' She was crying now. 'I'd told myself he was a good man, a man who did so much wonderful work for the charity – but then when I found out that he was married, suddenly I saw him in a different light.'

'That was important?'

She wiped her eyes with one finger. 'I'm not stupid,' she said. 'I know I'm fat and plain. But you see, my father was very old-fashioned. He tied up my trust fund so that I could only access the interest, not the principal, until I married. It was just me, you know, because I was a woman. There were no restrictions on my brother, though there certainly should have been.'

He could hear the bitterness in her voice. 'So what's the position with your money?'

'Quentin is my next of kin. I told him that when Adam married me I would give it all to him, and Adam knew that too. Oh, I know he didn't fancy me the way he did those girls but they were an interest that would pass. I was prepared to wait for the real, true, for ever love – we were lovers once, you know. I could have had his child. It was just, I didn't.'

There was real pathos in the way she spoke. Strang had been wondering about the doll he had found; now, with sudden insight, he understood. He hesitated for a moment, then took pity.

'It seems the call from his "wife" was just a hoax. There's no record that he was ever married.'

She had been sitting up as she told her story; now she fell back against the pillows as if he'd punched her. 'He – he wasn't?' she said faintly.

'Not as far as we know.'

Suddenly her eyes narrowed. 'Quentin,' she spat. 'That phone call – it was him who set it up, wasn't it? Oh God – he didn't kill Adam, did he?'

'Not as far as we know,' he said again.

Beatrice's face turned a dark, blotchy red. 'You're not suggesting *I* did it, are you? I didn't, truly I didn't. All I did was open the door and the dog attacked me. I could never do something like that – the blood—'

She seemed ready to turn hysterical. 'We have absolutely no reason to suppose you did, Miss Lacey,' he said soothingly.

She gave him an uncertain look but it calmed her down enough to allow him to say, 'You will be prepared to make a formal statement on the basis of what you've just told me?'

She blew her nose. 'Oh – yes, I suppose I have to. But you do understand that I didn't really know – not *know* what Adam did. Otherwise, of course—'

He didn't think he could take much more of this self-justification. He got up. 'Thank you, madam. You've—'

'There's something else,' she said. 'It's about Harry Drummond. He killed Adam, you know.'

Astonished, Strang sat down again. 'Really? You have proof of this?'

'No, no, of course not,' she said impatiently. 'But I know he did. He accused me of doing it to cover up that he'd done it himself. He and Adam were having the most dreadful rows over the past few days. I've no idea what they were about – it was perhaps about some sort of business thing.'

She was being blatantly disingenuous. 'Business thing?' Strang prompted.

'Oh, it was nothing to do with me. But if Harry thought poor Adam was going to get him into trouble, he would be totally ruthless, I tell you.'

Poor Adam! It turned Strang's stomach. Now she knew Adam hadn't deceived her about being married, the two dead girls didn't matter. But Beatrice was going on.

'The thing is, I'm frightened. Of course, *as I said*, I don't know anything at all about anything that Harry and Adam might have done, but Harry – well, Harry might think I did. Wrongly,' she added hastily. 'And if he thinks I'm some sort of danger to him, he'll do to me what he did to Adam. I want police protection.' Reading a refusal in his face, she said stiffly, 'Speaking as a taxpayer, I think I'm entitled to demand it.'

He couldn't take this any longer. He got up, saying coldly, 'I don't think you're in any danger right at the moment, madam. You're safe enough here and there are police officers everywhere at the Lodge. I'll send someone to take your statement. Thank you for your cooperation.'

After all that it was a considerable relief to get out, and he took great breaths of clean fresh air as he went back to his car. Her self-justification, the distortions to protect herself, the carefully calculated admissions – they were all disgusting.

Beatrice was a sad, pathetic creature, almost tragic in

her delusion that buying Adam Carnegie could ever have made her happy, he thought as he drove back to Balnasheil. But she hadn't genuinely believed what Adam had told her. She'd known perfectly well what he'd done, twice over, but her selfish romantic obsession had been her excuse for wilfully blotting it out.

And there was nothing at all romantic about the bloated corpse that was even now being shipped round to the concrete cell at the police office.

As the police helicopter was making its approach to Balnasheil, DCS Borthwick leant forward to speak to the pilot.

'Can you do a circuit above the cliffs there? I want to see what the coastguards are doing. They were hoping to be out at first light.'

She had been up promptly herself this morning. When she informed the chief constable of the latest developments, he had called her to a meeting immediately in some alarm. This was certain to bring the media down upon them and at the moment Police Scotland couldn't afford bad publicity.

When she arrived, he was clearly in a difficult mood. The First Minister, apparently, wasn't happy and didn't like to suffer alone, and the CC worked on the 'pay it forward' principle. Borthwick wasn't feeling too chipper herself now.

It was hard to see how this could have been handled differently but the press, with the advantage of 20/20 hindsight, would undoubtedly be able to find something. However professionally Kelso Strang might be running the investigation, he could be used as a stick to beat the Serious Rural Crime Squad with – newly promoted, bereaved . . . She could write the script and she wouldn't be given a starring role.

They were crossing the cliffs now and the pilot circled so that she was able to look straight down. From the air, the surly grey sea looked flat, the only movement the waves creaming white against the darker rocks. The scene had a sort of unreality, the boats far below like toys peopled with tiny figurines.

She could see two of them, one heading off round the headland, obviously on its way in to Balnasheil, and another still working between a curved ridge of rocks and the cliff. There was obviously some activity going on there, but she couldn't see what it was.

'Round again, ma'am?' the pilot asked, but she shook her head. The sooner she could touch base with Strang the better.

He must have heard the chopper. He was waiting in front of the house when she landed.

'They're bringing her in, ma'am. We're just preparing an incident room at the old police station across in the village and there's a cell there that'll do as a makeshift morgue,' he said.

'That was quick,' she said, surprised. 'To be honest, I'd thought they could search for days and we might never recover a body at all. The pathologist came up with me but more in hope than expectation.' She indicated the man who was just getting out of the helicopter.

'I spoke to the officer in charge,' Strang said. 'It's a curious configuration there, apparently. The rocks have created what's almost a sort of semi-lagoon and with the way the current runs, the body got driven in and caught in an underwater crevice. Not in a very good state, admittedly.'

'Even so, that's more than we expected,' she said. 'So—'

'That's not all. One of the divers spotted what could be bones when he was down. They've brought in another boat to investigate.'

'Good grief! The other girl? The same thing happened to her too?'

'A bit early to say that, but it's at least possible.'

'Right.' Borthwick assimilated that. It didn't make her feel any happier. 'So where are we going now? Here or across the bay? It would certainly be more convenient there.'

'Don't think they'll be ready for us yet, ma'am. The place was all but derelict but we'll manage once the cleaners have done their stuff.'

The site was quieter today. The SOCOs who had come in the chopper had gone to the patio and were putting on their white overalls but the pathologist came across to join them.

Strang briefed him on the situation and pointed him towards the jetty, where a motorboat was just coming in. He saw, with some annoyance, that PC Murray was in it.

'Excuse me, ma'am,' he said to Borthwick, then walked down to speak to her. 'I thought you were to oversee the cleaning at the police office, Murray?'

'Yes, sir. Just came to tell you it's finished. I got started last night.'

Performing penance, was she? *No harm in that*, he thought, and said more kindly, 'Good. Do you know when the equipment is arriving?'

'They're unloading that now.'

'Excellent. Thanks for letting me know.' He turned away, but she was still hovering.

'Was there anything else, sir?'

'No, that's all. You can get back now.'

He swung round, and almost bumped into Borthwick as she spoke over his shoulder. 'Good morning, PC Murray.' She was smiling. 'So – what has DI Strang got in store for you this morning?'

Murray didn't miss a beat. 'He hasn't had time to tell me yet, ma'am.'

Borthwick looked at him enquiringly.

Strang hesitated. He could say that tasking her was Sergeant Buchanan's business, not his, but not without sounding thoroughly pompous. He wasn't going to be bounced into letting her attach herself, though.

'I don't have anything for her at the moment. With the Carnegie investigation in abeyance—'

Borthwick pulled a wry face. 'I'm afraid it's not – not any more. Forensics have done their tests on the knife and unfortunately the one on the desk beside Carnegie wasn't the knife that killed him.'

Murray gaped at her. Strang said, with obvious satisfaction, 'Ah. I wasn't at all convinced, myself. The SOCOs weren't pleased but yesterday I ordered a full-scale crime investigation anyway.'

Borthwick was impressed. 'That's good, Kelso. It's vital we keep ahead of the game. No, they've established that it was one of his own knives placed beside him to mislead. The fingerprints showed he had gripped the knife, all right, but that could have been at any time and the clincher was that it's not the right shape of blade. So now, with the bodies from the sea as well, it will all have to be massively scaled up. I need to go over your ideas for the operation, so let's go to the room we were using yesterday. PC Murray, could you seek out the housekeeper and see if she can be persuaded to make coffee for us?'

'Yes, of course, ma'am.' She hurried away across the grass.

He and Borthwick followed more slowly while he filled her in on what Beatrice Lacey had disclosed. The case was snowballing. Strang should be feeling nervous but what he actually felt was anxious – anxious that now it was a serious, high-profile case he'd be demoted. It would be a false move; if the SRCS model was shown to be inadequate at the first major case it had encountered, the failure wouldn't go unnoticed by the media. And she'd said, in effect, that he 'had the ship'. If she wanted to take over, she'd have to prise his hands off the wheel.

He tried to assess from her manner what she was thinking but she was hard to read. Calm, cool, on top of whatever happened – that was her shtick.

But if things went wrong, it wouldn't only be his head on the block, it would be JB's too.

She'd got another chance. And there was going to be no fancy footwork this time; honesty would be Murray's watchword and she was going to keep her opinions to herself too.

Vicky Macdonald wasn't in the kitchen and Murray went along the corridor to tap on the door of her room, looking at her sympathetically when she said, 'Come in.'

'Sorry to dig you out,' Murray apologised.

Vicky had dark shadows under her eyes and she looked as if she'd been crying, but she gave a resigned smile. 'Looking for coffee? It's all right, you're not the first. Sergeant Buchanan and the other guy from Portree were in earlier. They've – they've found poor Eva, haven't they?' Tears sprang to her eyes.

Murray said gently, 'I guess they have. Not official yet, but—' She shrugged.

'At least she'll get a decent burial.' She took out a tissue and blew her nose. 'Well, I suppose everything will be winding down here now.'

Murray hadn't thought that might come up but she couldn't say yes, it would, because it wasn't true – and anyway, everyone would know soon enough. As she followed Vicky along the corridor into the kitchen, she said awkwardly, 'I'm afraid it's not as simple as that. They've discovered that Mr Carnegie didn't kill himself, after all.'

She said it just as she stepped into the kitchen, and heard Harry Drummond's voice say, 'Ah, Vicky, there you are—' and then stop short, just as Vicky spun round, saying, '*What*?'

'What did you just say?' Drummond echoed.

'I can't go into detail,' Murray said, wondering if she'd gone into too much detail already. She certainly wasn't authorised to question them and she was determined to watch her step. 'I understand his death is now being treated as suspicious.' That was what they always said on the telly so presumably it was all right.

Drummond, she noticed, seemed to have aged

overnight and the way he sat down on a kitchen chair suggested he'd done it so he wouldn't fall down. Vicky was looking aghast.

'You mean – they think now that one of us did it – me or Beatrice or Marek, or you, Harry? That's – that's awful! I can't believe it.'

'Not necessarily,' Drummond snapped. 'We're not in some Agatha Christie novel, you know – the isolated house with no communication with the outside. We're ten minutes from the mainland if you've a boat – and they're not hard to come by around here. And you said yourself someone came up by car, Vicky.' He licked his lips, as if they were dry, then addressed himself to Murray.

'You lot should probably know that I was a bit worried about some of Adam's connections. Wouldn't have cared for some of his acquaintances, myself. That's probably the direction you should be looking in.'

She was starting to get a bit out of her depth here. 'You'll have to talk to DI Strang. Which reminds me – I'm meant to be getting coffee for him and DCS Borthwick. Can you manage that, Vicky?'

'Of course,' she said automatically, and switched on the kettle though she was looking a bit shell-shocked. 'What were you wanting, Harry?'

Drummond took a moment to collect himself. 'It was just about meals, that was all. Are you going to be cooking tonight, or should I make other arrangements?'

'Oh, I see,' Vicky said vaguely. 'Of course I can do something for you – in fact, there's that hare needing to be cooked before it goes off. I could—'

Drummond said hastily, 'No, no, no, don't bother. I don't really feel like jugged hare. I'll just go to the hotel.'

A little silence fell when he had left. Then Vicky said, 'It's so awful – and scary, too. Someone killed Adam in cold blood and even if he was a murderer and totally deserved it, this makes it all much worse.'

'Mmm.' Murray wasn't up for an ethical discussion, right at the moment. Conscious of DCS Borthwick waiting for her coffee, she said, 'I'll set out the mugs on a tray, shall I? Oh, and I don't suppose you've any of that fab shortbread left?'

Vicky gave a wan smile. 'I think there's some in the larder.' She opened the door at the other side of the kitchen, then stopped. 'That's odd,' she said.

'What is?'

'I can't smell the hare. It was stinking the place out, getting high enough for Adam's taste. But – hang on, I'm just going to look.'

A moment later she reappeared. 'The hare's gone,' she said blankly. 'Someone's taken it.'

Borthwick's meeting with Strang had finished and the activity in the grounds at Balnasheil Lodge had been stepped up again. Uniforms were to be bussed in from Broadford and Portree to begin a fingertip search of the grounds, and the police boats, along with a couple of local ones, were running a shuttle service from Balnasheil Harbour.

PC Murray, using dispensing coffee as an excuse for staying in the room, had reported the mysteriously missing hare and had definitely done herself a bit of good with the

DCS by suggesting that it might have been laced to drug the dog. Even DI Strang had broken the habit of a lifetime and looked impressed when she'd pointed out that if so, Miss Lacey getting blood poisoning from the dog bite would hardly be surprising.

She was feeling a lot better about herself today; she'd told the cleaners to have an office for the DCS organised as top priority and it should be ready by now, so she'd demonstrated both ingenuity and efficiency. She just hoped the DCS was noticing.

It was Murdo John Macdonald's motorboat that was waiting ready at the jetty. He was standing ready to give a hand if needed as they climbed aboard; DCS Borthwick took it, Strang spurned it and she accepted it herself, quite deliberately, looking up into his face as she did.

He stared steadily through her. He was haggard-looking and his longish hair was untidy, as if he hadn't bothered to comb it this morning. She could even feel his hand trembling, just slightly.

He would know by now that they were bringing in Eva Havel's body – had probably even seen it arriving. Was he haunted by the image of his own beloved Veruschka, having suffered the same fate?

Not that there'd be enough of her by now to bring in, poor girl. There'd been a fisherman lost off a trawler in the spring whose body had been washed ashore three weeks later; Murray hadn't seen it herself but the description that went the rounds had given her bad dreams. Put her off crab completely.

As she watched him casting off she could almost feel the emotional tension in every line of his body. She couldn't read his mind – but he'd opened up to her a bit before. Perhaps he might do it again. She'd been warned off doing unauthorised interviews but there was a stubborn part of her that just wasn't listening.

A murder case was a challenge. She might feel Carnegie had got primitive justice, but to succeed in this would be validation for her ambitions. Officially and unofficially, she was going to give nailing the killer to be handed over for justice – of the legal sort – her very best shot.

Beatrice Lacey, much against her will, was discharged from hospital early in the afternoon. They disregarded her protests about not being fit and her complaints about stiffness and bruising; she had responded well to the antibiotics, they said, and as long as she finished the course of pills they had given her, she wouldn't need any further treatment. And exercise, a nurse had pointed out with what Beatrice felt was unnecessary emphasis, was the best treatment for stiffness.

She'd told the ambulance driver that she didn't want to go back home but he wasn't disposed to be sympathetic.

'Look, love, that's where I've been told to take you so that's where you've got to go. This isn't a taxi. Right?'

'But it's dangerous!' she said wildly. 'I could be killed too!'

They hadn't told him she was a nutter. 'You're all right, dearie. Don't worry,' he said in an elaborately patient voice and drove on down the Balnasheil road, muttering under his breath. If she just squatted there it'd be a bugger trying to get her out.

The police presence was apparent as he reached the harbour and an officer stepped forward and held up his hand to stop him.

'Where are you headed? The road over to Balnasheil Lodge is blocked.'

'Well, isn't this your lucky day?' he said to his passenger. 'You can tell the policeman here all about your problems.' He went round to open the door.

Beatrice ignored his supporting hand, gave him a cold look and walked past the officer and into the hotel. She pinged the bell on the reception desk several times until Fiona Ross appeared from the back.

'Yes? Oh, it's you, Miss Lacey! Are you all right? I heard you were in hospital.'

'They've turned me out. So I shall need a room here, Mrs Ross.'

Fiona Ross felt conflicted. On the one hand, having a direct in to the big story would be gratifying indeed, but she didn't owe Beatrice Lacey any favours, snooty old cow, and there was considerable satisfaction in saying sweetly, 'Oh, I'm so sorry! I'm afraid any free rooms are booked in case they're needed by the police.'

Beatrice glared at her. 'But surely you can make room for me? Balnasheil Lodge has always given you our patronage.'

Fiona gave her a tight little smile. 'Awfully sorry.'

'Surely, one room—'

'I'm afraid not.'

'Oh!' She caught her breath on a sob. As she turned away, she said, 'And if I'm the next one to be murdered, it's all your fault.'

Fiona stared at her. 'She looked quite wild,' she told her husband afterwards. 'I don't know what's going on in that place, I'm sure.'

CHAPTER TWENTY

The police office was buzzing now, with cars and vans parked outside and uniformed and plain-clothes officers coming and going. There were interview tables set up in the waiting room and when DCS Borthwick and DI Strang arrived, DC Tennant was sitting at one, talking to Harry Drummond, who jumped up as soon as he saw them arrive. He was looking thunderous.

'Inspector! Good,' he said. 'Perhaps you can explain to this man that I need to get back to Glasgow. He is insisting I remain here at his convenience. I gave him full cooperation when he asked to see the charity's records and we're just going round the houses all over again. And I simply can't see that what he is asking me now has anything to do with my friend's murder.'

Borthwick's eyebrows went up and she and Strang exchanged glances. 'News travels fast,' she said dryly.

Murray, who had come in behind them, took a step

backwards, trying to make herself smaller. She felt her cheeks go hot as Strang gave her a sharp look. Well, what was she meant to do? She'd got in trouble before for telling a lie and now she was going to get laldy for telling the truth. He didn't say anything, though, just waited while Borthwick introduced herself and explained that while they had no authority to keep Drummond there, she was sure he would not want to hinder the investigation by being unavailable for immediate questioning.

'As you can imagine,' she said, 'we will now have to conduct more interviews in depth. In fact, if DC Tennant can spare you now I'm sure DI Strang can arrange for you to make a full statement that can be given to you tomorrow at the Lodge to read through before you sign it.'

Drummond was emollient. 'Of course, of course. I'm not sure there's anything I can add to what I've told you already but I'm naturally anxious to help, not least since the thought of a knife murderer loose in my immediate vicinity isn't exactly reassuring.'

Strang turned to Murray. 'You can do that, Constable. Can I remind you that this is a simple process of recording information, not sharing it?'

'Yes, sir,' she said meekly. *Sarcastic sod!* But if that was all he was going to say, she'd got off lightly.

Tennant, his face set, yielded his seat to her without glancing in her direction.

'Thank you *so* much,' she cooed. She heard him say to Borthwick, 'May I have a word, ma'am?' and then they went out.

'Now, sir,' she said to Drummond. 'Can you take me through your movements from the time you arrived at Balnasheil Lodge?'

Tennant was white with anger. 'We have a major operation going on here. This is a money-laundering outfit we have been working to crack for months, almost a year. At last we have the opportunity to make real progress and you're putting obstacles in our way—'

Strang admired his courage – or perhaps he was just marvelling at his folly in taking on a DCS, particularly when that DCS was JB. He must be tired of life.

'DC Tennant!' Borthwick's voice cracked like a whip. 'Despite the fact that I have had no direct, formal approach for our cooperation we have given you every opportunity to investigate the accounts, have even requested a search warrant for Drummond's flat in Glasgow. I've been told that you still haven't found the smoking gun you were looking for – is that right?'

'Yes,' he said savagely. 'Because somehow he knew we were coming. That's why I need to keep up the pressure on Drummond—'

'Sorry.' Borthwick's voice was flat. 'Now that it's been established that this is a murder investigation—'

Unwisely, Tennant said, 'And why wasn't I told? I had to learn it from Drummond—'

Strang winced for him as Tennant encountered a look that stopped him dead. He bit his lip. 'Sorry, ma'am. I beg your pardon.'

'Yes. As I was saying' – she gave that heavy emphasis –

'now that this is a murder case and you have to be considered a suspect, I am withdrawing cooperation for the moment at least.'

He looked thunderstruck. 'You can't!'

'Oh, I think you'll find I can. DI Strang will arrange for you to be interviewed – with a view to eliminating you from our investigation, of course.'

Strang seized the moment. 'In fact, there's something I want you to do for me now. The body that has been brought ashore – we're assuming it's Eva Havel, but obviously it needs official identification. We can go through right away, if you're ready?'

Tennant turned first pale, then a queasy shade of green. 'Identify her? Now?' he faltered.

Strang was aware that Borthwick, like him, was studying the man's reaction closely. 'Of course, if it's too emotional, we can give you a bit more time to prepare yourself.'

'No, no,' Tennant said very hastily. 'Not at all. I hadn't been expecting it, that was all. I'll be fine. Where is she?' There was still the sheen of sweat on his forehead.

'Through the back, I understand,' Strang said. 'I think the pathologist is still here.'

As they went along the back corridor to what had been the police cell, the pathologist was just leaving, a heavy, old-fashioned key in his hand.

'I was going to lock up. Want to see her?' he said with the cheery insouciance of those whose days are spent in company that would give most normal people nightmares. 'She's not too bad, actually. Bloated, of course, but the crabs hadn't got to her yet.' He opened the door and waved them forward.

347

It hadn't occurred to Strang that he might be expected to go in. He'd never done it before; there was no longer a requirement for anyone except the senior investigating officer to view a body, and the visceral reaction hit him without warning. He wasn't ready, just at this time, to face again the brutal finality of death.

He felt his head getting light, as if it might float away, and for a terrible moment he thought he might faint. Tennant was ahead of him; as Strang reached the doorway he paused, leaning against the lintel, looking in to satisfy the technical requirement but directing his eyes downwards, forcing away the memory of his Alexa, also cold and dead.

He heard Tennant say, 'Yes, that is Eva Havel.' His voice was impressively steady. He turned to come out and Strang was able to step back into the corridor.

As the pathologist, with a hospitable gesture, invited him in he said, 'I've seen all I need to,' a little hoarsely and turned away. The man locked up and followed them.

'They're bringing in some bones now,' he told them. 'Picked clean, of course, and we can't hope for ID. We'll take DNA samples and check the register, but I wouldn't be optimistic.'

'The other one?' Tennant said. 'What was she called again – Veruschka?'

'Yes,' Strang said, but still not sure he could trust his voice, he didn't elaborate. What was certain was that the signs of distress Tennant had shown earlier were no longer visible. He must have iron self-control – useful, if you had something to conceal.

As they walked back to the incident room to record

the identification formally, Tennant said in a low, urgent voice, 'Look, Kelso, you know I'm useful. I've had a lot of experience and you need all the help you can get. Keep me in the picture – don't shut me out of this, even if that old battleaxe—'

'Stop right there,' Strang said coldly. 'She's a highly effective and very senior officer and you'd better show some respect. And anyway, why are you so anxious to be "kept in the picture"?'

'Don't be bloody stupid,' Tennant snapped. 'This is a big one for me – if I can wrap it up it would mean promotion. If your lot are blundering around you could take away the stuff I'm looking for without recognising it and bury it for years in the files. I need to know what's going on, Kelso!'

It sounded logical enough. But somehow Strang was uncomfortable: the two reactions, before and after viewing the body, didn't square. He was very thoughtful as he went back to Borthwick's office.

One of the police boats took Beatrice across to drop her at the jetty. She didn't protest; there was nowhere else for her to go and she limped painfully up the lawn to the house. There were a lot of police officers around but some seemed to be packing up; it was a gloomy afternoon now and the light was going, the threatening sky heavy with muddy-looking clouds and streaked with sullen purple and dull orange as the sun faded.

She went over to a man with stripes on his arm who seemed to be organising their departure. 'Good

349

afternoon, Sergeant. I trust you will be leaving a police presence here tonight?'

The man looked blank. 'I'm sorry, madam, I really couldn't tell you.'

Beatrice's voice rose. 'You mean I am to be left here, unprotected, to be knifed in my bed?'

'I haven't any instructions about that, madam. I suggest you just lock your door if you're nervous. Or you could take it up with headquarters.'

'Oh yes,' she said bitterly, 'and speak to someone in Glasgow, who tells me my complaint has been logged? What use will that be?'

Not waiting for his reply, Beatrice walked up to the house and let herself in. The hall was empty and silent. Perhaps she should just follow his advice; there wasn't much else she could do.

She was very, very afraid. If Adam really had – well, done something with Eva, Harry had been in on it: he'd come rushing up just after her disappearance and started checking through everything she might have seen when she was spying. And that was another thing Beatrice hadn't wanted to admit to herself – that there had been something – well, not quite right about the charity she had dedicated herself to.

Her heart was fluttering as she dragged herself upstairs to the safety of her flat. She didn't actually know anything about the paper files she'd never had access to – except, of course, that she'd seen Adam taking them away somewhere. To destroy them, maybe?

But Harry might certainly believe that she did – and there

were the other things that she actually did know about – those strange house parties for men who didn't seem to have any interest in hearing about the work of the charity, the 'distribution' office in Africa . . .

Oh yes, that was her problem: she knew too much. Adam had known everything there was to know about their secret arrangements, then he'd fallen out with Harry and now he was dead, horribly murdered – she gave a convulsive shudder as she thought about the blood.

She unlocked the door of the flat and almost fell into the room, sighing with relief as she locked it again behind her. Then her eye fell on the little white-draped crib, empty now. She burst into tears and collapsed into a chair, sobbing with grief and misery. And terror.

'Sarge! Over here!'

One of the uniforms engaged in the search of the grounds was standing looking down at something and Sergeant Rab Buchanan hurried across to him.

What he was looking at was the remains of an animal – hare, rabbit, probably. There wasn't much more than the bones, scraps of fur and a fine collection of maggots on what rotting flesh was left.

'Well done, laddie! We were kinda looking for that,' Buchanan said. 'Now bag that up and then get it taken across straight away.'

The constable looked at it with revulsion. 'Touch it? With my hands?'

'Not going to work if you use your feet, is it? Oh, for any favour, use your initiative – scoop it with a spade or something. But do it properly – it's got to go to the labs at once. If it's doped and the dog ate it, it wouldn't have been able to protect its master.'

He was impressed with that. 'Right, Sarge.'

He went back to look for a spade and a bag then came back and, gagging a bit, managed to guide it in. It was touch and go when a maggot dropped onto his hand but, thinking of the mockery he would get from the men around him if he threw up, he gulped and shook it off.

The boat waiting at the jetty was Murdo John's. He glanced at the bag the constable was carrying, then glanced again. 'What have you got there?'

The constable shrugged. 'Rabbit, or something. But they think it's been spiked and the dog mebbe ate it so it wouldn't attack the killer.'

'Oh,' was all Murdo John said.

It was a disappointing reaction to a prime piece of evidence, but then, the constable reflected, Murdo John Macdonald was a surly sod. No point in trying to pursue a conversation when they were almost across anyway.

It was good news that they seemed to have found the carcass of the hare – though of course they wouldn't know for sure that it wasn't just the remains of some fox's supper, or that the doping theory was right until the forensic report came through, but it was certainly promising.

With deliberate provocation, DCS Borthwick said to DI Strang, 'Your little Murray's useful, you have to admit.'

He didn't rise, only saying mildly, 'I dispute the possessive pronoun. Yes, she's not stupid but she's a worryingly loose cannon, ma'am. I certainly agree she's wasted in a place like this – ought to be back in Glasgow, learning her trade.'

Borthwick smiled and didn't pursue it. 'So – progress today, wouldn't you say?'

Strang pulled a face. 'Some, certainly. And there'll be a lot more coming in. But they haven't found the knife that killed Carnegie – at the bottom of the sea, is my guess. And unless there's something very definite once the SOCOs come back with the warrant to search the whole house tomorrow, we're dependent on just working the ground – knocking on doors, mainly. And that's slow and uncertain.'

'Yes. Of course, there's the big problem.'

She didn't have to explain. 'Yes,' he said heavily. 'It's not hard to guess what they'll be saying in the Black Cuillin bar tonight – that Carnegie had it coming to him. They're not going to be falling over themselves to offer us any incriminating evidence they might happen to have.'

'You know this place better than I do. Would they actually cover up for someone?'

'Wouldn't say I knew it at all, really, except that the jungle drums are frighteningly efficient. Murdo John Macdonald's one of their own – Vicky too, I suppose. But the rest of our most likely list – can't imagine it. Even so—'

She nodded. 'Yes. The public conception of what justice means is certainly a lot closer to Carnegie getting his throat cut than him being put on trial and getting out without even completing a full life sentence. And that's always supposing we'd managed to find enough to satisfy the fiscal.'

'There's certainly been no response at all to the

questioning about boats that might have been out on the bay last night.'

The sound of rotor blades whirring overhead cut him short. He looked at her sharply. Was she going to go back with it, or was she going to want to stay to oversee his work – or worse, send in someone more senior to take over?

She laughed. 'I can read you like a book, Kelso. Yes, I'm going back.'

He flushed, muttering something, and she laughed again.

'Funny thing, power. It gets addictive, doesn't it? Oh, I see in you a lot of my own attitudes – and as a matter of fact in little Murray as well: so enthusiastic, so keen to learn.

'You don't need me to point out that this is a big case and I'm ready to admit I'm very anxious that we don't screw up – I've got the CC on my back, apart from anything else. But I'm going with my gamble. You seem to have a grip on things, for the moment anyway, and politically it suits us better to follow it through on the SRCS pattern.'

Borthwick gathered up the papers on her desk. 'I'd better get out there. So it's over to you, Kelso. What's next?'

'Marek Kaczka,' he said. 'We need the second ID and I want to use that to talk to him, if he'll cooperate. I suspect he's using lack of English as an excuse for stonewalling.'

'Keep me in touch,' she said, and then she was gone.

When the police told her that Beatrice was back, Vicky Macdonald ran upstairs to knock on her door. When there was no answer, she called, 'Beatrice, are you there?'

'Oh, it's you, Vicky. Just a moment.' She heard a groan,

then heavy footsteps before the door was unlocked.

Beatrice looked terrible. Her right arm was in a sling and one side of her face was cut and bruised. She had been crying, too; her nose was red and her eyes puffy and swollen.

'Oh, poor you!' Vicky cried. 'You don't look well at all. I thought you would still be in hospital but one of the policemen said you'd come back.'

She followed her in as Beatrice said bitterly, 'I should be, of course, but they turn you out the moment you can stand upright nowadays. It's the Third World in the modern NHS.'

Tactfully, Vicky didn't enter into a discussion, just went to help her to sit down. 'Do you have painkillers and so on? Your arm must be painful.'

Beatrice snorted. 'Yes, it is. So they've given me paracetamol, which doesn't look at the problem.'

Vicky perched on a chair opposite. 'What happened after you left here, Beatrice? They were saying something about mountain rescue.'

'Oh, it was so awful, just like a nightmare. I remember crashing the car on the bridge – a policeman said the road was blocked now. Is that right?'

'Yes,' Vicky said. 'It's made it difficult for the police too. Were you hurt?'

'I – I don't think so. The thing is, after that everything is a sort of blur. I was climbing up the mountain in the fog – I don't know why. I think I was delirious, really. But then they were after me – the dog again, you know, and then—oh!'

She stopped, her hand across her mouth. 'There was this – this black monster, gigantic, stalking me, looming up out of the mist. When I tried to run away, it followed me. That was real, Vicky – I know I didn't imagine that! It was horrible, horrible.' She shuddered.

Vicky leant forward to pat her hand. 'I know just what that was. It happened to me once when I was hillwalking and it scared me witless. It's a sort of light effect when there's fog and the sun comes up – they told me afterwards it's called a Brocken spectre. It's your own shadow and when you move, it does too. But that's all.'

Beatrice started at her. 'I ran away from my own shadow? And then because of that I tripped, and lost Rosamond' – her voice broke – 'and then I fell myself – oh God, how could I have been so silly?'

'You were ill,' Vicky said, 'and shadows – well, shadows are frightening things. But you're all right now. You need to rest, though. Do you want me to help you to bed?'

But the other woman shook her head. 'No. I must be on my guard.'

'On your guard?'

Beatrice leant forward to whisper. 'You see, *I know too much*. I'm a danger to him.'

It sounded like something out of a B movie. 'Who – Harry? What do you know about him?'

Vicky had raised her voice in surprise and Beatrice put a finger to her lips. 'Sssh! He could be standing outside right now. I want him to think I don't know anything at all that could be a threat to him but I'm afraid he might work it out. And then—' She drew her left hand across her throat in a graphic gesture. 'Vicky, I'm scared.'

It was obvious that she meant it. 'What are you talking about?' Vicky whispered.

Beatrice didn't answer immediately. Then she gave a sigh that was almost a sob. 'Human Face. It's so important. It does so much good work for these poor little creatures – hungry, sick, abandoned. I knew there were things I wasn't told – that filing cabinet I was told not to touch, those strange house parties for donors who didn't really seem the philanthropic type. But the money would come in afterwards, the donations for the charity. And if the taxpayer lost out a bit, well . . .'

She looked up at Vicky. 'Oh, I know what you're thinking – I'm stupid. But I'm not stupid. I just – just didn't want to be smart. And I told you about the girls.'

'Yes,' Vicky said heavily. 'They've found Eva, you know. They recovered her body from the sea and brought it in today. She'd been pushed off the cliff.'

'Oh no! How – how dreadful.' Beatrice bent her head, putting a hand up to cover her face. 'I – I should have gone to the police sooner. Much sooner.'

'Yes, I think you really should.' There was a certain grimness in Vicky's tone, but she went on, 'Anyway, I don't think Harry's going to creep up here and murder you. It would be a bit obvious, don't you think, with all the police around?'

'But will they still be around tonight?' Beatrice quavered. 'Once they've all gone home—'

'Look, you lock your door, and if I hear Harry trying to break it down I promise I'll rush up and rescue you, all right? Shall I bring you up something to eat meantime? You probably missed your lunch.'

Having persuaded Beatrice to accept her offer, Vicky went back downstairs. It was hard to be sympathetic to someone whose wilful self-deception had caused so much death and misery – not that she had any brief for Harry either. The sooner she got out of this awful place the better. Surrounded by horrors she was beginning to feel like the prisoner in 'The Pit and the Pendulum', with the walls closing in around her.

Marek Kaczka only nodded when he was told what was required, viewed Eva's body in silence, apparently unmoved, and said, 'Yes, is her,' when he came out.

In the office DI Strang produced the form for him to sign. 'I need to take some details first. Age?'

It was slow work. He was fifty-six, he said. For nationality, he gave Polish, but he could give no more details. All his papers, he claimed, were held by Mr Carnegie.

'We haven't found anything,' Strang said. 'No papers, no employment records—'

Kaczka made a sound that could have been a laugh or a snort. 'No pay,' he said. 'Place to stay. Food. Sometimes money for beer. Sometimes.'

It wasn't unexpected. 'Look, we need to talk about this. Would you like a cup of coffee, sir?'

Kaczka looked at him. 'Why you say "sir"? To me?'

'I'm a public servant. You are a member of the public, so I call you sir. Wait here.' Strang wasn't sure he understood, but when he came back with the mugs and a pack of sandwiches held between his teeth, Kaczka actually smiled as he took them.

'Right,' Strang said. 'If you don't understand what I'm saying, stop me, OK?'

'I hear better than to speak.'

'Fair enough. It seems Carnegie was exploiting you – you know?'

He nodded. 'Like – slave.'

'Was it money? Did you have to pay him back for bringing you here?'

This made him obviously uncomfortable. He shrugged.

'Was there some reason you couldn't just come here for a job?'

Not even a shrug, this time.

'If you're Polish, you have a right to come here to work.'

Kaczka didn't meet his eyes. 'Yes, Polish.'

'Even if you weren't, after being treated so badly you would have a very good chance of being allowed to stay,' Strang suggested, but 'Polish' was the only answer he got.

They might have to bring in an interpreter to get this sorted out. If, say, the man had a criminal record, that might explain the hold Carnegie had over him.

He tried a new tack. 'How did you meet Adam Carnegie?'

'A friend. He knows.'

Strang jumped at that – people trafficking? – but got nowhere. The first sandwich was disappearing rapidly and Kaczka was using that as an excuse for not answering.

'Tell me,' he said conversationally, 'do you have a family? Wife? Children?'

Kaczka stopped chewing. His eyes, so dark they were

almost black, softened for a second, but only for a second. 'Not now,' he said.

It was often the little things, the passing comments, that got under the guard Strang had imposed on his feelings like a stiletto slipped between the ribs. His throat tightened as he heard the response he would have to give to the same question. He coughed.

'Back at home, perhaps?'

Finishing the second sandwich, Kaczka didn't answer.

He asked the next question more or less at random. 'So – why did you choose to come here? It's very remote.'

It was a comprehensive shrug this time, a shift of the shoulder with the hands outstretched, indicating a vast ignorance of anything approaching a reason. But as Strang decided to give up until they had the means of better communication and just ask him to sign the ID certificate. An idea formed in his mind.

'Were you fond of Eva?' he said suddenly as he held out the pen.

Kaczka took it. 'Is nice girl,' he said flatly, then took it to sign his name in a neat, old-fashioned copperplate.

'It's thanks to you we found her, you know,' Strang said. 'And the other girl, who disappeared before. Veruschka – did you know her?'

He was watching him carefully, but there was no sign of emotion. Kaczka laid down the pen. 'No. Is before I am here,' he said, then, 'I go now?'

Strang sighed. 'Yes. Thanks for your help, sir.'

'And you. Sir.' He gave an odd little bow as he left the room.

* * *

When Vicky Macdonald went into the kitchen, she saw that the door to the back premises was open and she could hear someone moving about. On edge anyway, she said sharply, 'Hello? Who is that?' and went to through to the back corridor.

Harry Drummond was standing there, his hand on the door of the game larder. It looked as if he'd been in the main larder too; the door to that was half open, as was the one to the old coal cellar where cleaning things were kept. He jumped, looking, she thought, like a schoolboy caught out raiding the fridge.

'Oh – Vicky!' he said awkwardly.

'Did you want to get into the game larder?' she said with polite mystification.

He reddened. 'Oh, I was just curious. How's the hare coming on?'

'It's gone. Disappeared the other day, bizarrely enough. You'd smell it if it was there.'

'Oh?' He didn't seem surprised. He opened the door anyway and peered inside at the bare room, the zinc-topped shelves and the wooden pegs. 'Yes, you're right. It's gone.'

He turned and went back into the kitchen, without explaining his behaviour. As he was leaving the room, Vicky said, 'If you didn't want to go across to the hotel tonight, I'm going to make an omelette for Beatrice so I could do one for you too, if you'd settle for that—'

'Beatrice?' He whirled round. 'I thought she was in hospital. Is she back?'

'Yes, they've discharged her. But she's still not very well and she's very tired,' Vicky said warningly.

'Of course, of course. Poor Beatrice,' he said and went out, leaving Vicky still more on edge. She really wasn't sure how much more of this she could take. Perhaps Murdo John – but no. That would create a whole other set of problems and it wouldn't remove the ones she had already.

She heard him coming across the hall below, recognising his firm, brisk steps. He was climbing the stairs two at a time. Beatrice shrank back in her chair as his knock came on the door.

'Beatrice, it's Harry. How are you?'

She didn't reply. He knocked again.

'I know you're there. Vicky told me you were back. Can I come in?'

He didn't wait for an answer, but tried to open the door. She sat, shivering as she watched the handle turn this way and that. He swore under his breath, but she heard him.

'Beatrice, this is ridiculous. I need to talk to you. I can't go on shouting through the door. You have to let me in. It's important.'

She could hear the temper in his voice. Perhaps she was making it worse by provoking him but she was so afraid that she didn't think her legs would carry her across to the door.

'You might just as well speak to me now.' He was making an effort to sound reasonable. 'You can't stay locked in there for ever. And the thing is, you might be able to help me save the charity. You don't want all these poor children to have no food, no blankets because we're stopped from helping them? Come on, Beatrice, let me in!'

The thing was, she wasn't sure now that she wanted Human Face to survive. There were other charities, bigger charities, that might even make her money work harder. She put her fingers in her ears, but even so she could hear him battering on the door with his fists, hear him shouting, 'Stupid, stupid bitch!' until at last, when her heart was racing so fast she thought it might fail at any moment, his footsteps retreated down the stairs.

CHAPTER TWENTY-ONE

After all the activity of the day, the police office seemed very quiet as Kelso Strang settled down to work at his desk. The local force had returned to Broadford and Portree and the pathologist and JB would be back in Edinburgh by now. PC Murray was presumably around somewhere but she'd probably retreated to the police house at the other side of the building.

The peace was welcome. Tomorrow would be more pressured than ever, with the SOCOs back for the search of Balnasheil Lodge, room by room. The warrant request for searches of Tennant's, Quentin Lacey's and the Macdonalds' residences had been turned down as speculative; irritating, but not unexpected. The work had been done already on the murder scene, though processing the information the experts had gathered would be a long job.

He clicked on the file of crime scene photographs. The forensic photographer was good at his job and Adam

Carnegie's flat leapt out at him again in minute and vivid – all too vivid – detail. He hadn't actually seen the body; here it was sprawled across the desk, and he spent some time studying the close-up of the wound. A neat cut, as the SOCO had said, right across the artery; not a random slash. Someone knew what they were doing.

It somehow reminded him of ritual slaughter, of sacrifice, like a goat placed on an altar – the altar of primitive justice, perhaps?

Then there was the blood – the blood everywhere, browning by the time the photo had been taken. The carpet was covered with bloody paw prints, dozens of them; the dog must have traced endless frantic circles in its distress and scrabbled at both the doors. From the photographed smears on Carnegie's trousers it had pawed at him too – trying to rouse him, perhaps, poor beast.

He'd had plenty of experience in looking at photos like these. Their professionalism had a distancing effect that certainly made it much less harrowing than visiting a crime scene itself, where even the smell was an assault. All the same, they always provoked a certain queasiness; Strang had to force himself to study them, concentrate on the story they might be telling him. That was the job.

The blow must have come from over the shoulder – right-handed, the report said. Had Carnegie been sitting down at the time, or could he have been standing by the desk and collapsed onto the chair? He wasn't a tall man; provided he was unsuspecting and had turned away it wouldn't be hard to draw a sharp knife across the side of his throat.

Supposing he had been sitting at the desk with his back to the person coming in, did that suggest someone familiar – Harry, say, or Vicky or Beatrice – or Marek, maybe, bringing back the dog from a walk? They'd established that he looked after it when needed. Carnegie might not even turn as one of them came in.

If it wasn't one of the household – Quentin Lacey or Murdo John or Daniel Tennant, or even some person unknown – he would almost certainly have got up to open it – but then, too, once Carnegie had let the visitor in he might have had some reason for going to the desk, to fetch something or even to look at something handed to him, something the murderer had removed when he left.

So that hadn't taken him very far. In any case, this sort of speculation was a waste of precious time. Establishing motive wasn't part of the professional job; it might be useful to the prosecution to suggest a 'why' once the facts were known, but if the evidence of guilt was solid, proving motive was unnecessary.

The next stage of the investigation, searching the house, would be concentrating on the results of the attack on the perpetrator. He, or she, would have been behind the victim, but it was unlikely that with a severed artery pumping out blood there would be no direct evidence – hands, clothes, surely, would bear at least some traces. But in the hours of darkness it was unlikely that there would be anyone to observe them, and out here disposing of bloodstained clothes would be simple enough: a weighted bag, and they would be at the bottom of the sea as the knife most probably also was.

The searchers tomorrow would be dismantling every sink and basin in the house, looking for evidence of blood in the traps underneath, but of course days had passed now and these traces too might have found their way into the convenient ocean. They could get lucky; every successful investigation Strang had ever worked on in Edinburgh had relied on a considerable slice of luck – luck and forensics.

Forensic evidence, though, was slow, no matter how much pressure JB could bring to bear, and at the back of their minds there was, as always, dread that the killer would strike again while they waited for results. If this was in some sense an execution rather than a murder, though, surely it was less likely? Of course, even if the killer believed this was justified revenge on an Old Testament scale – an eye for an eye, a death for a death – and had no other victim in mind, killing for self-protection was still possible. Yes, there was always that fear. He shifted uneasily.

And there was also the other possibility: Carnegie and Drummond had been aware that the net was closing round them and according to Tennant the thieves had fallen out, and now Drummond was doing his best to set Carnegie up to take the rap. His death was, to say the very least, convenient. And – the unwelcome thought came to him – if Beatrice had been in some sense complicit, she might be very inconvenient too.

On the thought, Strang picked up the phone to check with the Broadford station that there was an officer on duty overnight and was reassured to know that there was. With Vicky in the house too, surely there wasn't anything Drummond could do that wouldn't expose him to a worse charge than money laundering? So Beatrice should be safe enough meantime. Probably.

That wasn't good enough. They needed a breakthrough on this case, and soon.

Morally speaking, Strang was finding it a tough one. He'd thought sometimes how hard it must have been to do this job in the days when there was a hanged man on the other side of conviction, but presumably the inner dialogue was the same as the one he was conducting now; he was there to enforce the law, not approve of it.

But nailing Carnegie's killer . . . Strang could raise none of the passion for serving justice he had felt on previous cases he'd worked on. The fourteen-year-old girl who'd been raped and strangled and left on wasteland by the Water of Leith – that had generated the sort of desperation to bring in the man who did it that had every one of them existing on three hours' sleep a night and missing meals. It was all they could do for her.

This man, though? Carnegie had baited his snares with the cruel promise of freedom in the West to illegal immigrants with little hope of achieving it on their own. And being evil himself, it was looking as if he had contaminated another person and drawn them into evil too. If his executioner did escape the law, would Strang find himself haunted by it for the rest of his life? Morally speaking, probably not.

Professionally, though – ah, that was different. He hated to fail, hated it with a passion. Perhaps his father was responsible for the mixture of nature and nurture that had always made success so crucial for him, but he couldn't help it. And if he'd cared so much in the past, he cared even more now.

He'd been confident earlier when JB had left him in charge; now, alone in the silent room, dark apart from the pool of light from the desk lamp, surveying the inadequate evidence that lay before him, he felt the first frisson of uncertainty. What if he wasn't, after all, good enough to handle this by himself? What if he blew it, and brought JB down with him?

It would be the most public of failures too, with analysis of whatever mistakes he had made – even if he hadn't – running in the papers day after day. And worst of all would be knowing that his father would be reading them with a curled lip – his son, who couldn't even hack it in a job as lowly as this one.

Never mind the balance of rights and wrongs. Strang was going after the killer with all the skill and energy at his command and then it would be up to others to take account of the background to the crime. He did allow himself to hope, though, that whoever it was got a brief with a talent for the eloquent plea in mitigation.

And whatever you felt about Old-Testament-style justice, you had to remember that the lands where that writ still ran were not famed for peace and freedom.

Livvy Murray put the final full stop on the report, looked at her watch and swore. She had wanted to get down to the Black Cuillin before it opened in the hope of once more being able to persuade Murdo John Macdonald to say more than he meant to, but she'd been determined to make an impeccable professional job of Harry Drummond's statement, for her own self-respect.

He'd been slow to get the message that going off on rants, asking impassioned questions apparently directed to some person passing directly overhead and claiming loss of memory was only going to prolong things. Once the penny dropped, she'd been meticulous about limiting her questioning strictly to his movements, but she'd done it more or less minute by minute and when at last she'd finished he was looking like a lemon that had been squeezed until it was limp.

She was a fool to herself, of course. It had given her more than an hour of writing up to do and by now there would be customers in the bar to give Murdo John an excuse for ignoring her. So there was no need for hurry now; she sat back to read through Drummond's statement.

Perhaps Kelso Strang would make something of it, but it didn't tell her anything new. Drummond had sounded off, but when it came right down to it he'd been surprisingly precise, with no gaps left where you could slip in a chib to slice it open. It was creepy, really, as if all the noisy bluster was to cover up a cold, quiet reptile core. His bright blue eyes, she had noticed, were completely dead and she had little doubt that if slitting Carnegie's throat that night had been in his interests he'd have done it, then sat down next morning to enjoy his breakfast.

Her money had been on Murdo John, having glimpsed the passion he'd felt for his lost love. Passion was a classic when it came to motives for murder – but then so was greed. And self-protection. And revenge.

Whatever. She sighed. There was definitely no way she was going to get a dramatic confession out of Drummond and her opportunity to get to work on Murdo John had gone for tonight, at any rate. And there were the other suspects too – Tennant, Marek, Vicky. Even, she supposed, Beatrice and the feeble Quentin, though she just couldn't see him ever having the guts to do it.

There was something about Tennant that gave her an uneasy feeling, a tickle of nerves like a spider crawling across her back. If he worked undercover for the Met, he probably wasn't too bothered by scruples and he'd certainly been pretty distraught about Eva. Marek – well, it looked as if Carnegie had been exploiting him something rotten, but he'd been there for years, so why now?

Vicky – her thoughts lingered on Vicky for a moment. She liked her instinctively but that wasn't anything to go on. Vicky had been very upset about what had happened to Eva and even if that was hardly reason enough to take a knife to someone, there might be more to her relationship with Carnegie than met the eye. She and Murdo John had clearly fallen out over her decision to live in at Balnasheil Lodge; had she perhaps found that Carnegie's ideas of her duties were not what she had in mind? Had she snatched up one of his knives in self-defence?

But no, of course she hadn't. That knife hadn't been the one that killed her. Livvy was just wasting good drinking time, going round in circles.

She got up and went to the window. It was dark now and she could hear the wind getting up – a whiny, sighing wind that made the draughty building creak and whisper. There was foul weather forecast and she knew by now what that meant. She'd better get the buckets put under the leaks she knew about, though new ones kept appearing.

The light was still on in the office where Kelso Strang was working. He was certainly conscientious and he might be there till midnight. It must be a lonely kind of job with this new system of drafting in the experts when needed, but she knew better by now than to go and knock on the door to suggest he take a break to join her down the pub.

Maybe it was personal – and she knew she'd irritated him by screwing up a couple of times – but he didn't really seem the sociable sort. She pulled on her parka and set off in the chilly dark for the Black Cuillin.

He was there again. She had heard his heavy footsteps coming up the stairs and then stopping outside the door. She held her breath.

Beatrice hadn't dared to move from her chair since she'd locked the door after Vicky had brought her supper tray. She had dozed off a couple of times and then wakened with a jerk that made her stiffening muscles scream. She longed for her bed and the little white pill that would give her oblivion, but she dared not take it. She had to be awake, awake and ready to scream if Harry broke in to attack her.

The tap that came on the door was gentle, almost apologetic. 'Beatrice, are you there? Can you hear me?' Harry's voice said.

She didn't answer.

'Beatrice, I'm sorry I spoke to you roughly before.' His voice was gentle, cajoling. 'I can quite understand that with all that's gone on you're nervous and I'm so upset myself that I wasn't thinking straight. If you have the ridiculous idea that I might be going to harm you, I can tell you there's a policeman on duty outside and Vicky downstairs so one good scream would bring them rushing to your side. We need to talk – would you think about letting me in?'

It's like the Big Bad Wolf, Beatrice thought with a kind of nervous hysteria. *No, no, by the hair on my chinny chin chin* – she had to clamp her mouth tight shut on the words.

'No? Perhaps you can't hear me or you've gone to bed?'

He hadn't huffed and puffed this time. She still wasn't going to respond.

'But anyway, I'm just going to assume you're listening. Beatrice, Adam swore to me that he had destroyed everything he should have, the documents that could blow apart Human Face and everything we've worked for. But I've spoken to our lawyer and he said Adam had told him there was what he called "an insurance policy" and now I'm afraid there's something he's hidden away. They're going to search the whole house tomorrow and if they find anything like that it will be serious for us. And I don't just mean me, I mean both of us because no one will believe you if you say you didn't know. It's not just a smack on the wrist and a little fine, it's jail we're talking about here.'

Prison! Beatrice gave a little gasp of dismay and heard Harry's triumphant laugh on the other side of the door.

'Aha! You heard that, did you? So come on – do you know anything about that?'

She licked her dry lips. 'There were papers – a whole lot of papers—'

'Yes? Yes?'

'I saw him taking them outside.'

'*Outside*? Do you know what papers they were?'

'The – the ones from the filing cabinet, I think. The ones Eva was looking at.'

There was a silence, then Harry said, quite softly, 'Oh dear God. Outside. And you don't know where?'

She shook her head as if he could see her. 'No. Maybe – maybe he was just going to burn them.'

'Maybe. And maybe he wasn't. That treacherous bastard!' His voice was loud and harsh again. 'You have no idea, no idea at all, what this could land us in. And I can't even go out to search myself with a plod right outside the door. Better hope you're right that he burnt them. Goodnight.' He gave a harsh laugh. 'Sleep well – I certainly won't.'

There was nothing to stop her going to bed now but Beatrice was shaking so much she thought she might collapse on the way. She wasn't worrying about Harry now, she was worrying about her own foolish wickedness and the full majesty of the law.

The Black Cuillin was busy tonight. There was a party of the hardiest sort of hillwalker at the big corner table toasting their ascent of the Inaccessible Pinnacle before the weather closed in, and the regulars had turned out in force too. There would be good craic tonight; it wasn't often there was quality stuff like discussing murder available. There were also two strangers sitting among them but at opposite sides of the pub, ignoring each other.

It didn't take Livvy Murray ten seconds to identify them as press. Even wearing jeans and trainers they had the smell of the city about them, and the notebook one had open on the table in front of him was a dead giveaway.

That one glanced round as she came in and she saw him ask the man beside him, a mate of hers, who she was. As he opened his mouth to speak she gave him one of her high-octane, super-turbo-charged death stares and he got the message in time to shrug his shoulders with a blank, 'No, sorry.'

Murdo John wasn't behind the bar, so Livvy wouldn't have had a chance to talk to him anyway. Fiona Ross was serving instead, full of bad grace, with one of the waitresses from the dining room helping, but since she wasn't sure about prices she wasn't as useful as she might have been.

When Livvy reached the bar, Fiona was talking to one of the regulars as she pulled a pint. 'Oh, said he wasn't available tonight, just like that. No excuse, just that he wouldn't do it. And of course I can't sack him, because as you can see we haven't really got an alternative.'

She gave a contemptuous glance at the little waitress who was looking around her in a bewildered way. 'What's the matter, dear? Whisky Mac? Whisky and top up with ginger wine.' Then she gave a shriek of 'No!' as the girl went to a bottle of single malt. 'Blended, dear, blended – over there.'

'It's really too bad,' she finished as she put the money in the till and turned to Livvy. 'Yes? Oh, it's you, Livvy.'

'Yes, it's me. Glass of house red, please.'

Fiona lowered her voice, leaning across the bar confidentially. 'Do tell me, just between ourselves, how's it going? Oh, and have this one on the house. You deserve it – you're all working so hard.'

'Thanks but no thanks,' Livvy said. 'I'd need more than the price of a glass of house red to risk getting busted for selling information. Anyway, I'm off duty. Oh, and I'm wanting a bag of crisps too. Cheese and onion.'

Fiona pursed her lips and turned away to fetch them. A man who had been sitting along near the farther end of the bar got up and Livvy moved to take the stool, realising as she did so that the woman sitting by herself in the corner was Vicky Macdonald. She was looking pale and strained and she didn't turn her head when Livvy sat down until she spoke.

'Hello! I didn't expect to see you here. Just come across to get out the house?'

'Oh, hi.' Vicky gave her a wan smile. 'Yes, I suppose so.'

'Can't be easy, all this.'

'No. No, it really isn't.' She had what looked like whisky in front of her; she took a sip then said vehemently, 'Even here, everyone's avoiding me, even people I thought were my friends.'

Glancing around and seeing eyes averted as she did so, Livvy made a sympathetic grimace. 'They're not that keen on the polis either, you know.'

'Mmm. I suppose it was daft to have come, but—'

'Getting stir-crazy?'

'A bit. But I was hoping to see Murdo John too. He's not in tonight, though.'

Livvy hesitated. 'I sort of heard things weren't too good with the two of you.'

'Sort of heard?' Vicky gave a short laugh. 'You mean, you weren't given chapter and verse about every word we said to each other? They must be slipping.'

She emptied her glass and held it up to Fiona Ross, who, after a pointed pause, brought another whisky and set it down with a disapproving sniff.

How many had she had before? Livvy wondered. 'Are you trying to patch it up?' she asked tentatively.

'Oh, I don't know. It's just – well, contrary to the gossip we didn't actually have a proper showdown. We hardly talked about it at all, really. I said I was going to stay at the Lodge, he said if I did I needn't come back and that was about it. Perhaps I shouldn't have insisted but – well, you know. It's the money and I didn't want to lose my job. Murdo John didn't like that either – made him feel humiliated, I suppose.'

'So what are you hoping for?'

'After all this is over, you mean? I guess it will be, eventually. But for now I'd just like to come home, get away from that awful place – it's really getting to me now. I was hoping to talk to him, just chat – you know, nothing heavy. There are things we need to talk about, openly and honestly. We both know that.'

'He's probably at home,' Livvy suggested, but Vicky shrank visibly.

'I – I don't have the courage to go round, as if I was demanding he take me back. He could just slam the door in my face.'

'I can understand that,' Livvy said earnestly. 'But I think—'

'That glass looks empty,' Daniel Tennant's voice spoke at her shoulder.

Resisting the temptation to turn and grab him by the throat, Livvy said icily, 'I'm all right, thanks.'

'No, no, I insist. Fiona! Another of these and a vodka tonic for me.'

With the usual perversity of fate, the bar stool on Livvy's other side became vacant and Daniel slid onto it.

'I was actually talking to Vicky,' Livvy said, but before she had reached the end of the sentence Vicky had drained her glass and stood up.

'Time I was on my way back. It's getting a bit blowy out there,' she said, picked up the keys for the Lodge boat from the bar counter and left.

'Well, thanks a whole bunch,' Livvy said in a furious undertone. 'I was having a useful conversation about her and Murdo John when you butted in.'

He was unmoved. 'So which of them did it, then?'

'Probably you.'

Fiona set the drinks down in front of them and for a moment Livvy thought of ignoring it, but then she never had been one to cut her nose off to spite her face. He hadn't bought her a drink for the pleasure of her company and if he wanted something, it was only fair he should pay for it. She ignored it when he said, 'Cheers,' but she took a sip.

Daniel laughed. 'Oh, come on, Livvy. You know I didn't do it. For God's sake, I'm a copper. There's no way I'd do something like that. We're on the same side.'

'Not the way I see it, right at this moment.'

'You know I didn't do it. For God's sake, would I try to stage a suicide as pathetically as that? Puh-leese!'

He had a point there, and for a moment she hesitated. Then it struck her. 'Well, you might,' she said. 'You might, just so you could say that to prove it wasn't you.'

She saw the lines of temper appear between his brows. 'Oh, shut up. You've got a real talent for being irritating, do you know that?'

'I prefer to think of it as genius. Anyway, what do you want?'

He made an effort to smile. 'OK, cards on the table. I've got my career to think about and I'm being frozen out here. Kelso won't tell me what's going on and there's a huge operation at stake. I need to be in on it. Are you making any progress?'

Livvy said slowly, 'Exactly why are you asking me that, Daniel?'

He put down the glass he was drinking from with a thump that had Fiona turning to glare at him. 'Because, you stupid cow,' he said venomously, 'maybe if I'm allowed to help Police Scotland get its act together I can get back in to find some evidence before they mess that up.'

It was a solid excuse. Oh, he was good – you had to give him that. Maybe it was even a reason, but she didn't trust him. She said, 'And what about your Eva, down there providing food for the fishes? Maybe you felt she deserved revenge,' and saw his look of fury as she walked out. She even left the wine unfinished on the bar. There was a first for everything.

CHAPTER TWENTY-TWO

As Livvy Murray pulled up the hood of her parka and headed off home, her mind was on the conversations she had just had. Tennant was a toerag; she couldn't think of anything she'd like more than to see him banged up for killing Carnegie – but had he really cared that much about Eva? Could she see him going for a knife? It wasn't impossible but he seemed more the type to shrug his shoulders and say, 'Collateral damage,' like they did in war movies. Murder didn't look good on your CV.

She felt sorry for Vicky, though. She wasn't to know Veruschka had been the love of Murdo John's life and that she was a poor substitute. Marrying on the rebound was classic disaster, so maybe he'd even been glad to get out of it.

It was understandable, too, that Vicky didn't want the humiliation of turning up on the doorstep to be blanked. It was sad, though. They should at least end it right, look at what had gone wrong.

That was their cottage, just there. The curtains were drawn but there was a light on in the downstairs window and she walked slower, then stopped. Maybe she could help, just as a friend not a police officer; if she could explain to Murdo John the way Vicky felt, he might agree to what she wanted.

Maybe, on the other hand, she should remember that Murdo John was a suspect – not only that, but he was the suspect she'd worked out had pretty much the best motive. Bring them together again? Yeah, smart thinking.

But why not? He wouldn't harm her. It wasn't like the usual sort of case; if Murdo John had killed Carnegie it was because he believed he deserved to die – and in a way Livvy sort of thought that yes, he probably did.

She wasn't going to interview him or anything, after all, just tell him what Vicky had said. Just passing on the message – that couldn't do any harm. She knocked on the door.

Murdo John's face was set in hard lines when he opened the door. 'Yes?' But when he saw who it was his shoulders sagged and he said, with infinite weariness, 'Oh, it's you. What is it this time?'

She gave him a placatory smile. 'Look, I'm sorry to trouble you so late. It's not official – it's just a message—'

He stood aside, holding the door open. 'You'd better come in. They'll be saying you're here to arrest me.'

'No, no, it's nothing like that,' Livvy protested, but she stepped inside.

'So what is it?'

She'd hoped to work up to it a bit more, but Murdo

John wasn't really into small talk. 'I was speaking to Vicky in the Black Cuillin just now.' She thought he stiffened, but he didn't say anything and she went on, 'She's really wanting to come home, to talk to you.'

'What's stopping her?' His face looked as if it had been carved out of granite.

Ditching any idea of tact, Livvy said, 'Most likely she thought you'd look like that. You might as well punch her in the face.'

'You think so?'

'Well, no, of course I don't really. But it's not fair – you've never told her about Veruschka, have you? She's probably blaming herself because the marriage failed when all the time there was fat chance it'd work, was there?'

'Did she say that?' His tone was uncompromising.

Oh God, she was making a right mess of this. She could even be making things worse. 'No, no, she never,' she said hastily. 'What she said was' – she paused, trying to recollect the exact words – 'she said she'd realised there were things you needed to talk about honestly and openly and that you knew that too.'

Clearly that had made him think and it was a moment before he spoke. 'Yes, I do.'

'So I can tell her if she comes back you'll listen?' Livvy said eagerly.

'For what it's worth.'

If that was what Vicky wanted, it was a good result. Personally, she felt talking to the Black Cuillin itself would be more rewarding, but she'd done what she came to do.

'Thanks for listening to me. That's all,' she said and left.

Doubt assailed her along with the night air. She wasn't sure she'd done the right thing; Vicky might be furious that she'd interfered. But he had said he'd listen and that had to be good, didn't it? And maybe if she phoned Vicky and confessed what she'd done and told her that he wouldn't actually slam the door in her face, Vicky might not lie awake tonight worrying.

She had the Balnasheil Lodge landline number back at the police office. She switched on the torch she always carried and hurried on up the hill.

It was almost eleven when Kelso Strang stood up from his desk, stretched and yawned. He was as prepared as he was ever going to be for tomorrow and he'd better get some sleep. He locked the office and let himself out into the darkness.

He should have brought a torch and vowed to remember in future. All he could see was the small string of lights along the road down at the pier. There were no lights on in the building behind him; Livvy must be having an early night or else she was out, whooping it up – always supposing there was a whooping-it-up venue around here.

In the city there was always ambient light and Kelso was uncomfortable with darkness like this: it had an intense, almost physical presence. It seemed to wrap itself about you till the air itself felt thick and smothering. There were no stars, only a greenish pallor that was the moon, heavily veiled by cloud.

He couldn't claim that he couldn't see his hand in front of his face – he actually held his hand up to check – but he definitely couldn't see what was under his feet. He was walking all but blindly, splashing in puddles and stumbling into the verges, but somehow that made his other senses more vivid so that he was aware of the damp fresh scent of wet grass and the ranker smell of rotting bracken as well as the small rustlings and stirrings in the night about him. Under it all there was the insistent, threatening moaning of a rising wind. He pulled up his collar with a shiver.

Nearing the bottom of the hill there was at last light enough to see the pale ribbon of the road in front of him and he quickened his steps. His mind was on the bottle of Scotch in his drawer and a well-earned nightcap when he got back to the hotel. He glanced towards Daniel Tennant's cottage as he passed it and saw the man himself, sitting at the small square window, staring intently out over the bay towards Balnasheil Lodge. He followed his gaze: the place was in darkness apart from a light on the ground floor at the back and another on the first floor, and a bobbing light in the grounds – the poor wretched constable on duty, no doubt.

Kelso heard the urgent knocking on the window but walked on as if he hadn't. He was tired and there was nothing he wanted to say to the man. He wasn't going to get away with it, though; a moment later there were footsteps behind him and his name was called. He turned with an inward groan.

'Just knocking off?' Daniel said genially. 'You look like a man who's earned a drink. I've a bottle of Highland Park with your name on it.'

'Thanks, Daniel, but quite honestly what I want now is to get my head down. It's going to be another heavy day tomorrow.'

'I won't keep you long. There's something I really need to say to you. You'll want to know, I promise you.'

Kelso didn't even try to keep the irritation out of his voice. 'Oh, all right. But keep it short and never mind the whisky.' He followed him reluctantly into the cottage.

It seemed offensive to stand once Daniel was sitting down, but he chose an upright chair to stress that he wasn't settling in. 'So – what is it?'

'Look, I'm sorry to be keeping a weary man from his bed. I tried to talk to Murray earlier but she's impossible – the typical perfectly balanced Glaswegian with a chip on either shoulder. No wonder they've stuck her out here in the sticks where they thought she couldn't do any damage.'

Kelso's patience snapped. 'I didn't come in here to listen to you slagging off another officer. Get to the point.'

'Huh! Scots solidarity, I suppose – what did I expect? Anyway, I called my guv'nor today and he's given me permission to tell you what we're looking for. We believe Human Face is a front for money laundering—'

'No! You don't say? Well, blow me!'

Daniel gave him a look of distaste. 'I don't think being childish helps, do you?'

'No, I don't suppose it does,' Kelso acknowledged. 'My excuse is that I'm very tired and I don't really want to sit around listening to you repeating things you've said already that were statements of the bleeding obvious anyway. Just give me the basics.'

'Fine,' he said coldly. 'From what Eva told me, I know there are paper records – that's by far the most secure system nowadays. She found them for me and I think that's why the bastards killed her. So what we're looking for is paper files. They may have been destroyed already but if they exist at all I need to be able to search myself, in case some plod who doesn't realise what they are puts them in an evidence bag that will never see the light of day again. I know what your boss said. I'm sorry if I was rude about her – I was just frustrated. But you're in charge on the ground; you can bring me in on it. It's my guess you're not getting anywhere much – is that right?'

'I'm not going to comment on the investigation.'

The anger that Daniel had suppressed earlier erupted. 'For God's sake!' he shouted. 'You're still carrying on as if I were a suspect, when you know I'm not.'

'Do I?'

'Like I said to Murray, think about it. A copper, trying to stage a suicide by smearing the wrong knife with blood and leaving it beside the victim? Do me a favour!'

'It wasn't going to work, certainly.'

'So?'

'So nothing.' Kelso got up. 'I'll undertake to let you see any files that turn up. That should cover the problem you raised. I'll be sending someone to take your statement tomorrow in the hope that we may then be able to eliminate you from our enquiries.'

'I don't believe this! Kelso—'

'Sorry.' He walked out, hearing the man swearing behind him as he closed the door.

As he walked along to the hotel he thought over what Daniel Tennant had said and found himself wondering if

Murray's reaction had been the same as his was. Of course, it was true that no police officer would imagine forensic experts would be fooled by the wrong knife; it was equally true that if you wanted to divert suspicion from yourself that would be quite a smart move.

Did he really think Tennant had done it? Surely not – but from the start he had been so insistent about being included in the investigation, and now he remembered the look on the man's face, before and after he had viewed Eva's body, and it left him feeling very uncertain indeed.

'Not much of a night for a wee walk. Were you wanting something, sir?'

Transfixed by the beam of the constable's powerful torch, Harry Drummond froze. It was well after midnight; he'd watched the man from the window for half an hour to check out his routine, and he should at this moment have been right round the back of the house. But he wasn't, was he.

'Er – no, no, just – just a spot of fresh air before bedtime,' he spluttered, even though he knew it wasn't convincing. It was pitch-black and the air was damp and heavy with that nasty little wind blowing a bit stronger now.

'Oh aye. You won't be long, then?'

'No, no. In fact, I'm just turning in now.'

'I'll light your way back into the house, then. You'll not be wanting to trip or anything.'

The beam guided him back to the front door and with a falsely cheerful, 'You're doing a grand job, Constable,' Harry went back inside. When the door was shut behind him he clenched his fists and brought them down hard on the oak table in the hall, giving vent to a stream of obscenities under his breath.

After a night of the worst sort of dreams – the ones where Alexa was still alive – Strang was headachy and tired. He opened his bedroom curtains on a surly dawn, the low clouds bruise-coloured and heavy. There was something unsettling about the sea, lead-grey and heaving with a queasy motion, as if the tops of the waves had been shaved smooth by the wind that was blowing now with a deep, menacing groaning. The air seemed oppressive and he had to struggle with a sense of foreboding.

The pathetic fallacy, he told himself – the idea that nature was somehow in tune with human feelings. It was just that the forecast storm was taking longer to arrive than they had predicted and even though it might pose logistical problems, he thought he'd feel better once it arrived. This was – well, unsettling.

He skipped hotel breakfast. He could get a cup of coffee and a roll at the police office once the caterers arrived; he'd had too many cooked breakfasts and abstention was easier when you couldn't smell bacon frying. It would be good, too, to get ahead before the working day started. There might be reports in overnight; JB was keeping up the pressure on the labs to get the tests done and sometimes they worked late on priority cases.

When he switched on the computer there was nothing from forensics as yet. There was, though, a report filed late last night by what must be a very conscientious constable charged with interviewing Quentin Lacey's partner.

Or ex-partner, it seemed. Karen Prescott came across as a spirited lady. Her annoyance at having been persuaded to make the nasty little call to Beatrice was clear, even through the stilted language of the statement. She knew she shouldn't have done it, she said, but 'he just went on and on and on'. So she was anxious now to dissociate herself from the sordid goings-on at Balnasheil Lodge and, judging by the words she used, which included 'slob', 'sponger' and 'whiner', kicking Quentin out hadn't caused her too much heartache anyway.

Importantly, though, she was prepared to swear that on the night of Adam Carnegie's murder Quentin had said he was going out to see Beatrice, then returned in a very bad mood – 'with a right flea in his ear' – shortly before ten o'clock and hadn't gone out after that.

Pathology reports having established the time of death as being between 11 p.m. and 2 a.m., Quentin could be eliminated from the inquiry. Strang's own judgement had been that he was more likely to faint at the sight of blood than to slash someone's artery, but given this they wouldn't have to go through the motions. Costs were mounting and he knew JB was seriously twitchy about that.

PC Murray had filed Harry Drummond's statement too and he had to admit it was a competent piece of work. She'd been quite sharp about the business of the hare and JB seemed to be impressed with her; she had potential, admittedly, but she lacked judgement and he couldn't trust her not to get something badly wrong.

To be fair, this was evidence she'd taken on board what

he'd said about the difference between conducting an interview and taking a statement. She could be quite useful as long as she didn't overstep the mark. He'd applied for an interpreter to see if they could get a proper statement from Kaczka; Murray could go along and work that into a statement for him. It would stop her rushing off to 'use her initiative' and coming unstuck.

At 8.30, PC Murray knocked on the door of DI Strang's office. She'd heard him arrive just after seven o'clock but even though she was more than keen to know what would be happening today, she'd reckoned that interrupting someone who'd come in early to get some peace wasn't a smart move. But she didn't want to leave it too late, when everyone else would be clocking in. She was fizzing with ideas and she wanted the chance to run them past him.

She'd been thinking about motivation – the key to any investigation, surely? – and she'd worked out motives for all the obvious suspects. Some, admittedly, were stronger than others: all she could think of for Vicky Macdonald, for instance, was that Carnegie might have come on to her, but you didn't cut someone's throat for doing that – fortunately, otherwise every bar in every city would be knee-deep in blood every Saturday night. But there were others that were definitely worth discussing.

She took a deep breath. 'Reporting for duty, sir,' she said.

He was frowning at his computer. 'Oh, good morning, Murray. Do you think you could find me a cup of coffee and a roll if they've got the kitchen going?'

'Sir,' she said, trying not to show her resentment. It was

a perfectly standard request but it closed out any discussion and put her firmly back in her place. She was on the way to the door, sulking, when Strang said, 'Oh, by the way, good report on Drummond. And I meant to tell you they found the remains of your hare and it did look as if the dog might have been eating it. It's with the labs now.'

'That's good. Thank you, sir,' she said, though inwardly she was punching the air and shouting, 'Result!' She seized her opportunity. 'By the way, I was wanting to say I'd been doing a lot of thinking about motives for our list of suspects, sir . . .'

'Really?'

She tried to read his expression – irritated, but perhaps a little amused as well. She coloured. 'I thought it might be helpful—'

'That's doing it back end foremost. In real life it's once the evidence implicates a particular individual that it may be useful to consider why they did it but until then it's not good practice – if you dream up a convincing motive there's always the temptation to go looking for evidence to fit the theory. OK?'

'Sir,' she said, feeling crushed. He was more or less implying that she'd got all her ideas from TV detectives, and she probably had. And as she turned to go she remembered her row with Tennant the night before – that could be another black mark, if he made a complaint. She'd be better to get her side of the story in first.

'Er – I think I should maybe tell you I'd a wee bit of a run-in with Daniel Tennant last night. Sorry.'

'Yes, I heard.'

'Did he tell you? I was in the Black Cuillin and he just sort of butted in. Maybe I was rude.' Then she paused. 'Well, not maybe.'

'It's no business of mine what hobbies you pursue in your own time. He's having problems with accepting that he can't take part in the investigation before we've eliminated him from the inquiry. I'll arrange for him to make a full statement today – not to you, though, I think.'

He was actually smiling properly and she'd been right – he was very attractive when he smiled. She smiled back.

'I'll get your coffee, then, sir.' It did occur to her that perhaps she ought to tell him about her visit to Murdo John, but she wasn't sure it was a good idea. He was pleased with her for once and he'd never seemed too thrilled at the idea of her using her initiative, so it'd be a bit chancy. No, she'd keep quiet about that, for the time being at least.

When she opened the door, Sergeant Buchanan was standing there, his hand just raised to knock.

Strang looked pleased. 'You're bright and early this morning, Rab. Good – it's going to be a heavy day. Have the lads arrived to get on with the outside searches?'

'I gave them an early start time, sir,' Buchanan said. 'We want to get it done before the weather closes in. They've just gone across in the boats now.'

'Excellent. We'd better discuss dispositions, then.'

Murray didn't move. Maybe if she just stayed very still he might assign her to something more interesting than fetching coffee.

But no. He said, 'Thanks, Murray. Coffee? And can you bring a mug for the sergeant as well, please?'

'Sir,' she said, and went off with her spirits sinking. One day, she vowed, she'd get to be one of the ones who wasn't sent away when they got to the interesting stuff.

Marek Kaczka was sweeping leaves off the lawn. They were pretty much the last to leave the trees, lying in soggy, impacted piles of pale yellow and brown, with the occasional flash of flame-red from an ornamental maple. He was watching under his brows as the uniformed men and women spread out once more across the garden.

They'd been crawling around the lawn yesterday; today a line of them was doing that on the slopes on the farther side of the house. Others were beating the bushes, using rakes to drag away debris and check through the undergrowth. And going through the sheds and the barns.

There was a policewoman lifting the latch on the metal door to Amber's run. 'Hey, Sarge,' she called. 'You're sure the dog's not in here?'

The sergeant laughed. 'Sure as death,' he called back. 'Saw it stretched out myself.'

Kaczka raked more slowly. After a few minutes the woman came back out. 'Sarge! Come and take a look at this.'

CHAPTER TWENTY-THREE

In the Perthshire farmhouse that was her first ever home after forty years of living in army accommodation, Mary Strang sat in the country-style kitchen she had always dreamt of, reading *The Scotsman* over breakfast. At the other end of the table in the bow window looking out to her beloved garden, Roderick was absorbed in the *Daily Telegraph*; they didn't really speak in the morning until they had both had their second cup of coffee.

Otherwise, she might have said something when she read the report about a man who had been found dead on the Isle of Skye; the police, it said, were now treating the death as suspicious. It was only a small paragraph on the inside of the front page, but she read it again carefully.

Was it pure coincidence that Kelso had said he was going to be working in Skye? She knew that now with Police Scotland he could be posted anywhere, but from the way he'd spoken it had sounded temporary, so perhaps it was to do with this. Now she looked at it, though, the man's death seemed to have happened after Kelso would have arrived, so perhaps it had nothing to do with him after all.

She hoped it didn't. Murders always got a lot of publicity and Roderick would hate to see his son splashed all over the newspapers associated with something so sordid. Mary gave a little sigh as she glanced across at her oblivious husband. She loved Roddy dearly; he was a model husband, devoted and caring if perhaps a little unnecessarily protective. Soldiers, she had noted, were often like that about their womenfolk, perhaps as a result of their experiences out there in the very wicked world.

Unfortunately, they – or perhaps just he? – tended to extend that protective love into deciding what was best for their children, with the deeply disappointing results you might expect. Rory, the eldest, had dropped out of university and was now touring somewhere in the States with a band. Finella had made a promising start, training as a lawyer with a boyfriend who was another law graduate, but he had taken a job with Tesco and they weren't married despite having a child. Roddy hadn't dared use the word 'bastard' to Mary, but she knew he thought it.

Kelso had been his last hope; having seen him so well set on the path to glory, Roddy had been utterly crushed by his rejection of all that his father stood for, as he saw it. His subsequent behaviour had been inexcusable and for the first time in her life Mary had failed to pull him into line. It saddened her deeply to see the man she loved in such an ugly light.

She had set about him after what he'd said at the funeral;

he had looked abashed and she was reasonably certain that he wouldn't speak like that again. But she had a nasty feeling that what carried more weight was telling him that if he hoped that one day Kelso really might change his mind, this was the worst possible way to go about it; he hadn't given up. All she could do was go on trying to keep the peace between them, but the big problem was that in terms of determination – the Sunday name for sheer pig-headedness – they were far too much alike.

Yes, it was probably just as well to say nothing about the little paragraph in the paper. It was most likely nothing to do with Kelso anyway. She decided to call Finella after breakfast, though. She and Kelso had always been thick as thieves; if he'd spoken to anyone, it would be her.

But he hadn't. Mary didn't mention how worried she was about his emotional state and Finella didn't either. They didn't need to.

PC Murray had been disappointed again when she was allocated to scouring the grounds. Surely she was too useful to the investigation to be wasted on the lowliest, and most loathed, task of all, fingertip-searching, hands and knees in the wet grass. After all, she'd done a great job on Drummond's statement – Strang had said that himself – and they'd never have known about the hare if it hadn't been for her.

She'd protested to the Broadford sergeant who was in charge but got short shrift. 'Oh, all la-di-dah, now that we're hobnobbing with the high heid yins, are we? Get in that boat, Livvy, and do as you're told.'

Muttering, she stomped across to the boat and had to endure ten minutes of jeering from her colleagues – and that wasn't her only reason for being glad the journey wasn't longer. She was a rotten sailor and she didn't like this nasty, undulating motion one bit.

Still, she was in luck at the other side; the sergeant in charge over there was a mate and assigned her to checking the outbuildings, despite protests from the others about her getting the jammy jobs.

'Grub away, peasants!' Murray called cheerfully as she walked across to begin in the barn that also acted as a garage.

In fact, it wasn't as easy as she had thought. There was a lot of stuff piled around the walls and since there was no guidance on what they were looking for, she had to move everything and check behind it, and even climb on a ladder to go round the ledges under the roof. After an hour all she had unearthed was a prize collection of cobwebs, many of them festooned over her uniform and hair, and some particularly nasty creepy-crawlies. She'd given a small shriek when a sudden movement in one of the corners drew her attention to a thick, scaly tail that mercifully disappeared into a hole in the wall.

Maybe the outbuildings weren't such a doss after all. As a city lass, she hadn't really thought of the lower orders of livestock to whom they might be home and she came out of the barn when she had finished the search hot and filthy. She hated to think what she might find in the wood store.

Then she noticed the dog run. Surely rats wouldn't hang around where Amber, the killer of hares, lived.

With a cheery word to the sergeant, she went there next.

It still smelt of dog – a friendly smell, she thought, even if the animal itself had been far from that. The dog's bed against the back wall had a smart furry cover and there was a heavy water bowl, still full, beside it. The food bowl was sitting on a shelf beside a standpipe with a tap and it had been washed since the last time it was used – presumably that was one of Marek's responsibilities. He'd kept the place immaculate, a lot cleaner than he kept his own house; Adam Carnegie probably expected nothing less for his treasured pet. There was a leash hanging by the door and a travelling rug lying on the floor, covering a pile of something. Probably just dog stuff, she told herself, but her heart was beating a little faster as she went to lift it up.

Files. About a dozen thick files. She picked up the top one and opened it. There was a letter first, with some technical stuff about money that she didn't fully understand and a bank reference for deposits. It was addressed to someone she didn't know, but the signature at the bottom was familiar – Harry Drummond.

And when she riffled through the rest of that file there were more letters, all signed by Drummond, as well as bank statements, names and addresses, and accounts. Exactly what Tennant had been looking for, presumably.

And what Eva Havel had died for, too. With a shudder, Murray closed the file, picked up the rest and went out to tell the sergeant what she had found.

Beatrice Lacey still hadn't left her room. Sheer exhaustion had driven her to bed eventually but she had been afraid to

398

take a sleeping pill and with her various aches and injuries she had dozed only fitfully. This morning she was leaden-eyed and agonisingly stiff but at least the throbbing in her arm had stopped.

She was hungry; she made herself tea and toast in the tiny kitchenette area, the two slices of toast thickly spread with honey for energy. The comforting sweetness made her feel a little better and when she looked out of the window she could see that the garden was swarming like an ant heap with policemen.

She was still afraid of what Harry might do but surely nothing could happen to her with all these officers around, ready to be summoned by a scream? He simply couldn't risk attacking her now and she had to leave her room sometime. There was nothing to do here, except stare at Rosamond's empty crib and cry.

In fact, she wanted to leave more than her room. She wanted to get away from this godforsaken place immediately, find a truly comfortable hotel where she could recover and hide away from Harry. There were some very nice hotels in Portree, if the police would let her go. She was ready to insist; unless they actually arrested her, she was pretty sure they couldn't stop her.

It needn't, Beatrice thought suddenly, even be a hotel here in Skye. She could go back to Surrey, to that nice country house hotel near her old home. Harry wouldn't know where she was and she could look up the friends she'd ignored for so long, get back to the little bridge parties and theatre trips she'd always enjoyed. Then she looked down at her spreading girth; they would hardly recognise her, the way she'd put on weight here where there were no little treats except the ones that came in multicoloured foil wrappers.

Perhaps it might be better to go to a spa for a bit first, if she could afford it. She'd lost her lovely house, of course, but she'd get her trustee on to trying to recover what he could from the charity that would surely be closed down, and if she instructed the bank to stop the standing order today, that would cover the hotel bill. It gave her a real pang to think of the children looking to Human Face for help and not finding it, but she could donate to Save the Children instead.

She was feeling much more cheerful now. She could even do a little bit of packing before she went down and asked to see the nice inspector, but she stiffened when a knock came on the door. Harry, returning to pressure her?

But when she opened it there were two policemen standing there. 'Miss Lacey?' one said. 'We have a warrant to search this room.'

'Ah,' DI Strang said when PC Murray appeared in triumph and laid the bundle on his desk. 'So this is what DC Tennant has been hoping to find? Where was it?'

'In the dog's kennel. I reckon Carnegie thought no investigator would look there and if they showed any interest it would see them off. It certainly scared me stupid. So – can we arrest Drummond?'

Strang flicked through a couple of the files. 'Not on this – *we* can't, anyway. Not before the forensic accountants have assembled a case, unless Tennant can push it along. I'll tell him to come round.'

'But—' Murray stopped as he lifted the phone and held up a hand while he made the call.

Tennant was loudly pleased; she could hear him right across the desk. She wasn't happy. She couldn't stand the man, with his sneery voice and the way he had of treating them as if they were teuchters who hadn't heard about using a knife and fork. And whatever Strang might say, he was still a suspect in her book.

Strang caught the look on her face as he put down the phone. 'Yes, Murray? Was there something you wanted to say?'

She'd said it all about Tennant before and it wasn't going to be any different now. 'Oh, nothing.'

His lips twitched. 'Well, you could have fooled me. Anyway, you'll be pleased to hear that the analysis of the hare has come through and it was definitely doped.'

Brilliant! But all she said was, 'I was sure it had to be. The dog would never have let him be attacked otherwise. What with?'

He looked down at the paper. 'Zolpidem. In common use as a sleeping pill, marketed under several proprietary names.'

'They're searching the house now.' She couldn't help showing her excitement. 'If they find it on someone, that could be it, all wrapped up.'

'Hang on. That phrase, "in common use", remember? More than one person may be having trouble sleeping. And there's the question of who could have known the hare was hanging there too.'

That was certainly true. That was something else she

needed to learn – not to jump to conclusions. She'd said she was keen to learn, but she hadn't quite realised the education process would make her feel like quite such an effing idiot.

Tennant knocked on the door then came in without waiting for an answer. He nodded to Strang, ignored Murray, then snatched up the file on top of the pile without waiting for permission and flipped it open. As he flicked through the pages a broad smile spread over his face.

'Be my guest,' Strang said dryly.

'Oh – oh sorry, I suppose that was rude. But this' – he patted the papers in his hand – 'this is all our Christmases come at once.'

'I haven't looked through them yet and I'm not sure I understand what I'm looking at, really,' Strang said. 'I imagine it's the background to the money laundering?'

'Yes, of course.' Tennant sat down and started checking another file. 'And the names mentioned are gold dust – I recognise some as people we've had our sights on for a long time but there are new ones there too. The idea was that they donated to the charity, the money was sent out to an office in Zambia and then rerouted to the designated Swiss bank accounts. Hardly an original idea, really, but we've had difficulty pinpointing either Drummond or Carnegie as their contacts; their digital trails are very confused.'

'Double passports?' Strang said.

Tennant looked up. 'Oh, you were onto that one, were you?'

'Sometimes we manage to stumble on something, even up here in the wilds.' Strang's acid tone earned a grin from

Murray. 'The records said that Carnegie was in Paris at the time of Eva's death, when he couldn't possibly have been.'

'Well you see, that's my point,' Tennant said, leaning forward. 'If you'd told me that was a problem, I could have put you onto it right away. That's why you need me on the inside.'

The vulgar saying about people who were better there than outside came to Murray's mind but she decided not to push her luck. If she drew attention to herself, Strang might send her away.

'I'd like to help you get on with arresting Drummond,' Tennant went on. 'You've got his motive right here. Carnegie was trying to drop him in it.'

'His motive – really? I would have thought this would put him in the clear. If Carnegie had all this incriminating stuff, surely Drummond would have been mad to kill him and trigger an investigation.'

'Ah, but he didn't know, did he? He thought he'd purged the files. He was perfectly calm to start with, just banging on about the charity being Adam's business and he was only the official accountant. Beatrice was in on it too, according to him, and of course he did his best to blame her at the start. Something must have alerted him to the possibility that Adam had a little insurance policy tucked away somewhere. So – can I be absolved, and rejoin the team? Unless, of course, there's some other definite line of enquiry you're following?'

His question hung in the air for a fraction of a second too long. Then Strang stood up. 'Thanks, Daniel. That's been helpful and I'll get this stuff sent to Edinburgh when the operation support chopper comes in later today. I'll be speaking to my super so if your bosses want to contact her I'm sure they'll get this sorted out.' He reached forward to take the file that Tennant was still holding.

The detective clutched at it. 'Don't do this, Kelso! I've worked so long for this—'

'Sorry.' Strang held out his hand.

'Oh, for God's sake! Have it, then. Muddle along, nurse your stupid suspicions about a colleague and make a complete fool of yourself, why don't you?'

He handed over the file and walked out, slamming the door hard behind him.

Murray didn't speak, waiting for Strang to comment.

He didn't. Instead he said, 'Right. I'll have to put that in hand too. I'll need to speak to the fraud department in Edinburgh.' He was looking harassed. 'I've got a job for you, though, Murray. They've found me a Polish interpreter; she's in the waiting room. I want you to go across with her to speak to Kaczka. Get her to establish where he came from and why. But remember it's just a statement you're taking – don't start grilling him. What I'm interested in is if he had a wife, a family, and if he did where they are now.'

Murray's head came up sharply. 'A daughter, say – who might have come over here illegally?'

'Well, it's a thought.'

'Understood, sir. I'll pick her up now and get going. Sooner the better, really – it's getting worse out there. I was only a couple of minutes away from throwing up on the way back.'

'Better hope they gun it, then,' said Strang unfeelingly. 'Good luck.'

* * *

Strang looked after her as she closed the door, hoping he'd done the right thing. Buchanan was occupied with the logistics of getting personnel to and from Balnasheil Lodge – the road was still blocked and the council were in no hurry to clear it – and the local officers were an unknown quantity. Murray at least wasn't lacking in intelligence and she'd done a good job with Drummond's statement.

He'd done his debrief with JB this morning but he'd have to fill her in on the discovery of the files. It was progress of a sort, he supposed, but he couldn't really see that it got them any further forward with their own case. Tennant was right; the evidence on Drummond could be read in two different ways – and the same went for Tennant himself. It would be interesting to see what Murray came back with. They knew so little about the mysterious Veruschka that they might never be able to establish who she was, but he could construct a scenario in which she was Kaczka's daughter who had disappeared and he had somehow tracked her to this place and come to work more or less as a serf to try to find out what had happened to her. He had seen Carnegie take Eva away; had he then known what had happened to his daughter and taken revenge?

Strang sighed. It was far-fetched and even if it happened to be true he still couldn't see how he could prove it, unless the answer lay in the forensic reports – there were eight waiting for him on his terminal and he'd better read them before he phoned JB again.

He hadn't been hopeful and he was right: none, unfortunately, took them any further forward. There were unidentified fingerprints at the crime scene, naturally, and now they'd need to take prints from all of the suspects for comparison.

Would that tell them anything? Probably not. He was reaching out his hand to make his phone call to JB when it rang.

'Just thought you'd want to know at once, sir,' the voice of the sergeant leading the search team said. 'We've found sleeping pills in Beatrice Lacey's flat – Stilnoct, active ingredient zolpidem. That's what we were looking for, isn't it?'

'Yes,' said Strang. 'Oh yes.'

The wind was blowing quite strongly now and under a lowering sky the tops of the waves had broken peaks and were splashing ashore with little vicious slaps. As PC Murray and Marta, the interpreter, stood waiting at the pier for a boat, a great silver curtain of rain swept in from the sea with a hissing sound, obliterating the farther side. The raindrops were painful as nettle stings when they hit their faces.

Huddling inside her jacket, Murray complained to the sergeant in charge, 'For goodness' sake! Why is it taking so long? This is awful.'

'Patience, lassie,' the man said stolidly. 'We're one boat short today. Macdonald hasn't turned up – shut the door in my face when I went to speak to him. We're going to have fun getting everybody back across when they decide to call it a day.'

Murray looked at the rising sea and shuddered. 'Sooner the better, as far as I'm concerned,' she said and the woman beside her agreed with some fervour.

As the boat bounced its way across to them, her mind went to Murdo John. He'd refused to work last night too; what was he doing, sitting alone there in his house? Brooding about his lost love? Or was he considering how to save his marriage? She wondered suddenly whether Vicky might have come across to see him but when she asked the man at the wheel he said no.

She had briefed Marta with the questions Strang had wanted put to Kaczka, though she wondered if there was any point; both she and Strang had doubted Kaczka's claim to being Polish. Still, this would establish whether he was or not – and maybe that wouldn't take long and they could go back before things got worse. Even now she was concentrating on willing the boat to speed across the increasingly stormy stretch of water; it sort of helped to have something to think about apart from her stomach and she managed to reach the jetty without disgracing herself. She wasn't prepared to bet on the outcome of the return journey, though.

'I don't know where Marek will be but we'll try his house first. He surely can't be working outside,' she said to Marta as they hurried down the drive. 'The place is just minging, but at least it'll be out of the rain.'

She hammered on the door and they stood shivering for a moment, wondering whether he was there or not, and if he was, whether he would answer. At last the door was opened a reluctant few inches and Murray produced her warrant card hastily, before Kaczka could shut it again.

'PC Murray – could I have a word? I came before, remember?'

His face was dark and hostile but he swung the door back to allow them to come in. At least there was a log fire burning in the grate but the room seemed in worse disorder than before, the stink of soiled clothing and dirty sheets ranker than ever. There was nowhere they could sit and as she crossed the carpet the soles of Murray's boots stuck to it. She gave an apologetic glance at Marta, who was looking horrified.

'Mr Kaczka, this lady speaks Polish and she's going to be able to explain to you what we want to know. All right?'

It was clear from the expression of Kaczka's face that it was far from all right. He looked both startled and frightened, then he said, 'No, only English. I speak English.'

Marta began talking to him. She spoke for a few moments while he looked at her stone-faced, until she stopped and turned to Murray to murmur, 'I'm pretty sure he doesn't understand this at all. I think if he was Polish I'd have got some reaction.' She gave a little, wicked smile. 'I called him some very rude words at the end.'

Kaczka scowled. 'English!' he bellowed. 'Only English!'

Murray felt mixed emotions. On the one hand, she wouldn't be going back to Strang with the answers he had wanted; on the other, she was going to be able to go back right now.

'Sorry about that,' she said to Marta. 'We've dragged you out on a wasted errand. No point in pursuing this.'

'Wait a moment,' Marta said, and she started speaking again. Again, Kaczka didn't react, except with a black look. 'That was Serbian,' she said over her shoulder to Murray. 'I'll try Albanian next.'

Murray, who could just about order a beer in France if pushed, watched her, humbled. And this time there was no mistaking his reaction; he was alert, following what she said, even though he was making no response. Then she spat out a few words.

He was visibly shocked, rigid with anger. '*Jo!*' he snarled. Then he stopped.

'I don't know what you said to him,' Murray said with admiration, 'but it worked.'

'You don't want to know,' Marta said demurely. 'But he denied it very strongly.'

'So – Albanian,' Murray said. 'Illegal immigrant. Look, tell him that if he cooperates we'll do our best for him. He's been all but a slave here – the authorities are very sympathetic to people who've been exploited.'

Marta spoke at length and Murray saw the man's head bow and his shoulders sag, as if he was giving up a struggle that had become too much for him. He said something, his voice heavy and defeated.

'He says he'll cooperate,' Marta said. 'What do you want me to ask him first?'

Murray considered for a moment. 'Start by asking him if he killed Adam Carnegie and we can take it from there. You never know – he might say "Yes" and save us a lot of time.'

'It sounds as if that's quite definite progress,' DCS Borthwick said. 'You should be feeling cheerful – though it can't be easy, on a day like this. If it's as bad as this in Edinburgh I hate to think what it's like with you.'

'It's bad and getting worse,' he said gloomily. 'We're

starting to bring people back across here now and the SOCOs are packing up. The chopper's due any minute and they want a quick turnaround.'

'Can't blame them. Anyway – Beatrice Lacey? Is she a possibility?'

'No,' he said, then qualified it. 'I should say, hard to imagine. She's overweight, clumsy – could she have managed an attack like that? And then she walked straight into the dog attack in the morning – though I suppose she could have thought the dog would still be laid out.'

'It's not hard to get hold of, zolpidem. I think I was prescribed some myself once.'

'There's the Internet too, though I doubt if this was planned that far ahead. I think we'll start with who would have known about the hare. Vicky Macdonald certainly would and Murray said earlier that when she was there Drummond had made a bit of a thing about stopping Vicky looking for it to cook for supper, though she could be making too much of it. Can't stand jugged hare myself.'

'Not my taste either. And if it had been hanging a few days, anyone who passed within a hundred yards would have known all about it – not easy to eliminate anyone at all on that basis. So – just on with the routine stuff, I suppose. Whatever it takes to get a result.'

Borthwick, Strang thought, was sounding distinctly edgy, which wasn't like her. She'd have the chief constable breathing down her neck, of course, and he'd be looking for a success, preferably a quick one. 'Quick' meaning 'cheap'.

'We'll do our best, ma'am,' he said. He had just put the phone down when it rang again.

'Buchanan here, sir. Murdo John Macdonald didn't turn up this morning to help with the shuttle and he was downright rude when someone went to speak to him. Of course, it's not compulsory, but I thought I'd maybe have a wee chat and see what the problem was. He wouldn't let me in but he said he was wanting to talk to you. I told him you'd better things to do but he just shut the door on me. I wasn't sure what you'd want me to do so I thought I'd best check.'

'Absolutely right. I'm up to the eyes with all this stuff but with the weather deteriorating we need his boat, so if you think I might be able to talk him into doing it, I'd better get down there.'

He logged out with a sigh and fetched his boots and the weatherproof jacket that was unlikely to be proof against this sort of weather, and stepped outside.

It was blowing hard now, a gale coming in off the blackening sea and driving the teeming rain straight into his face, cold and stinging. There were white caps in the bay and the mountains had vanished, yet somehow he could feel the Black Cuillin's brooding presence, there in the heart of the cloud and mist.

Strang gave the little shudder that had become a reflex when he looked up at it. It spooked him, with that constant reminder of how puny and pathetic human effort was in the face of the implacable hostility of nature.

Visibility was down to a few yards and he did spare a thought for the officers who would be having to cross that menacing stretch of water. He hoped for Murray's sake that she'd be an early passenger; from what she said she wasn't much of a sailor.

The lights were on inside the cottage and when he knocked he was aware of Macdonald's face at the window, checking who it was. The door was opened promptly.

'All right, Mr Macdonald. What did you have to say to me that you couldn't say to Sergeant Buchanan?'

The man who was standing in the doorway looked a different man from the one he had seen in the bar when he arrived. His eyes were reddened and there were black circles below them as if he hadn't slept; his hair was wild and his black beard looked unkempt.

His voice was steady, though, as he said, 'I want to confess to the murder of Adam Carnegie.'

CHAPTER TWENTY-FOUR

'He says yes, he had a daughter,' the interpreter said.

PC Murray, who had been listening gloomily, looked at her sharply. 'Ask where she is, Marta,' she urged. *At last, something promising!* She could write the scenario – his daughter, the mysterious Veruschka; somehow he knows she was here, realises Carnegie killed her . . . This could be it!

There had been nothing useful so far, apart from his admitting that yes, he was Albanian. He'd denied having killed Carnegie – but then he would, wouldn't he? He said he'd come because he'd been promised a passport that would allow him to work in Britain but Carnegie wouldn't give it to him and he had no money and nowhere else to go. They'd guessed that already.

'He is afraid to tell anyone,' Marta said, adding in a rapid undertone, 'I think maybe he has a police record – that is perhaps why.'

Perhaps he had but unless they had good arrangements

with the Albanian police – unlikely – that wasn't particularly helpful either. But now they'd reached a breakthrough point. Though Murray didn't understand the words, she could tell what he was saying from his expression. The daughter was dead and he grieved for her. Could it be . . . ?

There was a long explanation; Marta was nodding sympathetically as she listened and Murray looked from one face to the other, trying to puzzle out what was being said. When Kaczka stopped speaking, he put his head in his hands and she could see that he was crying.

'It's very sad,' Marta said. 'He had a wife and a child. A little girl. It was a very bad winter and where they lived was cold, damp. He was away – maybe in jail, I don't know, but they couldn't pay for a doctor so then they both died. He wanted to leave, find a better life. The same as I did, but—' She gestured round the hovel. 'He found this. The guy who was killed – he was a bad guy?'

'You could say,' Murray said darkly. 'You don't know the half of it.'

'Maybe he deserved to die,' Marta said.

Murray pulled a face. 'In a way, he maybe did. But if you just let folk decide to kill anyone they reckoned was one of the bad guys it would get kind of messy – at least that's what I have to tell myself, doing this job.'

'Oh, you are right, I'm sure, but sometimes it's karma, you know? Anyway, what else do you want me to ask him?'

'I think that's all,' Murray said. 'For the moment, anyway. We'll report the exploitation so he can get proper help, so we may need you again. But I think we should be getting back across to Balnasheil now.'

Even in the time they had been talking to Kaczka the pitch of the gale had changed. It was howling round the walls of the cottage and the fire was hissing as raindrops came down the chimney and smoke belched out into the room, making them cough. The draught coming in under the door was lifting the filthy carpet and the door itself was rattling.

'Let's go,' Murray said.

Aware that a passing officer was standing with his eyes out on stalks and his ears flapping, DI Strang said, 'I think we'd better conduct this interview inside, don't you?'

Ushering Murdo John Macdonald before him, Strang went inside the cottage and shut the door. Then, very deliberately, he took off his wet jacket, shook it and hung it up on a hook by the door. He went to a chair by the fire and sat down, holding out his hands to the blaze. 'That's better. It's freezing outside.'

Murdo John Macdonald looked down at him, nonplussed. He had been standing squared up to the detective, like an animal at bay; now he looked confused. After a moment he said, 'Did you hear me? I said I was confessing to the murder of Adam Carnegie.'

'Oh yes, I heard you. I'm just wondering why you couldn't have said that to Sergeant Buchanan? I know he'd have been happy to bring you in at that point.'

'Er—'

'Not dramatic enough? I don't play games like that, Mr Macdonald. And before I indulge you in your wish to have me arrest you, we need to have a conversation. Unless you want to call your lawyer?'

The man shook his head and Strang went on, 'I suggest you sit down. I don't want to get a crick in my neck looking up at you.'

Macdonald stared at him, then very slowly took the chair opposite.

'I'm going to start with your movements on the night Carnegie was killed. Let's begin at 6 p.m.'

The pent-up tension burst out. 'For God's sake, man, I've made a statement about that already! Why are you wasting time with this?'

'I imagine that if what you're now saying is true, the statement was a lie. In which case I need to know what really happened, don't I?'

Deflated, Macdonald said, 'Oh – yes, I see. Well, I did my shift at the bar. Finished at eleven, then cleared everything and tallied up and came back here. I went out again later—'

'How much later?'

'*I* don't know.' The irritation wasn't far below the surface. 'I didn't look at the time – middle of the night, when no one would be around. I went to the boat—'

'Not worried that someone would look out when they heard the engine?'

'Rowed across. Anyway, they're early to bed here. I moored at the jetty, walked up—'

'Hang on. Did you take a knife with you?'

Macdonald paused, swallowed, then said, 'Yes.'

'Must have been quite a knife, to do that sort of damage.'

'I – I sharpened it before I went. Threw it in the sea on the way back.'

'I see. Go on.'

'I went to the glass doors of Carnegie's study. I knew no one locked them at night.'

'Dark, was it?'

He checked, sensing a trap. 'No – no, it wasn't. He was still up. He let me in and then I killed him.'

'Just like that? What about the dog?'

'The dog?' he faltered. 'Oh yes, the dog.' Then he took refuge in belligerence. 'Look, I've confessed. I'm not going to tell you any more. You can do your own work to prove I did it or whatever it is you have to do. I'm tired of this.'

DI Strang sighed, a heavy, elaborate sigh. 'Well now, Mr Macdonald, we're not just looking for someone we can arrest. We're old-fashioned enough to have a preference for seeing that it's the right someone and we really need quite a bit more than this to go on. With every murder, we get cranks and loonies coming in to say they did it. They get some sort of kick out of the attention, I suppose, and we can make right eejits of ourselves if we take them at face value. You haven't done very well so far. I don't believe you're either a crank or a loony, but I think you have made an assumption that may be quite wrong.'

Macdonald's chin jutted. 'I – killed – Adam – Carnegie.'

'You – not your wife?'

Avoiding Strang's eyes, he looked down to his left. 'No, not my wife. Why would she?'

'Good question. Why indeed? Anyway, let's talk about something else. Let's talk about Veruschka.'

The man's head came up so sharply Strang heard his neck crack. 'Veruschka?'

'The love of your life, according to PC Murray.'

'Oh God! Why did I talk to that woman?' It was a heartfelt cry.

'Perhaps because you just wanted to speak her name out loud,' Strang said. There was sympathy in his voice.

Macdonald bit his lip. 'There's nothing to add to what she'll have told you already. Veruschka disappeared; I believed she'd walked out on me. It was only recently I found out what had really happened. *And*,' he went on with sudden conviction, 'that's why I killed him – revenge for Veruschka's death.'

The way he said it made Strang think of a man whose boat has been wrecked suddenly noticing a floating spar. He said, very gently, 'What was she like?'

Macdonald had to clear his throat. 'She was – very lovely.'

'Do you have a photograph?'

For a moment he didn't move, then he got up and went over to a small, old-fashioned bureau that stood in front of the window. He let down the lid then pressed a panel to the right of three small drawers; it slid forward, disclosing a slim secret compartment. He reached in, took out a photograph, looking at it for a moment as if he didn't want to let it go, then handed it to Strang.

It had been handled many times; it was a little creased and one edge was dog-eared, but the print itself was clear. It was a dark-haired girl with pale olive skin who was looking at the camera as if it, or the person behind it, was a friend: smiling, wide-set dark eyes soft. She looked very happy, Strang thought with a pang, and she had been, as Macdonald had said, very lovely.

Then suddenly Strang tensed up. He looked again. And he knew.

Lightning flickered above the mountains as PC Murray and the interpreter came out of Marek Kaczka's cottage and Murray huddled into her hooded oilskin, looking anxiously at Marta's much lighter windcheater, wet through already. With the clouds so thick and sullen, daylight was fading fast.

Operations had been halted and there was a queue of officers waiting to be taken off in the boats. It was a slow business, with only two boats operating – still no sign of Murdo John, damn him – and the empty one coming back from Balnasheil was positively corkscrewing in the waves in a way that made Murray feel sick just looking at it. How long would it be, she wondered, before they decided it wasn't safe to run them any more? She was going to be almost the last in the queue, and little as she fancied the journey across, she liked still less the thought of being stranded over here.

There was Marta to consider, though. As a civilian she was entitled to preferential treatment and she led her up to the front of the queue to explain to the sergeant in charge.

'Yes, of course, madam. We'll get you onto this one that's coming in now.'

Marta squeezed Murray's hand gratefully. A space was made for her but in answer to a muttering of unrest, Murray said, 'All right, all right, don't get your knickers in a twist. I'll take my turn, you miserable sods,' and walked to the back.

At least three more trips needed at a rough count, she thought. She was cold, her face was red and sore and the force of the wind was frightening. She'd got used to the weather in her months here but she was still a city girl and she'd never been exposed to a storm like this. There was a crack of thunder that seemed to be right overhead and she flinched as a lightning flash followed almost immediately.

She didn't know the lads at the back. Two of them were up from Edinburgh but despite the storm they were in good spirits.

'Did you hear we got our man?' one said cheerfully. 'That should be it for us – you locals can clean up here. You're welcome to it.'

'Who're you calling local? I'm from Glasgow, myself,' she said automatically, but she was wrestling with profound disappointment. It was all done and dusted and she hadn't even been there. 'Anyway, what's happened?'

'The Macdonald guy. Someone actually heard him confessing.'

'Murdo John?' So she'd been right to suspect him – if only she'd had the courage to question him properly last night when she had the chance! But she hadn't.

Then she thought about Vicky. How was Vicky going to feel when she heard that the husband she'd been hoping to be reconciled with had been arrested, that he was a man who had killed in a hideously macabre way?

Murray looked at the queue. At this rate it was going to

be at least twenty minutes, probably more, before she was taken off and, turning her head, she could see the light was on in the kitchen. She made up her mind, said, 'Back in a minute,' and headed for the back door. She knocked on it then went in through the area where the larders were and tapped on the kitchen door.

Vicky Macdonald was standing by the sink, loading mugs into a dishwasher. She was moving listlessly, looking haggard and heavy-eyed but she managed a weak smile when she saw Murray.

'I'm guessing just one more request for a cup of coffee would be the last straw,' Murray said. 'You look absolutely exhausted. I've only a few minutes anyway—'

'There's still some in the flask. I'm going to have one myself,' Vicky said. 'Take a seat.'

She hesitated. Vicky was looking as if hearing what Murray had to say might make her fall apart completely. This was going to be much harder than she had thought.

'Well, you twisted my arm,' she said, sitting down.

'I think I can even find a piece of shortbread, just for you. I owe you one for trying last night.'

As Vicky went through to the larder, Murray frowned. There was something—

Then Vicky came back, poured the coffee, brought the tin and sat down.

She had to be told. Murray took a deep breath. 'Vicky, Murdo John's confessed that he killed Adam Carnegie.'

Vicky looked stunned. Then she said. 'Oh, for God's sake! The stupid, stupid idiot! What did he want to do that for?'

It was an odd response. 'Er – don't you believe him?' Murray asked.

'No – well, I don't know. Maybe he did. But it just seems, well, sort of unnecessary. Too dramatic, or something.' Vicky had picked up a piece of shortbread and was reducing it to crumbs with her restless fingers. 'What happens now?'

'He'll be charged, I guess.' But Murray spoke absently. When Vicky had gone through to fetch the shortbread it had reminded her of the last time, the time when she had come back immediately saying she couldn't smell the hare. But it had been removed before the murder happened and she must have been to and fro dozens of times since; why had she only mentioned it after Murray had told her they knew it wasn't suicide? Perhaps there was an explanation – she'd forgotten it was there, she'd only just remembered when she was thinking about making supper, but—

'Vicky,' she said, 'when did you realise that the hare had been taken away?'

Vicky's face went very still. The wide-set blue eyes were cold, defensive. 'What on earth do you mean? You know when I realised. You were there—'

'And it was just after I told you we were treating it as murder,' Murray said. 'You said it "stank to high heaven" – how come it was only then that you noticed the smell had gone? You go in and out of the larder all the time.'

'I didn't, that was all.' Her voice was high and unnatural. 'I just – didn't. Sorry.'

Murray felt a cold chill. The woman was lying and with a sudden deadly certainty she knew why.

'Vicky, did you kill Adam?'

Vicky picked up her coffee mug and walked over with it to the sink. 'That's such a stupid question I'm not even going to answer it,' she said, but her voice was shaking.

'You had means and opportunity.' Murray was surprised to find that her voice was quite steady. 'You understand about knives. I've seen your chopping skills. Was it one of the knives from here – the knives you use for chopping up hares and deer? Did you use that?'

There was another crash of thunder overhead and a huge gust of wind shook the window as it lit up with the blue brilliance of a lightning flash. Vicky cringed away from it; she was shaking violently.

'Vicky—'

The woman turned round, wailing, 'Yes, all right, all right! I killed him. And I'm not sorry I did. You've got to listen to me, Livvy. Once you know, you'll understand. Veruschka was my sister – my half-sister. That wasn't her real name; she was Nicoleta Gabor.' She gave a small, dry sob as she said it. 'My own name's Viktoria Gabor. My mother married a Romanian and when they divorced my father went back there but I stayed here. I used to spend holidays with my Tata, though.' She gave a short laugh. 'Couldn't be faithful for ten minutes, but a lovely man.

'He got married again, and then there was Nicci. I was eight and she was the most enchanting little thing. I adored her from the day I first saw her. She was so pretty, so charming. Oh, and so wilful, but you could never be cross with her for long – she had such a loving heart. She used to come to stay with us often and even my mother couldn't resist her. Nicci hated going back to Romania. "There's nothing there for me," she would say. "I want to live here, live like you do." I told her all she had to do was wait; Romania was in the EU, it would only be a year or two before she could move here legally. But Nicci—' She began to cry.

Murray said nothing, waiting as Vicky wiped her eyes and blew her nose on a tissue, while the thunder, a little further off now, rumbled around the mountains.

'Nicci didn't do waiting,' Vicky managed at last. 'From when she was tiny, her favourite words were "No, now!" She phoned me four years ago and said she was coming to Britain. She had a job, she said, but she wouldn't tell me anything about it. She was only eighteen; I was worried when she said I wouldn't approve – oh, I mothered her, I suppose. She had a wild streak, like my father, and I knew she had a frantic social life in Bucharest.

'Then she vanished. My father didn't seem too bothered – she'd called him and said she was fine. She texted me too occasionally, little teasing texts that told me nothing. That last one I got she sounded happy, excited. It said that soon she'd be able to come and see me – "Watch this space," she finished. Then – nothing.' Vicky picked up the damp tissue and dabbed at her eyes again. 'Nothing at all. My father told the police but you can imagine how interested they were – how many illegal immigrants come into the country every year and disappear? You weren't much bothered at first about Eva.'

It was true; she hadn't been. 'I know. I'm sorry,' Murray said humbly.

'The only clue I had was one postcard from Skye, a view of the Black Cuillin ridge on a sunny day, taken from here.

"The most beautiful place on earth and I'm going to stay here for ever," it said. That was all. So she was here, in Scotland! I smiled at the time; no doubt I'd hear from her when she felt like it. But then my mother died – she was only sixty – and I was on my own. There was no one else. Nicci was all I had left and I needed to find her.

'But there were no texts after that, and she didn't reply to mine. So I came here to ask if anyone knew a Nicoleta Gabor. They didn't, of course, but they said that foreign girls worked over at Balnasheil Lodge so maybe she had been one of them – they came and went, seemingly. No one was much interested.

'I drove out there and spoke to Beatrice. She was very frosty – there had been no Nicoleta Gabor, no Romanian girl, and no, there was no one else I could talk to. That was all. I don't think she even remembered she'd met me when I got Morag Soutar's job.'

She held out her hands pleadingly. 'How could I just give up, Livvy, when it was the only link I had with my little sister? There was a job going at the hotel so I took it. I tried talking to Marek, if he was in the bar – I even tried to ask Adam if he'd known anyone called Nicoleta but he just looked through me as if I didn't exist. Then there was Murdo John.' The name seemed to hang heavy on the air.

'Why did you marry him, Vicky?' Murray asked gently.

She gave a helpless shrug. 'Why does anyone marry? He was very attractive; I convinced myself I loved him. Oh, I still do, perhaps, in a way. But I was – sort of hollowed out inside by then, grieving for my mother, and finding Nicci had become an obsession. If I lived here, if I found out more about what had gone on at the Lodge perhaps there were clues I could pick up, work out where she'd gone.

'Of course I realised it was possible something had happened to her, but being Nicci she might just have decided to disappear. She had my phone number, if she chose to use it. But after Mum died I hadn't a home to offer her when she wanted to come back. If I married Murdo John – well,' she shrugged.

It was a chilling idea – marrying a man for a settled address. Murray was feeling considerable sympathy for Murdo John, especially since he seemed to have confessed to protect his wife.

'But how could you be sure Nicci was Veruschka?'

'Once I heard there was another girl who had suddenly disappeared from here, who else could it be? Dark hair, brown eyes, Murdo John said – that was Veruschka. She had said she was going to stay here for ever.' She gave a dry sob. 'And in a terrible way, I suppose she has.'

Murray glanced at her watch. If she was to get Vicky on the last boat back, she'd better hurry her up.

'Tell me what made you decide to kill Adam?'

'When Eva disappeared, I think I knew then that Adam had killed her, even if I didn't want to face up to it. And later, Beatrice as good as told me he had killed Nicci too. The man was a psychopath and I could see he was going to get away with it this time too.

'Oh yes, you lot were investigating but you wanted the sort of proof you simply weren't going to find. He was clever, he'd move away and then there would be another girl, and another. He'd learn from his mistakes this time and the next time there wouldn't be grounds for suspicion. And as long as he was alive, Beatrice would never get up courage to speak out against him, poor pathetic cow. She'd taken back everything she said even before I left the room.

'I owed Nicci revenge. So – I killed him. Just went in, hiding my butcher's knife up my sleeve, holding some papers, and said there was a problem with the household accounts and when he sat down at the desk . . .' Her voice trailed away.

The picture vivid in her mind, Murray gulped. 'Messy.'

Vicky seemed unmoved. 'Well yes, it was, a bit, but it had to be something he could do to himself, to look like suicide – you see? And I'd seen hogs killed on my grandfather's farm in Romania – it's quite easy to do.' She shrugged with chilling indifference. 'So that's what gave me the idea and I knew what to expect, where to stand. And then I just pulled down my sweater over my hand and took one of his own knives to put beside him. There was blood, of course; I had to strip off and go into the sea. God, I thought I would die with the cold! But then my clothes and the knife went into the sea – job done.'

'And the dog?' Murray felt almost proprietorial about the dog and the hare.

'Oh, I knew I had to dope it first, of course. Beatrice had sleeping pills so I just nicked them, laced the hare with them then left it on the lawn – and when I went into Adam's flat I didn't have to commit myself until I was sure it was out cold.'

She was sounding – yes, pleased with herself, admiring

of her own ingenuity. Murray gave a little shudder. And it was getting late; if she didn't move now they'd have stopped the boats. She stood up.

'Vicky Macdonald, I am arresting you on suspicion of murder—'

Vicky jumped up too. 'No, Livvy!' she cried. 'You understand – you know what sort of man he was. You know he deserved this – everyone knows that! What good is it going to do to lock me up for years for ridding the world of Adam Carnegie? If you hadn't worked it out, what harm would it have done? Don't tell, Livvy! You've been my friend; you're a woman. You know what it would feel like to be preyed on by a monster like Adam – how can you blame me for what I did? I'm going away. My bags are packed; I'm going to change my name. Please let me go. Don't stop me! You can say what you like after I've gone.

'Do you want to know how he killed Nicci? He turned the dog on her, to tear her to pieces. Beatrice knows that – she won't admit it to the police, though. Think about it, Livvy – you're helpless, in his power, and the dog's coming at you. How do you feel? You're terrified, helpless, then you suffer excruciating agony as it savages you to death, tears off your flesh, a bit at a time – while he watches. Didn't he deserve to die?'

Murray felt sick. She could almost feel the girl's panic in herself, see the dog, snarling as it went into the attack. The man had been evil personified and the world was a healthier place without him. Should anyone be made to pay for that?

Vicky seemed to sense her weakening. 'You're meant

to uphold justice, Livvy. Well, this is a life for a life – for two lives, and you'd be letting him steal my life as well. Please, Livvy, please! Look me in the eye – you can't say this isn't justice.'

The thunder rolled closer again; the lightning came almost simultaneously. Murray was shaken: all along she had found it hard to care about 'justice' for Adam Carnegie and her dogged working to find out the truth had been a combination of her natural curiosity and an ambition for professional success. It wasn't hard to view what had happened as savage justice – karma, as Marta had said.

She was actually hesitating when Cara came to her mind, Cara, who had been a friend of hers, stabbed to death in Glasgow when they were teenagers. When the man got three years and came out in eighteen months she'd felt like going after him. But even then she'd been streetwise enough to know what would have happened if she had: his friends would have come after her and the cycle of violence would go on and on. It was one of the reasons she had joined the force. Deciding what counted as justice was way above her pay grade.

She drew a deep breath, met the other woman's eyes squarely and said again, 'Vicky Macdonald, I am arresting you on suspicion of murder. You do not have to say anything—'

There was a thunderclap right overhead, a noise that made it sound as if the ceiling was coming down. The immediate flash lit up an eerie, livid landscape outside the window. There was a bang and they were plunged into darkness.

It was pitch-black. Murray could hear sounds of movement but couldn't place them. She turned her head to try to locate the direction. 'Vicky—' she said, then something hit her head and she knew nothing more.

CHAPTER TWENTY-FIVE

After DI Strang had sent Sergeant Buchanan in to take Murdo John's statement he headed straight to the pier, bending double under the force of the wind. There were real breakers in the bay now; he had to dodge the waves as they spilt over onto the street. Sandbags were protecting the doorways of the houses and the place was deserted apart from the personnel disembarking thankfully from a boat that had just come across – a few of them looking green and shaken – and hurrying towards the bus waiting for them.

With the noise of the sea and the thunder rolling all around it was hard to make himself heard as he told the sergeant on duty that he needed to get back across with the boat.

'I'll need a couple of men with me,' he shouted. 'I'm going to be making an arrest.'

The man shook his head. 'Sorry, sir – not now you're not. We've got everyone off and this is the last boat tonight – unless the storm eases back and I wouldn't hold my breath.'

He seemed to be taking a positive pleasure in refusing.

Counting to ten, Strang said, 'Look, you got over all right—'

'Can't do it. Health and safety, you know.'

Strang gave vent to his opinion of health and safety in terms that drew a dirty look from the sergeant but made the man who had been steering laugh.

'Right enough, sir, but it is nasty out there. And I daresay whoever you're going to arrest will be stuck there waiting for you meantime.'

Strang grudgingly acknowledged the truth of that, nodded and turned to face into the wind and rain that was driving in from the Atlantic. If he went back to the police office now he could download the appropriate forms and it would save time when the storm abated and he could get across to Balnasheil Lodge, so he tramped off up the hill.

He'd better take Murray along with him as a woman officer and he ought to phone JB as well. She'd be pleased to hear that the investigation was reaching its conclusion; it had been haemorrhaging money for the last bit.

DCS Borthwick was delighted with the news; he could sense a note of considerable relief in her voice as well. He filled her in on the developments and went on, 'The thing is, you'd be unlikely to notice it in real life unless they were standing side by side. The colouring's very different. Vicky's fair-haired with blue eyes and Veruschka was much more middle-European – olive skin, brown hair, brown eyes. But studying the photo I suddenly realised that the shape of the face and the set of the eyes was identical – they had to be sisters, or closely related, anyway. And then of course Macdonald crumbled. He claimed he hadn't known

432

about the relationship, though recently he'd wondered – there was a look his wife had given him that sparked a memory, I think. He may even have been attracted to her subconsciously in the first place because of the resemblance. Then she phoned him last night and told him she'd killed Carnegie, and why. He said he was very shocked, then decided he would confess to it himself.'

'Gallant, if misguided, I suppose,' Borthwick said dryly.

'Not according to him. He was mortified. I don't think he's quite up to speed with modern feminist thinking – it offended his male pride that a woman had done the job he ought to have done. He wasn't so much protecting her as trying to steal the credit.'

'I have to say that's a new one for me. So – arrest is imminent, can I take it?'

'Not in this weather. Can you hear the thunder? It's a serious storm and the boats have been stood down until it abates – not any time soon from the looks of it. But she won't be going anywhere either and I should get across tomorrow.'

'There's a press conference at eleven so it would be handy to have it tied up before that,' Borthwick was saying when there was a violent clap of thunder, a blinding flash, and Strang was plunged into darkness.

'Hello? Hello? Are you still there?' she said.

'Yes, amazingly enough. But the electrics have gone and I can't see a thing.'

'Hardly surprising. It may well be a while before you get the power back – the Western Isles are sometimes out for days at a time.'

'Oh, great, ma'am. Thanks for that.'

'Don't mention it. I like to do my little bit,' Borthwick said with all the cheerfulness of one sitting in a well-heated, brightly lit office in a city. 'Anyway, I'd better let you get on with sorting it out. Keep me in the picture.'

Strang rang off, looking helplessly about him. There was almost no light coming in the small window and the room was in darkness. He had the light on his mobile, but it was pitiful. He'd had a proper torch – it would be in the pocket of the jacket he'd hung on a peg to let the rain drain off, but he now had little sense of where the peg was. He stood up and was training the mobile light round the corners of his desk to get some sense of direction when he saw a sliver of light appear under the door. When it opened a constable came in carrying a paraffin lamp that lit the room with a soft amber glow.

'You have no idea how pleased I am to see you, Constable,' he told her. 'This is preparedness of the very highest order.'

She beamed. 'You get used to it round here, sir. There were a few of these in a cupboard and when the storm came in we got them out ready.' She set it down on the desk then went to the door, switching on the torch she had ready in her other hand.

'Thank you very much. Oh, by the way, could you send PC Murray to me? I left a message that I wanted to see her but maybe it didn't get through.'

'She wasn't in the incident room, sir. Maybe she's at the police house. I'll check and if she's there I'll send her in to you.'

Strang thanked her again and then sat looking at the blank, dead face of his computer with some dismay. That was the problem with modern technology; it was so efficient that you relied on it to the point that when something went wrong, you were hamstrung. If terrorists concentrated on taking out power stations instead of attacking shopping malls and pop concerts, the West would be on its knees in days.

Beatrice had been crying so much that her cheeks were red raw with the salt of tears. She had been interrogated – that was the only word for it – by two policemen about her perfectly ordinary sleeping pills, the ones her doctor always prescribed for her because she didn't sleep well. She had got so flustered she couldn't remember whether there had been another pack as well as the one she was using at the moment, and they had actually accused her of lying. That wasn't the way you expected policemen to behave; she'd actually thought they were going to arrest her, and when she asked if they were, they just laughed and one said, 'Well, not at the moment,' and the other said, 'But you never know.' It was just plain bullying.

Then they had gone away, but she was really, really scared now. Harry had told them before that she'd killed Adam, when it had been him all the time, and now there was something about her pills that had made it all worse, even if she didn't know what it was.

That was the trouble; she had no idea what was happening out there, and she didn't like the storm either. Up here it seemed terribly close and sometimes you thought the roof itself would come in. It had been right overhead at one point and she'd just cowered in a corner, but then it had moved a bit further away. From her window she could see lightning flickering all round the cloudy bulk of the Black Cuillin ridge.

Then it was back again, right over her head. Bang! Flash! Beatrice screamed as the light went out.

Power cuts happened, and there was a major one most winters. They'd been cut off for three days once which had been difficult, but then they'd all gone to sit together in the big sitting room with the fire blazing for warmth and it had been quite cosy and companionable. She hadn't been stuck up here all by herself in the darkness.

She knew where her torch was and she was able to grope her way to the drawer where she kept it. She switched it on and felt a little better. She could make her way downstairs and find Vicky to see if she would light the sitting-room fire. They'd have to keep warm and the house would cool down rapidly now the heating had gone off – and even if Harry appeared too it would be better than sitting up here alone. Shining the torch in front of her, she made her way cautiously down the stairs. 'Vicky! Vicky!' she called as she reached the bottom and went along the corridor leading to the kitchen.

Just as she reached it, the door to Vicky's room opened behind her and she burst out, carrying a small suitcase. She didn't look herself – positively *wild*, Beatrice thought with alarm.

'Vicky! You're not going somewhere in this weather?'

She didn't answer. She shoved Beatrice aside so roughly

that she stumbled against the wall, lost her balance and sat down, hard. The torch swung as she fell and she could see Vicky going out of the back door, slamming it hard behind her.

Tears of pain came into Beatrice's eyes. She'd hurt her injured arm and now it felt as if she'd twisted her back. She was in so much pain she wasn't sure she could get up by herself; she'd just have to stay here, getting chilled to the bone, and probably die of hypothermia.

Just then the kitchen door opened. She grabbed her torch again and saw, to her surprise and relief, a policewoman come out. She recognised her: she was PC Murray, the one who'd been asking questions about Eva. She was flinching away from the beam of light and she looked a bit odd and unfocused. She wasn't quite steady on her feet either; could she have been drinking? Beatrice wondered. She hadn't been much impressed with her anyway, but she'd do.

'Constable, I need you to help me to my feet,' she said. 'Vicky Macdonald has just assaulted me – pushed me right over.'

'Was that her going out of the door just now? Sorry, I'm going to need your torch.'

To Beatrice's astonishment and fury, the torch was snatched out of her hand and she was left there on the floor in the darkness as the back door slammed again. She was too angry for tears; surely there was something she could do about this appalling behaviour?

Then she remembered. She had her mobile phone in her pocket, and that nice inspector had actually programmed in his number in case she wanted to talk to him. If it worked, she could complain to him right now, and he could send someone to help her at the same time. There was an anxious moment as she wondered whether the mast had been struck as well as the power station, but no – there was the number ringing now.

'Inspector Strang? I have a serious complaint to make against one of your officers, PC Murray.'

Livvy Murray had opened her eyes on darkness and for a moment she thought she'd only dreamt that she'd opened them. But her head was throbbing and then she realised what must have happened – Vicky Macdonald had knocked her out and now she was lying on the cold tiled floor of the kitchen. She had no idea how long she had been unconscious, but by now Vicky was probably well away in the little motorboat that belonged to the Lodge.

The window was a lighter square, intermittently bright with lightning flashes, but it was deeply dark in the room. She tried to work out where she was; she had been sitting at the table and she'd stood up to make the formal arrest, so she must be somewhere near it. She swept her arm round in an arc and sure enough, it knocked against the sturdy table leg.

That felt like a small triumph, and Livvy grabbed it so that she could pull herself up. Mistake! The darkness swung around her; she swayed, and vomited. Concussion, then – but she couldn't give in to it. She had a job to do. Clinging to the table leg, she shuffled forward so she could rest her swimming head against it and gradually she felt steadier.

She risked levering herself up and thought she would be

sick again, but once she had steadied herself on the table for a minute or two she felt strong enough to take a step in what she guessed was the direction of the door. She was disorientated, though, and she still wasn't quite steady on her feet; once she let go of the table she'd have no point of reference and she wasn't even sure whereabouts the door was on the side wall. But unless she was going to just stand here like a stookie, she'd have to try.

She lurched off very cautiously, her hands spread out protectively in front of her. She didn't think she could bear it if she bashed into something; her head was throbbing like the bass beat in Adele's 'Rumour Has It'. But she hadn't been sick again and she was making progress – though whether in the right direction or not remained to be seen.

Then suddenly she saw light, faint but definite. It bobbed and flickered, but it outlined the door frame. Livvy hadn't been too far off, and as she made towards it she heard someone saying, 'Vicky! You're not going somewhere in this weather?' As she fumbled for the handle – *Not this side, no, the other side, try higher up* – she heard a thump and a cry, then the slamming of the back door.

At last her groping hand struck the handle and she wrenched the door open. Beatrice Lacey was outside in the corridor, sitting on the floor. She said something, but Livvy barely registered what it was. She asked if Vicky had gone out, grabbed the torch Beatrice was holding, with a brief apology, then dashed outside.

It felt as if someone had punched her in the face. Her head jerked back with the force of the driving wind and she gave a cry of agony, but she struggled on, following the slope leading down to the jetty. It was much lighter outside than in the house and with the lightning flickering in a dark and angry sky she could see where she was going; looking ahead she could make out, in odd, freeze-frame glimpses, Vicky bending over the small motorboat, rocking at its moorings. Beyond that there was only the glistening black of the boiling sea and the white caps on the waves that were breaking across the jetty. Salt spray stung her face as she hurried towards it.

There were no comforting lights on the other side of the bay. The whole area must have been hit and once the boat was launched it would be all but impossible to steer a straight course across.

'Vicky!' she yelled. 'Vicky, stop, for God's sake!'

Perhaps she hadn't heard her, with all the noise that was going on. It was only as Livvy approached, still shouting, that Vicky, now standing in the rocking boat, turned her head.

'I thought you were dead. Go away! You're not going to stop me.'

Livvy reached her, grabbed her arm. 'It's suicide, going out into a sea like that. And you're under arrest, so it's my duty to stop you.'

Unbalanced, she was too groggy to hold on and Vicky roughly pulled her arm free, saying nothing as she bent forward to put in the key and start the engine.

Maybe Livvy should just let her go. No one would blame her: she'd been wounded; she was really hurting. But if Vicky got herself drowned it would be a death in police custody and she had got to give it her best shot.

She climbed into the boat herself. 'I'm not going to let you go out there. See sense, Vicky – get back out and we'll talk.'

'We did that. There wasn't any point.'

'Look, you said yourself you didn't want Carnegie to claim another victim. That's what you're risking if I get out and leave you free to go.'

Vicky's reply was to swing at her, giving Livvy a violent push that made the boat rock still more, but it didn't topple her out. Instead she fell over, landing across the side, and was able to steady herself.

'It's not that easy, Vicky. I'm not going to get out until you get out too.'

In the light of another dramatic flash, Livvy saw her face, white and set and cold. 'With you or without you, it doesn't matter to me.' Vicky turned the ignition and the little boat roared out, out into the maelstrom of the bay.

DI Strang was having difficulty keeping his temper, and it showed. 'Look, I don't care what you say about health and safety. There's an officer out there who seems to have been injured and she is pursuing a murderer. She's entitled to support.'

'If it all went wrong it'd be me carrying the can, not you, sir. It's my duty not to put lives at risk. If something happened to you, I'd be the one got the blame and then I'd lose my job.'

Strang didn't trust himself to reply. He slammed down the phone and leant back. There was little that angered him more than a jobsworth; civilians had died because police officers had been told that the risk assessment didn't permit a rescue when it was the pride of the service that they put their lives on the line to protect the public.

On the other hand, putting your life on the line for any other reason was a different matter. He'd managed to establish from that ridiculous woman that PC Murray had looked odd, lurching as if she could be drunk. That sounded as if she was carrying an injury, probably because she'd worked things out too and misguidedly confronted Vicky Macdonald.

According to Beatrice, Vicky had been carrying a suitcase. If she was attempting to escape on a night like this when a small boat in a Force 8 was the only way out, she was desperate, if not actually deranged. For Livvy, injured already, to pursue her wasn't heroic, it was plain idiotic. Once he got her safely back, there would be a day of reckoning. *If* he got her safely back. He couldn't abandon her to the consequences of her folly, but with the best will in the world there was nothing he could do if he couldn't get across the bay.

Tennant! He had a boat. The thought came to him like one of the lightning flashes outside and he was on his feet, running out of the building two minutes later.

It was still barely five o'clock. The massing clouds – purple, dirty grey, sullen red – were underlit by the last faint hint of daylight, and with the flickering light of the storm he was better able to see the road in front of him than he had been the previous night. He took the slope at speed and only three minutes later he was banging on the door of Tennant's cottage.

Daniel Tennant didn't look welcoming. He listened, unmoved, to Strang's breathless demand. Then he laughed. 'Go out in that? Got a death wish, or something? Even if you do, I don't.'

'I need to get across. I think Livvy's in real danger.'

'Oh? What a shame. Not as much danger as I'd be in, taking a boat out in that.'

'Will you lend it to me, then?' Strang said desperately.

'Oh, sorry, mate,' he drawled. 'Not mine, you know. It's only rented. I could phone the owner and ask his permission, but I doubt if he'd give it.'

This was pointless. Swearing, he turned away, defeated.

The storm was moving further away now. As if it were reluctant to leave, there was still the occasional bolt of lightning but it wasn't directly overhead, as it had been. He turned to look across to Balnasheil Lodge, but the power cut had obviously affected them too; he couldn't even make out the shape of the house in the darkness.

He was looking out to sea when a particularly bright flash highlighted something in the water – a small boat, bucking and corkscrewing in the waves. Who would be mad enough to take it out in these conditions?

As if he didn't know. He stared, aghast; there were two figures on board. And it wasn't heading straight across to the harbour here; with the street power cut there was probably no way of knowing out there where it would be. The waves were breaking right over it; how much water could a boat like that ship before capsizing? But what could he do – just watch them drown?

Murdo John's cottage was just behind him, his boat moored right there in front. He spun round and hammered on the door.

Livvy was sick before the boat had even left the moorings. The terrible thing was that it left her so weak she couldn't even try to pull Vicky away from the controls so that she could turn the boat back.

'For God's sake, Vicky,' she screamed. 'You're going to kill us both!'

Vicky didn't answer. She was wrestling with the wheel as the force of the waves battered the little boat, directing it one way and the other. They didn't seem to be making any progress at all, just going up and down in ever more sickening circles.

'Turn back,' Livvy wailed. 'We're not getting anywhere!'

Vicky turned her head. Her frightened face gleamed white against the darkness. 'I don't know which is back now. I can't steer against this sea.'

Another bout of retching took Livvy. The boat was broadside to the waves now and water was coming in; there was a great pool in the bottom already. She thought of trying to bail with her hands but she had no strength left. And anyway, if she drowned she wouldn't be sick any more.

CHAPTER TWENTY-SIX

Murdo John Macdonald had listened silently to Strang's gabbled request, nodded, then, pausing only to grab a halogen lantern torch, an oilskin coat and a couple of life jackets, he strode across the street. While Strang climbed aboard, struggling into one of the jackets, he put on his own, unhitched the boat from its moorings and launched it into the stormy waves. It was old-fashioned, clinker built with a large outboard motor, and he took the tiller with what appeared to Kelso Strang to be calm confidence.

'You don't seem too much bothered by this.' Strang, soaked by the flying spray, turned to shout as a surge of power took them out into the bay, cutting through the waves.

'Seen worse.'

Strang had lost sight of the little boat and as the thunderstorm moved further away the visibility was growing worse. He switched on the powerful torch, swung it in great arcs to try to find it again. It ought to be somewhere on a line between the other shore of the bay and the village, but he couldn't pick it up. He swung it wider and wider in increasing frustration, but it was Murdo John who spotted it first.

'To your left,' he called.

Strang got a fix on it. The boat was no longer under any sort of control; it was being pitched about on the breakers, bucking and dipping as it hit the cross-waves. It was sitting low, shipping water. Their own boat was powering towards it now but it was dependent on the whim of the waves whether they could reach it before it sank. It would be when, not if.

'Lifebuoys. In the locker,' Murdo John shouted.

It wasn't easy with their own boat bucking as it smacked the wave crests but Strang had them ready, attached to the boat by their orange lifelines, as they approached.

'Boat hook. Along the side there,' Murdo John instructed.

Aware of his own inadequacies as a boatman, Strang picked up the long pole but was far from sure of his ability to keep his footing while he did anything with it. He could see clearly now in the wide beam of the torch: Vicky was still holding the wheel but when she turned her head towards the light he could see terror and despair in her face. Her mouth opened wide as if she was screaming but he couldn't hear her.

But where was Livvy? His heart skipped a beat. Had she been swept overboard already? Then her head came up; she must have been lying in the bottom of the boat. He remembered she was a bad sailor; seasickness was no joke and in conditions like this it would have laid her out.

They were almost alongside now. He half stood, trying to grapple the side of the motorboat while Murdo John manoeuvred for position, but their own pitched sharply as a rippling, deadly wave powered over them, throwing him back onto his seat.

When he looked, the other boat had vanished. Gone! He stood up again, not sure what he was going to do – plunge in to the rescue, and probably drown?

'*Sit down*!' Murdo John snarled. 'Lifebuoys, for God's sake!'

Feeling a fool, Strang threw them, first one, then the other, their flashing lights coming on as they hit the water. Frantically he scanned the waves, playing the torch across.

Then he saw white against the black of the sea; Livvy's face, then the yellow of her jacket. Pulling on one of the lines, he swung the lifebuoy through the waves towards her and saw her grab at it, but saw, too, her hand slip off the wet surface. Too weak to hold on? For an agonising moment he lost sight of her, but then she reappeared. Her oilskin jacket seemed to have trapped some air; perhaps that was giving her buoyancy. With what looked like a supreme effort she rose in the water and threw herself across the ring.

His heart in his mouth, he pulled on the lifeline, terrified that each wave would knock her off, but she was still holding on as he pulled it closer, closer, and at last she was at the side of the boat. He wasn't sure that she was fully conscious; he thrust the torch at Murdo John to let him keep searching for Vicky, then, keeping his own centre of gravity as low as he could, he reached over to grab her.

He couldn't get a proper hold. It was too far below and every time he touched her the swell of a wave pulled her out of his grasp; each time it subsided he expected to see that she had been swept off. She was still there, but sooner or later she wouldn't be; she would be drawn inexorably down by the savagery of the sea.

There was only one thing to do. He was afraid, very afraid, but he gave himself no time for reflection, just kicked off his boots, knotted a loop of the lifeline diagonally across his chest and round his arm and slipped over the side into the water.

It was deathly, deathly cold. He was chilled to the core in seconds, his chest so painful from the icy shock that he could hardly breathe. The life jacket buoyed him up and he was holding on to the side, but the force of the waves grabbed him and threw him contemptuously back against it, breaking his hold. For a terrifying moment he thought he would be swept away himself but the lifeline held and he pulled himself along it to where Livvy lay motionless on the buoy.

At last he had a grip on her, treading water frantically and relying on his jacket to keep him afloat. She was slight in build but her clothes were waterlogged and he was beginning to struggle. He was being dragged down and then they would both drown—

Then he felt something lift him. Murdo John had pushed the boathook through the hood on his jacket and, stabilised now, he managed at last to thrust Livvy over the gunwale, then with the boat rocking crazily climbed back in himself, teeth chattering so hard he thought they might break.

Murdo John said nothing in reply to his stammered thanks, only handed back the torch and again set the boat circling round the area where the boat had gone down.

He put Livvy in the recovery position and to his relief she began coughing, then vomited up seawater. She was very, very cold but she was alive and finding Vicky had to be the priority now. He went back to playing the beam across the dark expanse. Nothing but waves and the bobbing lights of the other lifebuoy. No sign of the boat; no sign of Vicky.

He gave Livvy a worried glance. It was a good sign that she was still shivering: when shivering stops, hypothermia has set in, but he wasn't sure how long it would take. They could lose her as they conducted a fruitless search for a woman who was almost certainly dead already. How long could anyone survive in water as cold as that? The Little Minch, in the winter, in a storm, with no life jacket? Ten minutes, maybe, and it had been that by now.

But how did you tell a man to stop searching for his own wife? What would he himself have done? Knowing with shame that if there had been any chance, however slight, of saving Alexa he would have ignored everything else, he said, 'Murdo John . . .' and shone the torch towards Livvy, who seemed, he thought with alarm, to be shivering less and less.

For a second Murdo John held his course. Then, with deep groan, he swung the boat round and headed back to shore.

They took Kelso to hospital in Broadford as well, seeming to find his protests that he was all right less than convincing given that he was shivering so much he couldn't properly form the words. They packed him into the ambulance, dry and wrapped in a survival blanket, then ignored him as they worked on Livvy, trying to raise her core temperature.

He remembered being told that core temperature actually drops after removal from the cold environment, and that post-rescue collapse was often the reason for death. The paramedics were experts, no doubt, and experienced too in this place where the sea and the mountains claimed regular victims, but it would have been good to see her stir, hear some sound to show she was still with them, even if it was only a moan of protest. He couldn't work out how long it had been before the treatment started; his waterlogged watch had stopped and time seemed to have developed a curious plasticity.

Certainly the journey through the darkness to the hospital seemed interminable; an ambulance is not the most comfortable mode of transport and though he had stopped shivering he was indeed feeling unwell by the time they reached it, queasy, headachy and with painfully strained muscles in his arms and shoulders.

It was a huge relief when the lights of the town appeared; they had either been spared the power cut or it had been short-lived, and there was a trolley waiting in the entrance for Livvy when the ambulance stopped. She was whisked away along a corridor while he climbed out shakily.

'Will she be all right?' he asked one of the paramedics.

'Oh, she will, right enough,' he said brightly. 'Don't you worry.'

Kelso gave him a sceptical look. 'I can recognise PR speak when I hear it. I'm a police officer and I'd prefer it straight. How is she?'

'Mmm. Well, not great. She wasn't responding much but we did get the core temperature up a wee bit and the guys here will be able to do a lot more for her. Odds on, if you're a betting man. Now, I'll take you along to A&E. You're looking a bit rubbish yourself.'

Later, in the peace of a side ward, Kelso found it hard to sleep even though he was exhausted. Everything ached and his tired mind kept rerunning the horrors again and again. Murdo John had gone back to the search once he'd put them ashore and they'd got other boats searching too but they would be looking for a body by now.

Was there anything he could have done to stop it happening? Vicky Macdonald's arrest could have waited if Murray hadn't been inspired to use her initiative. She hadn't been detailed to interview Vicky; he'd no idea what had happened except that Beatrice Lacey had said Murray had been chasing her, so he could only guess it was in trying to make an arrest.

Arguably, if she hadn't been in hot pursuit Vicky Macdonald would still be at the Lodge. She might have been planning an escape, but she certainly wouldn't have chosen the middle of a storm to do it. And what, for God's sake, had Murray been doing in the boat with her? It raised a lot of questions about her judgement. Surely she should have been smart enough to know that tackling a killer on your own was lunacy.

But she'd put her whole heart into it and you couldn't fault her courage. If she didn't make it – he shifted restlessly, trying to banish the thought. Too many women had died already. He mentally recited the litany of names: Veruschka, Eva and now Vicky. Perhaps even Livvy Murray as well. And Alexa.

He'd used all the skills he'd developed in the darkest days in Afghanistan to compartmentalise, to seal away the memories and the grief while he immersed himself in his work, but sooner rather than later he'd have to deal with it. Unconsciously he fingered the healing scar on his face.

Alexa had still been there, somewhere, in that sealed room in his mind. She would be in every room of the empty house when he returned, the echo of her voice, her laugh, still almost audible, the perfume she used a hint on the air. With her all about him, the lacerating grief would return.

He buried his face in the pillow to stifle a groan. The door opened softly and he looked up as a nurse peeped round the door. 'Still awake?' he said. 'Do you want that sleeping pill you wouldn't take earlier?'

'Yes, Nurse. Sorry,' he said meekly. Oblivion sounded wonderful.

Her throat felt as if someone had been hacking at it with a razor. Her tongue was sticking to the roof of her mouth and she had a splitting headache. Her eyes were so swollen that she could barely open them, her cheeks were stinging and every bit of her body seemed to be sore. She felt hot and it hurt to breathe; she coughed and that was so painful that tears poured down her cheeks, irritating the raw skin even more.

Livvy forced her eyes open. Bare walls. White bed. Drip stand – there was a needle in her arm. Hospital. Why was she in hospital?

It took a moment, but then it started to come back. Vicky. Darkness. Her head. She put up a hand to touch it:

a neat bandage. Yes, she'd arrested Vicky and then been knocked out. Then the boat – oh, she remembered that all right. She'd thought she could stop Vicky going by refusing to get out. She must have been mad.

The terrifying sea. The sickness – oh yes, the deathly sickness. She wouldn't have cared if she'd drowned, as long as it stopped. Then suddenly, the cold – the brutal, icy shock that was like knives going through her.

After that everything was patchy. She could remember weird lights in the water coming towards her, grabbing at them and her hands slipping off. Then she'd seemed to be skimming, somehow, on the waves, then . . .

Unwisely, she started up and yelped with pain. Kelso Strang's face – had she really seen Kelso Strang's face? Oh please, God, no! It was bad enough that he'd have to know what she'd done; if he'd been there, seeing it happen, it would be that much worse.

Her mind was clearing. She knew perfectly well what she ought to have done when she recognised Vicky's guilt: she should have said nothing, gone back and reported to the boss. But she hadn't. She'd wanted to keep all the glory for herself, wanted to show the Strangs and Tennants that she wasn't just some wee Glasgow hairy.

She'd screwed up, massively. She could hear her mother's scornful voice ringing in her ears: *You always do. You're useless.* She'd been trying to kid on she was worth something to the investigation, and look what she'd managed to do.

And Vicky – what had happened to Vicky? She felt sick. When the boat sank, had Vicky been saved along with her – or not? Her eye fell on a button on a flex, draped over her bedside locker. The nurses would know, surely.

'Oh, you're awake? That's good.' A nurse appeared, carrying a clipboard and a tray. 'I was just coming in to sort you out. How are you feeling?'

Livvy ignored that. 'Do you know if someone called Vicky Macdonald was brought in at the same time as me?'

The nurse was checking the drip. She shook her head. 'No. The only other person was your inspector. He's in the next room.'

She had been feeling feverish; now she felt very cold. 'My inspector? DI Strang? What was he in for?' As if she didn't know.

'Same as you, but not nearly as bad. You're a lucky girl – he went into the water to pull you out. Bit of a hero, really.'

And at that moment, Livvy wished he'd let her drown.

'Oh, thank goodness,' DI Strang said when Sergeant Buchanan appeared in his room, carrying a small suitcase.

He'd been told he'd be able to leave whenever his clothes arrived. He was desperate to get back, to try to take a grip on a situation that was likely to prove a media sensation. He still felt pretty rough; he was so stiff he could barely move but the doctor had passed him fit.

As he took the case he said, 'Have they—?' but from Buchanan's sombre expression he knew the answer and changed his question to, 'Not even the body?'

'There was some debris fetched up on the shore at first light,' Buchanan said. 'Looks like it's come from the boat. They reckon with the currents she'll wash up just this side of the point.'

Strang pulled on a shirt. 'Have you seen Livvy Murray this morning? They say she'll be all right – still suffering, but no more than that.'

'No, not yet,' Buchanan said. 'Terrible thing – poor lassie. Have you spoken to her yourself?'

'Didn't fancy turning up in a hospital gown, but we can go in together now. If she's recovered I'm planning to wring her neck.' He pulled on trousers and a sweater. 'For God's sake don't say anything to her about me going in after her – I don't think she was fully conscious last night.'

Buchanan was grinning. 'It's my bet that you're too late. The place is fair buzzing with it this morning and she'll have had it served up with her breakfast.'

Strang groaned. 'Oh, great! Anyway, our first task is to sort out a story for the press. Does DCS Borthwick know?'

'We contacted her first thing. She's hoping to get the use of the helicopter again.'

'Right.' He shut the suitcase. 'That's me. Let's go along and see how Livvy's doing.'

She was a sorry sight. Bruised and grazed, her face thick with ointment and her eyes puffed up and blackened, she looked like a waif as she lay against the pillows. Strang saw she was welling up.

'Sorry, boss,' she said stiffly.

'Know what my father used to say to me, when I said sorry? "Damn your sorrow – just don't do it again!" Cheer up, it's not the end of the world. How are you feeling?'

'Horrible, but I suppose it beats being dead, like

I would be if it wasn't for you. Don't know how you say thanks for something like that.' The tears were threatening to spill over.

He smiled. 'Aw, shucks, it was nothing. Don't cry – it'll hurt your cheeks.' He handed her a tissue.

Livvy dabbed her eyes cautiously. 'Is there – is there—' she said, then stopped, looking from one man to another. 'There isn't, is there?'

'I'm afraid not,' Strang said. 'But don't get eaten up with guilt. As far as I can make out, you were doing your best to stop her.'

'But maybe if—'

'If she hadn't taken matters into her own hands and killed Adam Carnegie, you wouldn't be in hospital now.'

It didn't seem to comfort her much. 'I got it wrong. If I hadn't . . .' Her voice tailed away.

'You just concentrate on getting well quickly,' Buchanan said. 'I'm lost without someone to argue with.'

That produced the wannest of smiles. Strang said, 'Put it out of your mind just now. We'll get the details once you're feeling better. Don't argue with the doctors, anyway – just do what they tell you and rest.'

They went out. 'Poor wee soul,' Buchanan said. 'She's a smart enough lassie, you know – wasted up here, in the general way of things.'

'Why did she get posted up here? She behaves as if it's some sort of exile.'

'No idea. They never told me and she's close as a clam about it. Maybe after this she'll be glad enough for a wee bit of peace and quiet.'

'Given the field day the media will probably have with all this, that may well be right,' Strang said gloomily.

When they arrived back at the police office in Balnasheil and had to run the gauntlet of shouted questions from people with fuzzy microphones, Strang realised that he'd have to assure his family he was all right before they got panicked by the headlines. If he phoned his mother, though, there was always the risk that his father would answer and he simply didn't feel strong enough to confess that the first time he had headed an investigation it had all gone hideously wrong.

Finella. He'd phone his sister. Her brothers always made use of her to break the news when there was something their father wouldn't like. She'd had her problems with him too but she somehow managed not to let that affect their relationship. She'd inherited her mother's imperturbability and finessed it to an almost catatonic calm, so he could rely on her not to overreact.

When he got back to his desk he called her number from the landline. 'Fin?' he said. 'It's Kelso.'

'Ah. Thought it might be. You've survived, then?'

He grinned. 'Seem to have.'

'Any bits dropped off?'

'Not so far. Hey, can you—?'

'Phone the wrinklies? Just because Dad will go ape? What a coward you are!'

'I resent that. Catch you jumping into the sea in a Force 8.'

'That's what Dad would call "unnecessary heroics". In his book you only appear in the papers when you're born, married, get a gong or die.' Then her voice sobered. 'Did you find the woman that was missing?'

'No,' he said heavily. 'I think there's going to be a bit of a fuss.'

'Right,' Finella said. 'Well, hang in there, kid. You know where to find me when you get back.' She hesitated, then added with a lightness that belied the seriousness of her concern, 'Apart from that, Mrs Lincoln . . . ?'

His throat constricted. 'Oh – you know.'

'Thankfully, I don't know but I can imagine. Tons of love.'

Strang rang off, blew his nose and then turned back to his desk. He'd better start marshalling something of a defence before he saw JB. She'd be carrying a lot of the blame for this disaster.

It was fortunate that exhaustion and a slight fever kept Livvy Murray dozing most of the morning, since every time she surfaced another wave of misery, humiliation and guilt swept over her. She'd all but murdered Vicky Macdonald and it was only luck that meant Kelso Strang hadn't drowned trying to save her. Far from being so impressive that she'd have to be returned to civilisation, she was going to be drummed out. It was just a question of whether they'd sack her before or after the excruciating torture of an inquiry.

She would have said she couldn't feel any worse but she realised she was wrong when she woke from a troubled dream to see Detective Chief Superintendent Borthwick coming in. Could she hope this was just another nightmare?

No. The superintendent was clearly all too real. As

Livvy struggled to sit up, she smiled, taking a seat by the side of the bed.

'Don't move. I'm not going to ask you how you are since you'd only feel obliged to sound upbeat. I expect you're feeling as awful as you look.'

It surprised a tiny laugh out of her. Then she said, 'Oh, ma'am, I'm so, so sorry. I don't know what to say . . .'

She was interrupted. 'Sorry? You're a heroine.'

'I'm – *what*?'

'A suspect was bent on a lethally dangerous course of action and you put your life on the line to try to save her from what unfortunately turned out to be a fatal decision. In what followed, DI Strang mounted a life-saving operation which at least managed to rescue you, though sadly not Mrs Macdonald. Heroism on every side – a wonderful tribute to our modern police force.'

'But – but' – Livvy spluttered – 'it wasn't like that.'

'Oh?' Borthwick had very expressive eyebrows. 'Wasn't it?'

'Can I tell you what happened?'

She desperately wanted to confess, to share the burden of guilt, and it was a relief when Borthwick, with a wry smile, reluctantly agreed that she could. She told her everything, right up until the moment when everything went black.

'She must have hit me. I don't know what with – the power went first.'

'A cast-iron frying pan,' Borthwick supplied. 'They found it on the kitchen floor this morning.'

'Oh. I suppose that would do it. But you see, ma'am, I'd put her under arrest. This was a death in police custody.'

'What?' Borthwick's expression changed. 'Oh. That's –

unfortunate, to say the least. You'd certainly need to admit that when you're questioned. Makes everything much more problematic. But I suppose you'd better go on and tell me exactly what happened.'

'When I came to in the dark I took a minute to find the door. Then I saw light underneath it and I think I heard the back door slam just then. Beatrice Lacey was sitting on the floor in the corridor – I think Vicky had assaulted her – but I just took her torch and ran after Vicky to arrest her and try to stop her—'

'Wait a moment,' Borthwick said. 'You said you'd arrested her already.'

'Yes, I had. At least I'd told her I was arresting her but I didn't have time to repeat the caution, so—'

Borthwick visibly relaxed. 'And what happens, Constable, if the caution isn't delivered?'

'Well, the arrest fails. Oh! I see what you mean!'

'You didn't arrest her, Livvy. You only tried to arrest her, so she wasn't in police custody, was she? She was fleeing arrest, and you did your best to stop her coming to harm.'

'I hadn't thought of it like that, but I suppose it is true. I know I was stupid, though. I should have—'

'That's your opinion. It's just possible that it may also be DI Strang's opinion, or even mine. You were an untrained officer who found herself unexpectedly in a difficult position and if you showed a lack of judgement, it's not surprising. But you showed a lot of courage too.'

Livvy sank back against her pillows, her eyes filling again with tears of weakness. 'I was sure I was going to be kicked out of the force. And I'd wanted so much to make my mark so I could apply for a transfer somewhere—'

'Like Edinburgh, say?' Borthwick was looking quizzical.

'Oh, I know I've probably blown it—'

'Not necessarily. You've shown a bit of promise and I think with training you could have a future as a detective.' She got up. 'Just work on getting better at the moment. All right?'

'Yes, ma'am. And thanks – thanks very much.'

Livvy lay back against her pillows, thinking. The super seemed inclined to give her another chance, but what would Kelso Strang say about that? From the way he spoke this morning he wasn't as inclined to view it all in such a favourable light as she had – and now she considered it, the way Borthwick had presented it sounded like a line you'd spin to feed to the media, and the inquiry that would have to take place might see it very differently.

Still, there was the hint of a light at the end of the long dark tunnel she was in at the moment – as long as it wasn't that oncoming train.

CHAPTER TWENTY-SEVEN

When DC Tennant appeared in his office, DI Strang found it hard to be civil. He gave up the attempt when the man said gleefully, 'All's well that ends well, eh?'

'I'm gobsmacked that you can describe a woman's death as a happy ending. And it's no thanks to you that PC Murray wasn't killed as well.'

'Oh, for God's sake, Kelso, I wasn't talking about that. And I can tell you that if I'd allowed you to talk me into going out in that last night, we'd all have drowned.'

The fact that there was a considerable amount of truth in that didn't improve Strang's mood. 'Anyway, what did you want?'

'Nothing, really. I just came in to say how pleased I am not to be a leper, now that you've reluctantly had to drop the moronic notion that I was a suspect. Of course, I forgot – I'm English. That was probably enough to damn me.'

'Don't be utterly ridiculous!' Strang snapped. 'We don't have a cover-up culture, that's all.'

'Oh, and the Met does?'

'Demonstrably.' He knew he shouldn't have said that, but he didn't care.

Tennant gave him a look of profound distaste. 'There's obviously no point in trying to do this on a friendly basis. Detective Inspector Strang, I am making a formal request to have Adam Carnegie's files released to me to facilitate the arrest of Harry Drummond.'

Strang smiled. 'Oh, I'm afraid it's too late. He was arrested this morning by our own fraud squad. They're dealing direct with yours.'

Tennant gaped at him. 'And what about me?'

'I daresay they thought it was simpler to cut out the middle man.'

'But it was me that told you about the money laundering!' he protested. 'It was my case – and I've spent months on this, stuck up here!'

'Then I expect your bosses will wonder what you can have been doing,' Strang said with sweet satisfaction. 'You didn't find the files. We did. I can only hope that book you were supposedly working on is going to be a bestseller.'

Tennant had turned crimson with rage. 'This is outrageous! I—'

Strang cut across him. 'I'm sorry, DC Tennant, I'm afraid I'm very busy this morning. If you have a complaint I can only suggest you take it up with the appropriate authorities.'

For a moment he wasn't sure if the man was going to hit him. Then Tennant swore at him and walked out, slamming the door behind him so that it rocked in its frame.

Strang grinned to himself. That hadn't been professional, but it was certainly satisfying. Then the grin faded. It was likely to be downhill from here on in.

The helicopter had put down at the hospital in Broadford where JB was going to see Livvy Murray before she was driven down here. He could hear from the noise outside that the media scrum was getting worse; JB had called a press conference for midday, and she must be worried about that. He still couldn't think of a way to present this in a better light.

She looked, however, remarkably cheerful when she came in. Having made the conventional enquiry about his health, adding with her usual bluntness that he looked pretty rough, she accepted his terse, 'I'm fine,' with a nod then took a seat and said, 'So – just the finishing up to do?'

He looked at her askance. 'What are we going to tell them?' he said bluntly.

'Oh, don't worry about that.' She produced a sheet of paper and handed it to him.

He read it, then said, 'But – but we can't say that!'

'No? Why not?'

'If Murray hadn't gone after her—'

'Ah – if! We're in the realms of speculation here, aren't we? We just have to deal with the facts. PC Murray attempted to arrest Mrs Macdonald perfectly properly when she discovered evidence of her guilt then acted very courageously in attempting to prevent her coming to harm, though sadly her attempt failed despite your bravery in trying to rescue both women. With, of course, the help of Mr Macdonald, who after reporting her confession to you did all he could to save his wife.'

Strang looked revolted. 'And Murray's going to say that to the inquiry, is she? It could come badly unstuck—'

'Why? Point to a word there that's untrue.'

Strang studied the statement again. 'I suppose there isn't. But if she hadn't—'

'Tsk! There you go again, Kelso. I shall get quite irritated in a moment. You'll have to go out there with me, looking suitably modest and self-deprecating. The chief constable is very excited about this. We need all the good publicity that we can get.'

Oh, if the CC was pleased, that was it, then. He felt a stirring of rebellion at the slickness of it all; he had somehow thought better of JB than that.

She read his reaction. 'Yes, I'm deplorably cynical, amn't I? You feel we should say that a very junior officer took the bit between her teeth and caused a disaster – oh yes, and in a spirit of self-flagellation you would claim that somehow you should have seen to it that she didn't. And throwing you both to the wolves would accomplish – what, exactly?'

Strang muttered, 'Nothing, I suppose,' but inside a small spark of rebellion still flared.

Borthwick looked at him with an ironic smile. 'Ah – you want the luxury of a totally clear conscience. With your years of service, I'm amazed that you still have one. Anyway, the CC is keen to stand down this operation as quickly as possible. It's been expensive but cost-effective as against keeping a full-scale department for something like this that hasn't happened in ten years and won't happen for another ten. We've done the heavy lifting; the lads here can take over the tidying up. Do a handover, then appear at the press conference. After that, you can get on your way back. Oh, and if they talk about a medal, do you think you could manage a simper?' She laughed at his expression of disgust. 'Could we settle for lowered eyes and a shrug, then?'

Reluctantly, he laughed too. 'Lowered eyes aren't a problem. Couldn't look anyone in the face, posing as a hero of spin.'

'I'll settle for that.' She got up. 'I'll be in Edinburgh this afternoon. Report after you get back.'

'Yes, of course. Thanks, ma'am.'

'Excellent. I'll leave you to get on with that. I'm going across to Balnasheil Lodge to oversee what's happening there – thank goodness the sea's gone down. It's a lovely day now.'

Beatrice Lacey was feeling sorry for herself this morning. She had sneezed four times and she had the prickle at the back of her throat that presaged a cold – no wonder, after getting so thoroughly chilled last night.

She was angry, too. Her 'nice' inspector – huh! – had seemed totally uninterested in the failure of his constable to help her at the time, and he hadn't even sent someone else to look into it. She'd had to scrabble to get herself up off the floor and this morning her bad arm was definitely worse as a result. Then, having lost her torch, she'd had to grope her way back up to her bedroom and she'd bumped her head painfully on the post at the foot of the stairs. With no heating she'd been freezing cold even once she'd got to bed, and then been wakened in the early hours by the lights coming back on.

At least she'd been able to make herself toast and a comforting hot chocolate for breakfast and now she was on her way down to find out what was happening. If they were going to arrest her because of the sleeping pills, she couldn't stop them, but she was going to make her complaint anyway to a higher authority.

She could hear voices downstairs and as she passed the first floor she saw the door to Harry's room standing open. That was unusual; she'd never known him do that before. Could he have been allowed to go, just as she was hoping to do? Or – her heart leapt – could he possibly have been arrested?

There was a group of people standing in the hall, two policemen in uniform along with a woman, who wasn't. They turned their heads as Beatrice reached the bottom of the stairs.

'Who is in charge here?' she demanded.

After a brief hesitation, the woman came towards her. 'I'm Detective Chief Superintendent Borthwick. Are you Beatrice Lacey?'

'Yes, I am. And you are exactly the person I want to see. I wish to make a serious complaint. I was treated quite disgracefully last night. I'm looking to you to deal with it.'

'Of course,' the superintendent said soothingly. 'Sergeant Buchanan will talk to you and get the full details. But for the moment, we have some questions that we need to ask you. Are you aware that Mr Drummond has been arrested?'

'No! Really?' Suddenly Beatrice's day had started to improve. 'I *knew* he had killed poor Adam – I just knew it! And for him to try to pin the blame on me—'

'No, Miss Lacey, not for murder. He has been arrested for alleged fraud. We will be wanting you to answer some questions about the finances of the Human Face charity.'

Her face fell. 'But – but I don't know anything about that! Harry did all the finance stuff. I just kept the books and there was nothing wrong with them – nothing.'

'No, I'm sure,' the superintendent said. 'But perhaps you would be willing to help us with our enquiries by making a formal statement at Broadford Police Station?'

Beatrice felt sick. 'I – I suppose so. But I'm not very well, you know.' Then another hideous thought struck her. 'You're not going to charge me with murder when I get there, because of the sleeping pills?'

The superintendent gave a wry smile. 'No, we won't be charging you with murder,' she said.

That, at least, was a relief. Then, 'Oh! Could I get some things together and go and stay somewhere – Broadford or Portree, maybe? You won't make me stay here?'

'No, Miss Lacey, there's no reason why you should.'

That was something, at least. And as Beatrice climbed the stairs she heard the woman say, 'Can't blame her. I wouldn't want to stay here either – ghastly place, at the best of times.'

It hadn't been fair, had it? She'd only wanted to do the best for those poor kiddies and as a result all this had happened to her. She hadn't known the things that were going on – well, not really – and yet she'd had to suffer. Now the police were going to ask her all sorts of difficult questions and she'd have to keep her wits about her to make sure that they understood she was blameless and it was all nothing to do with her. Sooner or later, as the saying went, one must pay for every good deed.

But now she'd get her trustee to sort things out and she could go back to the comfortable life she'd had before all this. It had just been a sort of madness, the whole Adam thing – she realised that now. And nothing like that would ever happen again.

DI Kelso Strang emerged from the Balnasheil Hotel feeling he ought to go back in for a shower after Fiona Ross's farewell.

'I don't know how you could do it, Kelso – even going out in a boat on a night like that would terrify me, but actually going in to save a subordinate – well, that was just simply heroic,' she gushed.

Yes, usually we leave them to drown if they're below inspector rank – no, he couldn't say that. He produced one of the non-committal grunts he had perfected since coming here and she went on, 'It was just – just so brave! But we're really disappointed you're leaving now. You know there will be so many people wanting to interview you, and we'd be more than happy to invite you stay a few more days – on the house, of course. A token of our admiration.'

Oh, I bet you would, he thought grimly. Free advertising, chance to be on the telly, bar takings soaring . . . 'I'm afraid I have to get back,' he said coolly.

He escaped and walked along to where he had parked his car. The sea was almost insultingly tranquil today, a deep navy blue with a gentle breeze blowing that barely ruffled the surface. Gulls were swooping and calling and further out there were gannets diving, piercing the surface like white arrows. The straggle of whitewashed houses was glittering in the sun and the colour of the sea, the lush green of the fields and the hills on the other side of the bay that were grey-purple shading into misty blue were an exquisite harmony, impossibly perfect like a delicate watercolour in a tourist gift shop.

But when he turned his head, there it was, the Black Cuillin ridge, bare today of even a softening wisp of cloud, looming over the prettiness like a death's head at a wedding party. Strang shuddered. How could anyone live here, in the shadow of that eternal reminder that the hills remained while human life was no more than a brief flicker of light, soon extinguished. He was in a sombre mood as he drove up the hill and turned his back on the mountains, heading home.

But he'd better drop in at the hospital to see Livvy Murray. JB hadn't really said anything about their meeting except to imply that Livvy would fall in with the political version, just as he had, but he needed to make sure they were singing from the same hymn sheet.

She was sitting up in bed when he arrived, still looking battered but definitely stronger, though he saw her quail as he came in.

'Hello, sir,' she said nervously. 'Look, I just want to say—'

He sat down. 'Let's have a pact, Livvy. We don't talk about any of that now, not any of it. We've been told what happened and there's no point in arguing, is there? Not with JB.'

'Is that what you call her? She was quite scary today when she was sorting out what we're to say.'

'She's a good boss. But don't try to take her on about it; she's very tough.'

She gave him a sidelong look. 'Think I'm daft?'

He laughed. 'Anyway, how are you feeling? You look—'

She held up her hand. 'Part of the pact. We won't talk about that either, right? What happens now?'

'It's up to you guys to finish up. I'm on my way back to Edinburgh – just stopped in to say goodbye.'

She looked surprised. 'You're not staying on? I thought . . .'

'So did I, but it's economics. Keeping me here costs money and CID Portree can do whatever needs to be done now.'

'So, that's it. Back to the police office, I suppose.'

She looked so glum that he felt sorry for her. She'd got it wrong, certainly, but she was worth more than that. 'Look, why don't you apply to join the CID? I'll put in a good word for you with the lads at Portree if you like.'

'Thanks very much,' she said dully.

She obviously wasn't thrilled about that suggestion either, and it occurred to him that she might have been hoping to prove herself in this investigation as a way back to Glasgow again. There was nothing he could do about that.

He rose, a little awkwardly. 'Well, I'd best be on my way back home. You just get well, all right?'

'Sure.' Then she paused. 'Do you mind me asking – have you someone waiting for you there?'

It caught him unawares. 'Not now. She's dead,' he said harshly, then as he saw her face crumple in dismay, stammered, 'Sorry – that came out wrong. Road accident. You weren't to know.' He floundered his way out of the room in a flood of half-phrases.

Oh God, her big gob! She wasn't even sure where that question had come from, just that she'd wondered a couple of times what his taste might be. Would she never learn?

Poor guy – and if the scar on his face was anything to go by, the accident was recent. She'd thought he was a cold, stand-offish bastard but it was probably taking him all his time to hold himself together. You weren't going to be a barrel of laughs in those circumstances and sometimes when he'd smiled and lightened up a bit she'd thought he'd probably be OK if you got to know him.

She wasn't going to find out now. The circus was leaving town and here she was, left behind, contemplating the trampled ground and the circles of blanched grass where the tents had been. The hint that 'JB' had given her was just that, not anything like a promise.

The thing was, she could go back to Glasgow any time she wanted if she left the force and got another job. She wasn't going to, though. Becoming a detective was obsessing her now and if that meant staying on in Skye, it was just what she'd have to do.

In one of its characteristic mood shifts, the weather had changed and it was getting darker now; the sun had vanished and as she looked out of the window, squally rain rattled on the pane. She groaned. She must be mad.

Kelso Strang could feel the clutch of nerves in his stomach as he drove along the Forth shoreline to Newhaven. It was dark; he could see the lights of the Fife coast winking on the other shore. He turned in and parked in the courtyard area below the little group of fisherman's cottages, fetched his bag from the back and slowly climbed the outside stairs to his front door.

It still looked the same. Alexa would still be there waiting for him, in the kitchen, in the sitting room, in their bedroom, in the little room they'd been decorating for the baby who would never occupy it now. He stood on the doorstep for a moment, bracing himself for the impact.

But inside, the house wasn't the same. It felt fusty, unaired, as he picked up the pile of mail from behind the door. It felt empty. Alexa wasn't there; she had gone.

Kelso had been living in a sort of suspended animation, keeping devouring grief at bay. He would have time to do his mourning now. He could take the compassionate leave he'd been offered and he wouldn't have to suffer alone. His mother, his sister – they were longing to give him any loving support he was prepared to accept.

He didn't want that, though. Only pausing to set down his case, he picked up his keys and drove off again to the police headquarters at Fettes Row. It was late, but he suspected that JB would be working on tonight anyway.

DCS Borthwick looked surprised to see him. 'This is impressive dedication, Kelso! I wasn't expecting to see you today. How was your journey down?'

'No problems. Thought I'd just come in and see where we are.'

'It's expanding in quite a dramatic way, actually. The fraud operation in conjunction with the Met is bringing in some big names and with the interest in the Balnasheil murders it's going to hit the national media in a seriously big way tomorrow. You may want to lie low for a bit,' Borthwick warned. 'Have you been pestered for interviews?'

'There wasn't anyone waiting on the doorstep and I haven't actually checked my messages.'

'The coverage has been very positive but it does no harm to play it down. I've persuaded the CC not to parade you and PC Murray for their benefit. Smacks too much of a hostage video, I always think.'

Strang laughed. 'How is she? She was on the way to recovery when I left.'

'Yes, they're probably letting her home tomorrow.' She paused. 'Kelso, I'm going to offer her a transfer here.'

'*What*!' He was horrified. 'Look, I'm not saying that she didn't make a positive contribution but it was a bit outweighed by the rest of it.'

'Speaking as the man who had to go into the water to fetch her out, you mean? I hear what you're saying, but I think she's got promise and I like to back my hunches. Someone took a punt on me, once. What she was lacking was training, but we can fix that.'

'I suggested she apply to Portree CID – that would be more her level.'

'You're forgetting something. She's a heroine in the eyes of the media.'

Strang compressed his lips, and managed not to say, 'For "media" read "chief constable".'

'I think we agreed we weren't going to theorise, Kelso.' There was a warning note in her voice.

She'd made her decision and there was no point in arguing. 'You're the boss,' he said without enthusiasm.

'Yes, I am. Anyway, there's going to be a lot of loose ends to tie up here, liaising with Portree CID and so on. Are you prepared to go on with that? I did offer you compassionate leave—'

'No,' Strang said, then, 'Thank you.'

'Right.' She gave him one of her penetrating looks. 'You're making quite a good job of coping, you know.'

'Am I? I don't know. How are you supposed to do it?'

'The way we all do – one day at a time. Don't look ahead. You keep your footing by checking the ground under your feet until the really bad days get further apart. Anyway, get an early night. We can talk about the next steps tomorrow. It looks as if we'll be getting the green light for further SRCS operations, so I'll want to know how you feel.'

'I—' he said, but she held up her hand.

'I don't want an answer now. Sleep on it. Scribble down a strengths and weaknesses list and come to a considered decision.'

* * *

It gave Kelso something else to think of apart from the empty house as he drove back to Newhaven.

Strengths and weaknesses – well, there were certainly drawbacks to having such a level of responsibility when you were isolated miles from direct support, and in this case at least there had been a local force to call on. In some of the wilder areas of Scotland there wouldn't even be that.

He'd had to go through a steep and sometimes painful learning curve and in the event it had stretched him to the limits. Indeed, Vicky Macdonald's death left him with questions he still wanted to ask himself about how far he had been responsible.

In the past, too, he'd enjoyed working closely with colleagues – the team spirit, the banter, the brainstorming. Had he only coped with being on his own because he'd put his feelings into cold storage for the duration of the case, and once feeling returned would that position be lonely and unsatisfying?

He'd been a sniper, though, another lonely job that had been satisfying too, and leading this inquiry had absorbed him totally, leaving him with no space to contemplate the black hole that was all that was left of his former life. For the foreseeable future, that would be an alluring thought – and if he was honest, he had thoroughly enjoyed the freedom of making a decision without having to persuade everyone else to go along with it. That could cut both ways; as his mother used to say to him when he was small, 'You can't have the penny and the bun.'

He would sleep on it and draw up his list for JB

obediently, but he knew already what his decision was going to be.

Kelso parked at the cottage and walked up the stairs to the front door again with dragging steps. This was where real life caught up with him – all those anxious calls from friends to return, the media blitz to deal with . . . He shut the door and looked round him, feeling his spirits sink. He'd kept the darkness at bay, but now . . .

Scotch. He had just poured two fingers into a tumbler when there was a knock on the door. He thought of ignoring it, but sooner or later he'd have to face the world again. It wouldn't take long for the *Daily Record* to find out where he lived.

But it was Annie, his elderly neighbour, who stood there. She was shrunken with age but she still had the brightest of beady dark eyes that swept across his face, then down to the glass in his hand.

She didn't say hello, didn't ask how he was, simply stepped inside, took the glass from his hand and set it down.

'You neednae be thinking you're starting that, right the very minute you're in the door. I'm telling you, Alexa would give you laldy for that. The pub's open so you can come right down there with me and buy me a wee bevvy as well. There'll be a good crowd in the night – there's that jazz group later – you aye liked them fine.'

The darkness lifted, just a little, and he laughed. 'Annie, you're a bully.'

'Oh, I am, right enough. So you better just do as you're tellt, before I put the heid on you. And I'm wanting salt and vinegar crisps with my dram.'

Looking smug at having got a laugh out of him, Annie led the way down the stairs and he followed her along. No matter what had happened to him, the little boats still bobbed, clinking, in the harbour there, the lights still shone from the houses over on the opposite shore and there were still the regulars in his local, laughing and talking.

Kelso fingered the scar on his cheek. It was healing, but it would never heal completely. And nor would he.

ALINE TEMPLETON grew up in the fishing village of Anstruther, in the East Neuk of Fife. She has worked in education and broadcasting and was a Justice of the Peace for ten years. Married, with two grown-up children and three grandchildren, she now lives in a house with a view of Edinburgh Castle. When not writing she enjoys cooking, choral singing, and travelling the back roads of France.

alinetempleton.co.uk